HANGMAN

HANGMAN

KAITLYN ELYSE

Published by BlackString Press

Published by BlackString Press
Dallas, Texas

First Edition: 2026

ISBNs: 979-8-9940755-0-0 (Paperback), 979-8-9940755-1-7 (Hardcover), 979-8-9940755-2-4 (Ebook)
Library of Congress Control Number: 2025925385

Developmental Editors: Ryan Landels and Caleb Garcia
Content Editor: Ryan Landels
Line Editor: Ryan Landels
Copyeditor: Ryan Landels
Editorial Oversight: Kaitlyn Elyse
Proofreaders: Amber Benton, Kaitlyn Elyse, Ryan Landels
Cover Design & Art: Jonathan Havard
Layout & Formatting: Kaitlyn Elyse

Printed and bound in the United States of America

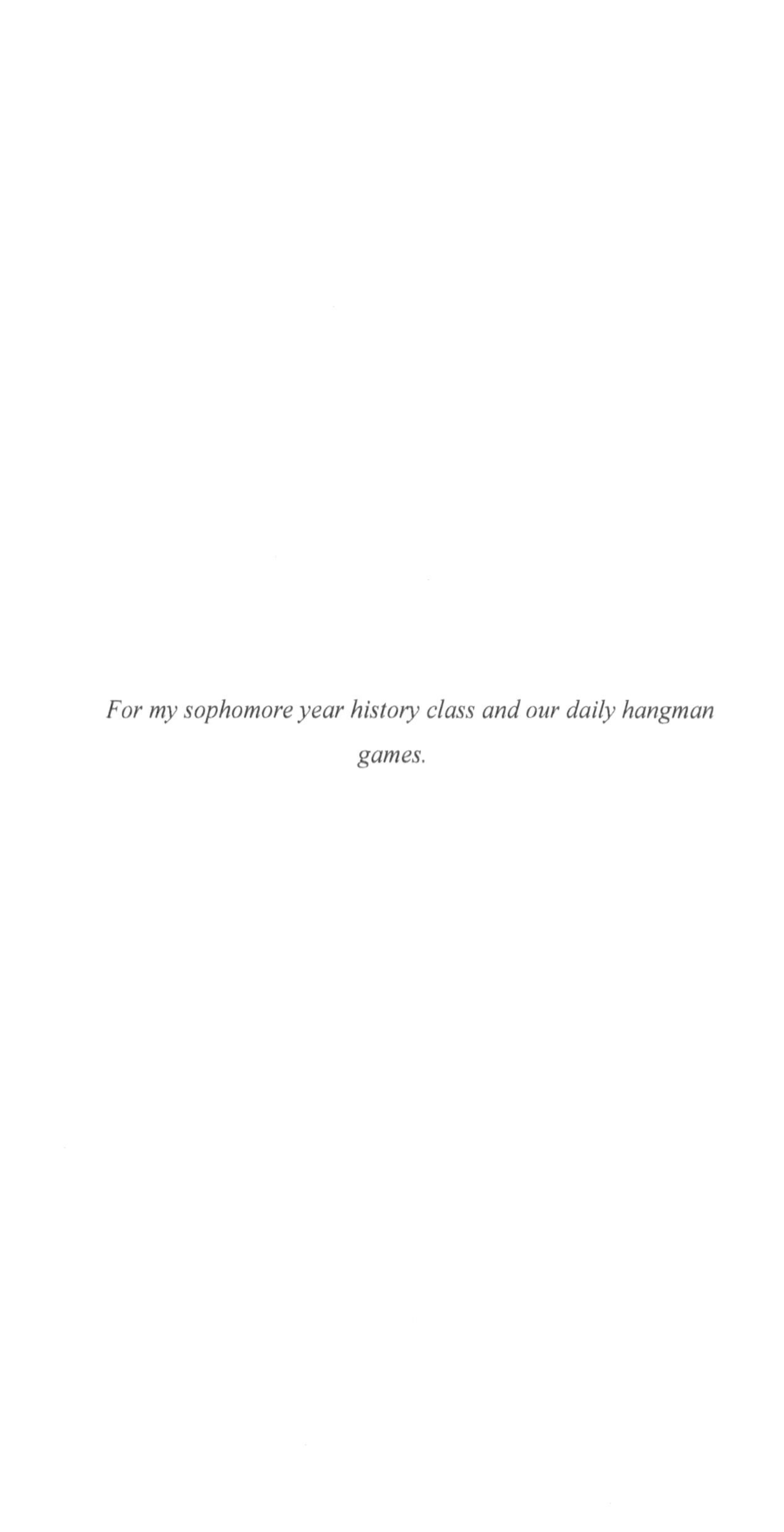

For my sophomore year history class and our daily hangman games.

"Though this be madness, yet there is method in't."

— *Hamlet* (William Shakespeare), Act 2, Scene 2

If you were to kill someone, how would you go about doing it? Would you lock them in a running car and shut the garage? Inject air into their veins? Plan something elaborate to make it look like a natural death? Or would you simply hang them from a tree?

Would you take orders from a hitman to kill some major businessman signing on to a deal people disapprove of? Would you kill a cheating spouse, and their lover, in a heat-of-the-moment rage? Would it be colder, cleaner, a technicality in a drug deal gone wrong? Or would you simply make killing a game where the least fortunate people die?

Would you kill someone with no warning? Shoot them while they are on their way to work or school? Follow them until they turn a corner where you can stab them or choke them without anyone seeing? Would you get close to the victim until they trust you? Or would you simply send them text messages telling them they are next on the list?

Personally, I would text the victim, tell them exactly what the game is. Once they have lost, then I tell them their punishment. The game is simple. It's a childhood game called 'Hangman'. Everyone has played Hangman. With every wrong letter, a new limb appears on the stick figure, head, torso, arms, legs, until, after enough mistakes, he dies.

But I gave it a twist: the game is the same, but now, the stakes are far higher. With every wrong guess, there's a punishment, and a limb drawn on the stick figure man. After all the limbs have been drawn, the unfortunate person who guessed the last letter gets the ultimate punishment.

Good luck.

Chapter One

You never really know what's in someone's heart. Not completely. What they tell you might be the truth. Or half of it. Or none of it at all. People lie. Sometimes to protect themselves. Sometimes to protect you. And sometimes just because they can.

That's what I've learned. Words are masks. Smiles are distractions. There's always something hiding underneath—motives, fears, desires they don't want anyone to see. Every truth has conditions. Every lie has a reason. Most of the time, we never ask what it is.

Everyone has secrets. Everyone lies. That's just how people survive.

And me? No one knows me as well as they think they do. They see what I let them see, nothing more. I've learned to be careful, to keep certain things tucked away where no one can touch them. Where no one can hurt them. Or use them against me.

I wish I could say I knew the people around me. My friends. My family. But the truth is, I doubt it more every day. I watch them laugh, talk, pretend... and I wonder what they're hiding too. What they'd do if they knew what I hid.

Honestly? I'm not sure how well I know anyone. Even myself.

"Sadee?" I'm pulled back into reality. "Have you heard anything I've said?"

I look across the table at the set of piercing blue eyes staring questioningly at me. "I, uh, yeah. Road runners. Trees. Yup."

Indigo sighs and brushes her long, jet-black hair away from her pale, angular face. "Sadee," she sighs. "Not at all." Her fork slowly pushes her food around her plate. "I don't know what I'm going to do with you. I was telling you about the movie my mom found for us to watch tonight."

"Oh. I'm good with whatever." I pick up a potato chip and crush it between my fingers.

"Um, okay. What are you wearing?"

I throw a potato chip at Indigo. "Indi, are you going through some mental checklist to make sure I'm ready for your party?"

"You can't blame me. You're late for everything and you always forget something. This is my eighteenth birthday. It's kind of a big deal."

"Alright, alright. Don't be late. Don't forget anything." Indigo rolls her eyes. "What? You think I'm going to show up, walk in and say, 'oops, guys, hold on—I forgot my shirt?' Indi, I'm not *that* irresponsible."

"Sadee, last year you showed up to the first day of school without a left shoe."

"Okay, well, ignoring that one circumstance, when have I forgotten something that was actually important?"

"You forgot to grab a fork for your salad, Sadee."

I look down to my plate. Salad, no fork. Shoot.

"Just face it, you can't remember to do anything unless I remind you. You're living in a different world. You're lucky you have me to remind you of everything, every single day."

"Okay, okay. I'm lucky to have you." I sigh.

She smiles, then nods behind me. "Your boyfriend's approaching," she teases.

I turn my head just in time to see Mason weaving through the crowded cafeteria, sunlight catching on his sun-kissed skin and sandy-blonde hair. Behind him walk two guys, his friends Eli and Finn.

Eli is lean and tall with a mop of dark-brown hair that's forever a mess. His deep-set, chocolate-brown eyes peek out from behind rectangular glasses. He wears a quiet smile that feels calm and thoughtful even in the noisy chaos of the lunch hour.

Finn follows closely, athletic and sharp-featured, with light-olive skin, and piercing gray eyes that seem to miss nothing. He's dressed in dark colors, blending into the shadows of the bustling cafeteria. A silver chain hung round his neck, catching the light at his collar, subtle but sharp, like everything else about him.

The room buzzes around us, chairs scraping, trays clattering, a mix of laughter and shouts bouncing off the fluorescent lights overhead. The smell of warmed-up pizza, stale fries, and something sweet from the vending machines lingers in the air.

Mason slides into the chair next to me with a grin. "Hey."

Indigo, sitting across from me, watches Finn with a flicker of something I can't quite place. They still look like a couple—his hand brushes against hers briefly before she pulls away, pretending not to notice.

Indigo pushes back her chair and stands up. "I think Cassie and Maya are in the bathroom. I'm going to go find them. I'll be back."

She gives Finn a quick look before weaving her way through the crowded tables, disappearing toward the bathroom doors.

The moment Indigo's gone, Eli starts to slide into her seat, but Finn gets there first: propping his sneakers up on the chair like a silent challenge. His gray eyes flick to Eli, calm but unreadable, and that's all it takes. Eli shrugs and sits on the edge of the table.

Finn leans back in the empty chair, arms crossed, his gray eyes calm but sharp, like he's quietly calculating every move in the room. The silence stretches, thick and steady around him, not because he says anything, but because he *doesn't*. It's the kind of quiet that makes you second-guess what you're about to say.

Then, breaking the silence, Ryan appears, dropping his backpack dramatically to the floor with a sigh like he just returned from war. He's lean and just a bit taller than average, his dirty blonde hair perpetually tousled as if he's been running his fingers through it all day. His sharp blue eyes dart around nervously behind his glasses, always analyzing, always curious. "Okay, fun fact. The vending machine ate my dollar again, and I'm convinced its sentient."

"That's the third time this week," I roll my eyes but can't stop the small smile tugging at my lips.

"Exactly. It's targeting me."

"Maybe it doesn't like conspiracy theorists," Eli offers, popping a grape into his mouth.

Ryan nods solemnly. "It's a government machine. They've probably flagged me already."

Mason laughs. "At least it's not your calculator this time."

Just then Liam strolls up, confident and easygoing, with a stocky build and sandy-brown hair cropped close to his head. His warm, round face breaks into a grin that shows off the dimples in his cheeks. "You won't believe what I saw," he says, shaking his head. "There was this absolute moron trying to pry open the vending machine with a freaking crowbar. I mean, who even does that?"

Ryan groans. "That "moron" would be me."

"Really? I never would have guessed." Liam plops down beside Finn, who finally lets a small smirk tug at the corner of his mouth.

Before anyone can say anything, Indigo strolls back through the crowd, Cassie and Maya trailing behind her like a mini parade. Finn moves his feet from Indigo's chair as she drops into her seat with a smirk. "Found them. Took absolutely forever to get them out of the bathroom."

Cassie, short and bubbly with curly, auburn hair that bounces when she laughs, plops down next to Maya. She pulls at her messy bun and grins. "Okay, sorry, but look at this bun. Is this not the cutest my hair has ever looked?" She gestures grandly to the space bun perched on top of her head.

Maya smirks like she's already over this conversation. "I told her it looked the same as yesterday,"

"Excuse you," Cassie gasps, "this one is structured."

"Your definition of structure is tragic," Finn mutters without any emotion.

"I didn't ask for your feedback, Finn."

Maya, with her, caramel complexion and thick, black curls pulled back in a high ponytail, laughs and shakes her head. "Also, you missed the best part, some kid was trying to break into the vending machine."

Liam raises an eyebrow. "Really? Who was this genius?"

Ryan buries his head in his hands. "I don't want to talk about it," he mumbles.

I glance around the table, watching them all. Laughing. Teasing. So alive in this moment, like the world doesn't stretch much further than this cafeteria. Like the outside doesn't exist.

In a way, it doesn't. Not here.

Our town is the kind that slips under the radar, barely a speck on any map, a dot that most people wouldn't bother to notice. It's small enough that you can drive from one end to the other in under ten minutes, and quiet enough that the loudest noise is usually the distant rumble of a train or the occasional bark of a dog.

Here, everyone knows your face. And your business. And your history, even the parts you wish they didn't. Secrets don't stay buried for long in a place like this. They bubble up, whispered behind closed doors, passed around like currency in the grocery store aisles or at a Saturday night dinner.

The streets are lined with houses that have seen better days, paint peeling, porches sagging, yards wild with weeds. The sidewalks crack and crumble, forgotten by the county, and the streetlights flicker like ghosts after dark.

Most nights, the town goes to sleep early. By eight, the streets are empty, and the only signs of life are the occasional porchlight or the distant hum of a television behind drawn curtains.

It's the kind of place that feels trapped in time. Nothing much changes here. And maybe that's why some secrets refuse to stay quiet.

But that's the thing about small towns. They remember everything. And they never forget.

"Sadee," Mason says, nudging my knee under the table. "You good?"

I nod automatically. "Yeah. Just tired."

He studies me for a second longer than I like, then drops it. That's how we work now, close, but not too close. Just enough.

Indigo's voice cuts through the hum of the cafeteria. "So... tonight. Who's bringing what?"

"Oh, I've got chips," Maya says, pulling her phone out. "Also, I'm making a playlist. Thoughts? Vibes?"

"Nothing too upbeat," Finn mutters.

Cassie leans in so she's face to face with Finn and whispers, "that's because you hate joy."

"I just don't need music to scream at me."

"We'll find the middle ground," Indigo interrupts, already typing in her notes app. "Sadee, you're coming early, right? To help set up?"

"Yep," I say, even though I'd kind of forgotten. "Wouldn't miss it."

The table falls back into conversation, half-planning, half-chaos, and I sit there, half-in and half-out, listening to their voices swirl together like static.

The bell rings, loud and shrill, cutting through the noise like a blade. It signals the end of lunch and the start of the awkward ten-minute shuffle where everyone pretends not to be in a rush but still bolts toward their next class.

Indigo groans, gathering her tray. "Can't believe we still have two periods left. My soul is tired."

"You have drama next," Maya says, rolling her eyes. "You're literally going to lie on a stage for ninety minutes. You're the corpse."

"That's acting," Indigo says, pointing dramatically toward the ceiling. "It's called *theater,* Maya."

"Same thing."

"Blasphemy."

I stand slowly, slinging my backpack over one shoulder. Mason reaches for my hand, and I let him take it, even though it feels like a reflex now instead of a choice.

"English next?" he asks, already knowing the answer.

"Yeah."

Eli and Ryan head off toward AP Chem, bickering over some podcast Ryan swears predicted a government experiment. Liam splits toward the art wing, Cassie trailing behind him with her sketchbook tucked under one arm. Maya and Indigo exchange one last teasing glance before disappearing down the hall toward the auditorium.

Mason squeezes my hand once more, then lets go. "Ready to survive English?"

I manage a small smile. "As ready as I'll ever be."

The bell's echo still rings in my ears as Mason and I head down the crowded hallway. Lockers slam shut around us, sneakers squeak against the shiny linoleum, and the chatter of students ebbs and flows like a restless tide. I'm trying to focus on Mason's easy smile, but my eyes keep flicking toward the walls, the faces, anything but the ground beneath my feet.

Out of the corner of my eye, I catch a glimpse of Ms. Davis, our history teacher. She's leaning against the lockers, arms crossed, that sharp look in her eyes cutting through the noise. Her gaze latches onto me for a second too long, and I feel a chill crawl up my spine.

I force my shoulders to relax as Mason notices the change. "You sure you're okay?" he asks quietly.

"Yeah, Mason, I'm fine. Just... tired," I say, brushing past Ms. Davis without meeting her eyes. There's something about the way she watches me that's off, like she knows something I don't want her to.

We slip into the English classroom just as the teacher, Mrs. Weller, begins her lecture. The room smells like old books and chalk dust, and the afternoon light filtering through the blinds leaves stripes across the desks.

Mason takes the seat beside me, nudging my shoulder playfully. "Try to stay awake this time, will you?"

I manage a small smile. "No promises."

Mrs. Weller's voice cuts through the chatter. "Alright, everyone. For our next assignment, I want you to explore the theme of madness in *Hamlet*. How does Shakespeare use it to reveal deeper truths about his characters?"

I stare at the question, feeling the weight of those words settling into my chest. Madness. Truths. Things hidden beneath the surface. Nothing new.

Chapter Two

Indigo is going to kill me.

Not in a dramatic, horror-movie kind of way. More like a slow, soul-crushing glare across the room that says, *you have failed me for the last time.* Which is honestly worse.

I woke up fifteen minutes ago to the buzzing of my phone and the very distinct, very noticeable sensation of dread. The party started at seven. It is now… too late for math. Definitely past when I was supposed to be there.

I sit on my bed for exactly three seconds, just long enough to stare at my ceiling and mourn the life choices that led me here. Then I launch into motion, scrambling through the mess of my room like I'm searching for oxygen.

I grab the first pair of jeans that don't smell like gym socks, and a Nirvana shirt that's halfway between vintage and destroyed. It's got holes near the hem, the sleeves are curling, and there's a mysterious stain I choose to ignore. Would Indigo approve? No. Do I have the time to care? Also no.

The floor is cold under my bare feet. I step on something sharp, probably a rogue paperclip or my brother Jack's spy gear, and yelp before hopping over to the dresser. My hair is a disaster. I try to run a brush through it and immediately regret my choices. The knots fight back. The frizz fights harder. I mutter something that would get me grounded if Mom heard and shove the chestnut mess into a ponytail. I don't even try to make it look nice. This is war, not fashion.

Shoes. Backpack. Keys.

I race down the stairs, except I don't. I *trip* down the stairs because someone left something on the third step.

"JACK!" I yell, slamming into the railing hard enough to see stars. The cool wood smacks into my shoulder, and I wince at the sting.

My little brother appears in the doorway. He's holding a tiny notebook and looking entirely too innocent. His dark brown eyes are wide, too wide, like he's rehearsing a lie.

"That's a tripping hazard," I snap, jabbing a finger at the pile of junk littered across the step, socks, an action figure missing an arm, and something that looks like it *used* to be a PB&J but is now more abstract art than food.

Jack blinks at me from the hallway like *he's* the offended party, then straightens his tiny shoulders with all the importance of a field agent. "It was part of a trap," he says calmly, the corner of his mouth twitching like he's trying not to smile. "I was testing to see if the hallway monster was still active."

I stare at him. "You're testing *what* now?"

His face breaks into a proud grin, dimples flashing, eyes gleaming with mischief. "You triggered it. So… yeah. Still active."

The breath I exhale is part frustration, part admiration. He's so annoying. He's so *me*.

I grab my keys off the counter. They feel slick in my sweaty palm. "Tell Mom I'll be back by lunchtime tomorrow."

"You're leaving for that long?" Jack gasps.

"Yeah."

Jack's eyes widen slightly. "Where are you going?"

"To Indigo's party."

He gasps like I just told him I was heading into battle. "*Can I come?*"

"No."

"I'll be quiet."

"Still no."

"I'll bring *disguises.*" He's dead serious now, clutching his little notebook like it holds state secrets.

"You are *nine,* Jack."

He follows me anyway, bare feet slapping the tile as he hustles to keep up. "What if you need backup?"

I stop at the door, hand on the knob. The porch light filters in through the window, casting soft gold across his face. I pause just long enough to meet his eyes, big, wide, warm and brown like mine. He's got that same warm honey-brown skin that I do, the same freckles splotched across his nose, and that same clever spark behind it all. And just like me, he never stops talking when he *really* wants something.

The kitchen light above him flickers slightly, casting a soft yellow glow over his tangled mop of curls. I sigh.

His voice softens just a little. "What if you need me?"

My throat tightens. I crouch to his level and tap his notebook. "I'll report back, Agent Jack. Full intel, mission summary, maybe even photos."

He nods solemnly, then salutes me like we've just sealed a pact.

I smile and ruffle his curls before stepping outside, the heavy door clicking shut behind me.

Outside, the air is muggy, thick with the scent of cut grass and the fading heat of the day. I climb into my car, shove the keys in, and, of course, nothing. Not even a sputter. Just the click of failure.

"Crap." I hit the dashboard like that'll do something.

I rest my forehead against the steering wheel.

Whisper a prayer.

Threaten the dashboard.

Try again.

Still nothing.

I throw the door open, storm back inside, snatch Mom's keys off the hook, and ignore Jack's smug little face as I leave again.

"Looks like you needed backup after all!" he yells after me.

After getting situated in Mom's car, I finally take off for the party. Still late.

Indigo's still going to be mad.

Seven minutes later, I'm pulling into her driveway, heart racing, breath short. The music thumps softly through the windows, muffled but still pulsing like a heartbeat. I slam the door behind me, grab my bag, and jog up to the porch, steps thudding against the old wood.

I step inside without even bothering to knock.

The house smells like popcorn and vanilla candles, a weird but cozy mix. Fairy lights glow along the walls, casting golden shadows over the furniture. The soft murmur of voices filters in from the living room, layered over the beat of some indie pop song I don't recognize.

"Sadee!" Indigo calls from the entryway, arms crossed, expression tight like she's been practicing it in a mirror. Her pale skin glows under the string lights, blue eyes narrowed just enough to show she's annoyed, but not furious. "I reminded you of everything at lunch today. How could you be late?"

"Look, Indigo, I'm sorry. I fell asleep after school and then Jack ran a monster trap on the stairs, and then my car didn't even pretend to care, and then..." I trail off, lifting my hands in surrender like I'm waving a white flag.

Indigo's eyes narrow, but there's the tiniest twitch of a smile at the corner of her lips. I glance at her, hope flickering.

"I know. I suck," I say, dragging the words out, voice dripping with mock drama. "Worst best friend certificate is awarded to none other than your very own Sadee Hart." I sigh, lowering my voice into a mock-announcer tone, like I'm making some grand declaration. My fingers nervously twist a loose strand of hair from my ponytail.

Indigo lets out a slow breath, then rolls her eyes with a shake of her head. "You really are impossible."

"But you love me anyway," I add quickly, stepping closer and nudging her shoulder.

Her smile finally breaks free, softening the tension in the room. "Yeah, yeah. Don't push it." Indigo steers me toward the back of the room where the music is louder, and the air smells faintly of spilled beer and something sweeter, maybe the punch Maya keeps refilling. I grab a bottle of water off the countertop.

Liam and Mason are lounging on the couch, each holding a red solo cup that clinks when they toast. Eli's nearby, nursing his drink with a quiet smile, while Finn leans against the wall, eyes sharp but relaxed. Indigo's already mid-laugh, tossing back a sip from her cup, and Maya's perched on the armrest, grinning as she refills her own glass.

Ryan's sitting cross-legged on the floor next to Cassie, both with cups of punch. Ryan's animated as usual, talking about some wild theory, while Cassie listens with an amused smile, doodling in her sketchbook.

I clutch my water bottle like a lifeline, feeling the cold condensation against my palms. The faint buzz from the others' laughter and the dull warmth of the room press in on me. I catch Mason's glance, no judgment, just quiet understanding. I nod slightly and turn my gaze back to the floor.

"Come on, Sadee," Maya calls, holding up her cup. "One sip won't kill you."

I offer a tight smile. "I'm good, thanks."

She shrugs but doesn't push.

The music dims to a soft hum as Indigo claps her hands together, making the last whispers in the room fade into expectant silence. "Okay, okay, everyone. Charades time. Prepare yourselves for a show you'll never forget." Her voice is loud, theatrical, the kind of voice that fills the room without trying. She walks around and hands everyone a slip of paper, then motions at Liam to go first.

Liam, cheeks flushed with a rosy glow, takes his place at the front of the room, and squints down at the paper he's holding like it's a foreign language. "Uh, I can't read this. Is this English? It looks like my math homework," he grumbles, then crumples the slip and tosses half of it on the floor. "Wait, wait—oh no, I tore it. How am I supposed to act now?"

Eli, sitting next to Liam with a goofy grin and a glassy-eyed stare, holds his slip upside down and furrows his brow. "Okay... my word is 'spaghetti,' but it kinda looks like 'elephant.' Does anyone want to guess what I'm supposed to be?" He shrugs and leans back, chuckling at his own confusion.

Across from them, I'm curled up on the carpet with Ryan and Cassie. Ryan's already whispering conspiracies about the game, something about coded messages hidden in the cards, while Cassie tosses popcorn kernels into the air and catches them effortlessly. Her curls bounce with each laugh, golden light from the fairy lights making her auburn hair glow like embers.

Indigo suddenly sweeps to the center of the room and freezes in an exaggerated pose, hands on her hips like a Shakespearean queen. "Behold, the majesty of my talents," she announces, voice dripping with mock grandeur.

She launches into a wild performance of walking a tightrope, arms stretched out, her foot wavering dramatically. Her eyes widen like she's about to fall, and then she spins, falling to the floor with a theatrical thud.

Laughter rippled through the group like a soft wave, bouncing off the cracked plaster walls and filling every corner with warmth. The air hung heavy with a sweet, buttery aroma, mingled with the sharp fizz of soda and the faint metallic tang of punch. Finn leaned casually against the wall, arms crossed as if only half interested, but the small, amused smirk tugging at the corner of his mouth told a different story. His short, dark hair was tousled just enough to look effortless, sharp features casting subtle shadows in the dim light. His light-olive skin caught a muted glow from the fairy lights, and those intense gray eyes flicked over the room with an unsettling confidence, like he saw everything but wasn't quite ready to share. It was the kind of look that lingers in your peripheral vision and makes you wonder what he's thinking when he's quiet.

Finn's smirk widened just a little as Indigo burst into another exaggerated gesture, her arms flailing dramatically as she silently acted out the next charade. She was a whirlwind of energy, every movement big enough to fill the room, drawing laughs and groans in equal measure. Mason rolled his eyes from his spot on the couch, lips twitching into a lazy grin, clearly amused but way too chill to join in.

Liam was doubled over beside Eli, who was squinting at his card as if it were written in a secret code only decipherable after several drinks. "Okay, wait, wait, 'Star Wars' or 'war stars'? Because if it's the latter, that's a whole different battle," Eli whispered, voice thick but sharp with effort, his glasses slipping down his nose.

Liam hiccupped softly, then pointed at the card with a goofy grin. "War stars. Definitely war stars."

Ryan sat cross-legged on the floor next to Cassie and me, nervously adjusting his glasses every few seconds. He was quiet, but his eyes darted between Indigo and the two drunk boys struggling to read their cards. "I'm pretty sure the whole point of charades is that you don't say anything," he muttered, voice low but clear enough for us to hear. "This overthinking thing? It's just making it harder for everyone."

Cassie, her curly auburn hair catching the soft light, laughed quietly beside me. "Yeah, Ryan, just relax. It's supposed to be fun."

I nodded, feeling the warmth of the group settle around me like a soft blanket. The sounds—the laughter, the shuffling of cards, the scrape of Liam's chair as he tried to stand without toppling over—were familiar, comforting. The taste of cold water on my tongue and the faint whiff of popcorn from earlier reminded me that, for now, this was just a normal night.

Indigo suddenly dropped to her knees, throwing her hands over her face in mock despair before leaping up to mimic an alien invasion.

"The invasion! The invasion!" she mouthed loudly, eyes sparkling with excitement.

Finn, barely containing a chuckle, threw up his hands in surrender. "Okay, okay, that's a classic," he said dryly, but the grin said he was loving every second.

Maya, sitting cross-legged beside Cassie, clapped her hands and cheered. "Come on, Mason! Your turn!"

Mason lazily shrugged, leaning back into the cushions. "I'll pass," he said, voice low and amused.

"Boring," Indigo teased, nudging him playfully.

As the game went on, the room filled with a mix of groans and cheers, whispered guesses and wild gesturing. Even the clink of glasses and occasional pop of a soda can couldn't disrupt the chatter. Outside, the faint hum of crickets drifted through an open window, mixing with the muffled bass of music from another room.

I sank a little lower onto the carpet, watching my friends with a smile I didn't quite trust. This was the kind of night that felt like it could stretch on forever, like we were wrapped in a bubble separate from everything else that threatened to pull us apart.

Maya, sitting beside Cassie with her legs crossed and a sly grin, nudges me gently. "Your turn, Sadee. Don't chicken out."

I swallow hard, heart racing a little from the sudden spotlight. Mason gives me a lazy thumbs-up from the couch, like he knows I'll mess it up but he's rooting for me anyway.

I stand, fingers trembling as I reach into the bowl and pull out a slip. *Butterfly.*

I clear my throat, trying to focus. The room feels warmer suddenly, the thick mix of sweat, perfume, and spilled beer mingling in the air, mingling with the faint scent of vanilla candles flickering on the side table.

I start by fluttering my fingers, awkward and tentative. Nothing like the graceful wings I want to mimic. Liam snorts from across the room, and I feel my cheeks burn.

"That's not helpful," Mason teases, though his smile is easy and encouraging.

"Yeah, Sadee, you're going to have to give us more to work with," Maya laughs, eyes bright as she watches me try again.

I lift my arms, trying to catch an imaginary breeze, moving slowly, then faster, hoping the motion looks natural. Cassie claps softly, and Ryan gives me an awkward thumbs-up, mumbling something about "wing aerodynamics" under his breath.

Indigo suddenly gasps, clutching her chest like I'm giving a performance worthy of Broadway. "Ooooh, the delicate wings, the fluttering dance of life!" she says, eyes sparkling.

"It's a butterfly, you idiot!" Eli yells. "Not everything is a dadgum metaphor!"

Liam, stumbling to his feet, trips over the rug and falls back down with a soft groan, but laughs it off. "I'm never getting up again. Acting is hard, guys."

Eli leans over to Ryan, whispering loudly enough for me to hear, "I think I need a manual for this game."

Ryan gags slightly at Eli's liquor-laced breath, and adjusts his glasses, eyes flickering nervously as he scans the room like it might explode into secret government agents any second. "I'm telling you, the Illuminati designed charades to control the masses."

Cassie giggles, resting her head on her knees. "You're ridiculous, Ryan."

"But maybe," Ryan insists, "the words on those slips aren't random. They're coded."

Maya rolls her eyes but smiles, shaking her head. "If so, I want the decoder ring."

The group's laughter fills the room again, loud, unselfconscious, warm.

The mood shifts effortlessly, like we've been doing this forever. It's chaotic and imperfect, but it's ours. A bubble of comfort in the messy noise of growing up.

Suddenly, Mason calls out from his spot on the couch. "Alright, Finn, your turn."

Finn, leaning against the wall with an almost unreadable expression, shrugs but moves to the front of the room anyway, grabbing a slip with a sharp edge and smooth finish. He reads it, nods once, then strides to the center.

He moves with a quiet intensity, the kind that makes you pay attention. His first gesture is subtle, a slow, deliberate step forward, hands outstretched like he's holding something fragile.

The room goes quiet; eyes locked on him.

He begins to act out *rowing a boat,* arms pulling back and forth with a steady rhythm.

Cassie whispers, "Boat?"

Indigo nods emphatically.

Liam shouts, "River!"

"Canoe!" Mason says.

Ryan looks baffled. "Is it a metaphor for life?"

The laughter returns, louder this time. Mason shakes his head, smirking. "No, it's a boat, Ryan. Not a life lesson."

"Yeah, Ryan." Indigo sighs. "Why didn't you listen to drunk Eli earlier when he got onto me for using metaphors?"

The game continues, slipping into a rhythm, small cheers, bursts of laughter, teasing glances.

I settle back on the floor, relaxing. The room hums with the scent of popcorn, faint hints of citrus soda, and the sweet, clean smell of Cassie's shampoo.

The glow of the fairy lights casts soft halos around faces, flushed, glowing with the warmth of the moment.

Indigo catches my eye and winks, her earlier annoyance forgotten.

And for the first time all evening, I feel like I belong.

I've waited long enough. It's time to play.

Chapter Three

One by one, the party starts to thin out. The music still hums low from the speakers, the faint scent of vanilla and popcorn lingering in the air, along with the last traces of laughter. The chaos of charades has given way to sluggish movement and soft goodbyes.

Mason tosses his keys into the air and catches them with an easy grin. "Alright, boys. Let's go before Liam passes out on the porch."

"I'm *fine,*" Liam says, swaying slightly as he leans on Eli for support.

Eli squints at him, then mutters, "you're literally not."

"Bro, I'm the picture of stability," Liam insists, nearly falling as he tries to stand straight.

Mason rolls his eyes, gently steering them both toward the door. "Come on. I'm getting you two home in one piece. Try not to puke in my truck."

"I make no promises," Eli mumbles as they disappear into the night.

Cassie gathers her sketchbook and hoodie, slinging her bag over her shoulder. "Maya's forcing me to work on our history project tonight," she says with a sigh, but there's a fond smile playing at her lips.

"I'm not forcing you," Maya retorts. "I'm just saying if we don't finish it, we fail. And you know I'm not failing anything that requires glitter."

They wave and duck out the door together, bickering playfully.

Ryan is already halfway down the porch steps when Indigo calls, "Hey, Ryan! You need a ride?"

He shakes his head, adjusting his backpack. "Nah, I'm good. Finn's giving me one."

From the hallway, Finn lifts a hand in silent confirmation. His gray eyes flick to mine for a second, unreadable, and then he's gone, the door closing behind them with a soft *click.*

The quiet is immediate.

Just me and Indigo now.

The silence only lasts a beat before Indigo grabs my hand and pulls me into her room, grabbing a speaker that's still playing music. "Let's go, loser." She starts dancing and singing to the music playing.

I jump in, laughing, and we twirl around the room like idiots. My socks slide on the hardwood floor, and for a second, everything is light again. Then we collapse onto her bed, giggling breathlessly and staring up at the ceiling.

"I think we need to watch the new *Scream* movie," Indigo says suddenly, propping herself up on one elbow.

I groan, sliding off the bed and onto the floor with a dramatic thud. "I don't know, Indi. You know I don't like those movies."

"Come on, Sadee, just give into the culture of the ghost town we live in." Indigo whips out her phone and shoves it in my face. "Just watch the trailer."

I push it away, laughing. "No way."

"Why not?"

"What if something like that happens here? I almost think it would be worse to know how it would end, you know?"

Indigo throws a pillow at me. "Right, because some psycho is coming to our nobody town to kill all of us. We barely even make it onto regional maps, we're so unimportant! 'Hey, I'm a mass murderer from New York. Oh, lookie! A nobody town filled with people who aren't even worth my time to kill. Let's stop here!'"

I gasp and throw the pillow back. "It could happen! You never know!"

"And when it does, everyone here will be prepared except for you." Indigo crosses her arms with an exaggerated huff.

"Last year the mayor hired a guy to wander around dressed like a plague doctor. He handed out candy from a bucket labeled *poison*," I point out. "Weird things happen here—what if someone decided to take it too far?"

"Yeah, but how long have we lived here? Eighteen years? How long have people lived here before then? A lot longer. And guess what? Nothing's ever happened."

"*Yet*," I whisper.

"Whatever, Sadee, just be boring then. It's whatever." Indigo rolls her eyes and flops back onto the bed.

I sit up, trying to shake the growing unease in my stomach. "Plus, I don't think I'd count *Scream* as a horror movie. I think it's what you'd get if a thriller and a comedy had a baby."

Indigo sits up so fast her hair whips around. "How do you know anything about *Scream*?"

"I've seen them."

"Even the new one?"

"Yeah, it's always the romantic interest or the best friend. In this case, it's both."

"Sadee, come on! You just ruined it!"

"How so? Haven't you seen them all a thousand times already?"

"I hadn't finished *that* one yet!" Indigo grabs another pillow and hurls it at me. Then she jumps off the bed, grabbing her laptop. "I'm finishing it right now, and I'm forgetting who you say Ghostface was in this one."

"Sam's boyfriend, Richie, and then there's Sam's sister, Tara, right? It's also her best friend, Amber."

"Right." Indigo slowly closes her laptop, clearly for dramatic effect. "Thanks, I don't even have to watch it anymore."

"You're welcome. It was too predictable anyway; I just saved you over an hour of your time." I stand and start to head for the door. "I'm going downstairs for a snack. Join me or don't. I don't care."

"I'm staying here, thanks." Indigo calls after me. "But bring me back some pickle spears."

Her phone rings just as I reach the stairs.

"It's Ghostface! Be careful, Indi, you're the next victim!" I yell.

Within seconds, she's magically by my side, clutching my arm. "And I thought *I* was the scaredy-cat," I laugh.

She sits at the bar while I open the fridge and pull out the pickle jar. She starts scrolling on her phone as I dig through the pantry for peanut butter and grab an apple off the counter.

Her phone dings at the same time mine vibrates in my back pocket.

I glance over. She's staring at her screen, brows furrowed.

"Did you get this too?" she asks.

I pull out my phone.

Welcome to the game.

My stomach drops.

Indigo looks up, slowly chewing on a bite of pickle. "What in the world?" she mouths, still mid-chew.

I shrug, my pulse ticking up as I wait for a follow-up text that doesn't come.

Indigo flips her phone over and drops it on the counter. "Whatever. Just ignore it. This isn't the first weird thing that's happened here.

Remember when half the senior lockers were filled with fake blood last year?"

My apple slice hovers midair. Indigo might be the horror movie expert, but she's not cautious. Meanwhile, I'm practically ready to pack up and leave this ghost town.

"Yeah, I remember," I say.

"I think it's just some creep who dumped a bunch of numbers into a group chat, hoping someone would respond. You know, start a conversation, lure someone out, classic online predator behavior." She pops another pickle in her mouth.

"What if the person who texted was a girl?"

"Then she's probably either bored or trying to get attention."

"Right." I take a bite of my apple. "What if it's something else though, Indi?" I rest my forearms on the counter and look at her.

"And what would that something be?"

"You know."

Indigo bursts out in laughter, almost falling out of the barstool she's sitting in. "Sadee, I think you've officially lost it!" She tries to contain her laughter. "There's no way we're being thrown into a horror movie. That's not how it works."

"That's what they all say," I mutter, a half-smile tugging at my lips.

"You know what, I have to pee," Indigo announces, stretching as she stands. She heads down the hall, then pauses dramatically at the bathroom doorframe. Gripping it with both hands like she's about to be sucked into another dimension, she lowers her voice and says, "I'll be back," in the creepiest tone she can muster.

"That's what they all say," I call again, louder this time, as she disappears behind the door.

I take another bite of my apple, chewing slowly as I scroll through my Instagram feed with my free hand. The usual selfies and sports recaps flash by until I notice a post from someone in my chemistry class. Then another from someone in my English class. And another. And another. All saying some version of the same thing:

Did anyone else get this weird text?

Okay. Breathe.

Don't spook yourself. It's just a coincidence. Probably.

Indigo silently appears back in the kitchen. "Are you seeing all of this?" She asks, shoving her phone in my face, giving me a glimpse of all the Instagram posts. "Sounds like the message was just sent to people in this area."

"Starting to believe me now?"

"Nope." She dances around the kitchen, making her way back to the barstool. "I think you're overthinking it."

"And you're underthinking it. I mean think about it, Indi. A group text with all the seniors in this small town, all thrown into some 'game'? What are the chances that's an accident?"

"Maybe it's just the senior prank?" Indigo suggests, her mind clearly rethinking the entire situation. "Or maybe it's just a way to scare us into staying in town and not leaving?"

"How would this scare people into staying here? This would scare them away."

"Then go with my senior prank idea. It is that time of year." Indigo shrugs and pulls her phone back out. "Plus, even if it is any of that weird stuff, I don't want to believe it. So please, let's not talk about it."

I lean against the counter and watch Indigo's facial expressions grow increasingly more worried as she scrolls through more and more of her Instagram feed. I can't help but to grab my phone and scroll through all the comments and reposts.

For a town so obsessed with all things horror, people really are too terrified about this whole thing. Really, it's just a simple text. How much harm can it do?

Indigo tosses her phone facedown again, harder this time. "Okay. Enough creepy. Let's cleanse our brains with something stupid."

I raise a brow. "Like what?"

She grins. "TikTok fails. Or those old ghost-hunting shows where the guy screams at the walls like the ghosts owe him money."

"Both sound better than focusing on this text. Let's do it."

We retreat to her bedroom, dragging snacks and pillows with us. Indigo props her laptop on her knees while I curl up in the nest of blankets at the foot of her bed. The screen glows blue as she pulls up a video titled "Top 10 Dumbest Paranormal Investigations."

A dramatic voiceover immediately fills the room: *"In this episode, our team returns to the haunted mansion where a demonic entity once allegedly threw a couch down a flight of stairs."*

"I mean," I say between chews of a granola bar, "if a couch flew down the stairs, I'd move out. Like, instantly."

"Honestly," Indigo agrees. "I'd just be like, 'Hey ghost, you can have the lease.'"

We laugh, but it's softer than before. The kind of laughter that knows it's covering something up. I catch her sneaking glances at her phone every few minutes, even if she doesn't unlock it.

Halfway through the third video, she pauses it.

"Okay, but what if, hypothetically, this game thing is real," she says slowly, like she's trying to feel out the shape of the thought before fully saying it. "What would that even mean?"

I shift, the blanket slipping off my shoulder. "Like… someone watching us? Or setting something up?"

She shrugs. "Maybe it's just a test. Like some weird social experiment."

"Or it's the start of something worse."

Silence.

Then she snorts. "Sadee, we sound like the kids in the first half of every horror movie."

"Yeah," I mutter. "And you know what happens to them."

She pulls the blanket over her head. "Stop. This is why I watch this stuff, it makes it less scary. Like, if you know the tropes, it can't get you."

"Tell that to the guy in the ghost show who got knocked out by a bookshelf."

Indigo re-emerges from her blanket cocoon. "Okay, new plan. We're not sleeping tonight."

I groan. "We still have school tomorrow. Those stupid history presentations are due." I rub my eyes.

She waves that off. "I'll write you a note. *'Dear Ms. Davis, please excuse Sadee from class as she has contracted a deadly virus for the next hour and a half. Thank you.'"*

I roll my eyes. "Very official."

There's a long beat where we just sit there, the video still paused on a grainy image of some guy screaming at a dark hallway. Then, as if syncing up, we both sigh.

"I hate that this is bothering me," Indigo finally says, quieter now. "It's probably nothing, but it's just… the not knowing."

"Yeah." I pick at the seam of a pillowcase. "It's the kind of thing that worms into your brain."

"Like a horror movie you can't turn off."

We don't say anything else for a while. She hits play again, and we keep watching, fake ghosts, clumsy camera guys, a guy named Kyle who claims he can hear demons whispering his name.

By the fifth video, the tension's mostly drained out of the room, or at least shoved to the back of our brains. Indigo's curled up next to me, the glow of the laptop flickering across her face, and I feel myself relaxing too.

My eyes drift toward the window. Outside, the sky is a deep, bottomless navy. Crickets chirp in the grass. A streetlight flickers at the end of the driveway, humming softly.

Safe. Normal.

Except… my phone buzzes again.

This time, it's not a text. It's a notification from the school IG chat.

I sit up a little straighter, nudging Indigo. "Hey. Look at this."

She squints at the screen. Then her jaw tightens.

This better not be part of a senior prank.

No one even knows who started the group.

Indigo and I exchange a look.

Neither of us is laughing now.

Chapter Four

The sun feels too bright for how little sleep we got. It's like it's mocking me, shining in through the windshield with this harsh certainty, while I'm still running on a memory of maybe two hours of restless shuteye and pure existential dread.

Indigo's car smells like cherry air freshener and cold hash browns, the kind of lingering smell that makes me almost nostalgic for the night before, even if it was full of late-night demon-hunting videos and way too much anxiety.

She's driving one-handed, sunglasses on, humming softly like she wasn't up until 3 a.m. watching videos about demons and curses. Like she's some kind of expert, or maybe just trying to convince herself nothing real is happening.

I don't say anything, just grunt in response when she offers, "I'm just saying, if we end up cursed or whatever, I better at least get cool powers. Telekinesis. Invisibility. Something." I press my forehead to the cool glass of the window and let my thoughts spiral. This is bigger than we are. I'm sure of it.

The gravel crunches under our feet as we step out of the car and head toward the school. Indigo pulls her hood up without a word, casting a shadow over her face in the early light. I follow, my mind already spinning faster than I can catch. School feels different today. Familiar chaos swirls around us, but every step feels heavier, like the quiet before a storm, like we're walking into something no one's ready for.

We slip inside just as the second bell clangs, and the noise swallows the last traces of silence between us. First period drags on through Calculus, but my mind is miles away, looping back to that strange text and the feeling that everything's shifted. Indigo sits a few rows ahead, her hood pulled low, eyes flicking to her phone every few minutes. The teacher drones on, but I barely hear a word.

When first period finally ends, Indigo slings her backpack over one shoulder, hood still up, and I follow her into the hallway. Near the door to our second period history class, Finn and Mason are already waiting. Mason's leaning casually against the wall, hands stuffed in his pockets, his easy grin flashing as we approach. Finn stands a few feet away, scanning the hallway with his usual quiet intensity.

"Hey," Mason nods. "Rough morning?"

Indigo pulls her hood down just enough to smirk. "You could say that."

I shrug. "Two hours of sleep, plus whatever is going on with that text."

Finn raises an eyebrow. "Yeah, got it too. Weird timing."

"Probably just some prank, right?" Mason says, shrugging.

Indigo shakes her head. "I hope it's just part of some senior prank."

Mason laughs and runs his hands through his hair. "I'm sure it is." He nods toward the classroom door. "We should head in. Are you guys ready for the presentations?"

"Not at all," I sigh, stepping into the room. Indigo and I find our seats at the back, pressed against the wall.

The door creaks open just as the second bell rings again. The air shifts. I can feel Indigo go still beside me. Her foot, which had been bouncing just seconds ago, halts mid-tap. She stiffens, then slowly reaches for her hood and pulls it over her head, not like she's cold, but like she's hiding. Like fabric is enough to shield her from whatever just walked through the door.

A sharp pop breaks the silence—the crack of a Red Bull can.

Nick Donovan walks in.

It's the first time we've seen him since "the incident".

He's tall. Too confident. The kind of confidence that doesn't come from self-assurance but from something colder, something practiced. His black leather jacket stretches across his shoulders like a second skin, creased just right at the elbows, perfectly worn to his figure. His dark hair is slicked back with surgical precision. His pale, flat eyes skim the room like he's counting who matters. Which is no one.

And that smile, that awful, cocky not-quite-a-smirk, is always glued to his face. Like he knows something you don't. Like he's been waiting for you to figure it out and is already bored of your slow progress.

He doesn't look at Indigo. He doesn't have to.

She flinches anyway, shrinking back into her chair like just breathing the same air as him makes her skin crawl. Her fingers disappear into her sleeves. I hear her inhale, sharp and small, like she's trying to keep it in.

No one else reacts.

But I notice.

And Finn notices. He's tucked in the corner seat by the window, forest green hoodie half-zipped, the frayed cuffs stretched over his wrists. His legs are stretched out under the desk. He hasn't moved in minutes. But now his knee starts bouncing, fast and erratic, like something's winding up inside him. His fingers twitch. Once. Twice. Sharp jolts, like he's holding back an electric current.

He doesn't look up.

But his jaw tightens. I see the tension flicker in his face, even from across the room.

Nick strolls past without a glance at Finn or Indigo. He moves like he owns the place, tossing himself into the back seat and kicking his boots up onto the chair in front of him. Red Bull in one hand, phone in the other, like this is all one big joke. Like we're just extras in his movie.

The teacher doesn't acknowledge the disruption.

Ms. Davis clapped her hands once. "Alright, presentations today. You know the drill, no whining, no last-minute excuses, and yes, you have to go up front."

A groan rolled across the room. Papers shuffled. Someone sighed audibly. Maya muttered under her breath about how she knew she should've stayed home.

Indigo didn't move. She curled in on herself; arms crossed tightly around her stomach. Her hood cast shadows over most of her face, and if I didn't know better, I'd have thought she was asleep. But I knew better. She was bracing herself.

Ms. Davis glanced down at the seating chart again. "Let's start with… Sadee and Indigo."

My stomach lurched. I nudged Indigo gently. "Hey. We're up."

Her eyes stayed locked on the desk, distant and unfocused. Then, barely above a whisper, she said, "You go."

"It's a group project," I reminded her softly.

She closed her eyes and let out a shaky breath. "I, I can't… Just, just do it, um, do it without me."

There was something fragile in her voice, beneath all the usual fire I knew so well. This wasn't just nerves. This was something else entirely.

Still, I couldn't do it alone.

"No one's expecting you to give a speech," I said, my voice low. "Just come stand next to me. You don't even have to talk if you don't want to."

There was a long pause. Then, slowly, she nodded. Her hood stayed pulled up, her arms crossed. But she stood, moving almost robotically, as if her body obeyed out of habit while her mind was somewhere far away.

We walked to the front together, and I could feel Nick's eyes sliding across us. They didn't linger, but I felt them, cold, measuring, like we were lab rats in some experiment only he understood.

My hands trembled as I clicked the remote, the projector flickering to life. The blue light from the title slide cast a faint glow over our faces.

I cleared my throat. "Um. So… our topic is the effect of media framing on public perception."

My voice sounded robotic, stiff and uncertain.

Indigo stood slightly behind me, her hands shoved deep into her sleeves, her shoulders hunched as if trying to disappear. But she was there, barely, but there.

I kept talking, forcing my voice to steady with each slide. Glancing toward the back row, I saw Finn still bouncing his knee, eyes locked on the room like a laser grid. He didn't look up, but I could feel his tension radiating across the room.

Nick looked completely amused. One hand held his Red Bull, the other lazily spun a pen between his fingers. He leaned back, watching the whole thing like a sitcom, like this was some entertainment meant for his amusement.

I swallowed hard and flipped to the next slide.

Then, unexpectedly, Indigo shifted beside me. Her voice was barely louder than a breath when she said, "The media often distorts narratives depending on the outlet's bias."

I turned to her, surprised.

She didn't meet my eyes, but she kept going, quiet, but steady. "It's not just what they report. It's how they say it. Headlines, word choice, even image selection. It shapes how people react—sometimes before they even read the article."

Her voice gained a little strength with each word, pulling herself into the moment.

Ms. Davis nodded approvingly. "Good. Keep going."

We finished together, awkward, a little shaky, but we finished.

As we walked back to our seats, I glanced over my shoulder. Nick was watching Indigo. Just for a second.

And even though his usual smirk was gone, somehow, that silence felt worse than anything he could have said.

The rest of the school day passed in a quiet haze. Classes went on, conversations hummed softly about the strange text, but no one had any answers. By the time the final bell rang, the weight of everything settled heavily over me.

After school, Indigo drove me back to her house to pick up some of the things I had left, including my car. I grabbed my keys from the desk in her room, thanked her parents for letting me stay the night, and slipped out the front door.

The drive home was calm, the evening light casting long shadows across the quiet streets. Once inside, I dropped my bag and tried to focus on homework, but my thoughts kept drifting, back to the text, to the weird feeling lingering in the air.

The smell of cooking food drifted up to my room, and my mom's voice called up the stairs, soft but insistent. "Sadee, it's time for dinner!"

I took a deep breath, letting the scent wrap around me like a soft blanket, and headed downstairs. The kitchen was glowing with golden light, the kind that made everything feel a little safer, a little more like home. The table was already set, plates neatly arranged, silverware gleaming, a small vase with wildflowers from the garden sitting off to the side. The air was thick with the rich aroma of roasted chicken, mingled with cinnamon and something sweet that I couldn't quite place, like baked apples or maybe pumpkin.

My little brother was sprawled across his chair, hands gesturing wildly, as he told some story from school that had Mom rolling her eyes, but laughing despite herself. She moved gracefully between the stove and the table, smiling as she passed around bowls of mashed potatoes and green beans. Dad sat at the head of the table, quiet but present, his tired eyes softening when they met mine.

I slid into my seat, trying to fold the day away beneath polite conversation and the comforting clink of silverware. My hands felt heavy, the exhaustion pressing down like a physical weight behind my eyes, dulling my movements. Two hours of sleep felt impossibly far away, like a distant place I couldn't quite reach.

The usual chatter circled around me, jokes and teasing, questions about school and plans for the weekend, but my mind kept drifting, caught somewhere between the warmth of the kitchen and the cold knot of unease coiling inside me. I watched Kirby, my goldendoodle, curled up at my feet, his curly fur soft against the floor, his steady breathing a quiet anchor.

After dinner, I grabbed Kirby's leash from the hook by the door and slipped out into the cool evening air. The sky was a deepening shade of purple, stars just beginning to prick through the darkening night. The neighborhood felt peaceful, the crunch of fallen leaves and gravel underfoot mixing with the distant hum of traffic and the occasional chirp of crickets.

Kirby bounded ahead, nose to the ground, ears twitching at every sound. Sometimes he'd stop suddenly, tilting his head like he'd heard something just beyond my notice. I looked around, but everything seemed still, just shadows stretching longer and longer, the night settling in slow and sure.

The walk wasn't long, but it gave me a moment to breathe, to let the quiet sink into my bones. The weight of the day pulled at me, but here in the cool air, with Kirby padding beside me, it felt just a little lighter.

Back home, I let Kirby off the leash in the yard, watching as he chased his tail for a few dizzy circles before curling up near the porch steps, eyes half-closed and content.

Inside, I moved through my bedtime routine with slow, deliberate motions. Brushing my teeth, the sharp minty taste a crisp contrast to the warmth settling into my body. Changing into soft pajamas, pulling the sheets back just right.

When I finally climbed into bed, I pulled the covers up tight around me. The ceiling fan hummed softly overhead, a gentle white noise that filled the quiet room. My eyelids fluttered, heavy with exhaustion, but sleep didn't come immediately. My mind buzzed with fragments, the day's tension, the strange text, the feeling that something was waiting just out of sight.

Eventually, the weight of tiredness won out, dragging me under into a deep, restless calm.

Tomorrow was waiting, whatever it held, I'd face it when the sun came up.

Chapter Five

The rules are simple. It's a game of hangman. I've chosen a word, and you all will take turns guessing letters. If you guess a letter that is in the chosen word, then I'll leave you alone. If you chose the wrong letter, then I draw a limb on the man, and you get a punishment. No one will know how many limbs are left to be drawn or who all has been told to take a turn.

We'll start off with a simple phrase. I'm sure you guys will know this one.

Good luck.

I startle as my phone starts buzzing. It rattles slightly against the nightstand, the sharp hum echoing louder than it should in the quiet of my room. I glance out the window instinctively, like I might find answers there. The moon hangs low behind thick clouds, a hazy silver disk waiting to disappear behind a storm. The clouds are bloated and slow, preparing to soak the town with a heavy downpour by morning. Everything looks like it's holding its breath.

I read the text from the unknown sender. Part of me, the smallest, most annoying part, feels smug for being right. I *knew* this wasn't random. I *knew* something weird was going on.

My phone buzzes again.

Sadee Hart, you're up. My entire body goes rigid. I re-read the message, once, twice, three times, as if the words might change if I just look long enough.

"What am I supposed to do with this?" I whisper out loud, my voice barely audible. My phone hovers in my shaky hands above my face as I roll onto my back, eyes fixed on the glowing screen like it'll go away in time.

_ _ _ _ _ _ _ _ _ _ _ _ _ _. I groan and set my phone face down on my bedside table. They know I'm not answering. Maybe that's all it takes. Maybe refusing to engage means I win.

I roll over, facing the window again. My cheek presses against the cool side of my pillow, and I close my eyes, letting the darkness settle around me like a blanket. I've always felt at home in the dark. People fear it for what it might hide—monsters, miseries, madmen—but I see something different. The darkness is honest. It doesn't lie to you. It just *is*.

What really lives in the dark? Secrets, maybe. Things people don't say. Feelings you can't explain. I let my mind drift, trying to find comfort in the familiar shadows.

Then the vibration hits again, loud, sharp, angry, rattling the hollow wood of the nightstand like a warning.

I roll over and face my window, closing my eyes and allowing the darkness to engulf me. I thrive in darkness. Where people fear the darkness for what it might hide, I see an unknown part of this world that we have yet to discover. What does live in the darkness?

My phone vibrates loudly against the hollow wood of my nightstand. *What letter do you want to guess? No answer is the same as guessing a wrong letter.*

I stare at the phone for a long time, the screen glowing in the corner of my vision. My fingers tremble slightly as I hover over the keyboard. I want to believe this is fake, just a game, just a hoax, but something deep in my gut is telling me otherwise. Something that's lived in this town long enough to *know* better.

I've grown up surrounded by stories that never made the news. Whispers of things that happened, but no one talks about. This town doesn't play fair, but neither do I. And this? This is another one of its games, and I'm ready to walk away victorious.

"*A*" I stare at my phone for a second, feeling sweat start to develop on the bridge of my nose, dreading the response I'll get. It comes quicker than I expected.

Third word. Third letter.

I let out a shaky breath. Relief floods through my chest like warm water. That's it. That's all. I guessed right. Nothing bad happened.

I set my phone gently back on the nightstand and push the covers off. Sleep feels impossible now. My heart's still racing, and the silence in my room feels different than before, heavier somehow. I make my way quietly into the kitchen and pour a glass of water for myself, holding it with both hands to keep them steady.

A floorboard creaks in the entry hall.

I freeze.

It's nothing, it has to be. Just the house settling, or maybe the wind. But then it creaks again. Sharper this time, like weight shifting. Like someone stepping carefully across a hollow rib.

My fingers tighten around the glass.

Please let it be Kirby.

But he's not barking. Not growling. Not making a single sound. That's what throws me off. He barks at everything, passing cars, mail carriers, his own reflection in the sliding door. This silence isn't normal.

Slowly, I back toward the counter, never taking my eyes off the hallway. My hand reaches behind me, fingers finding the knife block. I pull one out—the biggest one. I'm not getting killed tonight. Not tomorrow either. Or ever, for that matter.

I creep along the edge of the kitchen, each step slow and quiet. My breath is shallow, my grip tight on the knife. When I peek around the corner into the entryway, there's... nothing. Just empty tile and shadows.

See? I'm kidding myself.

I exhale shakily and turn back toward the counter to return the knife. Just as I start to slide it into the block, something nudges against my leg.

I let out a sharp cry and spin around, heart in my throat.

Kirby sits there looking up at me like I've offended him.

"Dumb dog," I mutter, lowering the knife. "You scared the crap out of me. What do you want?"

He lets out a soft whine and trots back toward the living room like he owns the place.

I stand there for a moment, letting my pulse come down, then head back to my room.

I'd guessed the letter. Nothing bad had happened. I'd done my part. This freak show? It's over. For me, at least. Thank God.

I crawl back into bed, pull the blankets up to my chin, and let my thoughts run.

How did this person know about senior prank week? It's not a huge deal outside of town, it's just something we do. Nothing that ever makes the news. So how would a stranger know it was happening here? Who even *cares* about some tiny town in the middle of nowhere?

They're not getting famous for this. They're not going viral. No one important is going to hear about it.

I don't get it.

I close my eyes and tell myself again that it's over.

But deep down, somewhere in the quiet space between one heartbeat and the next, I know that it's not.

I know that this game, whatever it is, hasn't even started yet.

Dawn could not have come any slower. A steady trickle of rain had begun within the past hour, leaving the sky dark gray, a perfect color to match this twisted prank someone was pulling.

At school, everything was loud again. The buzz of fluorescent lights and the squeak of sneakers on tile. Conversations bouncing off lockers like they'd never left. Someone shoved a poster in my face about the pep rally Friday. I nodded like I cared and kept walking.

Indigo found me at my locker, talking fast about something in English I barely caught.

"I swear if he makes us annotate *another* poem, I'm going to lose my mind. Like, how many metaphors does one dead poet need?"

I gave her a half-smile. "You love metaphors."

"Yeah, but not after lunch, I'm tired after I eat. And not while half the class thinks enjambment is a pasta." She looked at me then, more closely. "You good?"

"Yeah." I shut my locker. "Just tired."

She gave me a look, like she didn't quite buy it, but didn't press.

We walked to class together. I tried to keep pace, to match her energy, but everything felt two beats off. I kept thinking about the message. Not just the words, what *wasn't* said. No clue how long the word was. No clue what the punishment would've been. The Hangman is not playing fair.

In Government, someone had doodled a game of Hangman in the corner of the whiteboard. I stared at it too long. The stick figure was half-drawn, one arm raised like it was waving. No one else seemed to notice. Or care.

When the lunch bell rang, I flinched. The sharp clang against the silence of my thoughts felt like a gunshot.

I made it through the rest of the day on autopilot. Took notes I wouldn't remember. Answered a question I didn't hear. Laughed when someone said something funny even though I didn't catch the joke.

By fifth period, the rain had started again. Steady. Rhythmic. A wet soundtrack to a day that refused to feel normal.

I told myself it was over. I'd played the game, guessed the letter, nothing bad had happened. That should be the end of it.

Still, I double-checked the back seat before getting in my car.

Just in case.

I drove home with both hands clenched around the steering wheel, knuckles pale, tires humming over wet pavement. Rain hit the windshield in a rhythm that felt too deliberate, like it was trying to say something I couldn't understand. I had the wipers on low, just enough to smear the gray world back into view every few seconds. No music. No podcasts. Just me and my thoughts, looping like a broken record.

I kept glancing at my phone in the passenger seat, hoping, and not hoping, for another message. Something to confirm that last night wasn't just a vivid nightmare. But the screen stayed dark. No new notifications. The unknown number hadn't said anything else. Maybe that meant I was safe. Or maybe it meant I was being watched.

When I pulled into the driveway, I didn't get out right away. I sat there with the engine running, fingers still wrapped around the steering wheel, the sound of the rain thudding gently against the roof of the car. I wasn't afraid exactly. Just... braced. Like I was waiting for something to jump out. But nothing did. I knew it wouldn't.

Eventually, I popped the door open and jogged up the front walk, ducking my head against the drizzle. Kirby met me at the door like he always did, tail wagging, toenails clattering against the tile. I knelt to scratch behind his ears and felt the tension in my shoulders loosen just a little.

"Hey, buddy," I murmured.

He licked my hand and trotted off like everything in the world was fine. I tried to follow his lead.

Inside, I dumped my bag by the stairs and walked into the kitchen, suddenly very aware of how quiet the house was. My mom wouldn't be home for another hour or so. I'd never noticed how empty the place felt without her, without the low sound of a talk show in the background or the scent of something simmering on the stove. I grabbed a sleeve of saltines from the pantry and leaned against the counter, eating one without tasting it. The fridge hummed quietly. Rain streaked down the windows.

I pulled out my phone and unlocked it.

Nothing.

I opened the message thread with the unknown number and stared at it. The puzzle was still there, the line of blanks with only one letter filled in. The third letter of the third word. An "A." Just one correct guess and then silence.

The silence was somehow worse than the threat.

I switched my class group chat. Someone had sent a picture of cafeteria pizza from lunch, all soggy crust and weird orange grease. A few people had added laugh-reacts, some stupid caption about mystery meat. Totally normal. Completely disconnected from the night I'd had. I stared at it for too long, trying to decide if anyone else in the group was pretending like I was. If maybe one of them had gotten the message too.

I didn't ask. I couldn't.

Kirby wandered back into the room and looked at me expectantly, like he was waiting for me to get my act together. I sank down to the floor beside him and let my back hit the cabinets with a soft thud. He threw his head into my lap without hesitation, nearly knocking the crackers out of my hand.

"You think I'm going crazy?" I whispered.

He wagged his tail in response. I laughed, soft and tired.

When I stood up again, I wandered into the living room and threw a blanket over my lap. I turned on the TV, mostly for background noise, flipping until I landed on some old crime show I'd seen before. Nothing too intense. Nothing with jump scares. Just something to keep me from thinking too hard.

But my brain wouldn't shut up.

Every creak in the walls made me glance over my shoulder. Every flicker in my peripheral vision pulled my focus.

It was almost five. Still early. But the sky outside had turned a muddy gray, the clouds too heavy, the kind that pressed down on you. Thunder rumbled somewhere in the distance. Kirby barked suddenly, one short sound that made my heart leap into my throat.

"Really?" I muttered, peering down the hallway.

He was standing at the front window, tail rigid, ears forward. Staring at... nothing, as far as I could tell. Just the street and the trees. Maybe a squirrel. Maybe a shadow that didn't belong.

I got up and double-checked the front door. Locked. I checked the back one too. Still locked. All the windows. Every single one.

I wasn't being paranoid. I was being careful.

By the time I made it back to my room, I felt like I'd run a marathon without moving. I left the door open and clicked on my lamp, the soft yellow light casting long shadows on the walls. I didn't even bother changing out of my jeans. I just crawled under the blanket and laid there with Kirby at my feet, staring at the ceiling, my phone face-up on the pillow beside me.

Still no messages.

Still no explanation.

I knew I should've felt relieved, but I didn't. I felt like the quiet was waiting for something.

Chapter Six

School settled into its usual rhythm. The buzz of locker doors slamming, the sharp scrape of sneakers on tile, voices drifting down crowded hallways.

I moved through it all with that half-present, half-distracted feeling you get when you're thinking about a hundred things but none of them right now. Mostly, I was running through the math problems in my head, but the answers wouldn't come.

Instead, I pictured Kirby, waiting at home with that ridiculous golden-doodle grin, probably wondering why I hadn't fed him yet.

First period dragged on like it always did, a blend of textbook pages turning, teacher's voice fading in and out, and the low murmur of students who'd rather be anywhere else. I was halfway through my notes when the bell finally rang, a sharp relief. One class closer to lunch, one class closer to the weekend, one class closer to forgetting about this math test for a little while longer.

By third period, I was more awake, trading tired glances with Mason whenever our teacher went off on a tangent. He looked like he hadn't slept either. His hair was messier than usual, and there was this quiet tension in the way he sat, like he was trying to keep something tucked away just beneath the surface.

Lunch was the highlight, as always. We had our spot saved by the big window in the cafeteria, the one that let in the afternoon sun just right, making the peeling paint on the walls look warmer than it actually was. It was our corner, a little pocket of calm in the chaos of the school day.

Indigo was already there when I arrived, tearing into her sandwich with the kind of enthusiasm that made me smile. Cassie was setting out a small stack of sketchbooks, humming quietly to herself. Maya and Eli were in a low conversation that I wasn't quite paying attention to, while Finn leaned back in his chair, half-smiling like he was waiting for the right moment to say something.

Mason slid in next to me with a clatter, nearly tipping his tray.

"Easy," I said, reaching out to steady his drink.

He shot me a quick grin, but there was something distracted in his eyes. His phone buzzed softly in his pocket, glowing for a second before he slipped it deeper, like it was a secret he didn't want to share.

"Alright, Mason," Indigo said, eyes narrowing playfully. "What're you hiding? You're acting weird."

Mason gave a half-shrug. "Nothing. Just tired."

"Uh-huh," Indigo replied, raising an eyebrow. "Lying is your new hobby?"

I caught the way Mason's jaw tightened for a split second before he relaxed again. The way he hid that phone like it was some kind of ticking bomb was different from usual. Normally, he'd just pull it out and laugh off whatever was on the screen.

Cassie broke in, brushing a stray curl behind her ear. "Hey, anyone else completely lost in Mr. Crawley's class? I swear, some days it feels like he's just here to fill the chair."

Maya nodded, folding her arms across her chest. "Seriously. I think he's testing how long he can get paid without actually teaching."

Eli chuckled softly. "That might be the most accurate thing I've heard all week."

Finn's lips twitched into a smirk as he glanced at Ryan. "Or maybe he's an undercover agent. Teaching's just the cover story."

Ryan's eyes lit up with that familiar spark, taking the bait. "Okay, but what if the cafeteria food is part of some government experiment? Like, they want to see how long teenagers can survive on mystery meat before turning into zombies?"

Indigo snorted. "Ryan, you are just something, aren't you?"

Cassie wrinkled her nose. "Those mashed potatoes last week tasted like something out of a science lab."

I glanced at Mason again. His phone buzzed a second time, and his hand twitched toward it before he pulled back. He was quick to flip the screen down again, pretending to focus on his food.

"What's up with you?" I asked quietly, nudging him.

"Nothing," he said smoothly. "Just tired. Math test."

Indigo snorted. "Lame."

"Maybe I'm just old and wise now," Mason said, grinning like a kid caught sneaking out past curfew.

Maya laughed. "Old and wise? Since when?"

We all laughed together, and for a moment, it felt like the dark edges of the world softened. The weird messages, the eerie vibes, the creeping sense that something was off, none of it could reach us here.

The conversation shifted to more important things. Like whether dogs really run the world, my vote was yes, and if pineapple belonged on pizza, which I was firmly against. We argued, laughed, and made up ridiculous theories that made no sense but somehow fit perfectly.

Indigo made an exaggerated show of declaring herself queen of the pineapple debate. "Pineapple is a gift to the pizza world. Fight me."

Mason rolled his eyes. "You're wrong, and everyone knows it."

Cassie shook her head, smiling softly. "I don't even like pineapple, but I'm on Indi's side solely because I appreciate the passion."

Eli gave a rare grin. "This might be the most important lunch debate we've ever had."

Finn smirked. "Until someone brings up football, and then the stakes go way up."

Eli grinned. "Speaking of which, anyone catch last night's game? Or are we still too traumatized from the last play?"

Indigo groaned. "Don't remind me. That was brutal."

Just as the conversation was winding down, the cafeteria doors swung open, and Liam hurried over, backpack slung low. His cheeks were flushed like he'd been sprinting across campus.

"Sorry, sorry, I'm late," he said, sliding into the seat across from me. "Had to make up the last part of my calculus test. Didn't finish it this morning."

Indigo raised an eyebrow. "Calculus? You're officially a legend. I can barely keep up with Algebra II."

Mason grinned. "Calculus? That's some next-level math right there."

Liam shrugged, running a hand through his hair. "It's not so bad. Just stressful trying to cram it all in."

I noticed the tired edge in his voice, but he hid it behind his usual easygoing smile.

"Sadee, how did you finish that test on time? It was hard." Liam sighs.

"I told myself I have a high enough grade in the class to fail this test and still be passing, so I did as much as I could until I couldn't and then I just guessed on the remaining problems and turned it in. It was quite simple, really."

Liam nodded and we all went quiet for a moment.

Mason's phone buzzed again just as Ryan sat up. "Okay so imagine this, the pizza places are all in on some big government experiment and the pineapple is a mind control ingredient." He mimics an explosion with his hands and nods.

"Ryan," Cassie said, "please stop giving me nightmares."

"Hey," I jump in, "if he's right, then I'm safe from the mind control."

"Just because you're lame and can't eat pineapple on pizza doesn't mean you're all the sudden going to live longer than us." Cassie throws her arms up.

Maya groans. "For the love of… guys, its food. Eat what you want. Who cares?"

Liam glanced around, looking at all of us. "You know, sometimes I wonder what we'll be like in ten years. Still arguing over pineapple pizza?"

Finn smirked. "I'll still be right, probably. You all just won't admit it."

"Classic Finn," Maya said, nudging him. "Always confident, always wrong."

Finn rolled his eyes, but the hint of a smile softened his usual brooding.

I watched them, feeling something like warmth and dread tangled together.

"Weekend plans?" Cassie asked, breaking the silence. "Anyone doing anything exciting?"

Indigo rolled her eyes. "Exciting is not a word I'd use for my weekend. Probably just binge-watch horror movies and eat way too much popcorn."

"Sounds perfect," Mason said with a small grin. "I might actually join you on that one."

I bit back a smile, thinking about Mason's quiet smile and the way he sometimes looked at me, like there was something he wanted to say but held back.

Maya nudged me. "What about you, Sadee? Anything fun?"

I shrugged, feeling the familiar pull of the unspoken. "Probably just the usual. Work on some schoolwork, maybe take Kirby for a long walk."

Indigo gave me a pointed look. "Sounds like code for 'avoid all human contact.'"

I laughed softly. "Maybe."

Mason's phone buzzed again. This time, he glanced at it quickly, his face unreadable. He tucked it away without a word.

I wanted to ask, but I didn't. Some things felt better left unsaid.

The conversation turned again—somehow, it always did—toward a ridiculous story Maya had. Some kid in her and Cassie's history class got called out for sleeping through a presentation, only to wake up and confidently give a completely made up answer that somehow fooled the teacher.

Everyone laughed so hard I had to lean back to catch my breath.

As the bell rang again, signaling the end of lunch, we slowly packed up. The warm sun by the window had shifted, casting longer shadows on the floor.

A teacher walked past, calling out reminders about upcoming tests and school events, a dull noise that barely touched the bubble we'd created.

Mason's phone buzzed one last time as we stood up. He hid it quickly, but I caught the flicker of something, an edge to his usually easy smile.

As we walked out together, I glanced at him sideways. Maybe someday, I'd ask. But for now, I'd hold onto this, this normal, this quiet. It was enough.

We stepped out of the cafeteria, the afternoon sunlight catching on the glass doors and casting a warm glow over everything. The noise of the crowded hallway faded behind us, replaced by the steady shuffle of sneakers on the pavement and the distant hum of voices carrying across the schoolyard. It felt like stepping into a different world, quieter, slower, almost like the day was winding down just for us.

Mason walked beside me, his phone still tucked safely away in his pocket, like a secret he wasn't ready to share. I kept stealing glances at him, curiosity pulling at me, but something stopped me from asking. Sometimes, you can tell when a person isn't ready to talk and today was one of those times.

Ryan, trailing a few steps behind, was already firing off another one of his conspiracy theories—this time about the school's water supply and some chemical experiment supposedly going on without anyone's knowledge. His voice was loud enough to carry, but mostly it was met with laughter and playful groans.

"You actually believe that stuff?" Mason called back, shaking his head like it was ridiculous.

Ryan shrugged, grinning. "You never know. Stranger things have happened."

Indigo snorted from ahead. "The only conspiracy here is how we survive the cafeteria food without losing our minds."

That got a few laughs. It was easy to joke about the little things, the absurd things. Easier than facing whatever else was lurking beneath the surface. I liked that, the way laughter could hold off the dark just for a little while.

We crossed the courtyard, the sun low in the sky, casting long shadows that stretched out behind us like fingers reaching toward tomorrow. I breathed in the late-day air, slightly cool with the promise of evening, and for a moment, I let myself just be present. No weird messages, no hidden secrets, no questions unanswered.

Classes after lunch passed in a blur. The teachers talked, I took notes, but my mind wandered to the quiet moments, the sun through the cafeteria window, the way Mason's smile had flickered when he checked his phone, the sound of laughter bouncing off the brick walls outside.

By the time the last bell rang, I was drained. Not just from the school day, but from the constant hum of things that felt unfinished. I stuffed my books into my bag and headed toward the lockers, feeling the weight of everything settle deep into my bones.

Mason was already there when I arrived. He leaned against the lockers, hands shoved in his pockets, staring at the floor like he was working through some complicated math problem in his head. Maybe he was.

We walked out together, the path toward the parking lot stretching ahead of us.

The air had cooled even more, and the sky was streaked with pink and orange clouds, the kind of sunset that makes you think about all the things you don't say.

Halfway there, Mason pulled his phone out. His fingers moved quickly over the screen, eyes scanning something that made his face darken for a second. Then he locked it and slid it back into his pocket.

"Everything okay?" I asked softly.

He looked up, meeting my gaze for just a moment before looking away. "Yeah. Just… stuff," he said, voice low.

I wanted to ask more, to press for details, but I didn't. Sometimes, silence speaks louder than questions. Sometimes, you just have to wait.

We reached the school gate and split off, each heading toward our own paths home.

The evening air felt heavier now, as if the day's light was pulling back, making room for whatever was coming next.

When I finally got home, Kirby was waiting by the door, tail wagging like I'd been gone for days. His goofy grin always made me feel like I belonged somewhere, like things might still be okay despite all I've done.

I dropped my bag and sank to the floor beside him, running my fingers through his soft fur. The calm in his eyes was something I wished I could bottle and carry with me.

That night, lying in bed with the ceiling staring back at me, my mind circled back to Mason's phone, the way he tried to hide it, the quick flicker of something serious in his eyes. I wanted to ask what was going on, wanted to break the silence, but instead I held onto the quiet.

Some things are better left unsaid, at least for now.

The best deceivers often believe their own lies

Chapter Seven

The air smelled like the beginnings of rain, thick, heavy, and cold. I tapped my foot anxiously against the floor of my boyfriend's front porch, the old wood creaking with every jittery movement.

"Would you stop that?" Indigo asked, nudging me with her elbow. She stood beside me, arms crossed tightly, her breath forming small clouds in the cool night air. Her oversized hoodie did little to hide the tension in her shoulders.

I forced my foot to still. "Sorry. I just... I have a bad feeling."

"You always have a bad feeling," she teased, but her eyes kept flicking around the street, scanning the dark corners and quiet driveways like she expected something to leap out at us.

A low rumble of thunder rolled in from the hills, distant but promising. I couldn't help the involuntary shiver that crawled up my spine. Even the sky seemed to know something wasn't right.

We were supposed to be pulling off one of the biggest senior pranks our school had ever seen, coating the front of the school in hundreds of glow-in-the-dark balloons and stringing a massive "WELCOME TO THE PARTY" banner across the entrance. Dumb, sure. But harmless.

The front door creaked open, and Mason finally appeared, pulling a hoodie over his freshly bleached hair. "You guys ready?" he asked, a grin and shoving a duffel bag full of balloons into Indigo's arms. He winked at me, and I forced out a laugh that sounded more like a cough.

Indigo staggered backward under the weight of the bag. "Seriously, Mason? How many did you blow up?"

"Not enough." He slung another bag over his shoulder.

Mason draped his arm around my shoulders. I shifted away from his touch and turned to help Indigo steady the bag. "Mason, I don't know about this. What if we get caught?"

He shrugged and kissed my temple. "That's half the fun, Sadee."

"Yeah," Indigo added, grinning, "what the cops don't know won't hurt 'em."

Another rumble of thunder rolled overhead, this one closer, sharper. I looked up at the night sky, heavy with storm clouds that glowed faintly with the distant flashes of lightning. My stomach twisted again.

Maybe it's not the cops we should be worried about, I thought.

We piled into Mason's old rust-bucket of a truck, the inside smelling faintly of motor oil and fast food. I ended up in the middle, my knee awkwardly pressing against the gear shift as Mason started the engine. The seats squeaked as Indigo adjusted herself beside me.

A few minutes into the drive, Mason turned the radio down. "Hey, have you guys been seeing all the posts about the hangman game?"

I stiffened. Indigo perked up like someone had just handed her a microphone. "Yes! Everyone is talking about it. I've read every single post and theory. Honestly, it's kind of amazing. Creepy, but amazing."

Mason hesitated. "Well… I got a text last night. Said it was my turn."

Indigo and I both went silent.

"And?" she asked.

"I guessed the letter 'T' and got it wrong." He took a deep breath. "You think they're serious about punishments?"

My chest tightened. "I don't know. I want to believe it's just some freak trying to mess with us. But… he texted me, too."

"What?" Indigo turned on me. "And you didn't tell me?"

Mason raised an eyebrow. "Also, why are we assuming it's a 'he'? Could be anyone."

"Exactly," I muttered. "Texts don't have a gender. This could be some random sophomore who's seen one too many horror movies and has way too much time on their hands."

Indigo huffed, crossing her arms again, clearly annoyed. But she didn't argue.

The streets were nearly empty as we turned into the student parking lot. All the houses were dark; the town tucked into bed. Even the gas station was shuttered for the night.

"This is it," Mason said in a mock-dramatic voice as he parked behind the gym. "The point of no return."

I rolled my eyes. "You're so dramatic."

He smirked. "You love it."

I didn't respond.

We slipped out of the truck, grabbing the bags of balloons and banner materials. The mist had turned to a light drizzle, soaking my hoodie within minutes. My fingers felt stiff and numb by the time we reached the school doors.

Mason managed to jimmy the side door open with a bobby pin, something I didn't want to ask too many questions about, and we slipped inside. The school was dark and dead quiet. Only the occasional buzz of a dying overhead light broke the silence.

We worked fast. Indigo scattered the glowing balloons down the hallway, while I taped the edges of the banner together. Mason hung it above the entrance with a roll of duct tape he found in the janitor's closet.

"This is actually turning out really cool," Indigo said, her voice hushed but excited.

"Gives the place a weird vibe," Mason said. "Like a haunted birthday party."

"It's kind of... beautiful," I said, watching the way the balloons pulsed with light. "Like the kind of thing you'd see in a dream, just before it turns into a nightmare."

The glow wasn't just light, it was movement. The balloons shimmered in slow pulses, glowing green and violet and blue, their soft luminescence reflecting off the linoleum like ripples on water. The colors weren't harsh like LED lights, but strange and soft, more organic, like bioluminescence. They swayed slightly in the air currents from the vents, like they were breathing.

We paused for a moment, all three of us just... watching. The way the colors shifted across the lockers, how the shadows twisted and leaned in unexpected ways. The floor looked like it was underwater, bathed in a wavering pool of faint, shifting color.

Indigo spun slowly in a circle. "We should do this to the whole town. Imagine it—glowing balloons hanging from every mailbox and streetlight. It'd be like some kind of fever dream."

"It'd be a masterpiece," I whispered. "The kind that feels a little too perfect. Like the world's trying to distract you from something. Or cover it up."

I walked through the hallway, trailing my fingers along the edge of a glowing balloon. The rubber felt cold, a little tacky with moisture. For a moment, I could almost forget that this was supposed to be a prank and not some kind of warning sign. I turned and looked behind me.

The hallway looked... wrong.

Beautiful, yes, but also uncanny. The kind of beauty that makes your skin prickle. Like a porcelain doll's smile. Too perfect. Too still. Like it was holding its breath.

Indigo didn't seem to notice. She snapped a quick photo with her phone and grinned at the result. "I'm posting this if we don't get caught."

"Less talk, more blow," Mason said, dumping another armful of balloons at our feet.

We got to work. The sound of stretching rubber and duct tape filled the air, punctuated by soft laughter and the occasional muttered complaint. But beneath it all, there was something else, a hum, low and steady, barely audible. It felt like it was coming from the walls themselves, a vibration under the surface that made the hairs on my arms rise. I tried to shake it off, but I kept catching myself pausing, listening, waiting for it to fade. It didn't.

The lights flickered.

Just once. A sharp, buzzing pulse that made my stomach twist. For a second, everything held its breath. Then the glow returned, slightly dimmer than before.

"You saw that, right?" I asked.

"The lights?" Indigo said, glancing up. "Old building. Not a ghost."

Her tone was light, but her eyes betrayed her. She wasn't looking at me, she was scanning the ceiling, the hallway, the door at the end of the corridor. And she was standing a little too still. That half-second of hesitation told me all I needed to know: she felt it too. The electricity in the air. The shift. Something in the silence that wasn't there before.

I nodded slowly but didn't move right away. My eyes were drawn to a single balloon floating near the lockers. It cast a long shadow against the metal, far too long for the way it was hanging. The light bent in strange ways, as if unsure of how to wrap around the shape. The shadow looked stretched, distorted, like someone had grabbed the edges and pulled.

Still, we kept working. The rubber clung to my fingers, sticky from the mist and the chill, and the strange chemical smell of latex clung to the air. As more balloons were scattered across the hallway, the entire space began to shift.

Colors danced across the lockers, soft greens, purples, and icy blues that moved like reflections on water. At first it was beautiful, almost dreamlike, but as the light bent and shimmered around corners and cast unsteady patterns on the ceiling, the beauty took on a warped, unnatural edge. The shadows didn't behave like they were supposed to. They pulsed and twisted like something alive. Like they were watching.

At one point, I stopped mid-step, my hands full of half-inflated balloons, and just stared down the hall. I could've sworn the shadows moved. Not flickered—moved. One slid just a few inches farther across the floor, almost like it had reached for me. I blinked hard and looked again, but it was still.

A balloon popped somewhere behind me. The sound cracked like a gunshot, and I flinched so violently I dropped everything. Indigo looked over but didn't laugh like she normally would. Her shoulders were stiff, and she didn't say anything.

"This is dumb," I muttered. "Why does it feel like we're being... watched?"

"It's just nerves," Indigo said. "You always get like this before we do something risky."

"Yeah," I said. "But not like this."

We stood in silence for a beat too long. Then came the sound that made my blood run cold.

Footsteps.

Not close. But definitely not far.

They echoed down the hallway from the direction of the gym. Heavy. Measured. Slow.

"Tell me that was one of us," I whispered, barely able to form the words.

"I wasn't moving," Indigo hissed.

We stared down the corridor, not breathing.

Then something shattered.

The sharp crash of glass breaking ricocheted through the hall, sharp and raw, followed by the unmistakable sound of something metallic rolling across the tile floor. It clattered for several long seconds before disappearing into silence again.

Indigo's mouth opened slightly, but no sound came out. Mason, who had been crouched near the front doors with the banner, stood straight and dropped the roll of duct tape like it had burned him.

I was about to speak, maybe say we were overreacting, maybe say we should just leave, when another crash rang out, louder this time, closer. Too close.

We didn't wait.

Mason sprinted for the side doors, Indigo right behind him, and I followed without thinking.

The moment we burst outside, the cold smacked us in the face. Rain was coming down in sheets now, soaking us instantly. We ran across the lot, shoes slipping on the wet pavement, balloons trailing behind us like limp, glowing ghosts.

We threw ourselves into Mason's truck, gasping, dripping, shaking. For a second, there was only the sound of the rain hammering the windshield. Then Mason turned the key, and the engine sputtered to life. I exhaled in relief.

But the relief didn't last.

The second Mason tried to steer; the truck jerked violently to the right. The wheel spun in his hands like it had a mind of its own. The brakes did nothing.

"What the h—" he shouted, wrestling with the wheel. "It's not, the brakes aren't—"

The tires squealed and we spun out, headlights slicing through the storm like searchlights. The world outside twisted violently. Indigo screamed. I slammed my hands against the dash, bracing for the impact I knew was coming. We veered off the road and into the trees.

The crash was sudden, brutal. A bone-jarring jolt, a thunderous crunch of metal and wood and glass. The airbag exploded into my chest, knocking the wind out of me. My head snapped back. Everything went sideways.

For a long second, the world was nothing but ringing. I couldn't hear anything. Couldn't see straight. Just the taste of blood in my mouth and the blurred shape of the windshield caved inward.

Indigo was crying. Mason was yelling, but it all sounded underwater. Everything was too bright and too far away. Then it all dropped away, replaced by eerie, absolute silence.

None of us moved.

The only sound now was the ticking of the engine, and the rain beating down on the roof like a warning.

Eventually, Indigo whispered, "Sadee was right. This was a bad idea."

Mason swore under his breath and punched the steering wheel, hard enough that it echoed. He fumbled with his phone and called his mom, muttering something about a tow truck and being sorry. Then, he pushed open the door and stumbled out into the storm.

Indigo reached across the seat and touched my arm gently. "Sadee? Are you okay?"

"I think so," I whispered, my voice hoarse.

But I didn't look at her.

I was still staring out the back window, through the streaks of water and the fogged glass.

Because just before we lost control, just before the world went spinning, I could've sworn I saw someone standing by the gym doors.

Watching us.

Chapter Eight

The morning air was thick with the slow crawl of summer heat, even though it was technically still spring. Through the tall windows of the cafeteria, a bright but hazy sun filtered in, casting long, lazy shadows across the checkered floors.

The usual chatter hummed like background noise, scattered laughter, the clink of trays, the scrape of chairs sliding, blending into the restless energy that always seemed to swell around senior year. I sat with Indigo, Mason, Finn, Ryan, Liam, Cassie, Maya, and Eli at our usual spot, an island of quiet amidst the noise.

Indigo leaned forward, her jet-black hair tumbling over her shoulders, eyes sharp and alert as always. Mason lounged back casually, his bleach-blond hair catching the light, green eyes calm but watchful. Ryan nervously adjusted his glasses, his hair a little messier than normal today, while Liam chuckled quietly at something Cassie said, her auburn curls bouncing as she smiled softly. Maya twirled a strand of her curly black hair absentmindedly, Eli's dark eyes flicking around the room, and Finn sat still, watching everything and nothing all at once.

Across the cafeteria, the crowd shifted. The unmistakable cadence of heavy footsteps caught my attention—the arrival of Brady Carter and his crew.

Brady's tall, athletic frame cut through the noise like a beacon. His sandy-blond hair was perfectly styled, and his bright blue eyes scanned the room with the confident grin of a natural leader who expected attention wherever he went.

Following close behind was Trevon Wallace, massive and calm, his shaved head gleaming under the fluorescent lights. He didn't say much, but the quiet strength in his dark eyes spoke volumes.

Derek Nguyen, quick and lively, weaved through the crowd with a cocky smirk, his black hair sharply undercut.

From the cheer squad, Taylor Brooks strode in with an energy that almost demanded the room's focus. Her long blonde hair bounced with every step, green eyes sparkling with mischief and determination.

Jada Thompson followed, her dark skin radiant and curls piled high in a puff, confidence radiating off her every movement.

Maddie Lopez, the newcomer, still a junior, trailed slightly behind, shy, eyes wide, still finding her footing in this high-stakes social world.

Sophia Ramirez flitted around the group, her glossy dark hair and bold lipstick making her impossible to miss.

Brady's voice carried as he approached our table. "Hey, table eight. Mind if we steal a minute?"

Indigo raised an eyebrow, unbothered. "Depends. Who's asking?"

Taylor smiled, flashing perfectly manicured nails. "The senior class, actually. We've got something big in the works."

"Yeah," Brady added, "a party. The biggest one this town's seen in years."

Mason's jaw tightened. "A party? Sounds like trouble."

Sophia shrugged with a laugh. "Trouble's the point."

Trevon folded his arms, the quiet voice of reason in the group. "It's happening out by that tree, the one on the south side of town. The lonely tree."

A hush fell over our group. The tree, everyone knew the stories. Dark rumors and whispers, warnings ignored by all but a few.

Ryan swallowed, voice shaky. "That place isn't safe."

Jada stepped forward, her sharp eyes locking with mine. "You're not scared, are you?"

He shook his head.

Taylor's grin widened. "Senior year's about risks."

Brady's grin didn't waver as he leaned casually against the table. "So, what do you say? We're talking bonfire, music, the whole shebang. And yes, there'll be drinks. But nothing that's going to get you in trouble. Well, not too much trouble."

Indigo smirked, folding her arms. "Sounds like my kind of night. Count me in."

Maya's eyes lit up, and she nudged Eli with a playful grin. "You're not backing out, right?"

Eli shrugged with a lazy smile, "I'm in. Can't let you guys have all the fun."

Liam let out a low chuckle, leaning forward on the table. "A night under the stars with the whole senior class? How could we say no? There's drinks?"

Brady nodded.

Cassie glanced nervously between them, voice soft. "I don't know. That tree… it's kind of creepy, right? Maybe it's better to keep it small and safe."

Ryan pushed his glasses up, biting his lip. "Yeah, I'm not sure this is the best idea. I've heard stories about that place."

My heart picked up pace. "I don't want to be the buzzkill, but maybe we should think this through."

Mason gave a small shrug, voice calm but steady. "I'm down to go, but yeah, nothing stupid. We keep it chill."

Finn's eyes flicked from face to face, a small smile tugging at his lips. "I'm down for a good time."

Taylor clapped her hands, breaking the tension. "Look, it's senior year. Everyone's gonna be there. You don't want to be the one who misses out."

Jada leaned in, tone teasing but with a hint of seriousness. "Besides, if you chicken out, you're not getting a second chance next year. You won't be here."

I exchanged looks with Indigo. The excitement was infectious, but the unease lingered.

"I mean, yeah," Indigo said with a wicked grin. "Lonely tree, bonfire, open sky, it's practically begging for a party."

Taylor beamed like she'd just scored a touchdown. "Knew we could count on you."

Maya leaned over the table, hands splayed out like she was presenting a grand plan. "Okay but wait—*what's the vibe*? Are we talking like chill picnic vibes, or full-out rave in the woods?"

Sophia laughed, tucking her dark hair behind one ear. "Somewhere in between. You know, something that starts with music and s'mores and ends with dancing on truck beds."

"I volunteer Liam for DJ duty," Indigo added. "He's got that tragic music taste that somehow works."

Liam raised his soda can like a toast. "If I don't get booed off the aux cord, I'm doing something wrong."

While the others joked, I kept my gaze on Brady, who hadn't stopped surveying the group like he was piecing together some kind of social puzzle. I don't like the way his eyes flicked over me, not creepy, exactly, just… calculating.

"You're being quiet," Brady said suddenly, directing the attention squarely on me.

I straightened a little. "Just thinking."

"She's the deep one," Indigo said, patting my shoulder. "Doesn't mean she's out."

"I didn't say that," I replied quickly, but my voice was measured. "Just… what's the reason for the whole 'calamity' thing? Is it just a name, or is there a story behind it? You know the word calamity literally means an event causing sudden damage or distress. You're asking for a disaster."

Derek, who had been half-scrolling through his phone, looked up with a grin. "It's senior year. Everything's a calamity."

"We wanted something *dramatic*," Taylor said. "And let's be real, this town is cursed with boredom. So, we figured, why not throw a party like the world's ending?"

"That tree doesn't help the drama angle," Ryan muttered, not looking up.

Sophia leaned in closer. "You mean the one with the rope marks?"

Jada smirked. "Urban legends, Ry."

Eli, who'd been watching the popular group quietly this whole time, finally spoke up. "That's what makes it fun, though. A little creepy never killed anyone."

Everyone went quiet for a beat.

"Well," Trevon said, voice deep and flat, "not *yet*."

A few people laughed.

Maddie shifted uncomfortably beside Sophia, her tray barely touched. "So, like… is it actually safe out there?"

"It's not like we're hiking into the middle of nowhere," Taylor said, brushing it off. "There's a dirt road, and it's ten minutes past the edge of town. We'll bring lights, food, and music. It'll be great."

"And what's the backup plan when someone inevitably brings a bottle of something illegal and the cops roll up?" Cassie asked quietly.

"We don't get caught," Derek said simply, tossing a grape into his mouth.

"Look," Brady said, glancing at the time on his phone. "We're not forcing anyone. But we'll get you all the date within the next week and a half. If you're not there, you're missing out."

Taylor dropped a stack of glossy paper cards onto the table, handmade invitations with neon lettering and chaotic doodles. *Calamity.* No date, no time. Just a QR code in the corner.

"Nice touch," Liam said, flipping one over. "Real apocalypse-core."

"I'll be there," Maya said, taking one and tucking it in her backpack. "No way I'm missing this."

Eli nodded. "Same."

Indigo was already scanning the QR code. "Ooh, there's a party playlist?"

"Curated by yours truly," Sophia said with a wink.

Cassie turned her invitation over in her hands like it might sting her. "I'll... think about it."

Ryan folded his arms. "I don't drink."

"You don't have to," Jada said, shrugging. "There's soda. Marshmallows. The joy of human connection."

Ryan raised an eyebrow, unimpressed. "Pass."

I took and invite and shoved it in my backpack. I wasn't agreeing to going. Not yet. I just watched the way the cheerleaders glowed with excitement, the way the football guys looked so sure of themselves, like nothing could go wrong, even though it most definitely could, and will.

Mason gave me a light elbow. "You worried it'll be lame?"

"No," I murmured. "I'm worried it *won't* be."

Finn finally spoke, his voice low and amused. "We'll keep each other in check."

Mason nodded. "We're not showing up hammered. Just... relaxed."

"Exactly," Liam said. "Senior year's almost over. What's the worst that could happen?"

Another silence fell.

This one lasted longer.

Jada broke it with a whistle. "Well. This got awkward."

Sophia stood up, dusting off invisible crumbs. "Anyway, we'll see you there, or we won't. But the bonfire's going to be impossible to miss."

They turned and left as confidently as they'd arrived, Sophia already filming a TikTok of the walk away, Derek tossing grapes at Trevon, Taylor spinning in her cheer skirt like a girl in a music video.

Our table was quiet again.

"Okay," Maya said finally. "Tell me that wasn't the most *movie scene* thing that's happened all year."

"I hate that I kind of want to go," Cassie whispered.

"I hate that I definitely want to go," I muttered back.

The rest of the school day passed in a blur of barely processed lessons and mental reruns of the lunch table conversation. Teachers droned on about test dates and essays, something about finals week coming up, but my mind was fixed on that stupid invitation still tucked into my backpack. *Calamity.* Who names a party after a disaster?

The final bell rang, and the hallways flooded with bodies, locker doors slamming and sneakers squeaking against the tile. Someone was already blasting music from a phone. It felt like the whole school had been lit by some kind of fuse, anticipation crawling through the air.

Mason met me by the lockers, casually slinging his bag over one shoulder. "Still thinking?"

I didn't need to ask what he meant. "Yeah."

"You don't have to decide yet," he said, voice low and even. "Just... don't overthink it."

Which was kind of like asking the ocean not to be wet.

We walked out of school together, our footsteps falling into an easy rhythm on the concrete. Cars honked lazily in the pickup line. Someone yelled across the lot, and a burst of laughter followed. For a moment, everything felt normal.

But there was that invitation in my backpack. Still covered in pink glitter. Still burning a hole in the back of my mind.

Mason glanced sideways at me as we reached the parking lot's edge. "Want a ride?"

I shook my head. "I'm good. I think I need to clear my head."

He didn't push. Just gave me a little nod. "See you tomorrow?"

"Yeah. Maybe."

He raised an eyebrow at the *maybe*, but didn't press. That was the thing with Mason, he gave me space to me breathe.

When I got home, Kirby practically tackled me. His paws hit my thighs as I fumbled with the front door, barking like he'd been starving for my attention all day. I dropped my bag without thinking and crouched to scratch behind his ears. He licked my chin with his rough tongue, his whole body trembling as if trying to shake off some invisible weight.

"You wanna walk it off too?" I muttered.

The leash was already in my hand, as if it had been waiting for me.

We stepped outside just as the sun dipped low, the sky bleeding shades of gold and bruised pink. The streets were eerily quiet, but the breeze carried the sickly-sweet scent of cut grass mixed with hot asphalt and something else, faint, smoky, like burning wood deep in the distance. I couldn't tell if it was a neighbor's firepit or something else entirely.

A dog barked far off, slow and hollow.

Kirby moved ahead, nose glued to the ground, pulling me toward every mailbox and cracked sidewalk seam with obsessive focus. His tail twitched in nervous bursts, like he smelled something I didn't want to acknowledge. It felt like we were both walking into something, but neither of us dared to say it out loud.

We wandered without a plan through streets I knew by heart, but they felt different now. The sky stretched above, a soft, fake kind of calm that made shadows lengthen and twist, like fingers reaching for me.

My thoughts spun, frantic: the party, the Hangman, the message that will change my life.

We passed the grocery store. Mrs. Talbot was there, unloading a trunkful of paper towels and dog food, balancing a watermelon in one hand and waving with the other. Her smile looked the same, but her eyes were empty, like she was pretending just as hard as the rest of us. I wondered if she had seen something. If she knew what was coming.

The town hadn't changed. But I had. Every step felt heavier, like I was wading through water no one else could see. The easy pretending, the jokes about yearbook quotes and senioritis, it all felt like a fragile mask stretched too thin.

Because the game was still here. Always here.

People walked around like nothing happened. Like we hadn't all received the message.

Welcome to the game.

Like something wasn't watching, waiting.

But no new texts came. No new threats. Just a silence that wrapped around me, cold and suffocating. Worse than any noise. It felt like the Hangman was sitting right behind my skin, breathing slow and steady.

Maybe that was the point. To trap everyone in waiting. To make everyone doubt themselves. To keep everyone oblivious to what was really going on.

And now, a party? Out by the lonely tree? Of all places?

I thought of Indigo, already planning her outfit. Maya, buzzing like a live wire. Eli, steady as ever. Mason, calm, the rock I clung to. Even Finn, unreadable, was in.

And then there was me.

Caught between wanting normalcy and knowing too much.

Would the Hangman care if we partied?

Or was that exactly what he wanted?

Kirby stopped so fast I almost stumbled. His leash pulled taut.

At the park's edge, the sky stretched wide, warm colors fading into dusk. Trees loomed at the far end, black silhouettes twisting in the wind like something alive.

And then I saw it.

Someone.

Just where the cracked sidewalk faded into a narrow path slipping into the woods. Far enough that I couldn't see their face, but close enough to feel it, the way they moved. Slow. Unhurried. Deliberate. Like they knew I was there and wanted me to see. But why?

The world seemed to hold its breath. Birds stopped chirping. The rustling leaves stilled. Even distant traffic faded, swallowed by a heavy silence that pressed against my chest.

The figure stood at the edge of the trees, framed by clawing branches bleeding into shadow. They didn't turn, but I could feel the weight of their gaze, sharp and cold, crawling under my skin like icy fingers. The kind of look that burrows in your bones and won't let go.

For a terrifying heartbeat, I was certain that if I dared look harder, our eyes would meet, and something would snap.

Their dark green hoodie hung loose and worn; cuffs frayed with threads like spider silk caught on thorns. A silver chain glinted faintly across the fabric, catching the last sliver of dying sunlight like a warning.

My breath caught in my throat.

I knew that hoodie. The frayed cuffs. The way it sagged just so. The chain, worn outside the fabric instead of underneath. Not flashy, but unmistakable once you noticed.

Someone from school. Someone who belonged in daylight.

Kirby growled low in his throat, the sound vibrating through his whole body.

The figure didn't move or look back. Slowly, almost mockingly, they turned the corner and vanished into the blackness of the woods, swallowed by shadow like they'd never been there.

I froze, heart hammering in the sudden stillness.

Was that…?

The forest swallowed their footsteps, soft, deliberate, like a predator stalking its prey. My skin prickled as the chill in the air thickened, the scent of smoke now sharp and acrid, like something burning deeper, closer.

I swallowed hard, voice barely a whisper when I muttered, "Why?"

No answer. Just the rustle of dead leaves underfoot.

My fingers clenched tighter around Kirby's leash. The night seemed to close in, every shadow folding in on itself, hiding something just out of sight.

We didn't turn back the way we came. We walked the long way home, every step taut with tension, every shadow whispering threats.

The knot in my chest tightened.

The air grew cooler, thick with something sour and faintly metallic. I swallowed hard, hearing my breath loud in my ears as the dark swallowed the edges of the neighborhood. Each crunch of gravel underfoot sounded deafening in the silence, like the world had shrunk down to just me and Kirby.

I kept glancing over my shoulder, certain that the figure was trailing us, watching from the shadows. But every time I looked, there was nothing but swaying branches and empty streets.

But I knew better.

Because it was the Hangman.

The one who watched. The one who waited.

The one who decided who guessed right, and who paid.

Maybe I'd go to the party. To be with the people I trusted. To prove I wasn't losing it.

Or maybe I wouldn't.

Either way, the game was far from over.

And the Hangman was still watching.

Chapter Nine

The football field lights buzzed overhead, casting long, flickering shadows on the rain-soaked turf. The sticky scent of wet grass mixed with the faint, greasy tang of concession-stand fries and the harsh bite of autumn air. Even the chill in the wind seemed to hum with anticipation.

The crowd was smaller than I expected for a Friday night game, but every voice was loud and sharp, filled with that familiar mix of hope and desperation that only small towns can conjure. This was the kind of game where everyone you knew was here, or, at least, someone you knew was shouting in the stands.

We were winning. By a landslide, actually. It was the kind of lead that made the players relax just a little, but the energy didn't die down. Instead, it felt like the whole town was holding its breath, caught in the collective thrill of something simple and ordinary.

The student section on the other side of the field churned out chants that rose and fell in waves, their voices bouncing off the metal bleachers. I could see faces painted with school colors, mouths open in cheers, and hands clapping in unison.

Players huddled near the sidelines, streaked with mud and sweat, arms slung around one another's shoulders like brothers-in-arms.

The stands for the visiting team shook beneath my feet, filled with proud parents, siblings, and friends who cheered their team on with hopeful eyes and thunderous applause. They were thirsty for their first win this season, and you could feel that hunger like a current running through their ranks.

Mason stood nearby, leaning against the metal railing by the field, his hair damp and sticking slightly to his forehead from the drizzle that had started earlier. His arms were crossed, his jaw tight, his eyes locked on the action with a distant, almost haunted expression. It was hard to tell if he was proud or just lost in thought. I glanced at Indigo standing next to me. She caught my eye, raised one dark brow, and whispered, "You okay?"

I forced a small smile, though it felt brittle and fake. "Yeah. Just tired," I said, trying to keep my voice steady against the roar of the crowd.

She didn't look convinced. "Uh-huh. You're definitely not acting like you're having a good time," she said, glancing toward the field where the quarterback called the next play. Indigo bumped my shoulder lightly. "You remember last year when the band kid dropped his trombone on the field and the ref tripped over it?"

I snorted. "How could I forget? It was the only time we made it onto the local news."

"Honestly, top ten best moments of my life," she said, eyes sparkling.

"Your life is either extremely boring, or you have very low standards."

"Both can be true," she replied with a dramatic flourish, pulling her hoodie tighter. "Hey, if you had to die on this field, how would you want it to happen?"

I blinked. "That's... an intense question for someone holding nachos."

She shrugged. "I like to be prepared."

"I don't know. Maybe... struck by lightning in the middle of the halftime show. Go out with flair."

She nodded approvingly. "Respect. I think I'd want to be crushed by the scoreboard. Very poetic."

"You're unwell," I said.

"Fully."

I wanted to say something, anything, to explain the way my chest tightened when I saw Mason like that, so closed off, like he was carrying something heavier than the mud on his jersey. But the words caught in my throat.

 Instead, I just shrugged and took a slow breath, trying to steady myself. The game was fun, usually, but tonight my mind was elsewhere, caught in a loop of shadows and half-remembered details. The crash two days ago, the figure lurking by the gym doors after practice, the way everything had felt wrong ever since.

The crowd erupted again as another touchdown was scored. For a fleeting moment, I let myself get lost in the noise. It was normal. It was supposed to be normal. The lights, the cheers, the smell of popcorn and rain, they were the things that grounded me. But that uneasy feeling, like something dark was just beneath the surface, wouldn't let go. It was there. It wouldn't go away. It's been nagging at me, incessantly, and I can't ignore it.

I found myself glancing over at Mason again. His posture was rigid, the way he stood like he was bracing against something invisible. I wanted to ask him if he was okay, to tell him that eventually this game would end, and things would go back to normal.

But I wasn't so sure. Things will never be normal again.

"I'll be right back," I muttered to Indigo, my voice barely above the crowd. Without waiting for a reply, I slipped away toward the concession stand, hoping the cold bottle of water and the hum of the kitchen might distract me.

The hallway to the concession stand was quiet compared to the stands, the buzz of the crowd muffled through the walls. The faint smell of buttered popcorn mixed with cleaning supplies and the stale odor of damp clothes filled the air. I rubbed my arms, feeling the chill settle deep under my skin.

The hallway lights buzzed above me, flickering every few seconds like they couldn't decide whether to give up or try harder. My footsteps echoed on the concrete floor, and for a second, I was completely alone. No roaring crowd. No Indigo's voice cracking jokes beside me. No Mason's silence sitting heavy on my shoulders.

Just me and the smell of mop water and old hot dogs.

I thought about turning around. About going back to the noise and pretending I didn't feel the air shift when Mason looked away. Pretending I didn't feel that growing darkness in my chest, the sense that something was inching closer, waiting just out of reach.

But I kept walking.

Near the entrance stood Mr. Duvall, the town mechanic. His weathered face was half-hidden by the dim light streaming through the windows, and he held a soda bottle loosely in one hand. I hadn't seen him much since the crash. He was the one who took Mason's truck to the shop, and since then, Mason hadn't heard a word from him.

Mr. Duvall was a quiet man with a stutter who rarely talked. It made him seem more nervous than he really was. When he noticed me, his eyes flicked up with a mixture of surprise and hesitation.

"Hey, Mr. Duvall," I said, trying to keep my voice calm. "Enjoying the game?"

He gave a tight smile that didn't quite reach his eyes. "It's g-g-good. Y-your school's, your school's d-d-doing g-great, h-h-huh?"

"Yeah, we're winning," I replied, glancing back toward the roar of the field.

His gaze shifted. He looked past me, like he was waiting for someone else to appear. Or maybe checking to see if we were being watched.

"You okay?" I asked, suddenly aware of how stiff his posture was.

After a long pause, he leaned closer, voice dropping to a cautious whisper. "L-look, kid... I-I just w-wanted, I wanted to, to te-, to tell you... the wreck... it wasn't M-Mason's fault."

I blinked, heart pounding. "What do you mean?"

"T-those brake lines... they w-w-were, they were c-cut."

My breath hitched. "Cut?" I echoed. "Like... on purpose?"

Mr. Duvall nodded, slow and deliberate. "Y-yeah. Not a wear, not a wear-and-tear thing. C-clean slice. S-somebody, somebody knew, knew w-what they were d-doing."

A sharp buzz started in my ears. "Did you tell Mason?"

"I-I wanted to. B-but I wasn't sure if it was safe. Thought maybe, maybe it was just, it was some k-kind of prank at first. But... nah." He shook his head, his voice low and grim now. "This was precise. Deliberate."

"Why tell me and not him?" I asked, trying to keep my voice from shaking.

His eyes flicked to mine, and for the first time, I saw something that made my stomach twist: fear.

"B-because you l-listen," he said simply. "And you'll, you'll know, know what to do."

That didn't feel true. I barely knew what to do with my own thoughts lately.

"I d-didn't wanna start panic," he added. "But I c-couldn't sit with it either. You s-saw him after. That wreck... that was no accident."

The words repeated in my head like a broken loop: no accident, no accident.

My heart stopped. "Did you tell the police?"

He hesitated. "S-small town cops don't wanna believe in t-targeted crime," he muttered, eyes narrowing. "Said maybe a raccoon chewed through the line. A raccoon, can you believe that?"

I couldn't help it, I let out a breathless, disbelieving laugh as relief flooded over me.

"I'm g-gonna keep looking," he added. "See if the s-surveillance cam at the gas station caught, see if it caught anything. If s-someone messed with the truck there..."

He trailed off, rubbing the back of his neck. The soda bottle in his hand squeaked as he tightened his grip.

I looked at him, really looked. He wasn't just spooked; he was scared for us. For Mason. And maybe even for himself.

"If you see anything weird," he said, "y-you come to me. Not the cops. Not even your p-parents. J-just me."

I nodded slowly, too stunned to do anything else.

"Be careful, Sadee," he added. "Whatever this is... it ain't over."

I nodded; voice caught somewhere between numb and scared. "Thanks, Mr. Duvall."

He gave a tired smile, then turned his attention back to the window, his soda untouched on the ledge. But I could tell he wasn't really watching the game anymore.

As I walked back, everything felt... louder. The thud of footsteps, the slam of a bathroom door, the hiss of a fryer behind the concession-stand window. Like the world had cranked the volume up while I was gone.

Before I reached the bleachers, I spotted Indigo pacing by the snack booth, her phone held above her head in a desperate search for signal.

"Oh my, Verizon is actually the devil," she grumbled, waving her phone like a flag. "I've been trying to text Cassie for ten minutes."

I laughed, grateful for her voice, her presence. Something real.

"Want me to hold your phone higher? I'm like two inches taller," I said.

"You're like five-four, Sadee. Relax."

"Five-four and a half, actually."

She squinted at me, then offered the hot chocolate she'd been holding with a mock bow. "For surviving the port-a-potty, I assumed you got eaten."

"Much appreciated."

"May I offer you a french fry?"

"Please do."

She passed me her fries without hesitation. I bit into one, the greasy, salty taste oddly comforting.

"These are disgusting," I muttered.

She grinned wider. "And yet, you're still eating them."

I glanced back at the field where the home team had possession again. Even with the score so heavily in our favor, the quarterback lined up like it was the Super Bowl. The snap was crisp, the ball flying through the air to the waiting receiver—a touchdown.

The cheers in the student section swelled into a roar, echoing into the empty night sky. The cheerleaders jumped with white pom-poms that blurred in the light, their smiles bright and practiced.

Mason still leaned against the railing, arms crossed, jaw clenched tight. He hadn't said much since the crash, insisting he was fine, but I could see the invisible weight in his posture, the kind of burden that no one wants to carry alone.

He'd never believe it was sabotage. Not unless I told him. But I wouldn't. Not yet.

Indigo nudged me again, breaking into my spiraling thoughts. "You okay?"

I looked at her, a flicker of wanting to trust her flashing before I swallowed it down. Tell her what? That someone had cut brake lines? That a stupid game might, would, be a death sentence? She'd laugh. Or worse, she might believe me. And that meant facing what was really coming.

So, I said the only thing that felt safe. "Yeah. Just tired."

We sat in silence, the noise of the crowd rising and falling around us. The clouds parted just enough to reveal a sliver of the moon, casting a pale glow over the slick bleachers.

Somewhere behind us, a baby cried, a sharp, piercing sound that pulled at something raw inside me. Someone yelled too loud and was shushed by a man wearing a varsity jacket that looked like it belonged in a museum.

It was such a stupidly normal night.

By the time the final whistle blew, we'd won by nearly thirty points. Mason offered to drive us home, though he said his mom's VW Beetle was 'nowhere near as cool as his truck'. Indigo made him promise not to speed. He rolled his eyes but agreed.

The ride was quiet except for Mason's tapping on the steering wheel, keeping time with a faint song playing through the static on the radio. Indigo leaned her head against the window, earbuds in, fast asleep. I sat in the middle seat, hands folded in my lap, watching trees and shadows blur past.

The hum of the engine was steady, almost comforting. Headlights carved twin lines through the dark, catching bits of fog that drifted low across the road. Every so often, a mailbox or crooked street sign flashed by like a ghost. I tried counting them, like that might help me stay grounded, but I kept losing track.

Mason adjusted the heat, the vents clicking softly as warm air filled the car. My legs still felt cold from the bleachers.

Indigo shifted in her sleep, her breath fogging up the glass. She always fell asleep in cars, no matter the length of the drive. It was like her body trusted movement more than stillness.

I wished I could do that, let go like that.

Instead, I stared straight ahead, wondering how long I could pretend I didn't know what I knew.

"Remind me to never let you pick our seats again," I muttered.

"What?" Mason asked, glancing at me.

"You shoved me in the middle."

"I'm the driver. That's a seat of honor."

"Then *you* sit here next time," I said, poking his arm.

He chuckled. "You're just mad you can't lean dramatically against the window like Indi."

"She looks like a Victorian orphan," I said. "I aspire to that aesthetic."

"You could pull it off," he said. "You've already got the tragic stare."

I smirked. "Thanks. I try to keep it vacant."

He shot me a look, half a smile tugging at his mouth. "You okay?"

There it was again. That question. Everyone kept asking, and I kept saying yes. Even when it didn't feel like a lie, it didn't feel like the truth either.

I shrugged. "Yeah. Just tired."

He grinned, then lapsed back into silence, fingers drumming the wheel. Outside, a deer darted across the road in the headlights' beam, vanishing into the trees.

A part of me wanted to tell him what Mr. Duvall had said, to warn him, to protect him. But I didn't. The words stayed locked inside, hidden beneath everything else I was too afraid to say aloud.

Because once you say it, once you name the danger, it becomes real.

And I wasn't ready for real.

So, I stared out the windshield, forcing a smile at Mason's dumb jokes about how the other team "literally gave up by the second quarter." I rolled my eyes when he said we owed him gas money, even though it was his idea to come. I reminded him he still owes me $6 for the funnel cake last month.

He promised to Venmo me tonight. He wouldn't. He never did. I didn't mind. It was one of those debts people use as an excuse to stay in each other's lives.

And for just a little while, I let myself forget.

Forget that anything was wrong.

Even if everything was.

Chapter Ten

Saturday came soft. Not silent, there was the low hum of the A/C kicking on, the gentle rustle of trees outside my window, Kirby's paws clicking against the hardwood as he did his usual morning patrol. But soft. Gentle. A kind of quiet that settled into your bones instead of echoing in your ears, like a warm hand placed gently over your heart.

The cotton sheets tangled around my legs, cool in some places, still warm where my skin had pressed against them in others. The slight weight of the blankets was a comforting kind of pressure, like a quiet hug holding me steady.

I could hear the faint creak of the floorboard down the hall—a small, sleepy reminder that the house was still alive even when I was not quite ready to wake. The smell of the air was faint but distinct, that mixture of early morning coolness and the ever-present hint of lemon cleaner from Mom's obsessive Saturday ritual in the kitchen. It made me feel safe, grounded, like I was exactly where I was supposed to be.

Outside, the branches of the big oak tree scraped gently against the windowpane, a soft clatter that mingled with the distant chirp of birds waking up. The leaves flickered in the breeze, making shadows that danced quietly on the cream walls of my room.

Somewhere in the background, a car started up and rolled down the street, its tires crunching softly against gravel. It was the kind of morning sound you didn't notice unless you really listened.

I lay still for a while longer, my eyes half-closed, breathing slow and even. The quiet felt like a balm, pulling the tightness from my chest and loosening the knots in my shoulders.

For once, there was no tension waiting for me, no strange messages blinking on my phone, no cold fear creeping in at the edges of my mind. Just this soft, golden calm, and the slow, steady rhythm of Kirby padding back and forth behind the door.

The sun spilled in through the blinds in lazy stripes, painting thin lines of light across the carpet like delicate ribbons. I reached out, fingers brushing the warm glow as it pooled over my arm. The feeling was so simple, so ordinary, that it made my throat tighten just a little, the way a small thing can remind you that you're still here, still alive, still breathing.

Finally, I turned over and sat up, the sheets falling away like a waterfall. The wooden floor was cool beneath my feet, grounding me as I stretched with a slow, satisfied sigh.

I glanced at the nightstand and my phone blinked to life like it had been holding its breath, a pale blue glow cutting through the dim morning light. The screen reflected off the water glass beside it, catching a prism of tiny sparks like stars.

A text from Ryan popped up: *Cassie and I are getting lunch at 12:30. You should come.*

Just beneath it, Cassie's message appeared: *He's already planning a post-lunch trip to that haunted rock store. Come save me. Please.*

I stared at the messages for a moment, thumb hovering above the keyboard. My fingers felt heavy, like they didn't want to leave the warmth of the sheets. Then, with a slow exhale, I typed back: *Fine. But if he says the words 'chakra cleanse' I'm actually lighting myself on fire.*

A couple hours later, I stepped outside and into the kind of heat that doesn't feel like air at all, more like a solid wall pressing in from every direction.

The sun sat high, relentless and bright, hammering down on the pavement until it seemed to shimmer like a mirage. The sidewalk underfoot radiated heat back up in waves, making my old sneakers stick slightly with each step.

My shirt clung damply to the middle of my back, slick with sweat that made the fabric uncomfortable but somehow necessary, proof I was alive in the middle of this slow, simmering day.

Every breath I took tasted like dry dust and melted rubber, the kind of sharp, sour smell that sets in when asphalt melts under the sun and cars idle too long.

The cicadas buzzed somewhere in the thick, humid air, a steady, droning soundtrack that made the world feel both alive and just a little too heavy.

I pushed open the diner's glass door, and the little bell above it jingled in a high, tiny ring that cut through the low murmur of conversation.

Inside, the heat was replaced by the clatter of silverware and the sizzling pop of the fryer in the kitchen. The smell hit me instantly, a mixture of syrupy sweetness, the greasy tang of fried food, and the bitter bite of burnt coffee. It wasn't the kind of smell that made your mouth water; more like the smell of a place that had been here forever, a fixture of the town and all its weekends.

Ryan sat near the window, sunlight catching on his glasses, so they flashed like tiny mirrors. He was in the middle of a monumental decision, double-fisting two tall plastic cups, one root beer, one lemonade, and sipping both through bright plastic straws at once, like the stakes were impossibly high.

Cassie was beside him, hunched over the table and focused entirely on a tiny world of her own making, drawing detailed vines and mushrooms with a thick, globby blue ink that stained her fingers.

"You're late," Ryan said without even glancing up, his voice a casual jab that was somehow both irritating and familiar.

"You're unbearable," I replied, sliding into the booth with a mock sigh of defeat, wiping a stray bead of sweat off my temple.

"Both factual statements," Cassie said quietly, nudging a pink milkshake toward me. The straw stood straight up, waiting. "I ordered for you. Thank me later."

I lifted the straw, letting the cold liquid shock my overheated brain. The strawberry sweetness was sharp, almost painfully so, making my teeth chill and my pulse slow just enough to feel human again. The contrast between the heat outside and the creamy chill in my mouth was like a reset button pressed hard.

We didn't talk about school. Or the game. Or the slow, creeping dread that had been gnawing at the edges of my thoughts all week, the kind of unease that feels like it's always just beneath your skin, waiting to bubble up.

Instead, we drifted into something lighter, sillier. We debated who would last the longest in a zombie apocalypse, and the answer was obvious: Ryan. No chance. Cassie's earrings, tiny frogs wearing cowboy hats, became the center of a heated argument. Were they cursed? Iconic? Both, definitely both.

Ryan launched into a dramatic reenactment of a TikTok video where a man falls into a pond, complete with slow-motion flailing and exaggerated gurgles that made me laugh louder than I had in days.

It was ridiculous. It was loud. It was real. Exactly what I needed.

After lunch, we stepped out into the sunlight again, blinking against the harsh glare that ricocheted off cracked pavement and glossy car windows. The town was sticky with heat, as if it had been dipped in honey and left to dry. Everything felt slow and suspended, caught in that breathless pause where time stretches and sticks.

The thrift shop windows were fogged from the inside, blurring the faded mannequins dressed in once-colorful clothes, their forms ghostlike behind the glass.

A crate of bright oranges held the bakery door open, and with each beat of music spilling from a crackling speaker, a sweet, citrusy scent drifted lazily down the sidewalk. The song was some 2000s indie rock tune, familiar but distant, like a memory you couldn't quite place.

We slipped into the bookstore next, the transition from blazing sunlight to soft shadows immediate and comforting. The air inside smelled like a mixture of old paper, wood polish, and the faint metallic tinge of ink, a scent that felt like stories waiting to be told. The temperature dropped a solid ten degrees, and I let the coolness wash over me like a wave.

Ryan disappeared quickly, melting into the back aisles like he belonged there. Cassie and I wandered more slowly, our fingers trailing over cracked spines and frayed covers as if trying to read the history embedded in the paper and glue. She found a worn copy of *A Wrinkle in Time*, its cover faded and spine cracked and held it to her chest like it was a secret she had just uncovered.

I thumbed through a battered *Pride and Prejudice*, tracing the looping cursive of a previous owner's name inside: "Lucy C., 2006." I didn't buy it, but the thought of someone else holding this book a decade ago stayed with me.

Ryan reappeared silently, his expression soft but unreadable, and before we could linger, he tugged us toward the exit with urgent declarations about needing to check out the moldavite stones.

The rock shop was a sensory overload. The air was thick with the heavy, pungent scent of burning sage, mixed with floral hints of lavender and something spicy, clove, maybe? The fragrance wrapped around my face like a dense fog, forcing me to breathe through my mouth even as it settled deep in my lungs. The beads hanging in the doorway chimed softly, a gentle counterpoint to the thick scent, their tinkling like distant laughter or whispered secrets.

Inside, the dim, flickering lights made everything shimmer with an otherworldly glow. Polished stones sat in glass bowls like treasures, dried herbs filled jars that looked like they belonged in an old apothecary, and tarot decks were stacked in precarious towers.

A wind chime sang quietly even though the air was perfectly still, and the floorboards creaked underfoot, as if the shop itself had a story to tell.

Ryan headed straight for the moldavite display. "Still trying to summon things?" I teased, raising an eyebrow.

He was serious. "Those 'things' already know my name," he said, poking a bowl of smoky quartz as if it owed him money.

Cassie lingered near a rack of zodiac bracelets, her fingers brushing over each one thoughtfully. I drifted deeper into the shop, drawn by the quiet corner where the light was low and the air thick with possibility.

I picked up a chunk of rose quartz, smooth and warm, its soft pink glow pulsing faintly in the dim light. It felt alive in my palm, like it was breathing softly, waiting.

"You think this stuff works?" I asked when Cassie joined me.

She was quiet, watching the way light caught the crystal's edges.

"I think people want it to."

I nodded slowly. "Wanting feels safer than knowing, most of the time."

She didn't say anything else, but her expression softened. That was enough.

Evening slipped over the neighborhood like a warm blanket, stretching the shadows long and golden. The air cooled slightly, scented now with the smoky tang of backyard barbecues, freshly mown grass, and a faint sweetness drifting from an open kitchen window. The sidewalks still held the day's heat, radiating softly against my skin as I walked home.

The second I opened the door, Jack came at me full force, like a human cannonball.

"Sadeeeeeeee!"

I laughed, catching him as he crashed into me. His arms wrapped tight around my waist, and he was heavier than I remembered. "Oof, okay, hi," I said, breath catching from the impact. "You've gotten heavier."

"I've gotten stronger," he said proudly, chest puffed out like a tiny soldier.

Inside, Mom was busy curling her lashes using the toaster's reflective surface as a mirror, carefully perfecting each blink. Dad was in the hallway, wrestling with his tie in front of the mirror, his brow furrowed in concentration.

"Thanks for watching him," Mom said, slinging her purse over her shoulder as she headed out the door.

"Don't worry," I said with a grin. "We'll only burn half the house down."

Dad raised an eyebrow. "Make good choices."

"Define 'good,'" I teased back.

We took Kirby out first. The evening air was cool, touched with the smoky scent of grills and the fresh bite of cut grass. Somewhere nearby, a lawn sprinkler clicked rhythmically, its spray catching the last of the sun's rays.

Jack skipped ahead, humming a chaotic mashup of Minecraft and Mario Kart tunes, his energy boundless. Kirby trotted beside him, leash taut, tail wagging in time like a metronome.

"You think Kirby knows he's a dog?" Jack asked suddenly, eyes wide with curiosity.

"Nope," I said. "He thinks he's a disgraced reindeer trying to get his job back."

Jack giggled, the sound bright and clear in the quiet street. "That explains the prancing."

The world felt too still. The kind of quiet that makes you glance over your shoulder just in case. We passed the old McKinley house, the one with the sagging porch and shuttered windows. It had been empty for years, a fixture of whispered rumors and ghost stories.

A flicker of movement caught my eye in the upstairs window, just a shadow stepping back from the glass, barely more than a breath of motion.

I froze. Kirby tugged gently on the leash, oblivious.

"Did you see that?" I asked Jack, voice low.

"See what?"

"Nothing." I forced a smile, but my stomach clenched tight.

Back inside, the lights were warm and low, casting long, cozy shadows that stretched like fingers across the walls. Jack and I made popcorn, burning the first batch, nailing the second. He demanded a round of Uno, then Go Fish, and finally Spit, which dissolved into chaos when Kirby jumped onto the table, snatched a card, and paraded it like a trophy.

Eventually, we collapsed on the couch under a mountain of mismatched blankets that smelled faintly of detergent and peanut butter, a weird, comforting combination. Jack picked *How to Train Your Dragon 2* without argument, his head sinking against my shoulder, heavy and warm.

Halfway through, he shifted, blinking sleepily up at the screen, a soft frown pulling at his small features. He leaned his head a little further into me.

"Do you think you'd be brave," he whispered, voice small and serious, "if you had to fight a dragon?"

I paused, thinking. "Depends on the dragon."

"Like Toothless. But the scary version. Before Hiccup trained him."

"I think I'd try," I said softly.

He was quiet for a moment, then said, "I think you'd be good at hiding. Like a spy. You always notice stuff."

That hit me somewhere deep, and I smiled faintly. "Thanks. You'd make a good one, too."

Jack hummed, satisfied. His voice dropped further. "Spies get scared too, though. Even the really good ones."

"Yeah," I murmured. "But they do their job anyway. That's the brave part."

He didn't answer. Just sighed, melting fully into my side.

He fell asleep soon after, his breath slow and even. The room sank into quiet, only the faint hum of the fridge and the soft glow of the kitchen nightlight keeping the dark at bay.

I reached slowly for my book, fingers brushing the cover with the familiar roughness of well-loved pages. But then my gaze dropped, and I caught sight of Jack curled up against me. His small body fit perfectly in the curve of my arm, warm and soft. His mouth hung slightly open, breath shallow and even, like he was floating in a world only he could see. One tiny hand clutched a stray Uno card, the edges bent and crumpled, as if it was a talisman or a key to some secret world. The quiet vulnerability of that moment struck me harder than I expected.

The book could wait.

I scooped him up carefully, careful not to wake him. His room smelled like old crayons and Mom's lemon detergent, a little messy but perfectly his. I tucked him in, soft blankets pulled up to his chin. He mumbled something in his sleep, soft and lost in dreams.

Then I climbed in beside him.

Not because I was scared.

But because I wanted to be close to someone who didn't pretend they were fine.

The night wrapped around us like a soft, worn blanket, thick with the quiet hum of a sleeping house. The faint buzz of the fridge was a steady pulse in the background, a tiny heartbeat that reminded me the world was still turning even when everything else felt frozen in time.

The kitchen nightlight cast a pale, steady glow across the walls, muted shadows stretching and curling like the slow dance of smoke. It was the kind of light that felt like a gentle promise: no monsters, no surprises. Just peace, for now.

Jack shifted in the dark, turning toward me like a compass needle finding its true north. His tiny hand reached out and found mine in the quiet, fingers curling around like they belonged there. The warmth of his skin seeped into mine, and for the first time in days, the weight of loneliness that had been settling like dust in my chest began to lift.

The quiet didn't feel so alone anymore.

I lay there, listening to his slow breathing, the steady cadence of sleep pulling us both under.

Outside, the world was dark and still, but here, right here, was a fragile kind of light, a soft, steady heartbeat against the night.

I closed my eyes and let the peace wrap around me, holding onto the small, unspoken comfort of this moment. No worries about the game, no looming shadows. Just the steady warmth of a boy who trusted me enough to rest, and the quiet promise that maybe, just maybe, everything could be okay.

Chapter Eleven

The church bell chimed again, slow and steady, like a heartbeat rolling through the early Sunday morning. Its deep toll seemed to vibrate through the crisp air, mingling with the distant rustling of leaves and the soft murmur of birds greeting the dawn.

I stepped up the worn stone steps with Mom and Dad, the rough edges smooth from decades of feet pressing down. The sun was warming my back, a gentle heat that seeped through the light fabric of my shirt and made me squint against the kaleidoscope of stained-glass colors flickering on the sidewalk. Every step felt heavy with history, as if the stones themselves were holding stories I could almost hear whispered beneath the quiet hum of the morning.

The air smelled fresh, sharp like dew on grass, but it also carried that heavy, old-book scent that clung to the church walls. Faint hints of aged parchment, damp wood, and wax from countless candles burnt long ago, joined the olfactory symphony as I paused before the door. It was a smell that seemed to soak into your skin, wrapping around you like a secret the building itself was reluctant to share, as if holding onto decades of whispered prayers and forgotten confessions.

Inside, the coolness enveloped me instantly, a soothing contrast to the bright morning heat outside. It wasn't a cold chill, just enough to make the skin on my arms tingle slightly, and I could feel a faint draft slipping beneath the wide, heavy wooden doors as they closed behind us with a muffled thud.

I shuffled into a pew, the varnished wood a little sticky under my fingertips, rough in some spots where the shine had worn thin, smooth and polished in others from generations of hands. The cushions beneath me smelled faintly of lavender, the scent mingling with something older, a faint musk that spoke of years trapped in quiet corners and forgotten Sunday mornings.

My fingers found the worn hymn book lying next to me, its cover cracked and softened from years of use. The pages were crinkled, almost delicate, and the print was faded and smudged as if each letter had been kissed by countless voices raised in song. I traced the edges with my thumb, feeling the slight grain of the paper, the sharp corner of a folded page pressed flat, like a secret someone had left for another to find.

The choir started up, their voices weaving together like a slow river of sound, ebbing and flowing with a gentle power. The notes floated high into the rafters, soft and trembling, mixing with the deep hum of the organ and the occasional creak and groan of the old building settling into itself. The scent of polished wood and candle wax mingled with a faint, almost imperceptible trace of perfume from the congregants.

I glanced sideways and caught Mason sliding in quietly a few rows over, his presence almost a whisper. His bleach-blond hair was tousled, strands falling loosely over his forehead, probably from his usual rushed morning routine. The sunlight caught the golden highlights, making them shimmer like threads of spun honey. He gave me a small, almost shy smile, the kind that made my chest feel both warm and tight at the same time, a flutter that settled somewhere deep in my ribs.

Our parents exchanged polite greetings, nods and smiles that felt automatic, familiar. The soft shuffle of shoes on the wooden floor, the faint rustling of clothing, the occasional cough or clearing of a throat created a quiet soundtrack to the sermon. I listened without really hearing all the words, letting the calm rhythm of the church wash over me like a slow tide.

The pew creaked beneath us as Mason's dad shifted beside my mom, a subtle exchange of glances passing between them, a raised eyebrow, a smile held a moment too long, like a secret just out of earshot.

When the service ended, sunlight spilled through the doors in golden shafts, catching dust mites that floated lazily in the air like tiny dancers in the warm light.

Outside, the world seemed brighter and louder, the smell of freshly cut grass was sharp, mingling with the faint, smoky tang of barbecue drifting from a nearby backyard. The sweetness of blooming honeysuckle added a soft undercurrent to the air, carried on a lazy breeze.

Mason's mom waved over to my parents, and soon the two families were deep in conversation about church events, Mason's upcoming game, and the who-what-where of the neighborhood bake sale.

I stood there, feeling both like an outsider and somehow a part of something, a loose thread woven into the edges of a familiar pattern. Mason caught my eye and asked if I wanted to grab lunch, just the two of us.

My parents exchanged a quick glance and nodded, and I said yes before my brain could catch up.

The ride to the diner was quiet but comfortable. Mason fiddled with the radio, flipping through stations until a soft country tune drifted through the speakers, warm and steady like a friend's voice. We hummed along quietly, the silence stretching comfortably between us like a familiar blanket.

When we stepped inside, the heat hit me in a wave, thick and sticky, clinging to skin and clothes. The smells of the diner were a stark contrast to the ones outside. Grass and honeysuckle were replaced with grease and rancid oil. Barbecue traded for fried onions, sizzling bacon, burnt coffee, and the sticky sweetness of sugar. The clatter of dishes and soft murmur of conversations buzzed around us, filling the space with life.

We slid into a booth near the window, the vinyl seat cool and a little cracked beneath me. Mason's fingers brushed mine as he reached for the ketchup bottle, and I felt my heart skip.

We talked about everything and nothing, his touchdown last week, my failed attempt at pancakes, how summer felt like it was approaching too slowly but somehow too fast.

Outside, the street thrummed with weekend life, kids laughing on bikes, dogs barking, the distant revving of a lawn mower, but inside our booth, everything slowed down. I realized maybe this was what I'd been missing—a quiet moment with someone who didn't expect me to have it all together.

The sunlight through the diner window made tiny sparkles on the glass, catching the dust motes floating lazily in the air. I traced a finger along the condensation on my iced tea glass, watching droplets race each other down the side. The cold glass left a faint ring on the table, slick and cool against the warm wood grain.

Mason kept glancing over at me, that easy half-smile playing at the corners of his mouth like he was about to say something but wasn't sure how to start.

"So," he finally said, voice low and smooth, "how's the whole 'not officially playing the game' thing going?"

I bit my lip, trying not to let too much show. "It's... complicated." Code for: I'm terrified of what the Hangman is capable of, but I can't admit it to anyone, especially not Mason.

He shrugged, like that explained everything. "You know, you don't have to be brave all the time."

I wanted to say, "I know." But instead, I just nodded, pretending to be interested in the shifting pattern sunlight made on the table, a mottled dance of light and shadow, warm and safe.

Our food arrived, his burger sizzling with melted cheese, the scent of toasted buns and smoky bacon rising in tempting waves. My plate was a sloppy mess of fries and salad, the lettuce more jungle than garnish, leaves crisp and tangled with thin slices of cucumber and cherry tomatoes bursting with sweetness.

The ketchup bottle clicked open, and the smell of fried onions mixed with something sweet and greasy that made my stomach rumble.

Mason dug in without ceremony, jaw flexing, eyes locked on the fries like they were a prize. I laughed quietly, feeling the tension slip out of my shoulders.

"You're impossible," I told him between bites.

He grinned, mouth full. "Takes one to know one."

The diner hummed around us like a low, steady heartbeat, clatter of plates, soft murmur of other diners, occasional hiss from the fryer. Mason's fingers drummed on the table restlessly, like he was mulling over something heavy.

"So," he said finally, breaking the comfortable silence, "Mr. Duvall called me yesterday."

My fork paused halfway to my mouth. I set it down carefully, trying to keep my voice steady. "Oh?"

"Yeah." Mason's eyes sharpened, cutting past the easy banter we'd been circling all morning. "About the brake lines. Said he'd found some cuts, could've been sabotage."

I swallowed hard. The memory of that morning was still raw, the gym parking lot feeling too quiet, the acrid scent of burnt rubber hanging in the air, and the flicker of movement I'd caught out of the corner of my eye near the gym doors.

"What did he say exactly?" I asked, trying to keep my tone casual, but my heart hammered.

Mason shrugged but didn't look away. "He didn't say much, just that the police were involved now."

My heart stopped. "Police?"

"Yeah." Mason said with a mouth full of food. "But here's the thing, he thinks it might be connected to the Hangman game."

My breath hitched. The game, that sick, twisted shadow hanging over all of us lately.

"He mentioned your name," Mason added, voice low. "Said you might have info. Asked if you knew anything."

I clenched my jaw, not wanting Mason to know how much I'd seen, how much I'd kept to myself out of fear and confusion.

"I told him no," I said quietly.

Mason's gaze sharpened, suspicion flickering. "You didn't tell him everything, did you?"

I hesitated, then shook my head. "I didn't want to freak you out."

"But you knew," he said, leaning forward slightly. "You knew before he called me."

My stomach turned. "He told me at the football game," I admitted.

Mason leaned back, blinking. "You already knew? You didn't say anything?"

"I didn't know what to say. I didn't want to dump that on you in the middle of everything."

He stared at me, the space between us cracking. "So, you let me hear it from Duvall instead."

"I'm sorry," I said, voice low. "I just, I didn't want to say it was true yet. I didn't want to start a panic."

Mason looked away, jaw tight. "I could've handled it. I should've known first."

"I know," I said softly. "I messed up."

He was quiet for a long time, then said, "Was that all you kept from me?"

My fingers curled around the edge of the table, feeling the smooth grain beneath my skin. "No."

He blinked, sharp now. "What else?"

"I saw someone. Right after the crash," I said. "By the gym doors. Watching us. They slipped away when I looked straight at them."

Mason's brows drew together. "You saw someone and didn't say anything?"

"I didn't know who they were. It could've been anyone. And after that, I didn't want to scare you more than you already were."

"I wasn't scared," he muttered.

"Okay, fine. I was scared," I snapped, louder than I meant. "This whole thing, this game, it's not just weird. It's dangerous."

Mason stared at me, quiet.

"And there's more," I added. "I saw them again. Sort of. Twice."

He straightened. "When?"

"The first time, I was walking Kirby. I thought I saw someone watching me. Like, from the trees. They were wearing a hoodie or something dark, I don't know. But it felt wrong."

Mason's voice dropped. "And the second?"

"Last night. Walking with Jack. We passed the old McKinley place. I saw something, or someone, upstairs. Just a flicker. A shadow. I can't be sure, but it felt the same."

He pressed his hands to his face, dragging them down slowly. "Why didn't you tell me any of this?"

"Because I didn't want you to think I was paranoid. Or worse, right."

Mason exhaled, slow and deep. "Sadee… this isn't just your weight to carry. You don't have to do this alone."

"I know," I whispered. "But I'm used to doing things alone."

He reached across the table, his hand brushing mine, the touch light but grounding, warm and steady. "You don't have to anymore."

I looked up, eyes stinging. "You're not mad?"

"I'm… still kind of mad," he admitted. "But I get it. And I'd rather you be honest now than never."

I nodded. "I promise. No more secrets."

"Okay," Mason said. He squeezed my hand gently, then let go. "So, what do we do?"

"We pay attention," I said. "We talk to each other. We stop pretending everything's fine."

He nodded slowly. "Alright. Deal."

The tension broke a little. He leaned back again, letting out a breath that sounded like it had been sitting in his chest for days.

"You really thought I'd freak out?" he asked after a beat.

"I thought you'd try to protect me. And maybe get hurt doing it."

He smirked. "Well, that part's probably true."

I rolled my eyes, but I was smiling now too.

He gestured toward my plate. "You gonna finish that jungle of lettuce?"

"Not if you call it that again."

"Fine. Your charming collection of decorative greenery."

"Better."

We settled back into easy conversation, like the fight had shaken loose something that needed to break. Like we'd finally let the storm pass and now the air was clear again.

We fell into an easy rhythm, talking about the dumb stuff, the stuff that usually gets shoved under the weight of everything else. The sound of the jukebox clicking through songs, the low murmur of other customers, the clatter of dishes, it all wrapped around us, a soft cocoon that made the world outside feel distant and blurry.

At one point, Mason caught me staring at his hand as he reached for the napkins. I flushed, the warmth rising in my cheeks, and looked away, but he just smiled like he'd caught me doing something silly but sweet.

It was stupid, but I wanted to reach out, to close the small gap between us that always felt just wide enough to trip over.

When the check came, Mason insisted on paying, sliding his card across the table with a little flourish like he was pretending to be the hero of some cheesy rom-com.

"Are you sure?" I asked, voice low.

"Positive," he said, eyes bright. "Next time, you owe me."

I smiled, the kind that comes from something real and quiet, the kind that feels like it could grow if you let it.

By the time we stood to leave, the sunlight through the diner windows had softened into a gentle glow, the edges of the world blurring like a watercolor painting.

Mason reached for my hand without thinking, and I let him, the warmth of his fingers was a small but steady anchor.

We didn't say anything more about the crash, or the figure at the gym, or the shadow in the window. But we didn't pretend they weren't real either.

We just walked, side by side, both listening for footsteps that didn't belong.

The walk back to my house was slower, cooler now as the sun dipped behind the trees, painting the sky in streaks of pink and amber. We passed the same old houses with peeling paint and creaky porches, their weathered wood glowing softly in the fading light.

I felt like I was seeing everything through new eyes, the way the breeze teased Mason's hair, the way the air smelled like promises and something just out of reach, like the faint trace of a storm waiting on the horizon.

At my door, Mason hesitated, hands in his pockets. I didn't want the moment to end, but I also didn't want to say goodbye too soon.

"Thanks," I said softly.

"For what?"

"For… this. For lunch. For not making it weird."

He laughed, a low, easy sound that made me want to smile even wider.

"Yeah," he said, stepping back. "Anytime."

I watched him walk away, the last light catching his shoulders before he disappeared around the corner. And for the first time that week, I felt like maybe things weren't so tangled after all.

As Mason's footsteps faded down the street, I closed the door and leaned against it for a moment, the quiet settling around me like a thick, warm blanket. It was strange, how things between us felt both familiar and new all at once.

We were technically still dating, but some days it was like we were just friends who happened to know a little too much about each other. Other times, there was this flicker, something electric in the way he looked at me or the way my chest tightened when his hand brushed mine.

But right now? I wasn't sure where I stood. And I had no clue where Mason did either.

It was like walking a line in the dark, trying to guess if the next step would be solid ground or empty air.

I could remember the early days, when everything felt clearer, when the butterflies were loud and the plans were easy, and the world was all "us" in bright, sharp colors. But lately, those colors had softened, blurred around the edges, like an old photograph left in the sun too long. Sometimes I wondered if Mason felt the same shift, or if I was the only one holding onto the questions that didn't have answers yet.

I wanted to ask him, to say, "Hey, where are we? What does this mean?" But the words stuck in my throat, tangled up in fear and pride and the hope that maybe, just maybe, things didn't need to be figured out all at once.

So, I let the silence stretch instead, listening to the steady hum of the house and the distant sounds of summer settling in outside. Maybe, for now, that was enough.

There's no hiding from what's already beneath the surface.

Chapter Twelve

The sunlight threw scattered patterns across the floor of my bedroom. Small rainbows danced around the stacks of books and piles of laundry strewn about. Dust mites floated lazily through the air, turning in the light like tiny constellations. I rolled over to face the window, the soft linen comforter grazing my skin. The scent of detergent clung to the sheets, warm and familiar.

But familiarity didn't mean comfort anymore.

The air was cool against my skin as I sat up. For a second, I didn't move, just stared at the way the sunlight fractured across my wall, splintering through the blinds like prison bars. My chest felt tight, like something invisible had curled up between my ribs overnight and settled in. That weight hadn't lifted.

The comforter slid off my shoulders in a whisper of fabric. Every motion felt deliberate. Slow. Like if I moved too quickly, I'd wake something I didn't want to face.

From downstairs came the unmistakable smell of eggs and bacon, mingled with the sound of Jack's footsteps thundering down the hall and slamming down the stairs like a freight train.

We had eggs and bacon for breakfast last week. The day I went to Indigo's house. The day we got the text.

My phone buzzed sharply beside me, jerking me from thought. I groaned, squinting at the screen. "Who's texting this early in the morning?" I mumbled.

A notification flashed: *Congratulations to Jax Paar for solving the puzzle. "I see dead people."* I blinked at it. That was it? That was the answer? I let out a breath and rolled onto my back, staring at the ceiling fan spinning slowly above me.

It didn't feel over. It wasn't over.

I swung my legs out from under the covers. The hardwood was cold beneath my feet, grounding in a way I didn't want to admit I needed. I padded toward the hallway. The air smelled like breakfast and something faintly sweet, syrup, maybe. Something warm and normal.

But normalcy was a costume the world had put back on too quickly.

Downstairs, Jack was already at the table, shoveling eggs into his mouth like it was a race. His hair stuck up in wild spikes, a mess of curls that looked like it'd lost a battle with gravity.

"Morning," I muttered, sliding into the seat across from him.

"Mornin', honey," Mom called over her shoulder from the stove, flipping an egg expertly in the pan. She set a plate in front of me— perfectly cooked eggs, bacon, and toast with melting butter pooling at the corners.

"Thanks." I reached for the pepper shaker, hands still half-asleep, mind anywhere but here.

Dad wandered in next, wearing mismatched socks and sipping from his chipped travel mug. He kissed Mom's temple and ruffled Jack's hair. Jack whispered "ow" like it physically wounded him.

"Do I smell burnt toast or is that just the weather guy again?" Dad nodded toward the muted TV, where a stern-looking anchor gestured toward swirling storm clouds.

"Rain this afternoon," Mom said. "Don't forget your jacket."

Jack groaned dramatically. "Why does it always rain when I have PE?"

"I ask myself the same thing every Thursday," Mom replied, already handing him his backpack as the school bus honked outside.

Jack bolted for the door with a final bite of toast in hand.

I tried to eat, but the food just sat there, bright and greasy. My appetite was dulled by the thrum in my chest. I didn't know what it was exactly, dread? Anticipation? Something between?

"I need to get changed," I said softly, taking my plate to the sink. The clink of ceramic on steel echoed louder than expected.

Upstairs, I got ready slowly, like I was trying not to disturb the silence. Every drawer pull, every zipper zip, every brushstroke through my hair sounded too loud. My fingers hesitated at the collar of my hoodie before pulling it over my head.

The mirror caught me in its gaze. Tired eyes. Tense shoulders. A stranger who looked like me.

I walked to school.

The air was heavy with moisture; the sky smeared with dull gray clouds. Damp leaves clung to the sidewalk like fallen scraps of summer. Cars hissed as they passed, tires sending up fine sprays of water.

By mid-morning, school buzzed with restless energy. Lockers banged shut, voices rose and overlapped, the usual teenage chaos on full volume. The air was thick with cheap body spray, cafeteria grease, and the damp tang of floors recently mopped.

Jax was everywhere. His name floated through conversations like smoke. Jax Paar: the golden boy who solved the puzzle.

Even the local news had shown up, awkwardly dragging camera equipment through the crowded halls. I caught a glimpse of a camera light in my peripheral and flinched.

Everyone acted like it was over. The game. The mystery. The unease.

But the knot in my stomach hadn't gone anywhere. If anything, it had tightened.

The bell rang like a shriek, jolting everyone into motion. Bodies surged through the corridors. Shoes squeaked, backpacks thudded, lockers clanged shut in rapid staccato.

Indigo and Finn were just ahead of me. Indigo's hand brushed lightly against his as they walked, connected, even if slightly distant. They looked like they belonged together, even if their smiles were softer now, more careful. Tension clung to them. But the love was still there. I could feel it.

When Nick stepped into our path, it was like walking into a freezer.

He leaned against the lockers near the gym, arms folded, one boot propped against the metal. His expression was that same smug mask he always wore, but his eyes were sharp, scanning, calculating.

"Finn. Indi," he said with mock-casual confidence, pushing off the lockers and falling into step beside us.

Finn's body tensed so hard I thought his knuckles might snap through his skin.

Indigo's fingers twitched at her side.

Nick's presence was cold and heavy. He smelled like sweat and cheap cologne, and something sour underneath. The way he moved made my skin crawl, too smooth, too practiced.

"So," he said, voice too loud in the crowded hall, "Jax cracked the code. 'I see dead people.' That's what all the fuss was about? Really anticlimactic if you ask me."

"Guess the mystery's done," I said, keeping my voice neutral.

"Done?" He laughed, the sound dry and hollow. "You guys don't look like it's done. Still jumpy."

"Maybe you're just bad at reading people," I said.

Finn stepped forward, planting himself between Nick and Indigo. "Why don't you walk the other way, Nick?"

Nick raised an eyebrow. "You always play bodyguard now? That what you do since you and Indigo started acting like everything's perfect again?"

Finn didn't flinch. But I saw it, the flicker in his eyes, like a match trying not to catch.

Nick leaned in slightly, like he was sniffing for weakness. "You used to be chill, man. Like… surfer-boy energy. Now you're all stiff. Makes a guy wonder what changed."

Indigo stepped in. "You're not worth the energy. Leave."

Nick tilted his head. "Touchy. Guess I hit a nerve."

"You really want to find out?" I asked, stepping closer. My voice was low.

He turned his eyes to me. "That sounds like a threat, Sadee Hart."

I met his gaze. "It might be."

He blinked, thrown. His smirk faltered for just a second. Then he scratched at his eyebrow and gave a hollow laugh.

"Oh, whatever. I'm just messing." Then, with a glance that sliced through the noise of the hallway: "Heard someone's phone buzzed again last night."

That froze us.

He raised his hands. "Just saying. Rumors travel fast."

Then he turned and disappeared into the throng of students.

Indigo exhaled sharply. "He's such a creep."

Finn reached for her hand. She let him take it this time.

"We can't let anything slip," he murmured.

"No," I said, "not yet."

After school, Indigo and I found ourselves at Lou's Diner, one of the only ones left in town that still looked like it belonged to another decade. The booths were sticky, the lighting buzzed, and the coffee was always slightly burnt. But it was safe. Familiar.

We sat by the window. Outside, the rain had started, soft at first, then steadily soaking the sidewalks. Streetlights shimmered in the puddles.

A waitress in a faded uniform poured water into our glasses and didn't ask for our order. She knew us.

"I still can't believe Jax figured it out," Indigo said quietly, stirring a straw through her Coke. "Like… that's it?"

"It's not," I said.

She looked at me, eyebrows drawn together. "You feel it too, don't you? That… wrongness?"

"Yeah. Like something's watching."

She nodded slowly, her gaze dropping to the tabletop. "I know what you mean."

I didn't know what to say. So, I reached over and held her hand.

She didn't pull away.

"I keep thinking," she said, voice barely audible, "that we missed something. That this whole thing was just… the start."

My throat tightened. "It feels like a trap."

A sharp clatter from the kitchen made us both flinch. Just a dropped pan, but our nerves were drawn tight.

Indigo stared at her reflection in the window. "You ever feel like... someone pressed play on something and forgot to tell us we're still in the game?"

"Yes," I said. "All the time."

She looked over. "Can I crash at your place tonight? I don't really want to be alone."

"Of course."

We walked home through the drizzle, jackets pulled tight. The sound of our boots in puddles was the only noise for blocks. Somewhere in the distance, a train wailed like a ghost.

The old oak tree in our yard came into view. Its branches clawed against the side of the house, wind scraping them like nails on glass.

Inside, the house was warm. Safe. Mom handed Indigo a blanket and made tea without asking. It was nice, having someone know just what you need before you even know you need it.

Later, upstairs in the dark, we lay side by side in silence. I could tell Indigo wasn't sleeping. Her breathing was too even. Too intentional.

My phone buzzed once on the nightstand. I reached for it with trembling fingers.

New Message: 10:48 PM. From the same anonymous thread that started this all. *Ready for round two? Let's play again. This time... the stakes are higher.*

My pulse roared in my ears. A second message popped up, this time just for me.

What letter do you want to guess?

__ ___ ____ _____ ______.

The letters glared at me from the screen like open wounds. I stared, unable to blink.

Indigo turned toward me in the dark. Her eyes were open. She had seen it too. Her voice was hoarse, nearly a whisper. "It's starting again."

I nodded.

The game wasn't over. It had only just begun.

I didn't sleep that night. Not really. Not in the way that counted. My eyes closed sometimes, but my mind never shut off. It just circled and circled like a bird that didn't know where to land.

The message glowed in my brain like it was burned there. *What letter do you want to guess?*

I hadn't answered yet. This wasn't supposed to happen.

I couldn't. Every time I thought about picking a letter, my breath caught. Like guessing wrong would mean something worse than before. Like now the stakes were real.

Sometime around 2 a.m., I got up. Tiptoed to the bathroom, careful not to wake anyone downstairs. The floor was freezing under my toes. The nightlight cast long shadows along the hallway walls, stretching the shapes of furniture until they looked monstrous.

I stared at myself in the bathroom mirror. My reflection looked pale. Wide-eyed. Like I'd seen something I couldn't unsee.

I ran cold water and splashed my face. It did nothing.

Back in the room, Indigo was still awake. Her eyes were open, fixed on the ceiling.

"I can't stop thinking about it," she whispered. Her voice sounded too big in the quiet.

"Me neither." I crawled back into bed beside her.

"Do you think Jax got another message too?"

"I don't know. Maybe."

"Maybe he didn't," she said slowly. "Maybe he solved it, and that was the test. Maybe we failed."

The idea sat heavy in my chest. "Then what now?"

She turned to face me. "We guess. Or we don't. Either way, they're watching."

Rain tapped lightly on the windows. I tried to focus on the sound; to pretend this was just any other sleepover. But even the weather felt like it was holding its breath.

Eventually, sometime near dawn, we both drifted into shallow sleep.

When I woke, Indigo was gone.

Not gone-gone, just not in the room. Her blanket was folded neatly at the end of the bed. Her tea mug was gone from the nightstand. I found her downstairs, curled up in an armchair with Kirby's head in her lap, scrolling through her phone.

Her face was ghostly white. Her eyes gave away all the thoughts going through her head as she looked up at me. "They texted me last night. Same thing as you."

I sat down beside her. Kirby nosed my hand before settling against my leg.

I picked up my phone. The message still sat there, unanswered.

We stared at the screen together. The row of blank spaces. Twenty letters.

It looked like a graveyard.

"I'm not guessing yet," I said.

She nodded. "Me neither."

We walked to school together again. No words this time. Just the rhythm of our footsteps on wet pavement and the steady hush of traffic in the distance. Everything looked normal, but it all felt… brittle. Like the whole world was made of glass and we were walking through it barefoot.

At school, the air was buzzing again. But different this time. Less excitement. More tension. The kind that collects in the corners of a room before something bad happens.

People stared more. Whispered more. I saw Ryan at his locker, jaw tight, eyes scanning the crowd like he was waiting for something to jump out. Cassie stood beside him, chewing on the end of a pen, clearly nervous. She spotted us and waved us over.

"Did you get it?" she asked without preamble.

I hesitated.

Her eyes widened. "You did."

"Did you?" Indigo asked.

Cassie nodded. Slowly. "Late last night. It just popped up. Why are we going for a round two?"

"It's not." Ryan closed his locker.

I look at him questioningly. "What do you mean 'it's not'? The text itself said 'ready for round two.'"

"Don't you get it?" Ryan whispered. "It never ended."

Cassie shivered.

Indigo glanced around. "You think it's someone here?" She asked, her voice low.

I didn't answer.

In class, I couldn't focus. The words on the board blurred. My notes were just scribbles. I jumped every time my phone buzzed, even if it was just a reminder or a random group chat.

At lunch, Jax walked past our table. Everyone's eyes followed him. He didn't look triumphant. He looked pale. Drawn. Haunted.

Indigo nudged me. "He looks worse than we do."

"Maybe he's feeling bad. Him solving it didn't fix anything."

At lunch, no one ate much. Just picked at fries and pushed food around. At one point, Mason tried to speak, but he could tell something was off. He didn't ask. Just draped an arm around my shoulders and kissed my temple.

I leaned into him because it was safe. But my mind wasn't there.

My mind was stuck on those blank spaces. I wasn't supposed to get them again.

Back at home, after school, the house felt unusually quiet. I sat in my room next to Indigo, the overhead lights off, leaving the soft glow of our phones the only illumination.

Outside, Kirby's sharp barks pierced the calm as he chased squirrels through the backyard, his voice distant but urgent. From downstairs, I could hear Jack's fingers clicking rapidly on the controller of his video game, the low hum of the television blending with Mom's footsteps in the kitchen as she prepared dinner.

The sky had shifted since we left school, now a bruised shade of deep gray. Thunder cracked somewhere far off, a low growl rolling through the air like a warning.

I swallowed hard and opened the message again, the empty spaces blinking at me like a silent challenge. I stared at it for what felt like forever, my thumb hovering over the keyboard but frozen. I wouldn't be able to avoid it. Then, finally, I typed a letter. Just one.

"T."

I hit send, my breath catching in my throat. Almost immediately, the typing bubbles appeared, flickering across the screen like eyes watching me. I held my breath, every nerve on edge.

Then the message came.

Wrong.

My heart slammed against my ribs like a warning drum, nearly stopping altogether.

Before I could even process, another message popped up: a photo.

My stomach dropped. This *really* wasn't supposed to happen.

The image was taken from outside, from the street. It showed my bedroom window, the glass smeared with a single, horrifying mark: a red '*X,*' painted thickly, like blood that had been freshly applied. The color gleamed in the dim light, almost wet, and a streak of it trailed downward, dripping slowly like it was still fresh.

I leapt up, the chair scraping against the floor. Indigo was right behind me, her breath shallow, eyes wide. Together, we rushed to the window, and threw open the curtains.

Outside, the world was still. The sidewalk gleamed wet beneath streetlights, rain having fallen earlier. The asphalt shone like black glass, empty except for the faint, ghostly reflection of the red mark on the glass. No one stood there. No shadow moved. Nothing but silence and the soft, steady drip of rain sliding down the windowpane.

But the mark was real.

A fresh streak, dark and glistening.

Like blood.

I took a cautious step back, my skin crawling, breath shallow.

My phone buzzed again.

Thanks for playing.

I froze, every hair on my arms standing on end. Goosebumps erupted, my skin prickling as though I was suddenly exposed to cold wind. My whole body stiffened, muscles taut like wire.

"Sadee…" Indigo whispered, her voice fragile, almost breaking.

I turned slowly, eyes locking with hers.

"Indi, I guessed wrong. They know where I live." The words felt heavy, the truth sinking like a stone.

Then, without warning, Indigo's phone lit up.

One new message. Same format. Same anonymous sender.

She opened it, her fingers trembling. I watched her eyes dart rapidly over the screen. Her face drained of color, paling until she looked almost ghostly. A curse slipped from her lips under her breath, sharp and broken. She swallowed hard, her thumb hovering hesitantly over the screen as another message slid in.

"Your time to make a guess is running out. Not guessing is the same as a wrong answer."

Her whole body seemed to freeze for several long, agonizing seconds. Then, slowly, she typed.

"N."

The reply came back faster than mine.

Wrong.

And then, another photo.

We leaned closer together, eyes fixed on the screen.

The picture was grainy, blurred like it had been taken quickly, from a distance through glass. A girl in a hoodie stood in front of a living room window, her face obscured by shadows.

But there was no mistaking it.

That was Indigo's sister. Inside her own house.

Below the photo, a new message appeared.

Nice place. Hope the locks still work.

Indigo let out a strangled sound, a mix between a gasp and a sob.

"That's my living room," she whispered. "That's… she was home alone."

My stomach twisted painfully, a cold knot tightening deep inside me.

She turned her phone toward me, her eyes wide and glossy, shimmering with unshed tears. Her voice cracked as she spoke, barely audible.

"It's all just starting to mean something, isn't it?"

The quiet ones hide the loudest screams.

Chapter Thirteen

Indigo doesn't wait. She just spins on her heel and sprints out of my room, the sharp clatter of her keys cutting through the thick silence like a knife. Her footsteps thunder down the stairs—wild, uneven, like her body can't move fast enough, like panic is dragging her forward faster than she can process. The sound of her descent echoes through the hallways, magnified by the emptiness, each step a frantic drumbeat that sets my nerves on fire.

I bolt after her, heart hammering against my ribs so hard it feels like it might burst through my chest. My limbs feel disconnected from my brain, moving too fast, like I'm not really inside my body. The air in the house feels thick and wrong, pressing down on my skin, like it knows what we're running toward. I can feel it clinging to me, suffocating and close, as if the walls themselves are watching.

The front door slams open so hard it rattles on its hinges. The humid night air floods in, sticky and close, clinging to my skin like a second layer. I can hear the slow drip of a leaky gutter somewhere nearby, the distant bark of a dog two houses down, and a faint sprinkler ticking in the neighbor's yard. These normal sounds only make the silence around my house feel more suffocating, like reality is trying too hard to be calm, to pretend things are still okay.

Indigo throws herself into the driver's seat of her car, hands trembling as they fumble the keys. She misses the ignition once, then again, her breath coming in ragged gasps like she's struggling for air but can't catch it. Her chest rises and falls in uneven bursts. I can see her knuckles whitening around the steering wheel, like if she lets go, she'll fall apart completely.

I dive into the passenger seat, pulling out my phone with slick, shaking fingers. The screen flares too bright in the dark car, casting harsh blue light against the cramped interior. It reflects off the dashboard and glances against Indigo's profile, painting her in fractured neon shadows. My thumb finds Finn's name in my speed dial; he lives on the neighboring street of Indigo's, so he can get there faster than anyone else.

He picks up immediately. "What?" His voice is sharp and tired, like he just woke up but knows something's wrong.

"Finn," I shout, voice breaking before I even realize it. "You have to get to Indigo's house. Her sister—someone's inside. Just get there. Now."

A heartbeat of silence.

"Okay." Then he hangs up.

Indigo finally gets the key in. The engine growls to life, low and angry, and the headlights flare bright in the dark. The steering wheel jerks as she pulls out of the driveway, tires spitting gravel and squealing against the curb. My body slams hard against the door, shoulder colliding with the window. The glass is cold, but I barely register it over the roaring panic in my head.

She doesn't speak. Her face is carved in terror, eyes locked on the road but unfocused, glassy. Her breathing is shallow, almost mechanical. Her fingers twitch and clench too tight on the steering wheel, knuckles bone-white. Her lips press together in a thin, bloodless line. A sheen of sweat clings to her temple, catching faint traces of the passing streetlight.

My hands won't stop shaking either. I keep glancing at my phone, checking Finn's contact like it'll make the drive shorter. But the minutes crawl by, mocking me. Every second feels like a rubber band stretched too tight, about to snap.

The leather seat beneath me is sticky, sweat pooling on my back. The seatbelt bites into my collarbone, the rough fabric rubbing raw skin as I shift. I try to adjust, but every movement feels wrong, sharp, panicked, disconnected. The air inside the car smells faintly of Indigo's floral shampoo mixed with the stale tang of fast food from earlier. There's something oddly nauseating about that mix, something too human and too normal in a night that's anything but.

Outside, the engine hums, tires shriek softly on the asphalt, and the wind howls around us, rattling the open windows just enough to carry a whisper of tree leaves and late summer heat. The streetlights flash overhead in long bars of gold and shadow, casting flickering stripes across the dashboard and Indigo's tense face. It feels like we're driving through a strobe of memories, every light a flash, every second a snapshot we won't be able to forget.

My mind won't shut up.

What if we're too late?

What if we get there and it's already over?

Indigo gasps suddenly, chest heaving, and slams a fist hard against the steering wheel. The sharp crack of her nails against the leather echoes inside the car, a violent punctuation to the silence between us.

"This is my fault." Her voice cracks on the last word, brittle and raw.

"No," I say, even though I know it is.

"This is my punishment," Indigo whispers. "They're going after her because I got it wrong."

The green light ahead turns red, but Indigo doesn't slow. She barrels through it, eyes wide and wet and furious. I flinch as the car flies through the intersection, tires skimming the ground like we might lift off at any second.

The car skids sharply as she takes the turn into her neighborhood too fast. The street narrows, lined with towering trees and neat, quiet houses. Porch lights glow soft and warm. Curtains drawn tight against the night. It should be comforting, familiar, but the normalcy feels like a slap in the face. Too calm. Too untouched. Like the world hasn't caught up to what we know.

Nothing looks wrong.

And somehow, that's worse.

Everything should look wrong.

We spot Finn's car before we reach Indigo's house. It's parked perfectly in line with the curb, hazard lights flashing in slow, steady pulses like a heartbeat. He's already out, sprinting toward the front door with his phone in one hand, flashlight beam cutting a harsh line through the dark. His movement is fast and fluid, but there's something urgent in it, something terrified.

Indigo doesn't even bother to park properly. She slams the gearshift into park and stumbles out before the car stops fully. Her door swings open so hard it bounces back, and she rushes toward the house, every step frantic.

"CALL HER!" she shouts to Finn. "CALL MY SISTER!"

He doesn't answer, just disappears into the shadows on the porch. The front door is slightly ajar, just cracked enough to make the air inside congeal in my chest. That tiny gap feels like a threat, like a warning: something's already inside.

Indigo freezes beside me. "She always locks the door."

The night falls heavy and still. My mouth is dry; my legs feel like wet paper. I follow Indigo to the porch, every nerve screaming. The door groans as it swings inward. The air that spills out is stale and cold, despite the heat. It feels wrong, like something hollowed out the space and left it echoing.

Inside, the faint creak of floorboards echoes. The house smells like stale coffee and something sharp, metallic. I gag slightly, the iron tang catching in my throat. It clings to my skin, coats my teeth.

Indigo pushes past Finn and throws the door open wide.

"Ella?"

No answer.

The beam from Finn's flashlight dances across the entryway—walls hung with family photos, shoes tossed carelessly by the door. The silence presses in, thick and suffocating. The kind of silence that feels like it's listening.

My throat tightens.

This is what happens when you guess wrong.

Mason's brake lines. Mr. Duvall was right.

The beam from Finn's flashlight flickers uncertainly as he steps deeper inside, the narrow cone of light trembling against the darkness. Every inch it touches seems to hold its breath, waiting for something, some terrible thing, to reveal itself. The house is so quiet that I can hear the faint scrape of shoes against hardwood, the soft buzz of an old refrigerator somewhere in the back, and the distant hum of an air conditioner struggling against the heat.

The metallic scent thickens, sharp and sour now, making my stomach twist. It's not just stale coffee anymore, something else lingers, bitter and coppery, like blood. My breath catches, shallow and quick, as my eyes dart between the shadows beyond the flashlight's reach.

Indigo's shoulders are tense behind me, rigid like she's bracing herself for impact. I want to reach out, to grab her hand, but my fingers feel frozen in place. The air is electric with dread, heavy enough to make my chest ache. Every second stretches thin and taut, like a wire pulled too tight.

Finn's footsteps echo ahead, uneven and hesitant. I imagine his flashlight beam slicing through dark corners where secrets lurk, where whatever's inside might still be watching. A sudden creak makes me jump; a settling floorboard, or something more sinister? My pulse spikes so sharply it feels like a punch to the ribs.

I swallow hard, tasting the dry bitterness in my mouth, my tongue sticking to the roof like paper. My skin prickles under the cold crawl of sweat running down my back. The silence feels like it's wrapping tighter around us, squeezing until it chokes.

Indigo's breath is ragged now, shallow and quick like mine. She steps past Finn, moving with desperate urgency despite the fear radiating off her in waves. Her eyes flicker to the hallway leading deeper into the house, where the darkness pools thick and impenetrable.

The weight of the unknown presses down, heavy and suffocating. The house doesn't feel like a home anymore. It feels like a trap, a waiting thing, cold and hungry.

I follow, my legs barely keeping pace, every nerve screaming at me to run, to get out, but something roots me in place, an awful need to know, to find out if it's too late. If the worst has already happened. My breath comes shallow and fast, each inhale slicing at my chest like ice, but I force myself to keep moving. My hands tremble at my sides, and the air feels heavier with every step, like we're sinking deeper into something we won't come back from.

The hallway seems to stretch endlessly ahead, the beam of Finn's flashlight wavering as his hand shakes, casting distorted shadows that flicker and lurch like they might come alive. The wooden floorboards creak beneath our feet, long, groaning protests that echo too loudly in the stillness. Each step sounds deliberate, like the house itself is listening, like it's aware of our presence and waiting for the moment to snap shut around us. The air grows colder with every inch forward, thick with a dread that clings to my skin like wet fabric.

Walls lined with framed memories stare back at me, each picture a silent witness. Faded smiles, warm moments trapped in time, people who should feel close, familiar. But they don't. Not now. Now they seem like ghosts themselves, fragile, out of reach. Their eyes follow us with blank intensity, and I find myself wondering whether any of these people have any idea what's happening tonight. Whether they'd believe it if they did. The photographs should comfort me, should be proof of life, of normalcy. But instead, they remind me how quickly everything can break.

A sudden draft brushes past me, cold and ghostly, curling along my arms like fingers. I stop in my tracks. It smells faintly of something unfamiliar, like dust, old wood, and something sharper underneath. It carries a whisper, so faint I almost convince myself I imagined it. A sound like a sigh. A breath. Too quiet to be real. But I feel it, in my bones, and a chill ripples through me.

"Ella?" Indigo's voice breaks the silence again, softer this time, barely more than a whisper. Her tone is stretched thin, raw with desperation.

Nothing answers.

The house falls still again. But it isn't empty. It's watching. Breathing. Alive in a way that makes my skin crawl. Every creak, every shift of the walls, feels intentional; like we're being lured deeper, step by step, toward something we're not meant to see. I can't stop the cold wave of panic that crashes over me. It floods my veins like ice water, numbing everything except the ache in my chest. My hands curl into fists at my sides, nails digging into my palms hard enough to sting. It's the only thing anchoring me, the pain. Every instinct screams that we're too late; that whatever was going to happen has already happened.

Finn's flashlight catches something on the floor. We all stop short. A dark, wet smear, glistening faintly in the beam. My breath snags. For a moment, I can't move. My stomach twists in on itself, a sick knot of nausea and dread, and I clamp a hand over my mouth to keep the sob that tries to claw its way up from escaping. The smell hits next, sharp, metallic, unmistakable. It clings to the back of my throat, making my eyes sting. I know that smell. Blood.

Indigo stumbles back a step. Her face drains of color, lips pressed together so tight they've gone white. I think she might scream, but she doesn't. She just stands there, frozen, as if making a sound might make it worse.

My throat goes dry. I try to speak, but no sound comes out. It's like the house has stolen our voices, swallowed them whole. The silence is unbearable, thick and smothering. The house is a tomb, and we've just crossed the threshold into something terrible.

Then, a sound, soft, muffled, cuts through the silence. A whisper. A sob. It's impossible to tell. It comes from deeper in the house, from somewhere behind the walls or maybe from within the shadows themselves. We all freeze.

The hair on the back of my neck stands on end, a warning I can't ignore. My whole body goes rigid, caught between fear and hope, terror and the tiniest sliver of possibility.

"Did you hear that?" I manage, my voice barely a breath. It feels wrong to speak, like breaking the silence might wake something we don't want to meet.

Indigo nods without looking at me. Her eyes are wide and glassy, pupils dilated. She's holding her breath. I can feel it. So am I.

Finn raises his flashlight toward the sound, the beam jerking slightly with the tremble in his hand. He moves forward, each step slow and reluctant. The floor groans again under his weight, a groan that seems to echo too long, like the house is reacting to him.

The hallway twists, turning toward a closed door. It looms ahead of us, ordinary and sinister all at once. The muffled sound grows louder, clearer now. Not a whisper, not quite crying. A breath. A shuffle of movement behind the wood, soft but unmistakable.

Finn's hand hovers over the doorknob, fingers twitching. His flashlight beam stutters, bouncing around the frame, and for a moment it hits something, something small, something red, before settling back into darkness. My heart is pounding so loudly it drowns out everything else, a deafening rhythm that pulses in my ears.

He twists the knob slowly. His hand slips from the metal - maybe from the cold, maybe from sweat. The door creaks open with agonizing slowness, like it resents being opened. My breath hitches. I brace myself.

The beam of the flashlight cuts inside the room, slicing through the dark.

Nothing.

Just shadows.

A bed, messy and unmade, the sheets twisted like someone thrashed in them. A chair pushed back too far from a small desk. A cracked window letting in a thin shaft of moonlight, pale and ghostly.

The sobbing stops.

We all hold our breath.

Then, from the far corner, something stirs. A shape.

Small.

Ella.

She's curled up, knees drawn to her chest, her face streaked with tears. Her eyes catch the light, wide and terrified, staring at us like we're the monsters. Her body shakes. Her lips move, but no words come out at first. She looks so small. So, breakable.

"I thought—Finn—" Her voice cracks, breaking mid-sentence. She doesn't finish. She can't.

Indigo drops to her knees beside her, arms wrapping around her sister in a heartbeat. Her fingers clutch at Ella's back like she's afraid letting go will make her disappear again.

The weight of relief hits me so hard I almost fall to the ground. It steals my breath, buckles my knees. But tangled inside it is something else, something heavier. Because even though she's here, even though she's alive, the fear in her eyes tells me the story isn't over.

The punishment wasn't what I expected.

But now I understand exactly what this game is capable of.

What the Hangman is capable of.

And I know, deep in my bones, that it's far from done.

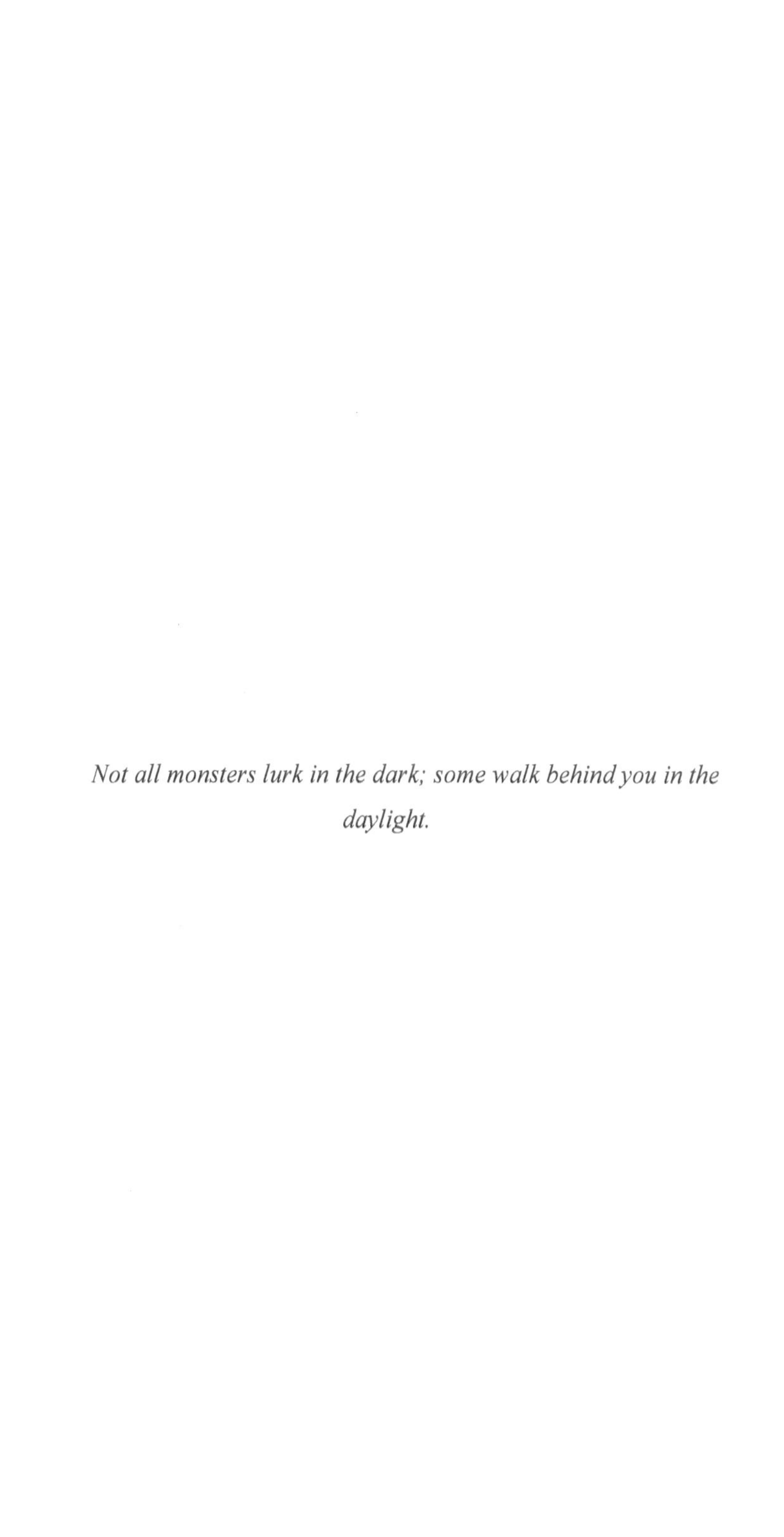

Not all monsters lurk in the dark; some walk behind you in the daylight.

Chapter Fourteen

I stepped outside to get air and ended up staring blankly into the dark, arms crossed tight over my chest like they might hold me together. The night wrapped around me like a heavy blanket, thick and suffocating, yet somehow brittle with tension.

Somewhere distant, an owl hooted, a mournful, lonely sound that made the silence feel even heavier. My breath comes out in shallow puffs, misting faintly in front of me before dissolving into the cold air. The crunch of gravel underfoot was swallowed by the overwhelming quiet.

The street was alive with red and white flashes, cop cars and an ambulance parked just crooked enough to tell you something awful had just happened. Their lights spun across lawns and rooftops, flickering through tree branches like lightning caught in slow motion, throwing jagged shadows onto the wet pavement.

The occasional sharp snap of a radio crackled through the night, voices too muffled to understand but full of urgency. The acrid tang of burning rubber mingled with the sharp metallic scent of antiseptic from the ambulance, weaving a strange, unsettling perfume in the air. The damp pavement glistened, reflecting the swirling red and white lights in fractured shards, like the broken pieces of a nightmare.

The air was thick with anticipation, as if the world itself was holding its breath, waiting for the next disaster to unfold. There was a faint hint of pine and crushed grass, grounding the surreal scene with a whisper of everyday normality. Somewhere nearby, a dog barked; a short, sharp yelp that echoed off the houses and pierced the fragile silence.

Finn stood on the porch, hands jammed into the pocket of his hoodie, rocking slightly on his heels. His shoulders were rigid, as if bracing against an invisible storm. His gaze was fixed somewhere beyond the flashing lights, eyes wide and unblinking, like his brain hadn't quite caught up yet. The faint hum of tension vibrated through the air around him, pulsing with every heartbeat. His breath came slow and uneven, the chest rising and falling with a barely contained tightness.

He looked like he hadn't blinked since we found Ella, like his mind was stuck in some limbo between shock and disbelief, fingers twitching in his pockets as if itching to do something, anything, to make this all go away.

Then Indigo stepped out.

She didn't slam the door like usual. Didn't say anything, didn't even look at us at first. She just stood there, silent, eyes fixed somewhere far away, like she was peering into a dark abyss that none of us could see. Her posture was stiff, almost brittle, the slight trembling of her hands betraying the storm raging beneath her calm facade. The soft rustle of her jacket was barely audible in the tense silence, mingling with the distant wail of sirens and the low thrum of the night.

Finn noticed her before I did.

He didn't say anything. He just walked over like he needed to be there. The gravel crunched softly under his shoes as he closed the gap between them. When he reached Indigo, he wrapped his arms around her carefully, holding her steady. Indigo didn't resist. She leaned into him, her breath shaky against his shoulder.

"I was so scared," she whispered, voice barely louder than the distant hum of the dispatcher's radio. "I thought I'd lost her."

Finn didn't say a word. He just held her tighter, resting his chin on her head, one hand slipping into her hair, fingers threading through the strands like he was trying to keep her grounded.

"I got it wrong," she breathed. "They could've taken her."

"We'll fix it," he said quietly. "We'll figure it out."

For a moment, everything else faded, the flashing lights, the distant sirens. It was just them. The silence between them wasn't empty. It was heavy with all the things left unsaid. The idea that whoever was behind this knew exactly where we lived, who we were close to, and maybe even more. It made the cold night air feel sharper, the shadows longer.

Finn's grip tightened just a little, like a quiet promise. Indigo didn't pull away. She just let herself be held.

The silence after that didn't feel empty. It was full of things we weren't speaking. Like the thought that someone who was playing games with everyone left threats at Indigo and my houses. They knew where we lived. They probably knew more too.

In the distance, a cruiser door slammed shut.

Sheriff Mike Dalton strode across the lawn like he'd already decided the whole situation was going to give him a headache. His boots sank slightly into the damp grass as he stepped up the porch, sending tiny droplets of water spraying up like brief sparks. Middle-aged and built like a linebacker gone soft, he carried himself with a resigned authority. The rough texture of his jacket caught the faint porch light, casting deep shadows into the creases. The silver badge pinned to his chest caught the porch light, gleaming coldly under the harsh white bulbs.

"You the three who found the kid?" he asked, voice low and flat, gravelly like worn leather. His eyes narrowed, scanning us like a predator sizing up prey.

I nodded, swallowing hard, the dry scrape of my throat echoing in my ears. Finn let go of Indigo slowly, stepping just a little in front of her, his jaw tight, fingers twitching at his sides. The tension radiating from him was palpable.

"She's inside," Finn said. "Ella. She's okay. Just scared." His voice was calm but brittle, like a thin veneer over fraying nerves.

Sheriff Dalton gave a short nod, like he already knew, like someone had radioed it in the second the EMTs got to her. He looked us over, me, Finn, Indigo, his eyes lingering a second longer on the red smear dried across the side of my shirt. It felt like a spotlight, burning cold and accusing. Then he pulled out a small notebook and flipped it open with a practiced flick of his wrist, the sound sharp against the quiet.

"I'm going to need statements from each of you," he said, already scribbling, the pen scratching fiercely across the paper. "One at a time. Just facts. No theories. No ghost stories. We'll start with the girl who called it in. That you?"

I raised my hand halfway, heart thudding against my ribs like a frantic drumbeat. The wetness of the grass soaked through my sneakers, cold and clammy against my skin. My fingertips tingled, numb from the chill.

. He nodded toward the front steps. "Let's talk over here."

I shot one last glance toward Indigo, who was still barely breathing next to Finn, her chest rising and falling in shallow, uneven waves. She looked small, fragile, as if the weight of the world had folded her into itself. I followed the sheriff to the bottom of the porch. My sneakers squelched in the wet grass, the smell of earth rising up in thick waves.

He flipped to a fresh page in his notebook. "Name?"

"Sadee Hart." My voice sounded weird, too thin, like it didn't quite belong to me anymore.

"And your relation to the Perez girl?"

"I was with Indigo, her sister, when we got the photo." The words felt flat, drained of color, like I was describing someone else's story.

"What photo?"

I pulled out my phone and showed him the screen. The photo still sat there in the message thread, grainy and terrifying. Ella, standing in her own living room, a blur behind the glass. The soft glow of the screen illuminated the worried crease in Dalton's brow.

Dalton looked at it for a long second, jaw tight. "And this was sent after a game prompt?"

"Yes. It's like... a hangman game. We get a blank word and we guess letters. If you get it wrong, you get punished. Or someone else does." My fingers trembled as I held the phone, the cool screen a stark contrast to my heated skin.

He didn't react. Just wrote it down like he was taking down a grocery list, the pen sliding smoothly across the paper.

"Who else has gotten messages?"

"A lot of people. Only people from the senior class though." The words felt heavy with unspoken fear.

Dalton didn't look up. "Has anyone gone to the police about it before tonight?"

"No," I admitted. "We didn't think it was serious." My voice cracked on the last word. But it was. Mason's brake lines had already been cut, sending him, Indigo, and me into a wreck that could've seriously hurt us. Or worse.

His pen scratched harder against the paper at that, like the sound was a warning.

After a moment, he clicked his pen shut and nodded once, sharp. "I'm going to need a copy of that message thread and any others you've gotten. Don't delete anything."

"I won't."

"Good. Sit tight. Don't leave the area tonight."

I nodded again. He was already turning back toward Finn.

Finn barely looked up as the sheriff headed toward him. Indigo shifted slightly behind him, like she didn't want him to go but knew she couldn't stop him. The faint rustle of her jacket whispered softly against his sleeve.

Dalton jerked his head toward the steps. "You next."

Finn didn't flinch. Just gave Indigo's arm a light squeeze before stepping away, the sound of his sneakers on the porch wood muted but steady.

They walked a few feet off toward the driveway.

Dalton flipped a page and started scribbling. "Name?"

"Finn Smith."

"You live nearby?"

"Yeah. Two streets over."

"How'd you end up here tonight?"

"Sadee called me. Said Ella was missing. I got here fast."

Dalton looked up. "You went in the house first?"

Finn nodded. "Door was already open. I didn't force anything. Just wanted to make sure she was okay."

"You find anyone else inside?"

"No. Just Ella. She was in the back room. Curled up. Not talking."

Dalton's voice lowered, almost suspicious. "She say anything at all?"

"She said my name," Finn said quietly. "That's it."

Dalton studied him for a second too long, then flipped the notebook shut. "Don't leave town."

Finn let out a short, humorless snort through his nose and walked back toward the porch, jaw tight, face unreadable. Indigo met him halfway, her steps tentative. Her fingers twitched like she wanted to grab his hand but didn't know if she was allowed to. He just looked at her once and nodded, barely a movement, but she relaxed a little, like it was all the permission she needed. She slipped her hand into his like she was testing the weight of it. He didn't flinch. Just held it like it was the most natural thing in the world.

They stood like that for a few seconds, saying nothing, doing nothing, just letting the weight of the night settle between them. Indigo leaned slightly into his shoulder, and he shifted without thinking, making room for her.

Dalton turned next. "Perez."

Indigo didn't move.

Dalton cleared his throat and spoke louder. "Indigo Perez?"

Indigo blinked like she hadn't heard him the first time. Then she squared her shoulders and stepped forward, eyes dark and stormy. She gave Finn's hand one final squeeze before letting go and following Dalton the same way Finn had, quiet and stiff, like her skin didn't fit right anymore.

I couldn't look away.

"Name?"

"Indigo Perez."

"Relation to the girl inside?"

"She's my sister."

Dalton clicked his pen. "Where were you when she disappeared?"

"At school. Then I went to Sadee's house."

"When did you get the message?"

"Forty-five minutes ago. A picture of her. In our house."

Dalton studied her. "And you didn't call 911 right away?"

Indigo didn't blink. "No. Sadee called Finn. He lives close—he'd get there before we did. I just, I had to see her. I had to know it was real."

"You entered the house after Finn?"

"Yes. I didn't see anyone else."

Dalton was quiet for a second, his pen hovering just above the page. "Anyone have keys to your house? Besides you and your mom?"

"No. Just us."

"You sure?"

Indigo's voice turned sharp, quick. "Yeah. I'm sure."

But there was a flicker, just a beat of hesitation in her eyes. She shifted her weight, looked past him for half a second too long. Dalton caught it. He lowered the pen slowly and raised an eyebrow.

"Are you lyin' to me?"

Indigo's jaw clenched. "No, no sir."

His stare didn't waver.

She exhaled, voice smaller now. "Sadee does. But, but she's not a part of this, sir. I swear. She was with me. She only uses the keys to let the dog outside when we're out of town."

Dalton nodded once, his face unreadable as he jotted something down.

"Alright. Stay close."

Indigo walked back like she was walking uphill against wind. Her shoulders were hunched, but her steps didn't falter. She didn't stop until she was next to Finn again. This time, she did take his hand. And he didn't wait; he tugged her a little closer and let her rest her head on his shoulder. No words, just steady breathing, the kind that said *I'm not going anywhere.*

A few minutes passed. The officers moved around quietly. One walked the perimeter with a flashlight; another spoke into a radio near the cruiser. Then Dalton went inside.

I watched through the screen door as he approached the couch. Mrs. Perez sat with Ella, wrapped around her like she could protect her from what had already happened. Ella looked small. Smaller than I remembered. Her face was pale, red around the eyes, mouth set in this tight, quiet line like she didn't trust herself to speak.

Dalton crouched in front of them. His voice was low, unreadable. He said something to Mrs. Perez first.

She straightened immediately. "She's not answering questions right now. She's in shock."

Dalton gave a slow nod. "I understand. But anything she can tell us helps."

Mrs. Perez hesitated. Then she looked down at Ella gently. "Sweetheart. It's okay. If there's anything you remember... anything at all."

Ella didn't speak.

She just blinked—once, slowly—like her brain was still buffering, trying to process a language the rest of them didn't speak. Her eyes were distant, fixed somewhere far beyond the room, like she'd been ripped out of her own body and left behind in something colder, something darker.

Then, without a word, she reached out, fingers dragging along the surface of the coffee table until they found it, a long scratch in the wood. Not new, but not accidental. It hadn't been there before.

A tree. Crooked. Carved deep into the table's finish.

Splattered with blood.

Ella's hand hovered above it like she was afraid to touch. Then, as if on instinct, she pulled her arm into view and held it out.

A long, deliberate slice ran across her forearm. Shallow, but fresh. The letter *N* carved into her flesh. Blood had bubbled along the edge and dried into flaking red. But part of it was still wet. Still alive.

The room fell into a heavy silence that pressed against the walls. It wasn't just quiet, it was the kind of silence that screamed, that filled your ears with everything left unspoken.

Dalton's gaze dropped to the wound, then flicked to the officer by the door. Between them passed a tension, unspoken, sharp, like a shadow stretching longer and darker.

This wasn't just a game.

It never had been.

Dalton turned back to Mrs. Perez, voice low and cold.

"Ma'am, I need to ask this next part clearly."

A pause thick enough to choke on.

"Was there any sign of forced entry?"

Mrs. Perez's lips pressed thin. "The back door was locked when I left this morning. I checked it."

"Was it locked when you got home?"

"I don't know." Her voice cracked. "I didn't go in. I just saw the ambulance. Saw—"

She couldn't finish. Ella pressed tighter into her side.

Dalton gave a short nod. "We'll have an officer sweep the house again before you go in. Just in case."

Finn, Indigo, and I sat shoulder-to-shoulder on the porch steps. No one talked. The world felt like it was holding its breath.

Then the lights started turning off. The ambulance pulled away first. Then one cop car. Dalton came out last; notebook tucked under his arm.

"We'll be in touch," he said to no one in particular. "And if anyone gets another message, don't play the game. Call me directly."

I nodded.

Finn nodded.

Indigo didn't.

Chapter Fifteen

The bell above the door jingled softly when I pushed into Lou's Diner, the warm air thick with the smell of fried eggs and stale syrup wrapping around me like a familiar, suffocating blanket. Saturday afternoons usually had this slow, lazy feeling, but today it felt off, like the whole world was holding its breath and waiting for something to snap.

Maya was already at the booth by the window, tracing the rim of her iced-tea glass with a finger, her curly hair pulled back into a loose ponytail. She glanced up when I slid into the seat across from her, giving me a look that said she didn't expect me to be much company, but she was here anyway.

"Hey," she said quietly, voice softer than usual.

I nodded, the weight of last night dragging at my shoulders. "Hey."

There wasn't much to say. Not yet.

The diner's hum was filled with murmurs from the few other patrons scattered around, older couples nursing coffee, a kid at the counter flipping through a comic book, the clatter of silverware against plates, and the occasional creak of the vinyl booths settling. Lou's had a kind of old-school charm that felt both comforting and a little out of place, like a set piece stuck in time.

Maya glanced at me again, then back down at her drink. "You okay?"

I tried to smile. "Yeah. Just tired."

"Yeah." She tucked a loose curl behind her ear. "It's… a lot."

The door jingled again, and Ryan walked in, backpack slung over one shoulder, eyes already scanning until they landed on us. His smile was a bit too wide, like he was trying to will some normalcy into the afternoon.

"Hey," he said, sliding in beside Maya. "Thought I'd find you two here."

"Lucky guess," Maya said with a small smile.

I didn't say anything. I just watched Ryan set down his bag and pull out his notebook, flipping it open.

"So," Ryan said, voice dropping. "Let's talk."

I shifted in the booth, the old leather creaking under me. The air felt tight, and the sound of the jukebox in the corner spun a slow, melancholy tune.

Ryan leaned forward, resting his elbows on the table. "Last night was crazy. Finding Ella. The message. The brake lines. We're not dealing with some random prank."

I nodded. "No. This is real."

"Exactly." Ryan's fingers drummed on the table. "So, theories. I've been thinking."

Maya raised an eyebrow. "Oh no, here we go."

Ryan grinned. "Hey, I have to start somewhere."

I let out a breath I didn't realize I was holding.

"Okay," Ryan continued, "First off: Mason. Those brake lines didn't cut themselves. Who else knows how to do that?"

I didn't answer. Mason's rusty truck was a joke at school, but no one questioned his mechanical skills, he kept it running with a surprising amount of know-how. If someone wanted to sabotage him, knowing exactly how to cut brake lines would be key.

"Mason's definitely got the skills," Ryan said. "But he's not the mastermind. Not the Hangman. More like… collateral damage or maybe even bait."

Maya shook her head. "Or a target."

"Could be," Ryan agreed. "Then there's Jax."

I flinched slightly at the name. Jax was the kind of guy who always seemed to be lurking just on the edge of things. Ryan leaned in closer, lowering his voice.

"Jax is the perfect candidate. No one would suspect him. He could have faked sending the messages. Maybe even claimed he guessed the last letter right. It's classic misdirection."

I swallowed, the knot in my stomach tightening.

Ryan's gaze flicked to me, sharp and steady. "What about Nick?"

I swallowed hard and looked down at my hands, twisting my fingers together like I could fold the truth into something softer. But Nick wasn't soft. He wasn't quiet. He wasn't just some background noise you could tune out.

Nick was loud. Too loud. Aggressive. The kind of guy who made your skin crawl without even trying, who thrived on making others uncomfortable. And what he did to Indigo… it wasn't just some messed-up secret we whispered behind closed doors. It was a shadow that stretched over all of us, whether we wanted to admit it or not.

"He lost it the other day, at school." I said, my voice dropping low, hesitant but real. "When I told him it wasn't over. Not just freaked out, he got angry. Like, furious. Like he wanted to make sure everyone knew he wasn't someone to mess with."

Ryan's eyes darkened, flicking to mine with a new kind of seriousness. "Yeah, I saw that. It's like he's scared, but he's also dangerous. That kind of rage usually means guilt or fear, sometimes both. Which makes him unpredictable."

I bit my lip. "He tried to make it clear he's not just scared. More like… pissed off. He was pacing, talking way too loud, threatening anyone who even looked at him wrong. It was like he was trying to scare *us* before we scared him."

Maya scoffed. "You're the opposite of scary, Sadee."

I blinked.

Ryan leaned back, folding his arms. "Focus guys. Nick's behavior is classic. People like that don't lose control easily, so when they do, it's a sign something's really eating at them."

"I think Nick knows more than he's saying," I admitted. "But he's not the kind to give it up. He likes having the upper hand. Likes knowing people are afraid of him."

Ryan nodded slowly, eyes sharp. "And with everything happening… he's probably feeling trapped. Like a cornered animal."

I shivered, not from the cold but from the thought of what someone like that could do when pushed too far.

"Indigo's scared," I said quietly. "Not just because of what happened to her, but because Nick's still around. Still watching. Still angry."

Ryan's jaw tightened. "Yeah. And that makes him a real threat, not just physically, but to the whole group. Because fear spreads. It poisons everything."

I nodded, glancing out the window at the dull gray sky outside, the world outside feeling like a cage closing tighter.

"Do you think he's involved with the game?" Ryan asked, voice low.

I hesitated. The hangman game was terrifying enough, but the idea that Nick could be behind some of it… that made my stomach twist. "I don't know," I said finally. "But if he isn't, he's definitely feeding off the fear it's causing."

Ryan's eyes darkened with thought. "Makes sense. He's the kind of guy who'd use chaos to cover his tracks."

The waitress came over, refilling our coffees, the clink of the cup pulling me back for a moment.

When she left, Ryan leaned in again, voice dropping to a conspiratorial whisper. "You're the closest to Indigo, right? What's she like now? After everything?"

I took a shaky breath, thinking of Indigo's stormy eyes and brittle silence. "She's holding on. Barely. She hides it well, but you can see it in the way she tenses. Every sound makes her jump. Every shadow feels like a threat."

Ryan nodded slowly, like piecing together a puzzle. "That's what makes it worse for you all. You're not just fighting some creepy game. You're fighting the aftermath, the damage Nick did, and whatever else is lurking."

I pushed my sleeves down over my hands, feeling the weight of it all pressing in.

"Do you think the others understand?" Ryan asked softly.

I shook my head. "Some do. Mason, Finn, Indigo herself, they get it. But most of the others? They want to pretend it's just a scary story, or that it's over. But it's not."

Ryan's voice was firm. "Sounds like you've got a lot riding on this."

I looked up, meeting his steady eyes. "We all do."

There was a pause, heavy and full of everything left unsaid.

Then Ryan pushed his coffee aside, rubbing his hands together like he was gearing up for a fight. "Alright. Let's talk through the suspects again. But Nick? He's one we keep a very close eye on. Dangerous doesn't even start to cover it."

I swallowed hard and nodded. "Yeah. No kidding."

Maya reached out and tapped my hand gently. "We all freak out sometimes."

I managed a small nod.

Ryan's fingers tapped his notebook again, the quiet rhythm like a metronome ticking out his thoughts. His eyes flicked over his scribbled notes, symbols, names, arrows drawn in looping ink that bled where coffee had dripped across the margin. He didn't seem to notice. "Then there's Duvall, the mechanic. People never look at the guy fixing their cars twice. But he's got the skills. Access. Plus, no one really knows much about him."

I looked up sharply. Duvall had always unnerved me in a way I couldn't quite name. Polite, but clipped. Calm, but unreadable. The kind of man who said thank you with the same tone you'd use to hang up a phone. He worked late, always had grease under his nails, and I'd never once seen him smile.

"Think he's involved?" Maya asked, twirling her straw in a glass of lemonade that had long since lost its fizz.

"Could be," Ryan muttered. He was still staring down at the page like the answers were hidden in the margin notes. "Or he knows more than he lets on. People like him… they see things. They're invisible until they're not."

I sipped my coffee. It was bitter and too hot, singeing the back of my throat as it slid down. The mug was chipped near the rim, a faded yellow diner logo barely legible through years of dish soap and use. I traced the groove of the crack with my thumb, grounding myself.

Outside, the wind picked up, rattling the big front window. A leaf smacked against the glass and stuck for a second before tumbling out of view. The sky was a washed-out gray, not stormy, just dull, like even the sun was tired of showing up.

Ryan's voice brought me back. "Who else knows about the game?"

"Only seniors," I said. "At least that's the extent of who's gotten messaged."

He nodded. "That narrows it down. If it's someone we go to school with, they've been close to us this whole time. At the parties. In the hallways. Watching."

Maya pressed her palm against her forehead, exhaling. "Feels like we're looking for a ghost."

"Or someone pretending to be one," Ryan said, eyes sharp now, his tone darker than before.

We all went quiet for a while. Not the comfortable kind. The heavy, uneasy kind that left your thoughts too loud in your head. The diner noise filled the space, dishes clattering, some old country song playing from a speaker mounted by the cash register, the faint sizzle of something frying in the back. A waitress walked past with a tray of burgers, and the smell of grease and onions made my stomach churn.

I hadn't eaten much. The pancakes on my plate had gone cold, syrup puddled and sticky. I cut off a small bite, more out of obligation than hunger. It tasted like cardboard.

Ryan finally broke the silence. "There's a pattern, I think. The way the messages are timed. Like someone's controlling the pace on purpose, letting it simmer."

"Simmer," Maya repeated. "Like it's some kind of sick game of chicken. How long can they keep us on edge before someone breaks?"

"Indigo and I were both texted the same day this time," I said quietly. "If there was a pattern, I think it's falling apart."

Ryan nodded. "So, our Hangman, or Hangwoman, I guess, is getting sloppy. Bored, maybe."

My eyes drifted to the window. The glass fogged at the corners. Somewhere out there, Ella was home. Alive. Breathing. But changed.

She'd looked straight through me when I saw her last night. As if some part of her hadn't come back.

And still, I knew this wasn't finished.

The air in the diner felt thick, like there wasn't enough oxygen for all the fear in the room.

"Maybe it is about control," I said softly. "Not revenge. Not chaos. Just... power. Someone who wants to see how far they can go before we break."

Ryan nodded slowly, his fingers flexing around his pen. "Then we don't give them that."

Maya tilted her head at me. "Are you okay?" she asked gently, and I hated how the question made my throat tighten.

"I don't know," I admitted. "I feel like I'm watching everything from underwater. Like I'm here, but not really."

Maya didn't push. She just reached across the table and touched my hand, a quiet gesture that didn't demand anything from me.

Ryan flipped back a few pages in his notebook. "So far, we've got a couple names with motive. A couple with access. And then there's the stuff we don't know yet, who's helping, who's watching, who's next."

"Do you think it's over?" Maya asked.

I swallowed hard. "No. Ella coming back wasn't the end. It was a warning."

Ryan looked like he agreed but didn't want to say it out loud.

He leaned in. "I'm still thinking Nick is our best bet."

I glanced down at my hands. This wasn't how it was supposed to be. We were seniors in high school—supposed to be worrying about college applications, scholarship essays, prom plans, stupid little things that didn't matter in the long run.

Instead, here we were, hunched over a diner table, trying to figure out which person in this entire town was twisted enough, cruel enough, to hurt us. I wanted to scream at the unfairness of it all.

Ryan pushed his coffee aside, rubbing his hands together. "Alright. One more thing. This is probably nothing."

Maya groaned softly. "Those are always something."

Then Ryan tapped his notebook. "Okay. Now—curveball."

Maya groaned. "I hate when you say that."

"Humor me," Ryan said. "Last night, before everything went to hell, I was leaving the school late. Had a meeting with a teacher. Place was basically empty."

I looked up. Ryan didn't usually volunteer details like that.

"I heard arguing," he continued. "Real arguing. Not joking around. Sophia Ramirez and one of the football guys—I didn't see which one."

Maya leaned forward. "About what?"

"'That night,'" Ryan said. "They kept saying it like it was a shared understanding. One of them accused the other of knowing exactly where someone was. The other one flipped. Threats. Real panic."

"That doesn't mean they did anything," Maya said.

"I know," Ryan replied quickly. "I'm not saying attacker. I'm saying witness. Or almost-witness. Someone who realized too late that what they saw mattered."

"The school is near Indi's house. Maybe Sophia or the other guy saw something?"

Ryan tapped his temple. "Or someone."

Silence settled over the table again, heavier this time.

"So," Ryan finished, flipping his notebook shut, "maybe Nick's the fire. But fires still need oxygen. Sometimes it's the people standing too close who get burned."

The conversation drifted after that, like someone let go of the thread. We moved from names and theories to things that felt less sharp. A girl who hadn't shown up to English all week. A rumor about someone's car being keyed in the student lot. Wild guesses about the Hangman messages and whether the clues had started earlier than we realized.

Maya leaned forward, turning her coffee cup slowly in her hands. "Do you think there's… an actual win condition? Like, if we solve all the prompts fast enough, does it stop?"

Ryan frowned. "If it's a game, it has rules. But if it's revenge, then no. Then it only ends when someone decides it does."

Something cold curled down my spine.

"That's not comforting," Maya muttered, and reached for her fork, but didn't eat.

I didn't say much. Just listened. Just watched them—watched Ryan's brain spin behind his eyes as he tried to line up events into a timeline like that could make it all make sense. Watched Maya fight her own exhaustion, still painting on a brave face like she always did, trying to be the calm one in the middle of the storm.

Ryan pulled out his phone at one point and got excited over a list of dates he'd typed in his notes app. "Okay, okay, hear me out," he said, leaning forward like a detective in a movie. "What if the first wave of messages, the ones from last week, aren't the real start? What if those were just the *public* start?"

Maya raised a brow. "You're saying it started earlier."

"Exactly. Look." He turned the phone to face us, pointing at a date two months ago. "That was the day Lexi's locker got broken into. And then a week later, that big party got canceled because of 'electrical issues.' I thought it was all random before, but now, what if that was a dry run? A test round?"

"You think they've been planning this since *then*?"

"I think it's been around longer than we realize." Ryan says. And he's right. It was around before it went public. Things like this, they spend forever bubbling under the surface where no one can see them.

Maya let out a long breath, pressing her fingers to her temples. "We sound insane."

"Do we?" I asked quietly. "Or does it only sound insane because no one wants to believe it's real?"

Silence fell again. Not heavy this time. It's the kind of silence that falls when everyone has something they want to say but no one wants to say anything.

The pancakes sat untouched. The coffee went cold. I watched a bead of syrup slide off the edge of Maya's plate, drip onto the table, and pool against the paper placemat. No one moved to clean it.

Somewhere between the hum of the diner lights and the soft scrape of forks against ceramic, the tension in my chest loosened. Just slightly.

Not enough to forget. Not enough to feel normal. But enough to breathe again without it hurting.

That was something.

The sky outside the window had shifted, pale blue bleeding into the peachy gold of early evening. The streetlamps flickered on one by one. I could see a man walking his dog across the parking lot. Just a normal person on a normal day. I envied that.

Maya smiled at me again, softer this time. "You'll be okay."

I didn't answer right away. I wasn't sure if I believed her.

But I nodded anyway.

Because sometimes pretending was the only way to make it true.

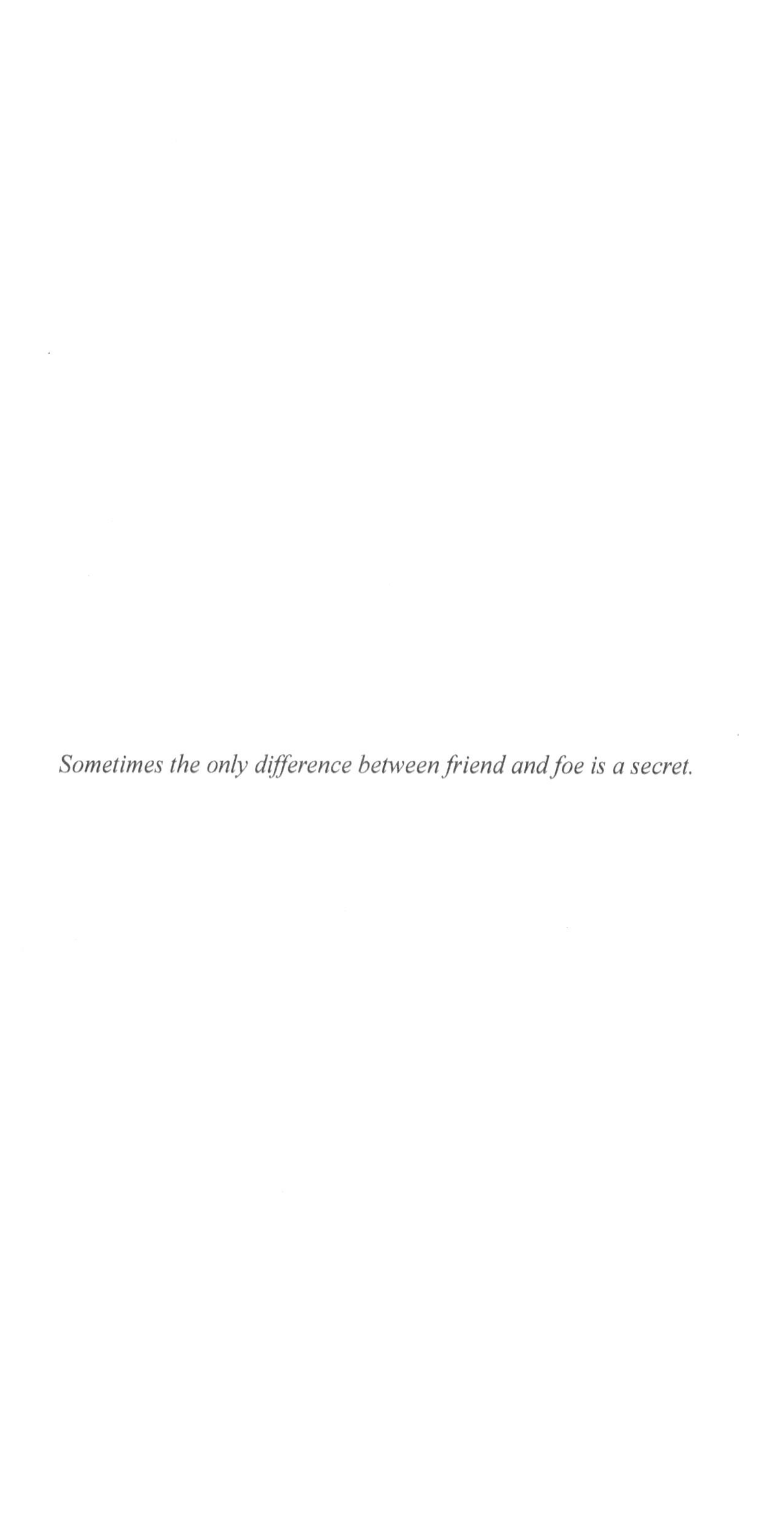

Sometimes the only difference between friend and foe is a secret.

Chapter Sixteen

Indigo left me on read at 6:47 a.m.

Not that I was expecting a real response. Not after three days of half-answers, delayed texts, and one-word replies. But seeing that tiny "Read" beneath the text bubble, still unread by her in every other way, twisted something in my chest. I shoved my phone in my pocket and kept walking.

This wasn't like her.

The hallway was alive, buzzing with Monday's usual energy. Too alive. People clustered around lockers, the air thick with the scent of hairspray, mechanical pencil lead, and hallway coffee. It felt wrong. Like the world should've slowed down after everything that had happened. After Ella. After the search. After she came back with more silence than skin.

Indigo's locker was on my route. Always had been. I used to stop there every morning without thinking. Today I didn't stop, but I still looked.

It hadn't been touched. Not since last week. A dusty pink hoodie still peeked out through the slats, and the taped-up photo was still there. A picture of the two of us, from way back, elementary school, maybe third or fourth grade. We were at some birthday party. I was in a tie-dye shirt with ketchup stains down the front, Indigo in a paper crown too big for her head. We both had missing teeth and frosting on our cheeks.

Written in glittery gel pen across the corner was Indigo's handwriting: *you're weird. i like you.*

I stared at it too long. Something about that version of us, loud, inseparable, unbreakable, felt like a ghost. That photo had survived dozens of locker cleanouts. She'd refused to throw it out, even when it curled and faded. "It's tradition," she used to say.

Now it just looked like a lie. I was her best friend. I'm supposed to be who she runs to when times get hard. But after Nick, after what he did, she never came to me again. She closed in on herself. Blocked me out.

And I hated him for that. I hated Nick Donovan. For taking her voice. For making her flinch when the hallway got too loud. For making her scared to sleep, to speak, to trust. For turning her into this version of herself that barely looked at me. I don't care what the rumors say. I don't care who defends him, or how many people whisper "misunderstanding" like it's some kind of curse word. He ruined her. I saw it happen.

It's Nick's fault. That's what I keep reminding myself.

I kept walking. Kept my eyes on the floor. Pretended my stomach didn't feel like it was crocheting itself into a tiny little ball.

Lunch felt louder than usual. Maybe because there were only seven of us.

One chair sat empty, Indigo's usual spot beside Maya, and even though no one mentioned it, we all noticed. The space felt too wide, the table too long, like someone had pulled it just a few inches farther apart than it was supposed to be. I kept glancing at the chair without meaning to.

Every time I looked, I half-expected to see her backpack thrown at her feet and a neon-red Monster can clutched in her hand. But there was nothing. Just a quiet absence.

Cassie was picking at the corner of her sandwich, tearing it into tiny pieces without ever eating a bite. Ryan was in the middle of explaining some weird fact about frogs eating their own skin when Liam cut him off.

"Hey," he said, and somehow it was louder than anything else at the table.

Everyone looked up.

Liam didn't make eye contact. He just stared at the table like it had done something wrong.

"My parents want to move."

Silence.

"To the city," he added, quieter. "They think it's safer."

Maya blinked. "Wait, what?"

"They're serious," he said.

Cassie's hand froze mid-braid. Ryan just closed his mouth and folded his chip bag slowly. Maya laughed, sharp and disbelieving.

"Is this a joke?"

He shook his head.

"Because it's not funny," she added, voice rising.

"I know."

Cassie was crying. Not loud, not dramatic. Just one tear, sliding down her cheek. She wiped it away fast, but her eyes stayed red.

Mason cleared his throat. "I mean… maybe it's for the best. If they think you're in danger."

"We're not," Maya snapped.

"Are we?" Ryan said quietly.

Finn stood up. Didn't say anything. Just left.

I watched him go, his shoulders stiff, back straight. The kind of silence that meant he couldn't sit with this moment. Couldn't let it fold into his chest and live there. I envied that in some way. I was stuck, cemented into the bench like gravity had decided I belonged nowhere else.

My heart was beating like I'd just sprinted. I hadn't said a word yet.

"It's not the worst thing that could've happened." Liam said, like what he was about to say would make everything better. "I get to finish out high school playing baseball for a bigger name high school than whatever we got going on here for us in this little podunk town. I'll have scouts watching me play."

"That's good for you," Maya said, sighing. "Not that it makes this any better."

"Liam, you've been a part of our friend group since second grade. You think we're going to let you go without putting up a fight?" Mason sat up straighter, forcing a laugh that turned into a cough.

"I'm going to quietly protest by burning a building down. Because that's how quiet protests work now." Ryan nodded, but his voice lacked its usual energy. He didn't smile.

"You'll need to work fast. We're leaving tomorrow morning." Liam looked down at the table.

No one said anything.

Tomorrow.

Not in a few weeks. Not "soon." Tomorrow.

No one said anything.

A fork clinked against a tray in the distance. Someone shouted across the quad. A gull screeched above us. The world, as usual, didn't care.

My throat tightened. I looked at Liam, really looked at him, his broad shoulders hunched forward, like he was trying to make himself smaller. His knuckles pale from how tightly he was clenching his hands. He was trying not to cry. And that broke something in me.

This wasn't like Indigo leaving. She hadn't left. She was still here. Somewhere. I was still holding on, stupidly, to the hope that she'd come back to us.

But Liam, he was leaving. For real. On purpose or not, it didn't matter. His parents were taking him away, and he wasn't fighting it.

"You can't just go," I said, finally.

He looked up at me. "I don't really have a say."

"You do," I said. "You could argue. You could stall. You could, I don't know, refuse to pack."

"That's not gonna change their minds."

"But it's not fair."

"I know."

I hated how calm he sounded. Like he'd already accepted it. Like the rest of us didn't get a vote. Like he wasn't tearing a hole in the fabric of our group and walking away without looking back.

"You're the glue," Cassie whispered. "You're the reason all of us ended up together. You introduced me to Maya. You made Ryan join our game night the first time even though he didn't talk to anyone for a week. You're the one who dragged Finn out of his I-only-sit-under-the-bleachers phase. You can't just disappear."

Her voice cracked on the word "can't."

Liam blinked fast. He looked like he wanted to respond but didn't know how. His silence felt heavier than anything else in the air.

Maya pushed her tray aside and folded her arms over it, resting her head down. "This year already sucks."

"Big time," Ryan echoed, monotone.

"No offense," Maya said muffled through her sleeve, "but you moving is like... the worst."

"None taken."

It wasn't like I hadn't imagined one of us leaving. Ever since the Perez's house was broken into, and Ella was harmed, physically harmed, the whole town had been vibrating with something, fear, paranoia, grief, that made people shut their windows tighter and check the locks twice. But imagining it and hearing it out loud were two very different things. Liam's words cracked something.

Cassie reached across the table, resting her hand over Liam's. "You can't just vanish."

"I won't vanish," he said, but it sounded like a lie. "I'll text. Call. Come down when I can."

"You think that's the same?" Maya said, her voice uncharacteristically fragile. "You think a FaceTime once a month replaces… this?"

Liam didn't answer.

I looked around the table, at our mismatched group. Ryan, fidgeting with a spoon. Mason, staring too hard at a crack in the table. Cassie blinking too fast. Maya trying to hold herself together with eyeliner and sarcasm. And no Indigo. Her absence felt more obvious now, like the ghost of what our group used to be was hovering behind her empty seat.

Liam leaving felt like confirmation that it was all coming apart.

"Does it even feel real to you?" I asked finally. My voice sounded too thin in the air. "Like… that you're really leaving?"

He shrugged. "It didn't until I packed my baseball glove last night."

And that did it. I felt something sting behind my eyes and blinked fast, biting my inner cheek. I wasn't going to cry at lunch. Not here.

"I don't get it," Maya muttered. "Like, sure, the town's been weird lately, but running away from it doesn't fix anything."

"No one's running," Liam said, but again, it felt like another lie.

"What about the calamity this Saturday?" Ryan blurted, uncharacteristically loud. "That's still on, right?"

The question hung there. Not because the party mattered that much, but because it was the only thing left to pretend about.

Maya gave a short laugh. "Honestly, after this week? We need that party."

No one agreed. Not out loud.

I just stared at the table. The wood was scratched and covered in initials carved over years. One of them might've been mine. Might've been Liam's. Now they were just marks.

Everyone started talking again, but it felt fake. Lighter than it should've been. Maya tried to spin a joke about getting Liam "city-proofed" with pepper spray and a glitter taser. Mason half-laughed. Ryan said something about learning how to throw a brick through a window if the city got too loud.

But underneath all of it was something unspoken. Something heavy.

Liam was leaving.

And once someone left, it was easier for others to follow.

This game was forcing people away. Was it worth it?

After lunch, we scattered. Some of us to class, some of us to nowhere in particular. I ended up walking alone.

The hallway felt hollow. Like everything was echoing too much.

By the time I pushed open the side doors after the last bell signaling the end of the day, the sky was that pale blue that comes just before sunset. It made the world feel colder, even though the air was warm.

I spotted Finn leaning against the fence by the lot, arms crossed.

The chain-link fence clinked softly behind him each time the wind pushed against it, a dull metallic tremble that matched the weight in my chest. The sun was beginning to dip, casting long orange shadows across the asphalt and staining the edges of the sky with tangerine and violet.

Heat rose from the concrete in waves, warping the air between us like a mirage. My shoes scraped slightly as I walked forward, each step crunching faintly over scattered gravel and old, sun-bleached leaves.

I hesitated.

Then walked toward him.

Finn didn't say anything right away. He just flicked a glance in my direction, the fading light catching the pale gray of his eyes. They looked colder than usual. His jaw was set, muscles twitching once, then going still. Behind him, the chain-link fence groaned again, whispering rust into the air.

"You good?" I asked.

He shrugged. "Better than Liam."

A passing breeze carried the sharp scent of warm asphalt, mingled with cut grass from the soccer field across the lot. Somewhere far off, a car door slammed, followed by the muffled thump of bass from a stereo. A sprinkler hissed to life behind the gym building, its rhythmic tick-tick-tick sounding like a countdown. We both turned instinctively toward the noise, though neither of us said anything about it.

There was a pause. We both watched a flock of birds move across the sky like they had somewhere better to be—sleek black silhouettes slicing across the orange canvas above. The faint rustle of feathers, like tissue paper tearing, drifted down as they passed.

Then, casual as anything, Finn asked, "You think Ella told the cops everything?"

I froze.

The words hung in the air like cigarette smoke, thin, acrid, impossible to ignore. A cicada screeched from a tree nearby, sharp and sudden, like the sound of something snapping.

"About that night?" he added.

I played dumb. "What night?"

Finn gave a half-laugh, low and humorless. It scraped out of him like something jagged. The fence rattled again as a gust pressed against it, and a dust devil spun up nearby, dancing in slow, eerie circles before collapsing into nothing.

"Don't do that."

I looked down at my shoes. Scuffed white sneakers. One lace coming undone, dragging slightly in the dust. My socks were too thick for the heat; my feet were already sweating. A small pebble lodged itself in the tread of my left shoe, grinding quietly with every micro-shift of weight.

"I don't remember much," I said. "Not enough."

Finn tilted his head. "That's what I was afraid of."

It should've felt ominous. But it didn't, not right away. Just felt like sandpaper against my skin. Something quiet and sharp. Like touching a metal doorknob and feeling the faintest shock.

The world around us kept spinning like nothing was wrong. Like it didn't matter that Liam was leaving, that Indigo wasn't speaking to me, that Ella had returned more ghost than girl. A leaf skittered past my ankle. Dried. Cracked. Forgotten.

"What about Indigo?" he asked. "Think she remembers?"

"Too much," I said.

A dog barked in the distance, sharp and desperate, and somewhere closer a siren began to wail. It sounded far away at first, but it kept growing, closer, closer, until the noise drowned out the beat of my heart. It cut through the thick heat, shrill and haunting. Then, just as quickly as it came, it faded, leaving behind a hollow ringing in my ears.

Finn didn't respond. He just looked out at the horizon again. The sun was dipping below the tree line now, slanting gold light across his face and casting the fence's diamond-shaped shadows across his jacket and onto the ground. It looked like he was behind bars.

I stood there beside him, feeling like the world was splitting open seam by seam—and no one else even noticed.

The light shifted again, one final stretch before dusk took over. The shadows grew longer, deeper. The wind picked up just enough to carry the bitter smell of distant smoke, someone's firepit probably, but it set my nerves on edge.

Dry leaves rustled at the edge of the lot. My skin prickled like it knew something I didn't. Like it remembered something I'd tried to forget.

Finn's arms were still crossed, but his fingers had tightened slightly, knuckles paling. The silence between us grew denser. Weighted. Like a fog pressing in from every angle. My throat was dry. I could taste the dust in the back of my mouth, bitter and stale.

Behind us, a car rolled slowly past, its engine humming low, tires crunching over gravel. The driver didn't stop. Didn't even look. The world moved on.

Finn finally shifted, pushing a hand through his hair. His fingers trembled, just barely, but I noticed.

"I didn't mean to ask it like that," he said.

"I know."

He turned slightly, just enough to glance at me again. His expression was unreadable. Eyes too dark in the fading light, face carved in stillness. For a moment, I wondered if he was about to say something else—something that would pull the thread loose and unravel everything. But he didn't. He just looked away again.

The sky was purple now. A deep bruise blooming overhead. The first stars blinked into view, shy and flickering. I focused on them. Let the quiet stretch longer.

Somewhere deep in my chest, something ached. Not sharp, not stabbing. Just steady. Like a muscle pulled too many times.

I didn't know what Finn remembered. I didn't know what Indigo saw when she closed her eyes. I didn't even know if Ella had really told the cops everything.

But I knew that something was coming.

I could feel it in the hush of the wind.

In the weight of Finn's silence.

In the way the shadows seemed to hold their breath.

And in the way I stood there, utterly still, like any movement might shatter the moment beyond repair.

Chapter Seventeen

Indigo hasn't looked me in the eye once today

She's been… off. Quieter than usual. Less dramatic in the way she tossed her bag into her locker or rolled her eyes at Eli's half-baked jokes. Her eyeliner's smudged at the corners like she didn't sleep, and she's picked her thumbnail raw again, it's bleeding, just a little, just enough to stain the cuff of her hoodie where it brushes her hand.

I notice all of it. I don't say anything.

The morning halls are electric with noise, metallic clangs from locker doors, bursts of laughter from groups of freshmen, the shrill squawk of the announcements coming on overhead, but Indigo walks through it like a ghost. Like she's slipped into a different frequency and none of it reaches her. She doesn't dodge a flying paper ball that whizzes past her head or react when someone yells out a greeting to someone behind us. Her boots strike the tile, dull and rhythmic, a far cry from her usual stomp that announces her presence like thunder rolling in.

We've drifted into the same hallway routine we've always had, walking side-by-side but not always saying much. It used to be a comfort. Now, the silence hums differently. It buzzes. Scratches. Chafes against my ribs.

There's an electrical charge in the air around us that I can't shake, like the moment before lightning, when everything is waiting to break.

Her footsteps are quieter today. Less stomp, more shuffle. Her boots, usually loud, statement-making, sound hollow against the tile. Like she's trying not to be heard. Like she's trying to disappear into the noise of morning announcements and slamming lockers and everyone else pretending everything's normal.

The fluorescent lights above us flicker for a second as we pass under them, throwing Indigo's pale skin into a strange, washed-out contrast with her black hoodie and smudged liner. Her face looks carved from something brittle. Porcelain, maybe. Or paper.

We pass a poster taped crooked to the wall, something about the Fall Talent Show for next school year, some glitter-glue monstrosity, and the corner brushes Indigo's shoulder. She doesn't flinch. Just keeps walking. Her hair is tangled at the ends, like she didn't brush it this morning. Or maybe she did, but her mind was somewhere else, and her hands didn't finish the job.

Her boots make a soft thud-thud-thud against the tile, steady like a metronome.

I match her steps without thinking, the muscle memory of friendship guiding me. But something about the rhythm feels wrong. Offbeat. Like we're dancing to different songs and pretending we're still in sync.

There's this tightness in my chest I can't shake. Like I'm waiting for a cough that won't come. Or a word. Or a scream.

"Are you gonna keep freezing me out forever, or…?" I ask it casually. Too casually. My voice wobbles in the middle.

She doesn't slow. Doesn't turn.

The hallway air feels thicker somehow. Like we've stepped into a different atmosphere. The kind that presses down on your shoulders and curls around your lungs and makes you second-guess your own heartbeat.

Indigo doesn't respond.

We stop at the edge of the quad, under one of the weird concrete overhangs that always smells like cigarette smoke and mildew. There's a hairline crack running through the wall beside us, one that someone wrote over in with black Sharpie to say "THE END IS NYE," except it should be 'nigh'. No one's ever fixed it.

The overhang blocks most of the sun, casting us in a grayish-blue shadow that makes everything feel colder than it is. The concrete beneath our feet is stained with gum and oil and something reddish-brown that no one's tried to clean.

Wind whips past us, tugging a stray lock of her black hair into her mouth. She spits it out with a huff. The wind keeps pulling, tugging at her hoodie strings, at the hem of my flannel. Leaves scrape across the sidewalk like they're in a hurry to escape.

I watch her hands. She has them balled up in her sleeves now, gripping the fabric like it's the only thing tethering her to this moment. Her nails are black with chipped polish, and I can see the red crescent of her thumbnail where it's split too deep. There's dried blood around the edge of it.

"You act like none of it happened," I say, trying to meet her eyes. "You won't talk about Nick. You won't talk about Ella. You've barely looked at me in a week, and when you do it's like I'm something you scraped off your shoe."

The wind dies for a moment. Everything feels too still.

Somewhere behind us, someone drops something. The clatter rings out sharp and jarring, but Indigo doesn't flinch. Doesn't even blink.

Indigo's face doesn't move. Her jaw is locked. Her arms fold across her chest like armor, and her fingers grip her sleeves so tightly I can see her knuckles turning white.

"I don't want to talk about that night. Either night," she says finally. Her voice is small.

I swallow. The words sting like rubbing alcohol poured on a cut.

"Why not?"

"Because if I say it out loud, then it's real. Then I have to remember every single detail. And I can't, I can't carry that around all the time like you do, Sadee. I'm not built like you."

Her voice fractures on the last few words. Like something splintering deep under the surface. Her arms fold tighter. She's trembling slightly, and I can't tell if it's from the cold or from holding something in for too long.

The clouds shift above us, and a pale beam of light slices across the pavement, catching the edge of her boot and my shoulder. Neither of us move.

A faint smell of wet leaves drifts in on the wind, earthy and sour, and I suddenly feel how cold my hands are. I rub them against the sides of my jeans, trying to bring the feeling back. Indigo's still staring straight ahead, motionless. Like a statue. Like if she moves, the entire illusion of stillness will shatter.

I look down at my phone. There's nothing new. No texts. No missed calls. The screen glares up at me like it knows I'm stalling. Like it knows how desperate I am for something, anything, that isn't this.

My reflection in the screen looks warped. Eyes too big. Lips too tight. Like I've been stretched and blurred at the edges.

Silence stretches. The wind returns, whistling through the breezeway, lifting a leaf into a slow spiral before dropping it again. There's a dull ache behind my ribs, like something pressing outward. Expanding. Growing teeth.

I glance at Indigo again. Her mouth is tight. Her shoulders are up near her ears. She's staring straight ahead like she's somewhere else entirely.

We've always been good at silence. The kind that says I'm here, even if I don't have words. But this isn't that kind. This silence is edged. Barbed. It hurts.

The cement wall behind her is cold and a little damp where condensation has crept in overnight. It leaves a dark mark when she leans back against it, and she doesn't seem to notice the chill that seeps through her hoodie.

I hear a bell ring in the distance, probably the five-minute warning for third period, but neither of us move. The quad is emptier now. People have trickled into class, into structure, into the illusion that everything's okay. We're still here, suspended in this pocket of time like a snow globe someone forgot to shake.

"Say something," I mutter. "Please."

She doesn't. Not at first.

Her breath fogs in the air, but mine doesn't. Or maybe it does, and I'm just not paying attention. Everything's buzzing too loud in my ears. My skin feels too tight, like it doesn't quite fit right.

Then, finally, finally, Indigo breathes in through her nose, sharp and shaky. Her fingers twitch at her sides, then curl into fists.

She looks at me.

Her eyes are rimmed with red, not from crying, yet, but from the pressure of holding it back. The kind of red that makes your throat tighten when you see it, because you know the person wearing it is barely holding themselves together.

"Sadee…"

I glance up from my phone.

"That night, that Ella—" a sob escapes her lips.

I nod. "Yeah?"

Her eyes are glassy. Her nose is snuffy. Her voice cracks like it's breaking open something buried deep.

The air stills again. There's no wind now. Just a cold heaviness, a breath held too long.

"Did I take the time to park my car perfectly in line with the curb?"

I hesitate. The question feels like it's carrying too much weight. Like a trap disguised as something innocent.

"No…"

Indigo breathes. "I just threw it in park, no matter where it was, and ran inside, right?"

"Yeah, you were worried about Ella. We all would've done the same thing."

She nods, slowly, barely.

Her lips part. She doesn't speak right away. Her eyes drop to the concrete, to the scuffed toe of her boot nudging a dried leaf out of its groove in the sidewalk.

"So why would Finn take the time to park parallel to the curb?"

The question drops between us like a stone in water. The surface of everything we thought we knew ripples.

The words vibrate in my skull. I can feel them echoing behind my eyes, like something rotten cracking open.

I turn away from her and press the heels of my hands against my face, trying to stop the tide of memory that's building fast now. I don't want to see it, but it's too late. It's already here.

I remember the headlights bouncing off the walls as we ran in. I remember Ella's cry, a broken, feral sound that still clings to my ribs when I try to sleep.

There's a silence that follows, not the quiet kind, but the kind that grows legs. That starts crawling up the back of your spine and nestles behind your ears. It pulses there. Heavy.

My mouth opens, then shuts. I can't seem to make anything come out. The words are stuck in my throat like splinters.

And then something shifts. Not in the air, not exactly. It's in my perception. Like I've been staring at one of those trick-eye illusions too long and suddenly the picture flips inside out. What used to be the background—Finn's headlights, the gentle hum of his engine, the curve of his tires against the street, it all rushes forward.

It wasn't just neat.

It was methodical.

Indigo's voice is barely more than a whisper, but it echoes. Inside me. Around me. Like the truth was already there, waiting for someone to say it out loud.

Why didn't that set something off in me? Why didn't I see it then?

But I did. In the back of my mind, I knew. I knew it.

"I didn't want to say it," Indigo says. "I kept thinking maybe there was an explanation. Maybe he just… parks like that. Maybe it was muscle memory."

But her voice is getting colder with every word. It's not rage. Not yet. But it's something older. Something heavier.

"It wasn't," I say quietly. "It couldn't have been."

The quad feels too quiet. Like the world's taken a breath and hasn't exhaled yet. A branch creaks overhead. Somewhere far off, a crow cries, one short, sharp note that sounds too much like a warning.

My thoughts start to spiral.

A camera has shifted. The angle's changed. And suddenly, I can see it, what I didn't let myself notice before.

I picture Finn's car. So stupid. It's a stupid mistake.

The glow of headlights in the dark. The smooth, symmetrical way it slid into place, lined up perfectly with the curb. Too perfect. Like he'd taken the time. Like he wasn't rushing.

Even though every second counted. Even though the rest of us had stumbled over our own feet trying to reach her.

I hadn't thought much of it before. Just a background detail. Lost within the chaos and fear of that night. But now… now it feels like a neon sign. A blinking light we'd somehow ignored.

My stomach turns. The wind slices colder now, sharp enough to cut through my jacket and raise goosebumps on my skin.

I glance at Indigo.

Her eyes are wide, unblinking. Pale face streaked with the faint residue of dried mascara. Her hands are balled into fists at her sides, trembling. There's blood at the base of her thumbnail, a vivid crescent of red where she's dug in too hard. She doesn't notice. Or she doesn't care.

And I, I feel it too.

That unraveling. That tilt. That slow realization seeping in through the cracks, cold and certain and quiet.

The world seems to slow around us.

A bell rings in the distance, muffled by wind and concrete. Neither of us flinches.

"He wasn't rushing," Indigo says. Her voice is steadier now, but cold. Detached. Like she's watching the memory unfold from somewhere else. She's putting the pieces together. "He wasn't scared. He wasn't coming to help."

The air presses down harder now. My skin feels two sizes too small. I tug at the sleeves of my flannel, suddenly desperate to feel anything but this numb, creeping pressure.

Even the shadows look different. Like they're stretching. Crawling toward us on elbows.

She looks at me again, and I see it, something sharp and terrified and furious flickering just beneath the surface.

"He knew," she says. "He knew before we did."

My breath catches.

I remember Finn's face when he walked in.

Too calm. Too collected. Everyone else was a mess, crying, shouting, shaking, but he was just… there. Standing in the doorway. Watching.

I remember how he looked at Ella, then at all of us.

How his eyes didn't match the panic in the room.

How he didn't ask what happened.

I told myself he looked like he was in shock. We all did.

But now?

Now that feels like a lie.

The horror blooms in my chest like black mold. Silent and suffocating.

Leaves rustle suddenly behind us. Sharp. Urgent. I turn too fast, heart in my throat, but it's just wind again. Just debris.

I feel stupid. Paranoid. But something about the way the wind moves now feels wrong. Off-key. Like it's imitating what it used to be.

Indigo hasn't moved. Her breath is coming fast now, but shallow. Controlled. Like she's holding herself together with the last thread of will she has left.

"He wasn't scared," I whisper.

"No," she agrees. "He was waiting."

The ground under me feels brittle. Like the pavement might give way if I shift my weight wrong. Like we're standing over something hollow.

Indigo's still staring at me, and I see it now, this moment is what's been eating her alive. The thing she's been holding. The weight she's been carrying in silence.

This isn't just guilt.

It's fear.

Fear that the people we trust aren't who they say they are.

Fear that one of them might've known something, done something, and said nothing.

The sky above us is gunmetal gray, heavy with unfallen rain. It presses down, thick and oppressive. The trees barely sway in the breeze, but the cold keeps biting deeper, threading under my collar and into my bones.

Indigo's eyes glisten. She doesn't wipe them.

She just breathes out, slow and unsteady. "Say something," she whispers.

But I can't. Because she's right. None of us were thinking that night. We were loud. We were frantic. We were moving without direction, trying to help, to fix something that was already broken.

But Finn—

He parked. He lined up his car.

The memory plays again. And again. And again. But it's different now. Off kilter. Warped. Like someone turned the contrast up and all the shadows are deeper than they were before. Why didn't Finn cover his tracks? Did he want to get caught?

And I don't have an answer.

And that might be the most terrifying part.

"What if he already knew what she was going to say?" she asks. "What if that's why he came at all?"

My pulse stutters. The thought made me uneasy. But not for the reason she knew.

"You think he…" I can't say it. The word won't form.

But Indigo doesn't need me to.

"I don't think he just found her, Sadee." Indigo's breath hitches. "I think he made sure no one else did first.

Chapter Eighteen

Indigo's coffee had gone cold.

The thin paper cup sat on the cafeteria table, no longer steaming, no longer offering warmth. Instead, it was a hollow vessel in her hands, an anchor, maybe, but one weighed down by a silence heavier than the entire room.

She hadn't touched her food; the tray still carried the cold remnants of the cafeteria's mystery meat sandwich and limp fries, untouched and forgotten. Her hands were wrapped tightly around the cup, fingers clutching like it was the only thing keeping her tethered to the moment, as if letting go would make her vanish.

Her fingers looked pale, almost translucent against the stark white of the cup, knuckles bleached as if the blood had fled in retreat. The jagged edge of her thumbnail peeked out from under her grip, torn, ragged, stained with a thin line of dried blood that followed the curve like a fragile scar. I'd seen Indigo bite her nails raw before, during long study sessions or stressful debates, but never with this kind of fury. Not with the storm brewing beneath her skin that seemed ready to break loose.

She hadn't once looked at me.

Indigo had been quieter all day. Not quiet, not like Cassie, who could go unnoticed for hours, but quiet for Indigo. That meant no sharp remarks tossed across the cafeteria table, no exasperated sighs or eyerolls when Maya launched into her melodramatic retellings of dream fragments, no sarcastic commentary about Mason's obviously terrible flirtations. The usual sharp edges she wore like armor had dulled to a numb sort of silence. Even when Liam's name came up earlier, offhandedly mentioned by Ryan in some joke about missing his loud chewing, Indigo didn't react. She blinked once and looked away, as if the words had bounced off an invisible wall around her.

Now, she stared past me, eyes unfocused, set on somewhere far away, a place I couldn't see, maybe even one she couldn't reach.

"I didn't get to say goodbye to Liam," she said suddenly, her voice low and rough, like it had been clawing its way out of her throat, raw and cracked from being held in too long.

I blinked. The words landed like a missed step on a staircase, abrupt, jarring, impossible to ignore.

"Last day. Just… gone," she continued, voice breaking slightly. "And I wasn't there."

She swallowed hard, and I saw the tense bob of her throat, like even speaking the truth was a weight she struggled to carry. Her gaze was fixed on something behind me, a scuffed section of wall, or maybe nothing at all.

"But I don't care. Not really. Not when Finn—" She stopped herself, jaw clenched tight like she was trying to lock her words away. She bit her lip until a bead of red welled up, then wiped it away roughly, like she hated that her body betrayed her with such weakness. Her next words came out quieter, cracked at the edges, fragile as glass. "Am I evil for that? For being so mad that I can't even miss one of my best friends after he moved?"

Her voice fractured again, dropping to a whisper so small I almost didn't hear it:

"Like… am I?"

I wanted to reach across the table. To grab her hands and tell her no, that she wasn't evil. That I'd felt that kind of rage too, the kind that fills your chest so tight there's no room left for anything else, not even grief. But I didn't say anything. Because she wasn't asking for comfort.

She was asking for permission to fall apart.

The silence between us stretched. The cafeteria felt like a war zone, not in the loud, cartoonish way it usually did, but in the aftershock kind of way. Everything dulled, like the colors bled out and the air thickened. We were sitting in the crater of something that had already exploded, and all the noise of the cafeteria had faded into a hollow echo.

I wanted to say something, anything, that would pull her back from the edge of whatever spiral she was in. But nothing felt big enough to reach her.

By the next passing period, I could barely keep up with her.

The hallway roared with life, the clatter of locker doors slamming, the squeak of shoes scraping across cheap tile, voices rising in every direction like waves crashing into each other. The smell of popcorn mixed with the sharp tang of disinfectant and the faint, sticky sweetness of spilled soda.

I walked beside Indigo, but she didn't seem to notice. She moved like a ghost; sharp edges and a storm bottled just barely under the surface. Her fists were jammed deep into the sleeves of her oversized hoodie, and her breath came out in short, quick bursts, almost like shallow gasps.

Then I saw him. Finn.

He was walking ahead of us, toward the science wing, calm, composed, quiet. Hands buried in the pockets of his jeans, head down as if the world was too bright to look at directly. No urgency in his steps. No sign of guilt weighing on his shoulders. No visible crack in the armor he wore every day.

My stomach twisted.

Indigo's voice sliced through the hallway noise like a shard of glass. "He's so sick. Walking these halls pretending he's not a monster."

Her words cut sharply, louder than the usual chatter and locker slams. I caught the edge of something raw and ragged underneath her voice, a bitterness that didn't quite mask the exhaustion. Around us, the usual chaos of passing students carried on, but for me, the sounds blurred into background static.

I didn't respond. Didn't trust myself to.

Because for a moment, I saw what she saw: Finn, unbothered. Untouched. Untouchable. The way he moved like he was wearing armor no one could pierce, calm and steady in the middle of an apocalypse. Meanwhile, Ella was still waking up from nightmares she didn't remember, her breath shallow and uneven, and Indigo was picking her skin raw in the quiet corners where no one noticed.

Indigo sped up. Her hoodie sleeves slipped over her hands as she shoved her fists deep into her pockets, shoulders hunched against some invisible weight. She didn't look at me, didn't say a word, but I knew where she was going.

I hesitated for half a heartbeat, then followed.

The hallway narrowed around us. The roar of voices thinned and grew muffled beneath the steady buzz of old fluorescent lights overhead. The stale, recycled air smelled faintly of burnt-out bulbs and forgotten lunchboxes; a scent that always made the place feel somehow smaller, more claustrophobic.

Finn was at his locker, twisting the dial with practiced indifference. His fingers brushed the familiar scratches in the paint like they were muscle memory, marks carved over years, silent testimony to the passing days, worn down by hundreds of restless hands.

Indigo didn't slow down. She stormed up behind him and grabbed his shoulder, yanking hard.

"Finn."

He turned, startled but not surprised. His eyes flicked up slowly, wary but steady.

Indigo's voice was low, sharp, and tight with barely restrained fury. "I've known you almost my whole life. I need you to give me one good reason why you didn't rush inside to save Ella. Why you took the time to park your car perfectly."

The hallway seemed to fall away around us. The noise dimmed to a distant hum, and all I could hear was the pounding pulse behind my ears, my breath shallow and ragged.

"I want to believe you," Indigo said, voice shaking now, all heat and heartbreak tangled together. "I need to believe you. But right now? I refuse to think you're behind all of this."

Finn looked at me, just for a second. Something flickered in his eyes. Uncertainty. Fear. A plea I couldn't answer.

I didn't move. Couldn't.

He took a breath.

"Because I thought I'd have to carry her out."

The silence that followed was total. It pressed against my eardrums like thick velvet. The whole hallway seemed to freeze, like even the buzzing lights were holding their breath.

Finn's voice was low, barely audible.

"I was scared. Terrified. But if I ran in blind, what if I made it worse? I didn't want to waste time getting stuck trying to back out of the driveway. I thought… if I had to carry her, I needed to be ready, and I couldn't waste time making a stupid three-point turn."

Indigo stared at him, eyes wide, the sharp lines of anger softening slightly under the weight of what he'd just said. "Why would you think you'd have to carry Ella out?"

Finn's jaw tensed, the tight muscles along his neck pulsing.

"Because this game is getting out of hand, Indigo. It's dangerous."

His voice cracked slightly. He was a good actor. He tried to hide it, swallowing hard like he was swallowing down a storm, but we both heard it.

Indigo's expression shifted, from fury to something sharper, more painful.

"Finn…" she said, quieter now. "Did something happen?"

His next words weren't loud.

"They took my mum."

Indigo's mouth opened, but no sound came out. Her hands, still clenched at her sides, trembled like she was barely holding herself together. The tension in her shoulders twisted tighter, like a coiled spring ready to snap.

Finn pressed on, voice raw and ragged as if he'd been carrying the weight of this secret for far too long.

"I guessed a letter wrong. Got a text with a photo of my house asking if I cared about the family I still had living." He took a deep breath and slowly exhaled, steadying his voice. "She disappeared a week ago. No note. No signs of struggle. Just… gone. The police think she left on her own, they don't know I'd been contacted by whoever's behind this. I left that part out. But my mum wouldn't leave. Not like that."

His eyes flicked up to Indigo's, haunted, darkened with exhaustion. "I didn't tell anyone because… I didn't want to make it worse. I didn't want to believe it had anything to do with this. But then what happened to Ella—" His voice broke again. "She's been like a little sister to me. I wasn't about to risk her getting hurt, not like—"

He stopped. Swallowed hard.

"Not like my mum."

Indigo's eyes brimmed with tears, but she didn't let them fall. Instead, she blinked rapidly, the red-rimmed edges glistening, and pressed her lips together until they turned pale. Her fists unclenched slightly, fingers curling like claws, trembling but still holding onto the fragile thread of control.

"And you never told us?" she whispered. "You just stayed silent?"

"I was trying to protect you," Finn said quietly. "All of you."

"Protect us," Indigo echoed bitterly. "Or protect yourself?"

Finn flinched. His hands curled into fists at his sides, knuckles whitening under the strain. "I'm not the monster you think I am."

The tension between them hung like a wire about to snap. The air around them seemed to thicken, heavy with unspoken truths and broken promises.

Indigo stared at him, her breathing ragged, chest heaving with the weight of everything she wanted to scream and couldn't. "I don't know what to think anymore," she said again, and this time it broke her. Just a little. Just enough.

She turned and walked away.

And I stood there, frozen between the two of them, the fracture yawning wide beneath my feet.

Finn looked at me again, eyes full of something I didn't want to name.

And I didn't move.

Couldn't.

The bell rang.

Students surged around us like water rushing past rocks in a river. Unbothered. Unknowing.

I watched Indigo go. Her shoulders hunched, her pace fast but uneven. Every step she took was a goodbye she hadn't meant to say. I wanted to follow. To fix this. But my feet stayed still, cemented by the weight of everything left unsaid.

Finn let out a shaky breath.

I didn't acknowledge it.

I didn't even notice Finn walking away.

One second, he was there, jaw tight, eyes full of something I didn't know how to name, and the next, I was standing alone in a hallway that buzzed with fluorescent light and too much noise. Lockers slammed. A group of freshmen laughed too loudly near the drinking fountain. The air smelled like pencil shavings and gum and too many bodies crammed into too small a space.

But everything felt... distant.

Like I was underwater, watching the world keep moving above the surface.

I turned.

Indigo was gone.

I didn't know where she'd gone until I found her outside in the school parking lot.

I sank onto the curb next to her.

A cloud passed in front of the sun, casting long, slanting shadows across the cracked pavement. The cool breeze tugged at loose strands of her hair, and the distant hum of cars idling and driving by blended with the faint murmur of voices echoing from the school doors.

Her arms draped over her knees, eyeliner smudging worse with each frantic pass of her hand across her face. The rage in her expression didn't match the trembling in her hands.

"I hate him," she said suddenly, voice low and hoarse, like it had been trapped in her throat too long. "Like I know that sounds dramatic or whatever, but I actually hate him."

She stared forward like she was talking to the air, not me. Her breathing was uneven, jagged like ragged breaths pulled from deep inside a chest full of broken glass. I sat down beside her without saying anything, letting the quiet stretch long enough that the sounds of passing cars and distant hallway chatter from the school started to feel deafening.

"You don't actually hate him," I said gently, trying to offer something solid amid the chaos swirling around us. "You're just angry."

She exhaled; sharp, shaky. "No. I mean it. I hate how he looks at me like I'm the one who's lost it. I hate how calm he's been through all of this. Like none of it touches him. Like Ella sitting in the corner of the back bedroom, hiding from whatever monster came into our house, wasn't enough to knock the stupid smug off his face."

I flinch at the mention of her name. Ella. Even though I saw it. Even though I was there. Hearing the events of that night said so bluntly still punches me in the chest.

Indigo pulled at a loose thread on her sleeve, wrapping it tight around her finger until the skin turned pale.

"I hate that he parked perfectly," she said suddenly, quiet again. "That's not normal, Sadee. Nobody parallel parks with that much care if they're running into a house because someone might be dying." She turned to look at me for the first time. Her eyes were raw, red-rimmed, wild with pain and exhaustion. "Right?"

I hesitated. And that was enough of an answer for both of us.

Her expression wavered, that flicker of uncertainty threading into her anger.

"You think I'm wrong."

"No," I said. "I think you're scared. And I think you don't want to be."

"I'm always scared," she snapped. Then her voice dropped. "I just don't show it. That's the difference."

She shivered and pulled her sleeves down over her fists. Her mouth twisted like she was about to cry, but she didn't.

And for once, I spoke without thinking.

"You believed him. In the beginning."

She jerked slightly, like the truth hit harder than she expected.

"I think…" I swallowed. "You still do."

Indigo blinked slowly, like her brain was trying to reboot.

"I don't know what I believe anymore," she said. "Except that I'm tired. I'm so freaking tired of pretending like I'm not falling apart."

I nodded. "Then stop pretending. Just for a second."

The silence settled again, thick and slow like honey. The sun's too bright for how heavy this moment feels, and the concrete is warm beneath my legs, grounding in a way I didn't expect.

"I think he's telling the truth," I said. "About Ella. About not knowing what happened. I think maybe that perfect parking job wasn't because he didn't care. I think it was because something else had already happened."

Indigo's head snapped toward me.

"Like what?"

"I don't know," I admitted. "But the way he looked at you today, like he was too tired to argue, like something else was weighing him down, I don't think it was guilt. Not the kind you're accusing him of."

Indigo blinked. Her brows furrowed slowly. Something shifted in her expression, just slightly.

"Oh no," she whispered.

I turned toward her.

"What?"

She stood up so fast the motion startled me. Her bag slipped off her shoulder, but she didn't even notice. She stared ahead like she was seeing something I couldn't.

"His mom," she said. Her voice cracked. "Sadee. Something happened to his mom."

I got to my feet too, heart thudding in my chest.

"Wait, what?"

"He told me—" She paused, breathing fast. "Earlier. In the hall. He said he didn't know what he was walking into because of his mom!"

My stomach dropped.

"Has he been acting weird?" she went on, more to herself now than to me. "When he came in to check on Ella. Not frantic, just… resigned. Like he'd already been through something that numbed him."

She grabbed her bag off the ground, barely even putting the strap on, and started walking backward like she was preparing to sprint.

"I have to find him," she said.

"Indi—"

But she was already turning, already halfway across the sidewalk. Her shoes slapped the pavement as she ran, dodging past a group of sophomores who barely glanced at her.

And then I was alone again.

The school felt quieter now. Like everything paused in the wake of her exit. A breeze rustled the trees lining the sidewalk, and someone's laughing in the distance, oblivious to the world falling apart around us.

I sat back down, knees pulled to my chest, heart pounding in the hollow space she left behind.

The school's usual chaos faded away behind me as I watched Indigo run. Her figure blurred slightly in the distance, like she was slipping through layers of noise and light that couldn't reach her anymore. The sharp slap of her shoes on the cracked concrete echoed loud in my ears, louder than any voice or locker slam.

I stayed where I was, sinking back onto the curb. The late afternoon sun warmed the concrete beneath me, but it couldn't touch the cold knot settling deep in my stomach. The air was heavy, almost sticky with the scent of drying grass and old asphalt. Somewhere nearby, a bird called, a single, lonely note that cut through the distant hum of traffic and laughter.

My fingers curled into fists on my knees, nails digging in just enough to remind me I was still here. Still breathing. Still caught in the middle of a storm I couldn't control.

I thought about Finn, the way his jaw had tightened, the flicker of fear in his eyes. The silence he'd kept about his mom, about everything that must have been crushing him inside. And Ella, fragile and broken, sitting in a room that smelled like antiseptic and blood, a scene seared into my memory like a nightmare I couldn't wake from.

The sun dipped lower, casting long shadows across the parking lot. The distant chatter from the school faded further, replaced by the soft rush of wind through the trees. I shivered, pulling my jacket tighter around me, the fabric rough and worn against my skin.

My mind raced with questions I couldn't answer.

What kind of game was this, dangerous enough to tear families apart, to leave friends bleeding on bedroom floors? What secrets were hidden beneath the surface, waiting to explode? And why was everyone so afraid to speak them aloud?

The weight of silence pressed down on me, thick and suffocating. I closed my eyes briefly, trying to push back the noise inside my head. But the images came anyway, Indigo's raw anger, Finn's haunted expression, Ella's pale face.

I opened my eyes and looked toward the school, the windows glowing faintly as the sun set. Somewhere inside, the story was still unfolding. And no matter how far I tried to step back, I was tangled in it.

And I can't help but think:

If Finn really was innocent, which, let's face it, he's not, but if Indigo's right, and something happened to his mom…

Then what did happened to Ella?

And why won't she talk about it?

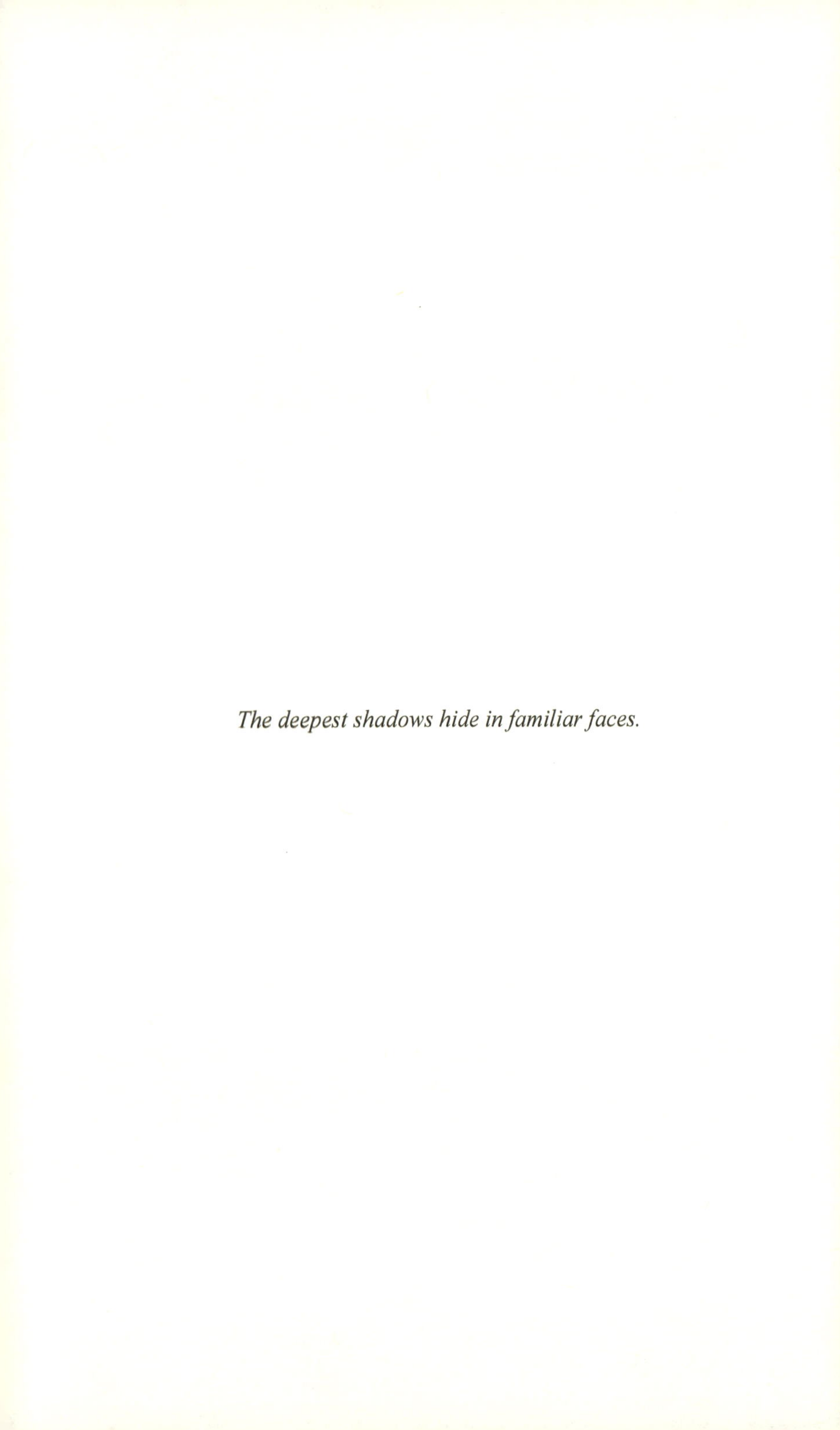

The deepest shadows hide in familiar faces.

Chapter Nineteen

Indigo was already in her room, the door cracked open enough for me to catch glimpses of her getting ready, that bright, fearless spark in her eyes as she fussed with a smoky eye look. When she finally emerged, she was wearing this sunshine-yellow dress that bounced with every step, covered in playful ruffles and soft cotton that matched her outgoing energy perfectly. It was the kind of dress that seemed to laugh as much as she did—light and bright and impossible to ignore. Her jet-black hair tumbled loose around her shoulders in wild waves, and she flashed me a grin sharp enough to cut glass while she lifted a silver flask. "Tonight's definitely for drinking," she said with a wink.

Maya was next, stepping into the room with that signature smirk, her camo-patterned dress clinging to her in all the right places, tough but with this wild softness underneath, like she was ready to crash a party or start a bonfire in the backyard. The faded greens and browns of the camo print stood out against her caramel skin and curly black hair, which she wore pulled up messily in a bun. Her eyes sparkled with that mischievous, daredevil glow, and when Indigo tossed her the flask, she caught it like it was a prize. "Let's see if you can keep up, Indi," Maya teased, voice low and full of challenge.

Cassie drifted in quietly, almost like a breath of calm in the storm. Her dress was a soft lavender shade, covered in tiny sequins that caught the light like stars in a summer sky. The delicate shimmer made her look ethereal, like she'd stepped out of a dream just to steady the rest of us. Her curly auburn hair was pinned back with little pastel clips, and she adjusted her silver necklace as if it were a talisman against the night's chaos. Cassie didn't drink, but her calm presence was a tether none of us could do without.

And then there was me, wrapped in a deep emerald green velvet dress that felt like a secret I wore on my skin. It was simple, but the richness of the fabric and the way it caught the fading light made me feel hidden and bold all at once. I'd pinned my chestnut hair back loosely, letting stray strands fall in soft waves around my face, hoping the freckles on my cheeks would soften the seriousness I carried around with me. I tugged nervously at the hem as I watched the others, feeling the mix of excitement and unease twisting in my chest.

Indigo plopped down on the edge of her bed with a grin that was way too wide for a normal afternoon. "Okay, so first things first, what's the game plan tonight? Besides fun, I mean."

Maya stretched out on the floor like she owned the place. "Well, we drink. We dance. Go out with a bang. This is it guys."

"What if we focus on that, and survival?" I ask.

"Way to be Debbie Downer," Indigo teases.

Cassie sat cross-legged on the carpet, her sequined dress catching the dim light like tiny stars scattered across the floor. "Surviving sounds… responsible." She smiled softly, looking between us. "Maybe we can avoid having a funeral for someone who drank too much."

I laughed, feeling the tension in my shoulders ease a little. "I'm down for that."

Indigo's eyes flicked to Maya and back to me. "Sadee's the responsible one. Like always. Someone has to keep us from setting the world on fire."

Maya snorted. "Pfft. No promises."

I rolled my eyes but smiled. "Okay, I have a question. Who's gonna be the first to make a complete fool of themselves tonight?"

Indigo's grin turned wicked. "Obviously, it's you."

"Excuse me?" I scoffed, folding my arms. "I'm the least likely to get plastered."

Maya smirked and rolled her eyes. "Famous last words, green dress."

Cassie giggled, tucking a loose curl behind her ear. "You never know."

The room was warm and smelled like a mix of lavender lotion, old books, and the faint hint of Indigo's vanilla-scented candle. Outside, the sun was dipping lower, the sky bleeding orange through the curtains.

Indigo bounced up from the bed, her yellow dress catching the light as she spun around like she was already the life of the party. "Okay, I'm calling it: Maya's gonna steal the show. Between the camo dress and that crazy laugh of hers? No contest."

Maya threw a mock glare at Indigo. "Hey! That laugh's a gift. Besides, you'll be too busy tossing back shots to notice."

I laughed, tugging nervously at the velvet hem of my dress. "You both make it sound so easy."

Cassie smiled softly. "It's the anticipation. That nervous energy before something big happens."

I nodded slowly, the twist in my stomach pulling tighter, like the first lurch of a rollercoaster right before the drop, that breathless second where you can't turn back, only fall. "Yeah," I said quietly, "like waiting for a rollercoaster to drop."

Indigo perched on the arm of her desk chair, golden fabric rippling like sunshine barely holding itself together. She leaned in, eyes bright but too sharp, like she was balancing on a ledge. "Honestly? I'm just here to have fun and forget for a bit."

Maya raised an eyebrow, a crooked smile tugging at the corner of her mouth. "Forget what? School? That we're all basically living in a horror movie now? That this stupid game spiraled into something actually dangerous?"

Her words cracked something in the room. The music kept playing, but it felt distant now, muffled by the weight of what we weren't saying.

Indigo shrugged, biting her lip, but her smile didn't reach her eyes. "Maybe all of it."

"We're not going to be able to forget," I murmured, not looking at anyone. My voice came out thinner than I wanted it to. "Not since it keeps getting worse."

Indigo's expression darkened, a flicker of something desperate flashing across her face. "Gosh, Sadee. We *have* to. Don't you see?

This game, whatever it's turned into, it's not just weird anymore. It's twisted. It's evil."

The word hung in the air, heavy and jagged. No one laughed. No one argued.

Cassie turned toward the window, her fingers absentmindedly tracing over the sequins on her dress. The glints of silver danced across her hand like scattered stars. "Sometimes," she said softly, "forgetting is the only way to keep going."

The next song dropped, the bass deeper now, almost like a heartbeat. It rattled in my chest. Not fast, but slow and ominous, like something creeping closer. My throat tightened.

It was getting harder to pretend this was just a normal night.

Indigo's grin widened. "Alright, enough of the scary stuff. Who's ready for some fun?"

Maya lifted the flask again, her smirk daring. "Cheers to that."

Cassie raised an imaginary glass with a soft laugh. "I'll toast with you in spirit."

I smiled, feeling the warmth of their friendship wrap around me like the soft velvet of my dress.

The evening was just beginning.

Cassie got up from the floor with a small grunt and smoothed her dress, the sequins catching the low light again as she moved. "Okay," she said, "last-minute mirror check before we go and potentially humiliate ourselves?"

"Potentially?" Maya scoffed. "I plan to. It's more fun that way."

"Plus, after two weeks, we won't ever see any of these people again." Indigo adds.

Maya stood and turned toward the long mirror propped against the wall. I followed her with my eyes, watching the way her camo dress clung to her. It wasn't an elegant dress, but it looked good on her. Her reflection grinned back at her like a dare.

Indigo slipped past me and peered into the mirror too, fluffing her hair with both hands. "Tell me I look hot. Lie to me if you have to."

"You look hot," Maya said, deadpan.

Indigo narrowed her eyes. "That wasn't very convincing."

"I'm not here to coddle your ego, sunshine," Maya said, but she bumped Indigo's hip with hers all the same.

Cassie leaned into the mirror next, tilting her head slightly as she adjusted one of her pastel clips. "Do you think it's too much?" she asked, quietly, like she was afraid to break the fragile joy in the room.

"Absolutely not," I said, moving to stand beside her. "You look like an actual fairy."

Cassie blushed and gave a small, self-conscious smile, but I caught the way her fingers stilled, like my words settled something in her chest.

Indigo leaned back on her heels. "We're a freaking dream team tonight."

"Hot dream team," Maya corrected. "Emphasis on dream. Emphasis on hot."

I laughed, the sound easing something tight inside me. "Okay, but should we, like… coordinate how we're arriving? I don't want to walk in and find out all the guys already started without us."

"They better not," Indigo muttered, grabbing her phone from the nightstand. "Finn said they were just meeting up outside Mason's car."

"Of course he did," Maya said, reaching down to grab her beat-up boots from where she'd kicked them earlier. "Bet Finn parallel parked like a psychopath again."

I flinched before I could stop myself. Did Indigo tell Maya? Of course she did, she couldn't keep anything to herself.

Indigo's fingers tightened slightly around her phone.

Cassie gently reached for her purse, her quiet voice breaking the tension. "Do we know who's all going to be there?"

Indigo's eyes flicked up. "Besides the guys? I think everyone. Even some seniors from our rival school. How crazy is that? Their head cheerleader, Savannah Lee, even she's made time for this. She's bringing someone sketchy, though, so keep your drinks close."

"That's comforting," I muttered.

"I'm *always* comforting," Indigo replied with a grin, slipping her flask into her small yellow purse. "Okay. Lip gloss check. Vibes check. Existential dread managed. We're golden."

Maya kicked on her boots and stood tall. "Time to go out with a bang."

"Final party of senior year, here we come!" Indigo cheers.

Cassie hesitated just a second longer, then nodded. "Let's go."

We filed out of Indigo's room in a line, each of us checking pockets, purses, and hair in the hallway mirror before slipping into our shoes by the front door. Indigo's mom was gone for the night, we had the place to ourselves, which made everything feel more dangerous and more exciting.

The evening air hit us as soon as we opened the door, thick with spring heat that hadn't quite lifted, the sky deepening into violet and gold. It was the kind of evening that buzzed in your bones, like the world itself knew something was coming.

As we stepped out onto the front porch, Indigo pulled out her phone again and tapped out a message. "Finn says they're already waiting by the corner."

"Already?" I asked. "Didn't we say seven?"

Cassie checked the time on her phone. "It's 6:47."

"Finn is incapable of being fashionably late," Maya said. "It's one of his many flaws."

We started walking, heels clicking and boots thudding in uneven rhythm across the sidewalk. Streetlights buzzed faintly overhead, not quite bright enough yet to matter. Our reflections danced in shop windows and parked cars, our laughter breaking across the stillness like glass shattering in slow motion.

"I feel like I'm in a movie," Cassie said, her voice soft and full of wonder.

"You *are* in a movie," Indigo replied, looping an arm through hers. "We're all the main characters tonight."

Maya bumped me gently with her elbow. "Even you, Sadee. Especially you."

I glanced over, the edge of a smile curling at my mouth. "Why especially me?"

"Because you look like you're about to uncover a murder and solve it in heels," she said, eyes glinting.

I snorted. "Only if I don't pass out from fear first."

We turned the corner.

And there they were, the boys, leaning against Mason's car like they were posing for a mixtape cover. Finn, brooding and silent, arms crossed, eyes flicking up the moment he spotted us. Mason, leaning casually against the passenger door, that trademark grin already on his face. Eli stood with his hands stuffed into his pockets, smiling like he wasn't sure if he belonged there, and Ryan already halfway through telling a story no one was listening to, his arms flailing in wild punctuation.

They looked up in unison as we approached.

Mason let out a low whistle. "Wow. You all showed up looking like a Vogue cover."

"Correction," Indigo said, sliding forward first. "We *always* look like that. Tonight, we're just making sure everyone knows it."

Finn's eyes lingered on Indigo for a second too long before he turned to me and gave a quick nod. I didn't look away fast enough.

"Ready?" Eli asked, pushing off the car with a sheepish smile.

"Born ready," Maya said, already stepping past him. "Let's do this."

Cassie gave me a small look, a mix of nervousness and excitement, and I nodded back.

This night was just beginning.

And we had no idea what it would cost us.

We all piled into Mason's truck and Finn's car, laughter still clinging to our voices, oblivious to the quiet shift in the air.

The road stretched out ahead of us, twenty minutes through the small dirt roads, out past the edge of town where the trees stood too still and the sky felt too wide.

To the lonely tree.

The one with rope marks.

Rubbed into the thickest branch for eternity.

The vehicles rumbled to life.

Mason leaned out the window, waving Finn on. "You lead. I don't wanna end up in a ditch again."

Finn nodded once, headlights sweeping across the driveway as he pulled ahead.

Cassie climbed into the space beside me, fiddling with the hem of her dress as she settled in. Her sequins caught the light from the dashboard, flickering like tiny stars. Mason drove, I beside him in the front, already queuing up a playlist. The bass thudded faintly through the speakers, something upbeat and fast, and Indigo stretched her hand out of the passenger window of Finn's car and waved.

In front of us, Finn's taillights glowed red through the trees as Maya's laughter filtered out faintly from the cracked window of his car.

Cassie glanced at me with a crooked smile. "You nervous?"

"A little." I shrugged. "I keep thinking this will be normal. Like it's just a party. But then…"

Her expression softened. "But then you remember everything happening in reality."

The road narrowed as we pulled away from town, houses thinning out until it was just trees and shadows. The sun had fully dipped by now, and the world was bathed in dusky blue and amber, the last hints of daylight clinging to the sky like smoke.

Branches arched overhead, forming a tunnel that swallowed the light.

"I hope there's actual food," Mason said suddenly, breaking the silence. "Not just, like, dry chips and whatever was leftover from someone's pantry."

"You didn't eat before we left?" I asked.

"He was busy, trying to look hot for you, Sadee. Aren't you flattered?" Cassie teases.

He snorted and turned the wheel. "Not wrong."

Cassie giggled beside me. "Sadee, you do look gorgeous, though."

I give her a shy smile. "Thank you." I'm never quite able to figure out why talking about how I look around Mason always makes me feel weird. But it does. I leaned forward, resting my arms on the dashboard. "Maya's dress is stunning."

"She better not blend in too well," Cassie said. "Actually, I want someone to accidentally flirt with a tree thinking it's her."

That got a laugh from Mason, the laughter bouncing off the windows, warm and a little too loud in the tight space.

Outside, the trees pressed closer, the road winding like a ribbon into the woods.

It wasn't far now.

I could feel it, that subtle shift. The way the air seemed heavier, like it knew something we didn't.

Mason flipped on the high beams as the road dipped. "Almost there."

The lonely tree wasn't marked on any map. Just a clearing in the woods near an old fire road, somewhere people only remembered when they needed a place to sneak off to. No neighbors. No cell towers. Just trees, stars, and miles of empty space.

We reached it just as the music changed again, something slower now, with a darker beat. Fitting.

Finn pulled into the clearing first, his headlights sweeping across the base of the gnarled tree at the center. Its branches twisted up like fingers, silhouetted against the bruised sky.

"Okay, that thing's haunted," Cassie muttered.

"No kidding," I said.

Mason parked beside Finn, tires crunching over gravel and dry leaves. I opened the door and climbed out, the night air cooler than I expected. It smelled like pine and smoke and distant dirt, like something freshly unearthed.

Maya hopped down from Finn's car, pulling a flask from her purse with a triumphant grin. "Party time!"

"I thought we were easing into the fun," I said, crossing my arms.

"We are. I'm just accelerating the ease."

Indigo joined her with a laugh. "Let's toast to terrible decisions."

"I'll drink to that," Maya said, unscrewing the cap.

Cassie lingered near me, her arms folded tightly around herself. "We're really doing this, huh?"

"Yeah," I said, my voice quieter now. "We are."

They disappeared into the clearing, Indigo and Maya already clinking flasks, their heels clicking against rock and root. Finn followed behind, hands in his pockets, unreadable as ever.

From the back of the truck, Mason lowered red cooler onto the ground with a grunt. "Help me with this?"

"Sure." I grabbed the opposite handle. It was heavier than I expected, filled with ice and who knows what else, and we started the slow trek toward the tree.

Strung-up lights blinked in the branches above us, some flickering battery-powered bulbs, others flickering lanterns hanging crooked from low limbs. They cast long shadows across the clearing, soft pools of light that barely held the dark at bay. The kind of glow that made everything look too still. Too quiet. Like a painting that hadn't dried all the way.

A mob of people stood around the lonely tree. That was our party. No turning back now.

We stepped past the first few cars and into the tree line. That's when I noticed it.

No music.

No thudding bass. No drunk karaoke. Not even the usual rustle of feet over dead leaves or that awkward shuffle when someone trips over a root.

Just… silence.

Thick. Suffocating. Heavy enough to press against my ears.

The air smelled like damp bark and ash. My skin prickled, and not just from the evening chill.

"Last time I checked," I whispered, "these parties were chaos."

"This is weird," Mason said beside me, voice low. He slowed his pace.

"Yeah." My throat was dry. "It is."

Up ahead, the rest of our group stopped short, Indigo, Maya, Cassie. Finn, Eli, and Ryan paused a few steps behind them.

Finn's head tilted slightly, his posture suddenly tense.

And then—

A scream.

Sharp. Gut-deep. Terrified.

It cracked the stillness like lightning on dry wood.

Indigo's voice.

High and cracking and not playful in the slightest.

Everyone froze.

The cooler dropped from Mason's grip with a hollow *thud*. Ice and cans spilled across the dirt.

I ran.

I didn't know what I was running toward, only that Indigo was still screaming. That the glow from the tree was wrong. That the lights looked dimmer now, like something had sucked the warmth from them.

Branches tore at my arms as I pushed past people, past shadows, past Finn's frozen form.

And then I saw it.

The tree.

The rope.

And what was hanging from it.

Chapter Twenty

The scream tore through the silence like a jagged blade ripping through glass, shattering the fragile calm of the night and echoing in our ears long after it had died away. My heart hammered painfully in my chest; each beat a cruel reminder that we'd crossed into something far more terrifying than we'd ever imagined.

I had dropped the cooler, its contents spilling onto the dirt with a sickening crack, forgotten in the frantic rush of my legs as I pushed forward, flesh and bone instinct overriding fear. Shadows stretched and writhed beneath the twisted, gnarled branches of the lonely tree, flickering like dying candle flames, alive with some silent, sinister rhythm.

And then I saw him.

Nick.

Hanging from the branches like a broken marionette, his body swaying gently in the breeze, a sick, silent pendulum. The frayed, blood-stained rope bit cruelly into his neck, a cruel scar glaring against his bronze skin.

His head lolled forward, hair tangled and matted, eyes staring into the abyss, frozen in a final, haunting silence. His mouth was slack, incapable of forming words, only the faintest trickle of blood slipping from the corner of his lips.

Blood darkened his shirtfront, pooling and staining the bark beneath him, thick and sticky, a grotesque blot of life spilled onto the rough, unforgiving wood. The sickly-sweet scent of blood and damp earth invaded my senses, making my stomach churn and my head swim.

My breath hitched, shallow, ragged, an instinctive gasp that felt like it might shatter my ribs. I staggered closer, every nerve alight with primal horror, the metallic tang of blood, the dampness of the soil, the rot of rotting leaves, every smell an assault on my senses. The air was thick with it, heavy enough to press against my skin, suffocating.

My palms were clammy, sweat pooling in my hands, trembling uncontrollably as I stared at the terrible sight.

Indigo's trembling figure was already in front of him, knees sinking into the dirt as she sobbed brokenly, her shoulders shaking with a raw, uncontrollable fear. Tears streamed down her face, her hands trembling as if she'd been struck by lightning. Her voice was a broken whisper; words lost in the chaos.

Maya's face was ghostly pale, lips trembling uncontrollably, her eyes wide and unblinking, frozen in a state of shock and disbelief.

Finn stood rigid, jaw clenched so tightly his teeth flashed in the faint lantern light, eyes fixed on the hanging figure as if willing him to vanish, to disappear like a nightmare slipping away at dawn. His fists were clenched so tightly that his knuckles gleamed white, muscles tense with helpless rage and dread.

The tree's bark was scarred with deep, jagged scratches, probably made by some cruel hand, or perhaps by the act itself.

I couldn't look away. My stomach twisted into knots, bile rising at the back of my throat. Tears burned my eyes, blurring my vision, yet I couldn't turn away from the scene, couldn't escape the visceral horror. The metallic scent of blood, the damp earth, and the panic rising inside me, all pressed against my senses, overwhelming and sickening. My skin prickled with icy dread, every hair on my body standing on end, as if some unseen force was trying to invade my mind.

My breathing grew shallow, ragged. A wave of nausea swept over me, threatening to send me to my knees. The scene before me felt like the climax of every nightmare I'd ever had, only this was real, raw, terrifying. Somewhere deep inside, a primal scream echoed, a mixture of raw fear, grief, and horror, an unspoken plea for this nightmare to end.

Mason's trembling voice finally cut through the stunned silence. "We have to call someone." His words sounded distant, as if from underwater, but I clung to them desperately.

Indigo pushed herself up, trembling violently, clutching Finn's arm like a lifeline, her face contorted with shock and horror. Her eyes weren't focused, they stared past us, into the eyes of Nick Donovan.

Indigo blinked and turned to look at me, and I saw the unspoken understanding pass between us—this was no accident.

The group was frozen, caught in a paralyzing mix of shock and dread. No one spoke, only the faint creak of the rope, swaying softly in the breeze, like a death knell. The flickering glow cast long, twisting shadows that seemed to crawl and stretch, reaching out to claim us.

Somewhere in the back of my mind, a primal scream echoed, fear, and shock intertwined into a single, suffocating wave. We had entered a nightmare, and I knew, deep down, that this was only the beginning.

The cold night air pressed against my skin, and I shivered uncontrollably. I could feel the tremble in my legs, the pounding of my heart, the beads of sweat cooling on my forehead. The scene before me was forever etched into my mind, the dark stains on his shirt, the wild, unseeing eyes, the cursed symbols flickering like dying embers.

I wanted to look away, to run, to scream, but I was rooted in place, unable to move, overwhelmed by the horror that had become real.

Then, a faint sound, a whisper, slithered into the edges of my consciousness. Soft, insidious, almost inaudible. I strained to hear it, to understand what it was. It was a whisper of wind slipping through dead leaves, or maybe a voice, straining to form words but fading before they could take shape. It slithered around my thoughts like a cold, unsettling murmur that sent chills racing down my spine.

I felt goosebumps rise, and an icy shiver traced a path down my neck and through my fingertips.

My gaze flicked to the symbols carved into the bark above Nick's head. The "H" pulsed, faint and irregular, like a heartbeat. The word "Wrong" beneath it shimmered, shifting as if bleeding ink into the bark. The symbols seemed alive, breathing, writhing. The glow was alive, dancing, flickering, trying to drown the faint light of the moon. I felt a coldness seep into my bones, as if unseen fingers were tracing over my skin, probing, trying to reach inside.

The horror pressed against my chest like a heavy weight, squeezing the breath from my lungs. I wanted to scream, to run, to hide, but my body was frozen, paralyzed by terror and disbelief. I looked around at the others, their faces masks of shock and horror, each of us caught in this sick display, a nightmare come to life.

Beside me, Finn's voice was urgent. "We need to get out of here. Now."

Indigo's face crumpled, tears flowing freely, and she stared up at Nick's hanging form, trembling so badly she looked about to faint. Her voice was a whisper, broken and raw. "This… this isn't just some sick prank. This is something… worse."

She looked at Finn, clutching him tight, her eyes pleading for reassurance. I saw her unspoken fear, the terror that this was only the beginning, that whatever force had marked Nick was now hunting us.

And I felt it too, an icy, creeping dread that seeped into my bones, into my mind. Whatever this was, it wasn't just a death. It was a message. A warning. A curse. Something ancient and unseen, lurking beneath the surface of our world, waiting patiently for the right moment to strike.

The symbols, the flickering glow, the blood, none of it was random. It was part of something bigger, darker. And I knew, with the sickening certainty that made my stomach churn, that this nightmare was only the beginning.

The wind whispered again, soft at first, then louder, like a chorus of unseen voices. Goosebumps erupted across my arms as I stared at the glowing symbols, their flickering light casting shadows that danced and writhed across the clearing. It was as if the very bark, the living, breathing wood, was whispering secrets, trying to tell us something we weren't meant to understand.

The night felt colder suddenly, as if the darkness itself had deepened, pressing closer around us.

Every sound, the distant owl's cry, the rustling leaves, the faint creak of the rope, became sharper, more insistent. It was as if the woods around them had thickened, closing in, trying to suffocate the very air they breathed.

The shadows stretched and writhed, but now, it felt as if they weren't just shadows. They were tentacles, reaching out, trying to grasp at something just beyond their sight.

Indigo pressed her trembling hands to her face, her shoulders shuddering. Her tears had slowed, but her eyes remained wide, unblinking, darting nervously around the scene as if expecting something to leap out of the darkness at any moment.

"This… this isn't real," she whispered again, voice cracking, but her trembling hands betrayed her. She looked as if she was trying to deny what she saw, yet her fear was undeniable.

Maya was clutching her arms, trembling so violently that her nails left marks on her skin. Her gaze kept darting toward the symbols, then back to the body, as if trying to decipher some hidden message that might explain all of this. Her lips trembled, but she didn't speak.

Finn's fists clenched so tightly his knuckles turned white, but his eyes flickered not just with rage or helplessness, they were emotionless.

His body was tense, ready to move, yet rooted to the ground. He looked as though every instinct was screaming for him to run, but he stood still. Frozen in place.

The whisper still lingered, layered in the air, layered in our minds. It was softer now, more insidious, like a voice just beyond hearing, whispering secrets that made my skin crawl. Not words, but a presence, something that felt disturbingly close, almost within reach.

And then a new sensation crept in, uncanny, almost impossible to ignore. It was as if the danger wasn't just nearby; it *was* nearby, so close that they could feel it breathing. The sense that someone, or something, was standing behind us, hidden in the shadows, observing with intent. The kind of presence that could be within the crowd, among the gathered friends, the witnesses, the people enjoying the aftermath of what had been done, someone blending into the darkness, watching us, waiting patiently for the perfect moment.

The scene around us didn't seem real anymore. Shadows stretched and flickered, but now they seemed alive, writhing, reaching out, trying to clutch at something just beyond sight.

The feeling grew sharper, more visceral. It wasn't just that the threat was close, it *was* within reach, embedded in the very fabric of the woods. Every instinct in my body screamed at me to flee, yet my feet felt glued to the ground. The danger wasn't just out there in the dark; it was *here*, among us, in the silence that stretched between our ragged breaths.

The silence stretched, thick and heavy, until someone finally broke it with a shaky voice, her words trembling like fragile glass. "This…

this doesn't feel right. I mean, it's just a game, right? Just some sick prank…" The voice cracked on the last word, but it tried to sound convincing, as if repeating the lie enough times would make it true.

Maya looked over, her face pale, eyes darting nervously to the symbols flickering faintly in the dim light. "Yeah… it's just part of the game. Someone's messing with us, that's all. It's probably some sick joke," she said, voice strained but trying to sound firm. "We've seen worse pranks before."

Mason's jaw clenched tighter, but his voice was quiet, almost a growl. "Worse than this? You think this is just a joke? Look at him," he said, nodding toward Nick's hanging form. "Look at what's carved into the tree. This isn't some prank. Someone's trying to scare us, sure. But this… this feels personal."

Indigo's eyes widened and she shook her head rapidly. "No, it's just—"

"Don't," Mason interrupted, his voice low but firm. "We're not going there. It's part of the game. That's what we tell ourselves. Someone's messing with us, trying to make us think it's bigger than it is."

But even as he spoke, I couldn't ignore the creeping sensation that the darkness was pressing closer, that the symbols pulsed with a life that was almost human—almost alive. The faint glow flickered irregularly, like a heartbeat fighting to stay steady.

Mason's voice softened as he added, "It's just the game. That's all."

No one responded immediately. The whispers in the wind grew louder, layered, layered, insidious. They seemed to seep from the shadows, from the very bark of the tree, as if the symbols were alive and whispering secrets meant only for the darkness. The sense of proximity was overwhelming now, like the danger was behind every shadow, lurking within the group itself.

Maya looked around nervously. "But it's too close, isn't it? I mean, I feel like… like the person behind this could be *right* here, among us." Her voice dropped to a whisper. "Like, they're watching, waiting for us to slip up. Maybe they're even in the crowd, blending in."

Eli scoffed softly, but his eyes darted around, suspicious. "That's what's got me worried. Someone's been in on this from the start. Someone's been playing us, every step of the way. And this… this isn't just some random sick joke. It's too personal."

Indigo's voice faltered. "You think… someone we know? Someone here?"

Mason hesitated, then nodded grimly. "It's possible. Or worse. Maybe it's something that feeds on our fears, something that's been waiting for a moment like this, to get inside our heads. I don't feel like we're just dealing with a game anymore. It's… it's like it's trying to reach us."

Indigo shivered, clutching her arms. "I swear… I feel like we're being watched. Not just by… whatever's doing this, but by something… *someone* else. Like we're part of the game, but the game's not just in the woods anymore. It's inside us."

Maya nodded. "Exactly. I don't trust it. I don't trust any of this. It's too personal. Like… like whoever did this, they're trying to tell us something. Or they're trying to scare us into doing something. I mean, *really* scare us."

Finn looked at her sharply. "Or maybe they want us to think it's just a game. That it's all fake. But I don't buy that anymore. Something's wrong. Everything's wrong."

Indigo's eyes flicked nervously to the symbols again. "And the way it feels… like it's right behind us. Like the danger's so close that it's brushing against us, inside the circle, outside the circle, everywhere. I swear I can feel it moving, breathing, like it's alive and waiting to pounce."

Mason finally spoke again, voice tight. "Whatever it is, it's not just in the woods. It's in the air, in our heads. Don't give into it. This is what they want." His eyes darted nervously toward the flickering glow, the shadows stretching and twisting. "We've got to stay sharp. Keep our heads clear. The moment we start panicking, we lose."

Indigo looked around, her voice trembling. "I keep thinking… what if this is personal? What if someone did this to him, to Nick, because they knew us? Because they wanted us to see this?"

Maya's voice was barely a whisper now. "Or because they want us to become part of it."

And the feeling persisted, more urgent than ever, that the danger wasn't just lurking in the shadows. It *was* the shadows. It was someone among them, someone hiding in plain sight, whispering in the darkness.

Someone who might already be part of this nightmare, waiting for the right moment to reveal themselves.

I felt it, a primal, visceral awareness that the threat was closer than it should be, more intimate. That the darkness had already begun to crawl into our minds, into their very bones.

And in the quiet, someone, perhaps the one standing closest, was listening.

And I knew this with unshakable certainty: none of us were safe anymore.

What if the hand that saves you also holds the knife?

Chapter Twenty-One

The sharp wail of sirens sliced through the heavy night air, a sudden, jarring sound that shattered the stillness surrounding the tree. Blue and red lights flickered against the twisted branches, casting long, twitching shadows that danced over Nick's hanging form like restless ghosts.

Voices shouted orders, urgent, clipped, professional, but none of us moved. Our limbs felt leaden, trapped in the thick fog of shock and fear.

The distant crunch of gravel under boots grew louder. Flashlights bobbed through the woods, sweeping across the faces of the group, pale, wide-eyed, frozen.

Officers shouted over the chaos, struggling to corral the restless crowd. "Move back! Clear the area! This is a crime scene!" Their radios crackled sharply in the night, calling for backup and medical aid.

The group stayed frozen near the tree, shadows pressed tight against the harsh glow of lanterns and flashlights. Faces pale, eyes wide, none of us wanted to move, not fully ready to leave the terrible scene behind.

From the edges of the crowd, other seniors peeked over shoulders, some whispering, some on their phones, alerts and rumors already spreading like wildfire through the tight-knit class.

Mason's voice cut through my stunned silence, low but urgent. "We have to stick together. No slipping away. No one leaves." His eyes flicked nervously toward the officers, then back to us.

Indigo wiped her eyes fiercely, trying to compose herself, but her trembling hands gave her away. "They don't get it. They never will."

A sharp-eyed officer barked orders to two younger cops, pointing toward the glowing symbols carved into the tree's bark. "See if forensics can get anything from those markings," he commanded. "And someone keep an eye on that group over there." His gaze flicked toward us.

I swallowed, a cold pit forming in my stomach.

Every single person from the senior class was here. At an illegal party, where there would be underage drinking, and someone turned up dead.

We weren't just witnesses anymore—we were suspects.

The night had shifted. The shadows that had danced around us were no longer just darkness. They were eyes. Watching. Waiting.

The officers started ushering students away in small groups, their hands firm but practiced as they tried to maintain control over a crowd growing restless with fear and confusion. Voices rose in whispered clusters, questions and accusations tossed between friends and strangers alike.

A tall cop with a notepad took charge of our group, his eyes sharp beneath the brim of his hat. "We're going to ask some questions. Stay close. Don't talk to anyone else about this." His tone was clipped, a clear warning.

Indigo wiped a tear from her cheek, trying to steady her breath. Finn's hand was firm on her shoulder, grounding her. Maya bit her lip, glancing around nervously. Cassie stayed close to me, clutching her jacket like a lifeline.

When the officer looked at Finn, his gaze lingered a moment longer than with the others. Finn's jaw tightened. His answers came short and measured, avoiding any detail that might unravel the story.

I stayed close to Mason, Indigo, Maya, Cassie, Eli, Ryan, and Finn, though Finn lingered at the edge, quiet as a shadow. No one wanted to leave, even though the officers kept ordering us to spread out, to answer their questions.

One cop came to me first. His face was stern but not unkind. "Where were you the last time you saw Nick?"

I swallowed, heart knocking against my ribs. "At school. Friday. After classes."

He nodded, jotting notes. "Did anything happen? Any fights or arguments?"

"No," I said, voice barely steady. "He seemed... normal."

Mason was next. He answered clearly, steady. "Passed him in the halls after lunch, before English."

Indigo trembled as the officer crouched beside her, his radio crackling faintly at his shoulder. The blue and red lights washed over her face in flickering pulses, painting her tears in crimson.

"You knew Nick well?" the officer asked, voice gentler now.

She shook her head, wiping her eyes with the back of her hand, not dainty, but fierce, like she was trying to scrub away the entire night. "No. But I hadn't seen him since school ended."

The officer's pen paused over his notepad. "Did he have any problems? Anyone mad at him?"

Indigo opened her mouth, but only air came out. She looked around for help, lips parting like she might lie, might bury it all again. "No," she finally whispered.

But around her, voices cut in, a quiet chorus of contradiction.

"Yes," I heard Ryan say under his breath.

"Obviously," Maya muttered, crossing her arms.

Eli gave a single nod, and even Cassie, normally silent in moments like this, looked down and mumbled, "Yeah."

The cop looked up sharply. "People were mad at him?"

There was a beat of silence. Then Maya stepped forward, hair wild around her face, earrings catching the flashing lights. "I mean, all of us are livid," she said flatly, staring the officer down. "A few months back, at a different party, Nick drugged Indi. Took advantage of her."

The air snapped. Cold. Still. Like the forest itself was holding its breath.

Indigo's whole body seemed to fold in on itself. Her hands balled into fists, knuckles white. She turned away from Maya slowly, eyes wide with betrayal. "Maya," she hissed, voice tight and raw, "shut up."

Maya ignored her. "She almost passed out on the lawn. I was the one who found her, barely conscious, mascara streaked, throwing up in the grass. Nick never admitted to anything, but he didn't have to. After that night, he hovered like a shadow. Smiling, watching her flinch whenever he came near. He *liked* it. Liked the way she shrank into herself whenever his name was mentioned; like her fear proved he still had power over her."

The silence that followed Maya's words was suffocating.

Even the wind seemed to hold its breath. The flashlight beams stopped bobbing. Footsteps slowed. A few heads turned.

The officer blinked, his expression shuttering. "That's a serious accusation."

Finn's voice barely scraped out of his throat. "It doesn't matter anymore. He's dead."

"That doesn't mean it didn't happen," Maya snapped, stepping slightly in front of him like a shield. "And it doesn't mean he deserves sympathy."

"Enough," Mason muttered under his breath.

The officer held up a hand. "We're not making judgments tonight. But if there's something we need to know, about Nick's behavior, past or present, it matters."

Indigo just shook her head; her gaze fixed on the ground like she might fall through it.

They pulled her aside gently for more questions, and I wanted to follow, to reach for her, but I didn't move. My legs still felt heavy. Cemented. Everything around us had tilted off its axis.

Cassie hovered beside me, her arms wrapped tight around herself, eyes locked on the tree like she still hadn't processed it was real. Her lips moved in a silent prayer, or maybe just a repetition of *this isn't happening, this isn't happening.*

Ryan sat on a nearby log, hunched over with his elbows on his knees, hands clenched together so tightly his knuckles had gone white. "They're gonna search our phones," he muttered. "They're gonna look at everything. Even the dumb stuff. They can't do that, can they?"

"They can," Eli replied quietly, standing beside him. "It's a homicide. They'll get warrants. Especially if they think it happened before tonight."

I glanced over. "What do you mean?"

Eli rubbed the back of his neck. "I heard one of the officers say rigor was already disappearing. And… lividity. That stuff happens when someone's been dead a while. Longer than just a few hours."

A new wave of cold washed over me. So, Nick… wasn't even alive when we got here.

I see the question etched into everyone's faces: then who brought him?

A scream broke the air from deeper in the woods, someone being separated from their friends, probably. But it sounded too close to panic. I turned instinctively, heart racing, but the flashlight beams quickly converged and revealed a pair of officers ushering a few stragglers back toward the main clearing.

"Go with your friends," one barked. "No wandering. Stay together until you've been spoken to."

Cassie pressed closer to Maya and me. "Why would someone bring him here like that?" she whispered. "Like, like some kind of… warning?"

Maya's jaw clenched. "Because whoever did this wanted us to see it."

A chill passed between us.

Nearby, a cluster of officers stood around a notepad, voices low but urgent. One of them tapped the carved symbols on the bark, pointing toward the strange spiral near Nick's head, then down to the rough, scorched patch of earth below him.

The officer from earlier returned, his face more serious than before. "We need to start separating you for questioning. One at a time. We'll be documenting everything from tonight, including when you last saw Nick."

He glanced down at his notepad. "Which, from what you've said, was yesterday afternoon?"

Everyone nodded slowly, except Finn.

He hesitated, just a beat too long.

Then, quietly, "Yeah. School."

No one seemed to notice, but I did.

I always noticed Finn. The way he rarely spoke unless spoken to. The way he watched people like he was listening to something none of us could hear. Right now, he stood behind the group, his shadow barely touching the edge of the flashlight beams.

I looked away before he noticed me staring.

One of the female officers stepped toward Mason. "You first. Walk with me."

Mason squeezed my hand before letting go, jaw set. "Be back," he said quietly, and followed the officer through the shifting crowd.

It was like the party had reversed itself. The laughter and music had once spilled into the trees. Now, dread trickled through the branches instead, slow and inescapable.

Another officer called my name.

I didn't realize I was trembling until I tried to stand.

"I just have a few questions," she said. "You don't have to answer anything that makes you uncomfortable. This is more of a general conversation."

"Okay," I managed. My voice felt buried in my throat.

She glanced down at her notes. "You were part of the group that found him?"

I nodded. "Well, kind of. Mason and I were the last people to see him. My friend group arrived late, and then Mason and I were carrying the cooler, so we were behind everyone. We didn't—this was supposed to just be a game." Tears well up in my eyes, I look away to try to hide them. "This is crazy. I just want to go home and hide under my covers until this is all over." I force a small chuckle. "I sound like a coward."

The officer gave a small nod. "That's not uncommon in situations like this. Especially with young people. It's... a lot."

Her sympathy didn't reach her eyes.

She continued. "How well did you know Nicholas Donovan?"

I shrugged. "Not that well. He was in our friend group's orbit. He'd show up to parties. Say weird stuff sometimes. I guess we all tolerated him."

The officer wrote something down. "Were there tensions? Fights?"

"Not... openly," I said. "But people didn't like him. Especially after what Maya just said."

"And you?" Her voice softened. "Did *you* dislike him?"

"I didn't trust him," I said, which wasn't a lie. I didn't trust him. I just figured it was smart to leave out just how much I hated him. "I always felt like I had to watch him. Like I couldn't let my guard down around him."

The officer leaned against the hood of a car, folding her arms. "Do you think anyone in your group—" she glanced over toward the others, "would be capable of doing something like this?"

My heart jumped.

"Sorry," she added quickly. "That's not an accusation. We're working with a few possibilities. It looks like the victim might have been dead before the hanging. That changes things. We're just trying to build a psychological picture."

"Dead before—" My voice caught and panic rose inside me. "Wait, how can you even tell that?"

"There are signs. Bruising patterns. Lack of defensive wounds. The lividity. It's not conclusive yet, but we're pursuing that theory seriously."

The edges of my vision started to blur. Not from tears, but from some weird, creeping fog in my mind. I felt like I was looking at the scene through a dirty window.

"I don't know," I finally said. "I mean we were all pretty mad at him. I won't imagine any of us being *violent*."

The officer tilted her head. "That's not always the kind of person who does this. Sometimes it's personal. Sometimes it's someone who holds things in for too long."

My stomach churned.

"I guess if you're asking if anyone's been *hurt* before? Yeah. Indigo. But that's not what you meant."

"No. But thank you for clarifying." The officer scribbled something else down. "When was the last time you personally saw Nick?"

"Yesterday," I said. "Friday. At school. He walked past us in the hallway between second and third period. Didn't say anything."

She nodded again. "Thank you, Sadee. We may need to follow up later, but that's all for now."

I stepped away quickly, almost stumbling back toward the group. Mason caught my arm.

"You okay?" he asked softly.

I nodded, but my jaw was tight, and my whole body felt wrong.

Why did we get cops involved again? Nick deserved to rot in that tree. He doesn't deserve a funeral and frankly, no one needs closure on this either. Nick was gone. End of story.

Cassie had her arms wrapped around Indigo, who was still sitting on the curb with her knees pulled tight to her chest. Maya paced. Eli had taken out his phone, though I doubted he was really looking at it. Ryan hovered awkwardly at the edge of the group like he wasn't sure where he belonged.

Finn leaned against a tree, arms folded. His face was unreadable.

I didn't want to look at him, but I couldn't help it. He hadn't said much since the cops arrived. His silence had weight.

Maya looked over suddenly. "You guys realize whoever did this had to get Nick *here* somehow, right? Like, his body didn't just show up out of nowhere. They either lured him or brought him already—" She broke off, voice sharp with disgust.

Eli finally looked up. "The police said it might've been someone he knew."

"That means one of us," Cassie whispered. "Or someone from school."

"No way it was someone from school," Ryan said. "I mean, Nick had enemies, yeah, but murder? No one's that far gone."

No one answered.

The silence pressed in again.

I blinked.

Finn's car.

The image came back sharp: His car, perfectly parked outside Indigo's house. So precise it looked almost staged. Too perfect.

He shouldn't have made that mistake.

My blood ran cold.

I turned, just slightly, to look at him again.

Finn's arms were still folded. His jaw tight. His gaze distant.

He looked calm. Too calm.

And I suddenly couldn't breathe.

A deeper voice cut through the quiet.

"Alright, listen up."

We all turned.

A different officer approached this time, taller than the woman who'd spoken to me earlier. Broader, too. There was something about the way he moved, deliberate, commanding, that made the air feel heavier.

"I'm Sergeant Alden," he said. "Forensics confirmed the estimated time of death for Nicholas Donovan. Looks like he died sometime between six and nine last night."

My throat tightened.

Last night. Friday.

Before the party even began.

A subtle ripple passed through the group, shifting feet, shallow breaths, a tremor in the silence that followed. Alden's gaze swept over us like a slow-moving spotlight, sharp enough to catch on every twitch, every flinch. His eyes narrowed slightly when he landed on each face, like he was taking inventory of our guilt before we even spoke.

"I need to know where everyone was during that time window."

Maya was first. "I was at home. My parents can confirm."

Cassie echoed her. "Same here. At home." She didn't cross her arms, but her hands dug into her sleeves like she wished she had.

Indigo shook her head. "Family dinner." Her tone was soft, almost careful, but she didn't look away from Alden.

Eli and Ryan exchanged a glance before Ryan spoke. "We were together. At my place. Mason was with us." Mason gave a stiff nod, jaw tight.

Then Alden's attention landed on me.

"I was home. Alone." My voice barely reached him; it sounded thin even to me.

He raised an eyebrow. One small movement, but enough to slice through whatever scraps of composure I had left. "Alone? Anyone who can confirm?"

"No."

A silence settled.

Then Finn stepped forward. He didn't make a show of it; he just moved, calm and steady, like he'd been waiting for precisely this moment. His voice, when it came, was quiet but firm enough to cut cleanly through the tension.

"Sadee wasn't alone."

I blinked.

He looked at me, briefly, just enough to ask without asking, then turned back to Alden.

"We were together Friday evening. Hung out, talked, got some food. She was with me."

For a heartbeat, Finn's words wrapped around me like a shield I didn't know I needed. The pressure in my chest eased, just slightly, like I'd been allowed one breath after too long without any.

But the relief didn't last.

Mason's eyes slid toward me, narrowing as if recalculating everything he thought he knew. His gaze lingered too long, heavy with suspicion, or curiosity, or something worse. Disappointment. Anger.

Indigo's stare was different. Hurt. Distant. Her dark eyebrows knit together just enough to sting. It wasn't judgment, it was confusion threaded with something that felt like betrayal, like she thought she'd missed some chapter in a story she thought she knew by heart. I met their eyes briefly, a flicker of panic rising inside.

I *was* alone last night. Finn was lying to the police to protect me. Surely, they'd understand that?

I swallowed hard and nodded just slightly.

Not now.

I'd have to face them later.

Right now, I just needed to keep breathing. To stay upright. To not fall apart under the weight of Finn's lie, and the truth it covered.

Chapter Twenty-Two

I didn't want to admit it, but the truth was simple enough. I really had been alone Friday night. After school, I went home, shut the door, and tried to forget everything. No one knew. Not Mason, not Indigo, not even Finn.

So, when Finn told the cops we'd been together, I couldn't say anything. I didn't want to drag anyone else into this mess. Part of me was grateful, he was covering for me, protecting me. But another part of me felt exposed, like I'd just made the line between us thinner, more fragile.

Mason's eyes had been sharp when Finn said it, like he didn't believe it, or maybe he wished it wasn't true. Indigo's hurt looked deeper, like I'd betrayed something between us. I couldn't face them. Not yet.

I kept replaying the moment over and over, wondering how long Finn had planned it.

The worst part was that he hadn't even looked at me when he said it. Just stood there, arms loosely crossed, voice level and disinterested. "She was with me," like it was the most obvious thing in the world. Like we'd talked more than we had this past week.

The officer had paused, scribbling something into a weather-worn notepad, eyes flicking between us. I'd forced a nod, quiet and shaky, and that had been enough. For now.

But everything after that was a blur, blue and red lights painting the pavement in stuttering pulses, Maya's voice rising and falling in outrage somewhere behind me, the crunch of gravel as students were herded toward their cars in pairs or kept back for more questions. The air had smelled like wet bark and something metallic. Probably blood.

Cassie had found me at one point. Her hands were trembling, her sequined lavender dress reflecting the red and blue lights. She didn't ask me anything. Just touched my shoulder and said, "I'm sorry," and I didn't know what she meant. For Nick? For everything? For the fact that nothing felt real anymore?

And Indigo—she stood stiff as stone on the other side of the caution tape, arms wrapped around herself like armor. Her face was blank, but her eyes weren't. They burned. At me. At Finn. At something deeper.

We weren't allowed to leave until after one in the morning. They let us ride with friends or parents, but I didn't want either. I sat on the curb and waited for the police to stop caring, for the tape to come down, for someone to give me permission to disappear.

When my phone buzzed with a message from Mason—*you okay?*—I didn't answer. I couldn't. What was I supposed to say? *No, but I'll lie about it tomorrow?*

By the time I got home, the sky was that inky black that swallows everything, no stars, no moon, just shadow stretching over shadow. I didn't turn on the porch light. I didn't even bother locking the door behind me.

Inside, the house felt too quiet. Too still. The kind of stillness that made the air feel heavier, like the walls had been listening the whole time and were now holding their breath.

I dumped my phone on the kitchen counter. The screen lit up with missed calls, Mason, Indigo, my mom. I turned it face-down.

My room hadn't changed, which somehow made it worse. My backpack was still slouched in the corner like it was waiting for me to pretend homework mattered. A hoodie I'd worn earlier in the week was still balled up on the floor. I sat on my bed and stared at the window, wondering if Finn had known he was going to lie for me. If he's rehearsed it or if lying just came that naturally to him.

He knew I hadn't been with him. He *knew*.

And why did it feel like it had been for *me*—not out of guilt, or strategy, but protection?

Or maybe I was just desperate to believe someone still wanted to protect me at all.

I pulled my knees to my chest, burying my face in the fabric of my jeans. The texture was rough against my skin, grounding. I wanted to cry, but the tears never came. My body was too drained, like grief had hollowed me out and left only the echo behind.

I stayed like that for a long time. Until the silence stopped being comforting and started feeling dangerous.

Somewhere past two in the morning, I finally moved. I locked the front door. Closed the blinds. Turned off the lights one by one like I was snuffing out parts of myself.

Then I crawled into bed and let the darkness swallow me.

I woke up to rain tapping against my window. Gray light filtered through the curtains, soft and sickly, casting long shadows across my room. For a second, I couldn't remember what day it was, or why I felt so hollow.

Then it hit me all over again.

Nick was dead.

It wasn't supposed to happen this way.

I rolled over and grabbed my phone. No new messages. Just the same unanswered ones from Mason, from Indigo. I left them unread.

Downstairs, Mom was already dressed for church. Her heels clicked against the tile as she moved through the kitchen with practiced efficiency. She looked up when I entered, her expression folding into something careful.

"You don't have to go, if you're not up for it," she said gently, pouring coffee into a mug she always meant to replace but never did.

"I'll go."

She didn't argue. Just nodded and slid the mug across the counter. "There'll be something said for Nick during announcements. I think the Langstons are helping coordinate the service."

My stomach twisted. Of course, Cassie's family would be involved.

I nodded, wrapping my hands around the mug even though the heat stung. I didn't drink it. Just held it.

The car ride was quiet. I watched the windshield wipers drag back and forth, slicing the rain into neat little halves. The clouds hung low, pressing against the town like they wanted to smother it. Everything looked washed out, like even the color had decided to give up for the day.

The parking lot was full when we pulled in. People were hugging tightly in the lobby, whispering things like *"so young"* and *"such a tragedy"* and *"he was always so funny, remember that skit he did when he was in third grade?"* like that could undo anything.

I didn't see Finn. Or Indigo.

But Mason found me after service, his hair still damp from the rain and a strange look in his eyes. He didn't look angry, not quite.

"Lunch?" he asked.

I hesitated.

"It wasn't a question." He grabbed my arm and led me toward Lou's diner.

Lou's smelled like syrup and burnt toast, like always. The booths were half-full, mostly families and old couples and kids still in their church clothes. Someone's baby was crying near the window. The usual chatter buzzed low, but it felt distant.

Mason didn't wait for a hostess. He slid into our usual booth in the back, the one near the jukebox that hadn't worked in months. I sat across from him, the leather seat sticking slightly to the backs of my thighs.

He didn't open the menu. Just stared at me.

"You looked like a ghost," he said finally. "When Finn said that. That you were with him."

His tone wasn't cruel, just observant, quietly cutting in the way only Mason could be. The kind of remark that made you realize how much he'd noticed even when you thought you'd kept your mask on.

I traced my finger along a crack in the table's laminate. "Yeah, well. I wasn't expecting it."

"Weren't expecting it, or it wasn't true?"

My gaze flicked up. His eyes were green, and too steady. He wasn't letting this go. Not until he carved out whatever truth I was hiding from him.

"I don't know why he said it," I said. Not a lie. Not really.

Mason leaned back. The leather of the booth creaked beneath him. The movement was slow, deliberate, like he was trying to take a step back emotionally, but his eyes never left me.

"You didn't correct him."

"What would you have done? Told the cops I was home alone, with no alibi?"

"Maybe," he said. "If it was the truth."

There it was again, that something in his voice, that thing he did when he wasn't yelling but still made you feel like you'd been slapped. He wasn't accusing me. But he wasn't *not*.

I picked at the corner of my napkin, nails scraping over the table as the silence between us started to stretch too tight.

The waitress came and left with our orders, two burgers, two waters, no small talk. She barely glanced at us, probably used to this kind of tension by now. Mason didn't take his eyes off me the whole time.

"I just don't get it," he said after she left. "Why Finn? Why would *he*, of all people, lie for you?"

"I don't know."

He studied me, jaw tense. "I don't buy that. You're not stupid, Sadee. You don't just let people do things for you without figuring out what they want in return."

I didn't answer. Mostly because I didn't have an answer.

Or maybe I just didn't want to admit what I knew.

I stared out the window. Rain gathered in tiny rivers along the edge of the glass, distorting the world outside, people blurred, trees bent out of shape, everything just a little wrong. The sound of it hitting the glass was soft and rhythmic, like a second heartbeat under the surface of everything.

"I didn't ask him to lie," I said.

"That's not what I'm asking."

Mason's voice had softened, but it wasn't any gentler. If anything, it felt more dangerous, like he'd put down the sword and picked up a scalpel.

I turned back to him. "Then what are you asking?"

He leaned forward, elbows on the table. "I'm asking if you *wanted* him to."

That caught me off guard. I blinked. "What?"

"You've been... distant. For weeks," Mason said. "Ever since winter break. And I kept telling myself it was school, or stress, or whatever. But now Finn's in it? Finn, who you barely ever looked at before December? You never cared about any of my friends until after that party, and suddenly he's lying to the cops for you like you two have some secret connection?"

"Mason—"

"No," he said, voice low but tight. "I'm trying, Sadee. I've been trying. But I feel like I'm always one step behind with you, and I'm tired of guessing."

I looked down at the table. "It's not about Finn," I said finally. "Not really."

"Then what is it?"

I hesitated. My mouth was dry. I took a sip of water, trying to steady myself, but it didn't help. I needed to change the subject, in a convincing way.

"You know how people keep saying maybe someone knows who's behind it?"

Mason stilled. "Yeah."

I didn't say anything else. Just looked at the table.

He looked at me carefully. "Sadee, what are you saying?"

"I'm saying I think he… I don't know for sure. The way he kept showing up. Hanging around. Watching people. Watching Indigo. He knew something."

Mason didn't speak. His eyes narrowed slightly, unreadable.

"And now Finn's making sure I'm not left without an alibi," I continued, "like he's trying to keep me out of something I don't even understand yet." My stomach churned at the lie. I hope Mason didn't notice.

"You think he knows more than he's saying."

"A lot of us do."

Mason exhaled, dragging a hand through his damp hair. His fingers left small trails of water on the tabletop, drops beading along his knuckles.

"This is starting to sound like a conspiracy theory." Mason chuckles. "You sound like Ryan."

"Is it?"

That quiet hung between us. Just the buzz of the other diners, the scrape of silverware on ceramic, the soft hum of old speakers overhead. Everything in the diner went on like nothing had changed.

But something *had*.

"You just sound too confident that people know too much."

"My subconscious is sure of it."

A silence settled between us and I wondered if I'd said too much. I'd just accused his best friend of lying to us.

"You trust him?" Mason asked finally.

"Finn?"

He nodded.

"I don't know," I said. "But I know he doesn't lie without a reason."

"And you think he's doing it to protect you?"

"I think he's doing it to protect *something*. I just don't know what yet." Also, not technically a lie.

Mason leaned back, arms folded. His gaze wasn't angry anymore, it was distant. Like he was trying to solve a puzzle without all the pieces.

"If you ever find out," he said, "promise you'll tell me."

I nodded. "Promise."

But even as the word left my mouth, it felt flimsy. Like a scrap of paper caught in the wind. I wanted to mean it. I wanted to trust that, if I ever did understand what was happening, I'd be brave enough to say it out loud. But the truth was, I didn't know what I'd do.

Because what if understanding meant seeing things I couldn't unsee?

The rain had slowed to a mist by the time I left Lou's. Outside, the world smelled damp and hollow, like it was holding its breath.

I walked slowly, feeling every step echo somewhere deep in my bones. The sidewalk shimmered with a thin sheen of water, reflecting the streetlights in fractured gold. My hoodie clung to my arms, sodden and heavy, the fabric dragging against my skin with every movement.

Mason's words echoed behind me as I walked, unsteady on the slick pavement. *"If you ever find out, promise you'll tell me."* I wanted to. I really did. But I didn't know if I could. If I really wanted to.

And Finn, he lingered in my thoughts.

He didn't have to lie. I can take care of myself.

And more than that, why did I want to believe he had a reason for all of this that I could live with?

I passed a house I'd trick-or-treated at as a kid, the one with the crooked porch and the blue door. A jack-o'-lantern still sat outside, collapsed in on itself, forgotten. The sight of it made something twist in my chest, like even the things that were supposed to be over had left their ghosts behind.

When I reached my street, everything felt too quiet. Like the shrill silence that came after a scream. I could feel the stillness pushing against me, trying to get under my skin.

At home, the door creaked louder than it should when I unlocked it.

I dropped my purse by the stairs and kicked off my wet shoes. The floor was cold against my bare feet.

In my room, the shadows pooled like ink beneath the dresser and the desk. I flipped on my lamp, but even the soft yellow glow couldn't push them all the way back.

I stared at the ceiling, trying to will the questions away, but they came anyway.

Who did Finn think he was protecting?

What did Mason really see in me?

And how much longer could I pretend I didn't feel like I was standing on the edge of something sharp and dark, waiting to fall?

I peeled off my wet hoodie and tossed it to the floor. My shirt underneath clung to my skin like it didn't want to let go. Everything felt tight. Suffocating. I ran a hand through my hair, tangled and damp, and sat on the edge of my bed.

For a second, I imagined walking downstairs and telling my mom everything. Just blurting it out: "I wasn't with Finn. I was alone. And I know something terrible is unraveling, and I don't know how to stop it."

But what would she say?

Would she believe me?

Would she even understand?

A memory surfaced, something small. One night, years ago, I'd had a nightmare and crept into my parents' room. My mom had pulled me into bed beside her and said, "There's nothing out there that we can't handle together."

I used to believe that.

Now I wasn't sure.

Outside, a distant dog barked. The wind rattled the windowpane.

I closed my eyes.

My phone buzzed. I willed myself not to pull it out and look at it, but something inside me felt like I had to.

The man hangs in the balance, his fate tied to your courage or mistake.

—— ——— —— — ——————— ——— ——————————.

My throat closed.

I stared at the words, rereading them until they stopped making sense.

Then I looked at the empty spaces below them.

And I knew, this wasn't over.

Not even close.

I read the message again. Then again. I held the phone so tightly my knuckles turned white, my fingers trembling against the edges of the screen. For a second, I thought I might drop it. Or throw it. Or smash it against the wall just to make it stop existing.

But I didn't. I just stared.

The message wasn't just cryptic. It was a threat wrapped in a riddle, soaked in something that felt almost... personal.

My stomach turned.

What was going on? Nick had been killed. That was supposed to be the end, right?

The shadows in my room stretched longer, as if the message had pulled them closer. I reached for the lamp and turned it off. Maybe it was childish, but the light made everything feel too exposed, like I was on a stage I hadn't agreed to step onto.

My pulse thudded in my ears

I set the phone down on my nightstand screen-up, though I couldn't stop glancing at it, like it might flicker again. Like there'd be another message. A correction. A clue.

Nothing came.

I crawled under the covers and lay on my side, facing the window. Rain streaked down the glass, thin lines like veins across a skin of shadow. I watched it until my eyes burned.

Somewhere in the distance, a car engine started. A door slammed. A dog barked again.

Life went on.

But something had shifted.

The game had started again.

And this time, I wasn't sure I was ready to play.

The ones who hurt you most often hide behind love.

Chapter Twenty-Three

I didn't sleep well.

Not because of the rain or the cold, but because my mind kept circling back to Saturday night; Nick, the cops, Finn's lie. I tried to push it away, but it sat heavy in my chest.

I stayed under the covers longer than I should've, staring at the ceiling until the first gray light seeped in. The room was quiet except for the soft patter of rain against the window. My phone buzzed on the nightstand, a sharp little sound that made my skin crawl. I didn't want to look.

At school, everything felt off.

People didn't say much. They looked past me, or at me, then quickly away. Whispered words hitched in the air but never made it all the way out. Indigo's eyes flicked over me when I rounded the corner, and I saw the question there—did you lie? Did you need him to?

I said nothing.

The hallways smelled like wet concrete and stale coffee, thick with the kind of silence that presses on your ears. Finn stood against a wall, hoodie pulled up, hands tucked deep in his pockets, eyes scanning but never settling. He looked distant, like he wanted to be anywhere but here.

I wasn't sure I wanted to be either.

I found myself drifting toward the usual spot near the lockers, the one where we used to laugh and plan and pretend like the world hadn't cracked open. But today, the space felt too small. Too exposed.

Mason was already there, leaning against the cold metal, eyes shadowed and tight. He caught my gaze and nodded once, no words, but I understood the message. We were all on edge, holding pieces of something none of us could say out loud.

Indigo appeared next, her steps sharp and deliberate. Her eyes swept the group, flicking past me and landing briefly on Finn, who stayed silent against the wall, hoodie still up like a shield. She stopped beside Mason, arms crossed, jaw clenched.

"Has anyone heard from Cassie?" she asked without looking at me.

I shook my head slowly. Cassie had been distant all day, barely speaking when she did. Probably avoiding the group, avoiding the game.

Ryan wandered in next, his usual nervous energy dampened, shoulders hunched like he was carrying something heavier than usual. He gave a small, forced smile when he saw me.

"Hey," he said, voice low.

"Hey," I answered, wishing it was easier than that.

The silence stretched, thick and uncomfortable. Someone cleared their throat, maybe Eli, but no one spoke up.

Finally, Mason broke it. "We can't keep ignoring it."

His words hung there, heavy. The elephant in the room wasn't going anywhere.

Indigo's voice dropped. "No one wants to play again. Especially after… everything."

Finn shifted but didn't say anything.

I could feel the eyes on me then, and the weight of the unspoken question pressed hard: Why were you with Finn? I wanted to tell the truth. But I didn't want to admit why he lied.

My throat tightened. I wanted to scream no, but the fear wrapped around my words like thick fog.

"It's not just a game anymore," Mason said.

It never was.

No one moved.

I swallowed hard, feeling the weight of every pair of eyes, on me, on Finn, on the fragile space between us.

Ryan shifted awkwardly, clearing his throat like he was trying to will the tension away. "Maybe we just need more time… to figure things out."

Indigo's gaze snapped to him, sharp and unforgiving. "More time? What good's that done so far?"

Her voice was low but fierce, cutting through the quiet like a blade.

Finn's hoodie slipped back, and for a second, I caught a glimpse of his face; tense, guarded, unreadable.

I wanted to ask him why.

Because maybe some truths are too dangerous to say out loud.

And maybe some games never really end.

The bell rang, hollow and echoing, but it didn't bring the usual relief. Instead, it felt like a countdown starting over. Another round in a game none of us wanted to play.

The hallway had emptied, voices and footsteps fading into distant echoes as the rest of the group scattered to their first period classes. I thought maybe the worst was behind us. That the silence between Indigo and me would disappear.

But then her hand came crashing against the locker beside me with a crack sharp enough to make my heart jump.

Before I could step back, she shoved me hard against the cold metal.

The sharp edge bit into my shoulder, pain blooming like fire through the dull ache of everything else.

Indigo's eyes blazed, wild and fierce, the storm inside her breaking free.

"Why, Sadee?" she demanded, voice ragged, lips trembling but fierce. "Why were you with Finn Friday night? Alone."

The pressure of her body pinned me, the harsh clang of the locker ringing in my ears. My breath hitched, panic curling through me in waves.

"I wasn't," I whispered, voice barely steady, throat thick. "I swear."

But my words felt small, fragile against the weight of her fury.

She leaned in closer, breath hot and ragged, eyes searching mine like she was trying to unravel a lie I wasn't telling.

"Then why did he tell the cops you were with him?" The question sliced through the quiet like a blade. "Why lie about it if it wasn't true?"

I swallowed hard, the pain in my shoulder pulsing with every shallow breath.

"I don't know," I said, voice cracking.

Indigo's jaw tightened so much I thought it might break.

"Are you lying to me? To yourself?" Her voice was barely more than a whisper now, but it cut deeper than before.

I shook my head, panic rising, tears burning behind my eyes.

The cold metal pressed into my back grounded me, but it wasn't comfort. It was a reminder; of the pain, of the broken trust, of everything I didn't have answers for.

I swallowed, the lump thick in my throat. My shoulder ached where the locker bit into my skin, but I barely noticed.

"I'm not lying," I said, voice tight. "I don't know why Finn said that. I wasn't with him."

Indigo's eyes narrowed. She didn't look convinced.

"Then what is it?" she said, voice low but hard. "Why would he lie?"

I shook my head. No answer. No defense.

She took a step back, the fury in her eyes still burning, but now mixed with something colder. Disappointment, maybe.

"I don't know if I can trust you," she said.

I wouldn't trust me either.

The silence that followed was worse than the shove, heavier than the pain.

The hallway felt impossibly quiet after Indigo stalked away, her footsteps fading into the distance like thunder retreating after a storm. My shoulder throbbed where the locker had bitten into me, every pulse a sharp reminder of what just happened.

I was still trying to catch my breath when a shadow shifted near the corner.

Finn stepped out, hoodie pulled low, but his eyes locked on mine with a steady calm that unsettled me more than anger ever could.

"I didn't mean for it to get like that," he said quietly, voice low. Too calm. Like he was keeping a secret.

I swallowed hard, the knot tightening in my chest. My voice barely found air. "Why did you lie Finn? I had everything figured out."

He hesitated, jaw tightening like he was weighing something heavy. "It wasn't for you. Not exactly."

Confusion twisted in my gut, sharp and bitter. "Then who?"

Finn scratched the back of his head, the flicker of something cold behind his eyes. "Clearly I didn't have an alibi either."

I blinked. "So, you lied to cover yourself. And me."

He shrugged, almost casual, but the weight behind it dragged the air from my lungs. "Sometimes the truth isn't the safest choice."

His eyes snapped back to mine; steady, unreadable.

"We don't have much time," he whispered. "Be ready."

Then he turned and slipped back into the shadows like he'd never been there at all.

The moment Finn disappeared, the hallway seemed to inhale a long, slow breath, leaving me stranded in a quiet I wasn't ready for. My shoulder throbbed where the locker had pressed into my skin, each pulse a sharp reminder that nothing felt safe anymore.

I pressed my palm flat against the cold metal, trying to steady the tremble in my fingers. My breath came out in ragged little bursts, uneven like my thoughts. Why did it feel like the truth was a weapon we were all too afraid to wield?

I slid down the locker, letting my back rest against the cold metal, but the chill didn't seep through the ache in my chest.

I'd made a terrible mistake.

My thoughts spiraled, twisting around all the pieces that didn't fit. Finn's lie, Indigo's fury, Mason's quiet despair. The game wasn't just a game anymore; it was something darker, something that clawed at the edges of every breath I took.

I wanted to scream, to throw the phone across the hallway and shatter it into a thousand pieces. But the silence around me pressed harder than any noise ever could. It filled the empty spaces, wrapping around my heart like cold hands.

What was I supposed to do? Who could I trust when the people I cared about looked at me like I was part of the problem? They were supposed to trust me. Believe me. They've known me for years.

A sharp pang hit my shoulder again where the locker had bruised me, grounding me back to the moment. I closed my eyes, willing the pain to dull, but it pulsed like a heartbeat, reminding me I was still here. Still caught in this nightmare.

I need an ibuprofen. I rubbed the tender spot through my shirt. It felt ridiculous to worry about something so small when everything else was falling apart, but the ache was a reminder I wasn't invincible.

I glanced up as footsteps echoed down the hall. A teacher paused nearby, concern flickering in his eyes. He hesitated, then gave me a small nod before moving on, leaving me alone again.

Why was I still here? Why hadn't I gone to class?

I needed to get out. To move. But something held me in place, a mixture of fear, confusion, and the creeping knowledge that I was avoiding something that was inevitable.

I decided I didn't have the energy for any of my classes today. Slowly, I pushed off the locker and started walking, the empty halls stretching ahead like a maze. The rain had slowed, but the air still hung heavy with that damp, cold weight.

When I got home, the familiar creak of the front door felt strangely loud in the quiet morning. Mom was alone, sitting at the kitchen table, her eyes lifting as I stepped inside. She studied me quietly, the kind of look that said she wanted to ask but didn't know how.

"Hey," I muttered, dropping my backpack by the door.

"You okay?" she asked, voice soft.

I shrugged, forcing a smile I didn't feel. "Just a headache. Still caught up on… everything with Nick."

She nodded slowly, but I caught the flicker of worry in her eyes.

I pushed the thought down, telling myself it didn't matter. *Served him right,* I thought bitterly, but the words felt like something I shouldn't say aloud.

I made my way to my room, the familiar walls both a comfort and a cage. I shut the door, slid down against it, and let the quiet swallow me whole.

The light filtered through the blinds, pale and hesitant, stretching long shadows across the floor.

I stayed on the floor for a while. Not sleeping. Not moving. Eventually, I crawled into bed and pulled the blanket over my head like it could protect me from everything outside it.

I don't know how long I stayed like that. Long enough for my mom to knock softly and slide a glass of water and two ibuprofen into my room without saying anything. Long enough for the rain to stop.

The quiet wasn't peaceful. It felt heavy. Like the house was holding its breath with me.

Sometime in the late afternoon, my phone buzzed against the nightstand. I didn't want to look. Not yet. Not now.

But it buzzed again. And again.

Like it was pulling me back, dragging me into something I wasn't sure I was ready for.

Finally, I reached for it, my thumb trembling as I unlocked the screen.

A message from Eli: *Anyone doing anything tonight? Feels like we've been in a graveyard all day.* I stared at it, my chest tightening. Feels like that.

Then Maya's message appeared: *I literally can't sit here and think about Nick anymore. I need a distraction.*

I wanted to type back, *Me too,* but I couldn't.

Cassie's message appeared next: *Same. This silence is worse than the game.* The silence was suffocating. Like the quiet was swallowing us whole.

I looked away from the screen for a moment, blinking hard.

Indigo's text came quickly after: *Agreed. Where?* I held my breath, waiting for an answer, hoping for something. Anything.

Eli replied: *Mason's? He usually doesn't care if we show up.* But then the screen went quiet. No one typing. No responses.

Maya broke the silence: *Did anyone ask him?*

Ryan: *I texted. No response yet.*

My thumb hovered over the screen. I could say something. I should say something. But I didn't.

Cassie tried to stay hopeful: *Maybe he's asleep? Or just off his phone.*

I swallowed hard. Maybe.

Indigo's message popped up, sharp and sure: *Unless he says not to, I'm going.*

Eli: *Same.*

Maya: *We'll figure it out when we get there.*

Cassie: *We always do.*

The chat went silent again. I stared at the screen. The last message glowing softly. My fingers felt heavy. Like they carried the weight of everything unsaid. Everything I couldn't say. I felt the pull. The need to be somewhere else. Maybe this was what I needed. I took a slow, shaky breath and typed: *I'll come too.* My thumb hovered for a moment. Then I pressed send.

I didn't know what I was expecting tonight to be. A normal hangout? A disaster? Maybe both. Maybe neither. But at least it was something.

A distraction.

I set the phone down, rolled over, and closed my eyes. Outside, the clouds started to part, just barely, and the gray of the day gave way to the slow creep of dusk.

A distraction sounded good in theory, something to break the silence, to shove the heaviness under a pile of noise and laughter. But the truth was, I didn't feel ready. Not really. Not yet.

Still, I told myself that maybe being around them would be better than being alone with my thoughts, those dark, twisting thoughts that circled back to Nick's lifeless eyes and the questions that had no answers.

I dragged myself out of bed and pulled on jeans and an old hoodie, the fabric soft but unfamiliar against my skin like a small comfort. My fingers trembled as I tied my shoes, and I swallowed down the knot tightening in my throat.

The rain had stopped outside. The sky was a bruised mix of purple and gray, heavy with the promise of more storms. I glanced out the window, watching the dark clouds crawl away like they couldn't quite decide if they were done.

The walk toward Mason's street was heavy with silence, broken only by the crunch of gravel beneath my shoes. Each house I passed stood still, shutters drawn and porch lights off, like the whole neighborhood was holding its breath. My heart pounded harder the closer I got, like my body knew something I didn't.

Mason's porch was dark.

His car wasn't in the driveway.

I stopped at the curb, stomach knotting. He wasn't home.

For a second, I just stood there, staring. My mouth opened like I might call his name; but nothing came out.

I turned, retracing my steps slowly, thinking I should call someone. Eli, maybe. Indigo. Anyone. But what would I even say?

Before I could decide, someone called my name. "Sadee!"

I looked up.

Everyone was sitting in Mason's empty driveway. Indigo, Maya, Eli, Ryan, Cassie. Scattered across the concrete like they'd just given up waiting on the porch. I hadn't even seen them when I passed.

I walked over, heart in my throat. "He's not home," I said, lowering myself onto the ground beside Indigo. She didn't look at me, just pulled her arms tighter around her knees.

"No," Maya muttered. "We've been calling him."

"Texting too," Ryan added. "Nothing. Not even a read receipt."

"That's not normal," Eli said. He had his phone in hand, screen dim. "Mason always texts back. Even if it's just a thumbs-up."

"I thought maybe he was ghosting me," Maya said, forcing a short laugh. "But then he didn't answer Indigo either."

Indigo finally looked up. Her eyes were rimmed red, lashes clumped like she'd rubbed them too hard. "He wouldn't ignore me," she said quietly.

Ryan shifted beside her. "Could he be out with someone?"

"Someone not in our friend group? Who does he hang out with that's not us?" Maya snapped.

"I dunno, the other football boys?"

"When it's not football season? This is stupid." Maya leaned back and looked up at the sky and sighed. "This is all just so, so stupid." She whispered.

"He would've said something." Cassie's voice was soft, but certain. "He always does."

The group fell quiet.

I stared down the road, willing his headlights to appear, wishing he'd come flying around the corner with some dumb excuse. "Forgot my phone." "Took a nap." "Battery died." Something. Anything.

"Maybe he went out for food?" Ryan tried.

"Without texting? He lives on his phone." Maya frowned. "No offense, but it's kind of gross."

"Maybe he dropped it," Cassie offered.

Eli rubbed his jaw. "And what, lost his car too?"

That shut everyone up again.

We sat there, a loose circle in a driveway that didn't belong to any of us. The air was starting to cool, but the heat from the pavement clung to my skin. Somewhere in the distance, a dog barked once.

"Did he say anything earlier?" Indigo asked, "Before school ended?"

"No," Eli said. "He seemed fine. Quiet, but not weird."

"He didn't show up to fourth period," Ryan said. "I just assumed he was skipping."

"He wouldn't," Indigo said. "Not with all this—" Her voice broke off. She pressed her lips together hard.

All this.

Nick.

The game.

Everything spiraling out beneath our feet.

"I should've said something," I muttered, my voice catching. "He wasn't acting like himself today. Barely talked."

Maya looked over sharply. "Why didn't you tell us that earlier?"

I shrugged, the guilt twisting tighter. "I thought maybe we just… fought. Maybe he was still caught up on our conversation from yesterday. Or he needed space. I don't know. I didn't think it meant…" I couldn't finish the sentence.

"Meant what?" Maya spat.

I didn't answer. I didn't have to. Everyone was already thinking the same thing.

Cassie's hands twisted in her lap. "If this is part of the game…"

"We don't know that yet," Eli said, but even he didn't sound convinced.

"What if it is?" Indigo's voice cut through the quiet like a crack of thunder. She wasn't yelling, but something about the way she said it made my chest go cold. "What if the game took him?"

"Don't say it like that," Ryan muttered, running both hands through his hair. "The game can't take people. It's not magic or some cursed movie script. There's a person behind it. A real person. Don't make it sound like some fictional scenario when it's very much real."

"She's not wrong," Maya said. "First Nick. Now Mason's just… gone?"

The word echoed in my head. *Gone.*

I stared at the spot where Mason's car should've been, half-expecting it to flicker into existence if I stared hard enough. Like I'd missed it. Like I'd imagined the whole thing.

"It doesn't make sense," Eli said. "He would've fought back. If someone came after him, we'd know."

"Unless he never made it home," Cassie whispered.

The silence that followed felt sharp enough to cut.

"I keep thinking maybe he's just hiding," Maya said. "Like… maybe he needed space."

"He'd tell us," Eli said. "He'd tell me."

And I believed him.

Eli always knew where Mason was, always. The two of them had this unspoken radar, like they were tuned to the same frequency.

If he was scared, we should all be.

I stared up at the house again. Porch still dark. No sign of life.

Cassie was the one to finally say what we were all thinking. "We should've never played. Every single senior should've ignored that first text. Everyone."

No one disagreed.

Then, like clockwork, like it had been waiting for the exact right moment to strike, all of our phones buzzed at once.

A group text. To just us.

A message from an unknown number.

And we hadn't guessed a letter.

What you see is never the whole story.

Chapter Twenty-Four

It was just a picture. No lines, or spaces, or dots, or ambiguously worded questions asking for letters.

It was just a picture.

Of Mason.

Bound, bruised, and slumped against a rough concrete wall. His shirt torn, smeared with dirt and dark, drying blood. Cuts crisscrossed his face, and his eyes stared wide and terrified, like he couldn't believe what was happening.

Seconds later, a single text followed the picture.

An address.

A pit opened in my stomach.

Indigo's fingers trembled as she held her phone, eyes fixed on the screen.

No one spoke.

The silence stretched between us, thick and suffocating.

"Guys..." Maya's voice was barely a whisper, fragile and scared.

"We have to get there," Eli said, his voice steady but urgent, cutting through the stillness like a lifeline.

I nodded slowly, swallowing the knot tightening in my throat so hard I thought I might choke. The game was far from over.

"Let's go," I said, already pushing myself up from the cracked driveway, heart pounding like a drum.

Ryan scrambled to his feet beside me, pulling his jacket over his head.

The tension was a living thing, wrapping tight around us as we scattered, scrambling into cars, the night suddenly charged with a wild urgency.

Somewhere in the chaos of scrambling into cars and shouting names, my eyes caught the empty stretch of Mason's driveway, the place where Finn should have been. But he wasn't. Not there. Not anywhere.

A cold knot tightened in my stomach.

Where was Finn? Had he ever been with us at all?

He *should not* have done this.

This had gotten too out of hand.

"Wait." The word slipped out, barely a breath, but my voice caught in my throat like it was choking on itself. "Where's Finn?" I desperately needed him to be in someone's car, ready to help us save Mason.

Indigo froze mid-step, the sharp lines of her face hardening as her eyes flicked over the shadows surrounding the house. Her breath hitched, and her fingers clenched into fists at her sides. The tension in the air twisted tighter.

"He wasn't with us?" Maya echoed, brow furrowing deeply, confusion and something darker flashing in her eyes.

"No," Ryan said slowly, shaking his head. His usual nervous energy was gone, replaced by a quiet seriousness that made my chest tighten even more. "He never showed up. I figured he was busy or… I don't know."

The weight of Ryan's words dropped like a stone into the deep water of my chest. The cold ripples spread, flooding me with dread I couldn't shake.

Finn wasn't coming with us. That means… no. *Do* not *go there, Sadee. He wouldn't have done this.*

For a long moment, no one moved. We just stood there, rooted to the cracked pavement, caught in the heavy silence that stretched between us like a widening gap.

The night seemed to press closer, shadows creeping up the sides of the house, the faint rustle of leaves stirring the chill that slithered down my spine.

Cassie bit her lip nervously, eyes darting around the group like she was searching for some impossible answer. Her voice was low, tentative, but filled with a strange mix of fear and suspicion. "Do you think… Finn sent it?"

The question hung between us, thick and heavy, stirring the silence into something fragile and dangerous.

Eli didn't look up as he slid his keys from his pocket, jaw clenched tight. "Does it matter?" His voice was steady, but every word held urgency. "We don't have time for this."

Whatever was coming next was already in motion, and waiting wasn't an option.

The air around us felt thick, charged with dread and adrenaline, each breath sharp and shallow.

Without another word, we scattered, some running to their cars, others piling into Eli's.

The night had turned cold, the sharp sting of autumn creeping into the air, but the heat of fear burned hotter beneath our skin.

Engines roared to life one by one, a cacophony of urgency and mechanical growls piercing the silence. Tires crunched against the gravel driveway, sending small stones scattering in every direction as the cars peeled away from Mason's house, headlights cutting through the dark like knives.

Inside the cars, the silence was almost suffocating, thick and heavy. No one dared break it. Not with everything still so raw, so fragile.

I jumped into the passenger seat of Eli's car. His hands gripped the steering wheel tight enough to turn his knuckles white. The weight of what lay ahead pressed down on me, heavier than the night itself.

The stakes had just skyrocketed.

Every mile we drove, the dread grew heavier. I wanted to turn the car around, to run away from it all, but something deeper pushed me forward. Guilt. Fear. A desperate need to face the nightmare we'd been dragged into.

The silence around me was suffocating.

I caught a glimpse of Eli beside me, jaw tight, fingers twitching as he held the steering wheel. None of us had the words to break the quiet.

I wanted to ask if anyone believed Finn was still on our side. But the question hung unsaid, drowning in the space between us.

What if he'd done this? He wouldn't. What if Mason's fate was tied to something none of us could understand?

The road stretched ahead, empty except for the faint glow of the moon hiding behind thick clouds. The trees arched over the highway, their twisted branches like clawed fingers reaching out to snatch us into the dark.

My breath caught in my throat as the car's headlights finally caught sight of the house; the place we'd been sent to.

The old house sat fifteen minutes past the edge of town, a lonely relic abandoned by time and the living. Its shadow loomed against the darkened sky, a crooked silhouette of twisted wood and rotting shingles. The windows, once glass panes reflecting sunlight, were now boarded up with weathered plywood, uneven and splintered, a patchwork of neglect. Paint peeled like shedding skin, revealing the layers of faded color—grays, whites, and streaks of stubborn brown— beneath. The entire structure seemed to sag, leaning slightly to one side as if burdened by centuries of secrets, secrets that had long since seeped into the cracked foundation.

We were alone. No other cars, no distant voices, not even the rustle of wind through the trees. Just us, standing in the shadow of something that refused to die. The night was thick, oppressive, pressing down on us like a weight that threatened to crush every ounce of resolve. The air smelled damp, earthy, and rotten, a mixture of mold, decayed wood, and something metallic that made my stomach churn. It was as if the house itself had been made of darkness.

The car slowed to a crawl, headlights piercing the darkness, sweeping across the house, illuminating the old worn-out boards. The engine's hum was the only sound for a moment, then silence fell again as the vehicle stopped. We stared at it, hesitant, unsure if we dared to approach. But there was no turning back now.

My shoes crunched on the gravel driveway, dry leaves crackling beneath my weight. The weeds had overgrown the path, tangling around my ankles, whispering stories of neglect and forgotten sins. Each step felt heavier than the last, as if the house itself was pulling us in, eager to swallow us whole.

My heart hammered as we approached the front door: splintered and hanging slightly off its hinges.

Finn was there. He stood just inside the shadowed doorway, his figure dark against the faint glow of the moon behind him. His shoulders were hunched, sagging under an invisible weight that had clearly worn him down over time. His face was a mask of exhaustion and sorrow, the lines around his eyes deepened by grief and fatigue. In his hand, a shiny revolver rested loosely, the barrel pointed downward, almost limp. His grip was trembling slightly, as if holding onto the weapon was the only thing keeping him tethered to some fragile sense of control.

My breath caught in my throat, a sudden constriction that made my chest tighten. I stared at him, trying to process what I was seeing, this boy who had once been full of fire, now hollowed out, haunted. His eyes, dull and sunken, flicked briefly to meet mine, and in that glance, I saw a ghost of the person he used to be.

Behind him, slumped against the wall, was Mason. His body was twisted and mangled, a grotesque testament to violence. His shirt was torn to shreds, ragged and soaked with blood. His skin was ashen, bruised purple and black, with streaks of fresh crimson staining his chest. Two dark, fresh holes marred his torso, flesh punctured and bleeding, the exit wounds still oozing. It looked as if a beast had torn into him, relentless and savage.

He was dead. No doubt about it.

No.

I stifled a scream.

The weight of that realization slammed into me like a physical blow, knocking the wind from my lungs. It was as if the air had thickened into a leaden substance, pressing down on my chest, squeezing the breath from me. The silence around us was deafening, broken only by the faint, irregular heartbeat in my chest, and the creaking of the wood under us as someone shifted their weight from foot to foot.

Finn's eyes met mine again, and in that fleeting moment, I saw something raw and unfiltered, pitiful, haunted, and utterly broken. An ocean of despair swirled behind those weary eyes, and I knew he was carrying a burden heavier than any of us could understand.

"He couldn't understand," Finn said softly, almost inaudibly. "He was supposed to stick with me through everything. But he didn't. He couldn't."

His words sounded like a confession, a plea. He moved slowly, almost carefully, as if afraid to disturb Mason's corpse or shatter the fragile calm that hung over the house. His hand, holding the revolver, trembled slightly as he raised it, the cold metal catching what little light remained. The click of the trigger was sharp, jarring in the heavy silence, an unspoken promise, a final act of despair.

He herded us inside with a steady, hollow voice. "Come in. We're not done yet."

The house seemed to close in around us, the walls pressing inward, the darkness swallowing the faint glow of the moonlight. It was as if the very structure was alive, hungry, eager to claim us as part of its cursed history. Each creak of the floorboards, each whisper of the wind outside, seemed amplified, echoing in the emptiness.

And in that moment, I realized how far this nightmare had dragged us. How little chance we had left to escape the shadows that clung to this place, to Finn, to Mason's lifeless body. Our footsteps echoed softly as we crossed the threshold, the air thick with decay and regret. The house was a catacomb of memories, secrets, and sins buried beneath layers of dust and darkness.

I felt a shiver run down my spine as Finn's grip on the revolver tightened slightly, his knuckles whitening. His eyes flicked around the dim interior, shadowy corners, abandoned furniture draped in tattered sheets, and the faint outlines of broken windows that let in slivers of cold, silver light.

He moved slowly, almost gently, as if afraid to disturb the stillness that surrounded Mason's lifeless form.

"Sometimes… friendship isn't enough," Finn continued, the words bitter and raw. "I didn't want this. But it had to be done."

His voice cracked, trembling with emotion, regret, pain, something darker I couldn't quite place. He took a slow, shuddering breath, then looked away, as if he couldn't bear to meet our eyes any longer. "He fought back. He didn't want to die. But I had to do it. I had to." He lowered the gun just slightly, the trembling in his hand betraying how much he was holding back. "He was my best friend," Finn said again, voice cracking into a whisper. "He was supposed to stick with me through everything."

He took a step forward, looking at my haunted expression. "You never know how far people will go, do you?" He chuckled a little bit, tears shimmering in his eyes. "But I couldn't let him tell," Finn said, voice barely audible now. "He knew too much. About me. About everything." Finn glanced at me. "Somehow he, he, he was piecing together my part in this." He trailed off.

A long silence stretched as he stared at Mason's body, as if trying to grasp what he'd done, or what he'd lost. "My best friend is gone. And I did it. I killed him."

We didn't speak. We couldn't. The shock hit us like a punch to the gut. Maya's hand flew to her mouth, eyes wide in horror. Indigo's face was pale, her jaw clenched tight as she fought back tears. Ryan's fists clenched, tears pooling in his eyes but held back, rage bubbling beneath the surface.

Eli sank to his knees next to Mason, who'd been his closest friend since first grade. Mason was everything to us.

And I just stood there, looking at him. He deserved better.

Finn looked up at us, his shoulders trembling, tears streaking his face. His voice was broken, pitiful. His eyes searched ours, pleading for understanding, for forgiveness, or maybe just for someone to see how broken he really was.

"He was my best friend," he repeated one last time, voice almost a whisper.

And in that moment, everything our group thought we knew shattered beneath that truth—Finn's darkness, his broken heart, and the terrible choices that had led to this nightmare.

I stepped forward before I could stop myself.

Just one step. Just enough to feel the weight of all their eyes shift toward me, then toward Finn. The silence stretched out, thick and suffocating, each second dragging like a heavy stone pressing down on my chest. I could feel my heart pounding loudly in my ears, a deafening drumbeat that seemed to echo in the stillness of the moment. My mind raced, trying to formulate some kind of defense, some way to diffuse the tension, but my body moved on instinct, a reflex I couldn't control.

"Finn," I said, my voice trembling slightly despite my efforts to sound steady. "You don't have to do this."

He didn't look at me right away. Instead, he remained frozen, as if caught in a moment of internal struggle. His gaze was fixed downward, watching Mason's blood pooling beneath him like a dark, glossy puddle that refused to stop spreading. The crimson liquid seemed to glow in the dim light, a stark reminder of how thin the line between friend and foe is. The revolver in his hand trembled minutely, the only sign of the turmoil raging inside him. His knuckles were white, clutching the weapon so tightly that it looked as if he might crush it at any second.

When he finally turned his head to face me, his expression was unreadable, like a mask hiding a storm of conflicting emotions. His eyes held a faint glimmer, a flicker of something unspoken. Was it regret? Resignation? Or perhaps a desperate attempt to hide his true feelings behind a veil? I couldn't tell. All I knew was that the silence between us grew heavier, filled with unspoken words and the weight of what was about to happen.

"You think I don't?" he asked softly, the words slipping out in a whisper. His voice was fragile, almost hurt, as if the question hurt him more than he was willing to admit. The softness contrasted sharply with the weapon in his hand, creating a dissonance that made my stomach churn.

I swallowed hard, trying to keep my composure. My throat felt tight, and my palms were clammy, but I forced myself to speak. "I think you're scared," I said, voice steady despite the tremor in my chest. "And I think you're not the only one."

Something flickered behind his eyes, but it was gone in an instant, replaced by a cold, distant stare that sent a shiver down my spine. It was like watching someone strip away their humanity, revealing only the barest core of who they truly were in that moment. Or maybe, just maybe, he was trying to convince himself that this was the right thing to do.

"I'm trying to help," I added, my voice softer now, more pleading. I wanted him to see reason; I wanted him to understand that there was still a way out, a path back from this brink of destruction.

But Finn's laugh cracked through the tense air like a whip, sharp and sudden. It wasn't amused or sarcastic; it was unhinged, raw with emotion. Not joy, not mockery, but something darker. Anger, despair, perhaps even madness. The sound made my skin crawl, and I took a step back, instinctively clutching my own trembling hands to steady myself.

"You're not helping anyone, Sadee," he spat, voice cold and venomous. He turned fully toward me now, the trembling hand that held the revolver no longer shaking but steady, controlled. "You're a liability."

That single word hit me like a slap across the face. Liability. A burden. A weakness that could get us killed. I could feel the sting of it deep in my chest.

He took a deliberate step closer, the gun lowered slightly but still threatening. An unspoken warning, a challenge. His eyes bore into mine, searching, judging. "You think you're good at hiding," he said, voice sharp and cold, "but you're not. You're sloppy. You're soft. You'll get us caught."

My breath hitched, my heart pounding harder now. The accusation felt like a punch to the gut. I had always strived to be careful, to be strong. But in this moment, I felt exposed and vulnerable. I wasn't used to that.

And then, the word that echoed in my mind—*us*.

The word reverberated through the tense silence, loud and undeniable. It was a collective, an unspoken bond we'd all shared, forged in the fires of our desperation. But now, hearing it slip from his lips like that, it sounded like a threat, a challenge, a warning of what could happen if anyone faltered.

From behind me, someone muttered it aloud, Maya, maybe, or Cassie. "Wait. Us? What do you mean 'us'?"

I didn't move. Couldn't. My body was frozen, caught between the need to protect and the fear of what might happen next. The atmosphere grew heavier, the air thick with unspoken truths and dangerous possibilities.

Finn realized what he'd said a split second too late. His lips parted, and for a moment, I saw a flicker of panic, perhaps regret, cross his face. His eyes widened just slightly, and I sensed a shift in his demeanor, a crack in the carefully constructed façade.

But then… he smiled.

Only a little, just a twitch of his mouth that barely registered. It was enough to send a ripple of unease through me. That smile was cold, calculated, a mask hiding something darker beneath. The kind of smile that didn't reach his eyes, a smile that said he knew exactly what he was doing, and he was enjoying the power he held in that moment.

My stomach twisted, bile rising in my throat. The scene felt surreal, like I was watching a nightmare unfold in slow motion.

He turned slowly, surveying the group with a new, calculating look. Like we were pieces on a chessboard, and he was the only one who knew the rules. The confidence in his stance was unsettling, the calmness in his expression a stark contrast to the storm raging inside him.

"Oops," he said softly, the mockery in his voice dripping with sarcasm. "Didn't mean to slip up."

The storm in his eyes was unmistakable now. And as I looked at him, I realized that I was standing on the edge of a precipice, too, unsure whether I could hold my ground or if I would fall into the darkness he was summoning.

In that moment, I understood that nothing would be the same again. The line between friend and foe had blurred, and no one knew who they could trust. The only thing I knew for certain was that the stakes had never been higher, and every second that ticked by brought us closer to an inevitable reckoning.

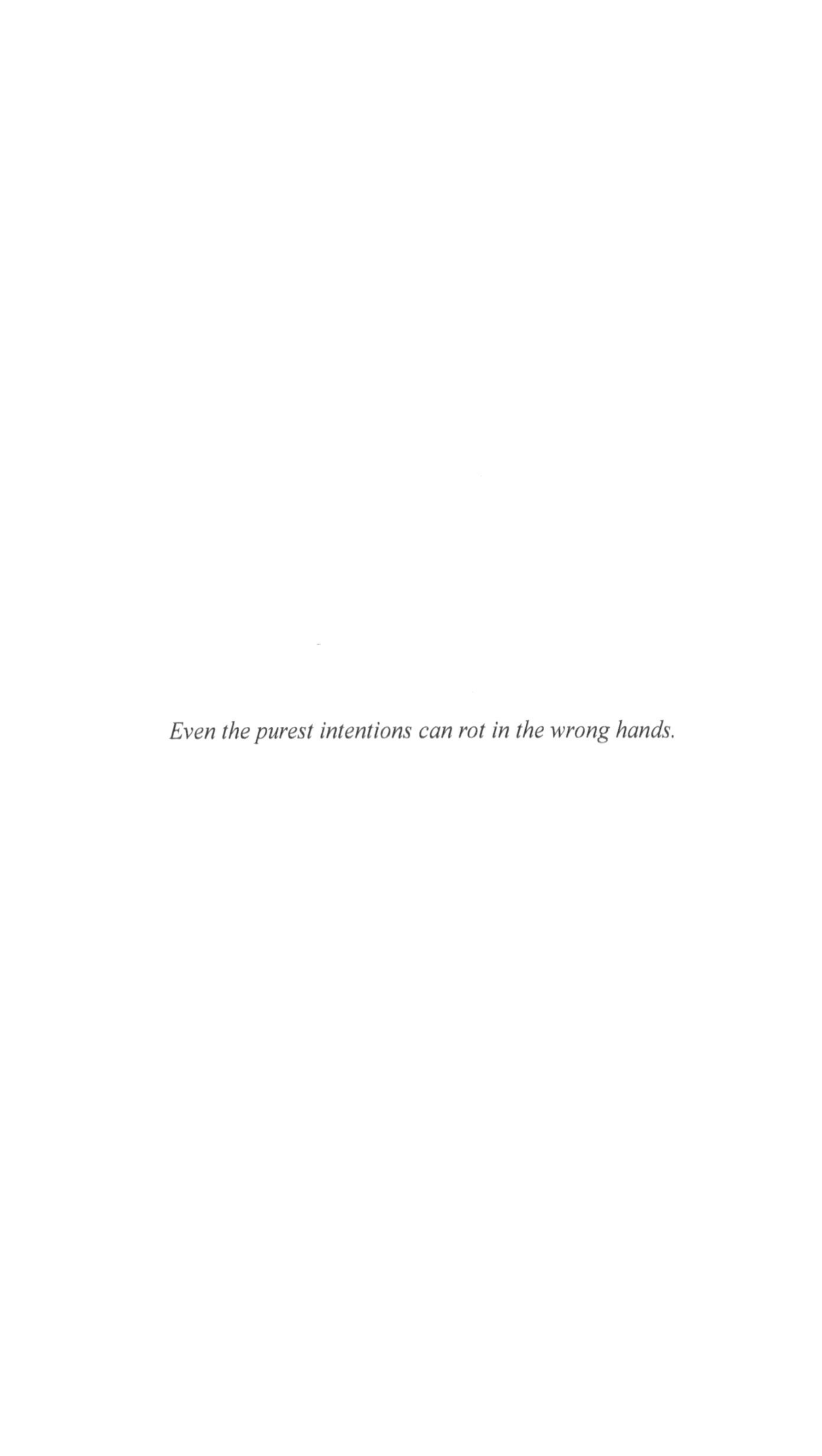

Even the purest intentions can rot in the wrong hands.

Chapter Twenty-Five

The house was heavy with silence, thick enough to suffocate. Finn stood in the dim room, the gun in his trembling hand aimed directly at Eli. His eyes, once calm, even protective, were now cold and unrecognizable. His face was a mask of rage and despair, and every muscle in his body tensed as if holding back a storm.

Indigo's mouth opened, then closed again, her face a mask of shock and heartbreak. Her brain struggled to process what she was seeing, her *"perfect"* boyfriend, the boy who had always taken care of her when darkness threatened, now pointing a gun with deadly intent. Tears welled up but she couldn't move, couldn't speak.

Finn's gaze flicked over her, his expression devoid of warmth. "I did it for you." He whispered. "After I realized what I'd done." He took a ragged breath. "You're going to get me in trouble. You're going to ruin everything."

Behind him, Mason's bloodied, mangled body lay sprawled on the ground, eyes staring unseeing into the void. Mason was gone, horribly, brutally gone, and Finn's grip on the gun was a trembling tremor of regret and rage. Every breath he took was a challenge, every heartbeat a countdown to something irreversible.

Eli took a step forward. "Finn," he extended an arm toward him. "Why don't you hand me the gun, and then we can figure out what to do about Mason's body."

But Finn didn't turn. His eyes were fixed on Indigo, and his finger was a hair's breadth from pulling that trigger. The room seemed to hold its breath, waiting for the inevitable.

Suddenly, from behind Finn, a voice cut sharply through the tension. "Finn, stop!" It was Cassie. Her voice was firm but trembling, desperate. "Put the gun down! Please—"

Finn glanced toward Cassie but ignored her.

"Did any of you know I was the one who sold Nick the drugs?" He spun toward us, a dark chuckle escaping him. Indigo's eyes widened in disbelief. "I bet you didn't."

Indigo's face drained of color, her breath hitching in her throat. Her eyes flickered from Finn to me, to Ryan, as if the room had started to spin and she couldn't quite catch her bearings.

Her legs gave out, and she slumped against the wall. "No…"

Her breath hitched, and then, without warning, she doubled over, hands clutching her stomach. The sound of her retching filled the room—loud and unrelenting. She couldn't stop it, her body betraying her in the worst way.

I could hear her struggling for breath, her body trembling as she emptied the contents of her stomach onto the floor. She was silent for a few seconds—silent except for the ragged breaths and the sound of her sobbing.

Her voice was barely a whisper when it came, shaking and hoarse. "You… you did this. Finn… *you*—"

But she couldn't finish. Her body shook too violently, the horror of it all cutting off her words. It was like her insides were being ripped apart, and she couldn't process it all fast enough.

Finn stared at her. "I didn't know what, I didn't—I swear, I didn't know what he was going to do with them. Never asked. Never cared. Until I, until I heard what he, what that monster, did." He scratched at a fresh scrape on his eyebrow, a souvenir from his fight with Mason.

Indigo's breath hitched, the weight of Finn's confession crashing over her like a wave. "Why... why didn't you say anything?" Her voice cracked, barely more than a whisper.

Finn's eyes darkened. "Because no one would've believed me. Nick had his grip on everyone, friends, dealers, cops, maybe even some of you." His finger twitched on the trigger, the gun's shiny metal gleaming faintly in the low light.

Eli took another careful step forward; hands raised like a shield. "Finn, this isn't you. We can fix this. We just need to calm down and talk."

A bitter laugh escaped Finn's lips, dry, hollow, and ragged. "Fix this?" He spat the words, venom thick in his tone. "I'm too... I'm way too far gone to fix." His gaze flickered toward Mason's lifeless body sprawled on the floor, twisted and broken in ways that words could barely capture. For a fleeting second, something like pain softened the hard edges of his face, but it was gone almost as fast as it appeared.

Cassie's voice trembled but grew steadier. "We're your friends, Finn. We're scared. Please, just put the gun down."

Finn's grip on the weapon loosened fractionally, the barrel dipping just a hair, but his shoulders stayed rigid, coiled tight like a spring ready to snap. The air between them seemed to freeze, every heartbeat echoing in the oppressive silence. The faint, uneven rhythm of Finn's breathing was the only sound, ragged and raw.

Indigo wiped a tear from her cheek, voice firm despite the quake inside her. "You have to let us help you. This isn't the way."

Finn's jaw clenched so tight I thought it might snap. His laugh came out bitter, almost bitter enough to taste; sharp and dry like cracked glass scraping down my throat. "Help?" The word hung in the air, twisted and dark. "There's no helping me."

The room suddenly felt smaller, like the walls were folding in, squeezing the air out of my lungs. My breaths came shallow, too loud in my ears, like they were the only sounds left in the world. Every heartbeat hammered in my chest, loud and irregular, a frantic drum signaling the storm I'd been trying to avoid for so long.

Then his eyes found mine.

Cold. Accusing. Piercing through everything I wanted to hide.

"I couldn't have done this all alone, right, Sadee?" His voice was low, dangerous, a poisonous thread woven tight with blame and darkness. He stumbled back a few steps, scratching the back of his head with the muzzle of the revolver.

My stomach dropped as if someone punched it from the inside. I swallowed hard, desperately holding back the scream rising in my throat. My voice felt like it was trapped, lodged somewhere deep and unreachable. I wanted to look away, to shut out the fire in his gaze, but I couldn't. My body betrayed me, frozen where I stood, pinned by those dark eyes.

Everything inside me screamed to run, but my feet refused to move.

Before I could say anything, Eli's voice cut through the thick silence. Angry. Hard. His words broke like a whip, sharp enough to sting.

"How dare you drag someone else into this?" Eli said, his tone laced with disgust and fury. "This is your mess."

Finn snapped his head toward Eli, eyes blazing with pure hatred. "Shut up," he snarled.

Eli didn't back down, not an inch. His chest rose and fell with steady breaths, the kind of calm that comes only with confidence. He took a deliberate step forward, closing the distance between them, and his voice dropped low, cold and dangerous.

"Make me."

I felt every second stretch out, slow and suffocating. The air trembled with tension so thick I could taste it, metallic and bitter on my tongue.

My heart pounded so hard I thought it might break free from my ribs and burst through the floor. My hands clenched into fists at my sides, nails digging into my palms.

Finn's finger twitched on the gun's trigger. It moved just slightly, the barrel dipping a fraction, and everything in me screamed *no*.

The gunshot ripped through the air like thunder, loud enough to shake the walls and shatter the silence that had strangled us. It was a brutal, sharp crack that echoed in my ears, ringing so loud it drowned out everything else.

Pain exploded in my chest, not from the gunshot itself, but from the crushing weight of what had just happened. My breath caught in my throat as the shock slammed into me, raw and immediate.

I blinked against the sudden brightness of the room, eyes wide and searching.

Eli's eyes went wide, shock and pain flashing across his face. His body jerked backward, stumbling as he collapsed to the floor, clutching his chest. Blood seeped from the wound, spreading across his shirt.

Finn's expression shifted; wild, raw, and almost unrecognizable. The rage hadn't left him; it had only fractured, cracked open to reveal something darker, colder.

He stepped back, as if shocked by his own actions, the gun shaking in his hand. His breathing was ragged, every inhale a battle.

"Eli," I whispered, voice breaking as I stepped forward. My legs felt unsteady, like I was wading through water, but I forced myself closer. "Eli…"

His eyes flickered to me, and he tried to smile, a small, broken thing that didn't reach his eyes. "Sadee…" he gasped, voice thin and strained.

Cassie rushed forward, hands trembling as she dropped to her knees beside Eli. She pressed a hand to the wound, trying to stem the bleeding, but the horror in her eyes told me it wasn't going to be enough.

"No," I breathed, shaking my head in disbelief.

"Stay with me," I whispered, my voice cracking. "Please, Eli, stay with me."

I swallowed back the tears that threatened to spill and looked up at the others, Cassie, Indigo, Ryan, Mason's lifeless form, the blood on the floor. None of us could forget what had just happened.

Eli's grip on my hand tightened for a moment, a fleeting spark of life and stubborn will, then faltered. His body shuddered once, small but violent, as if trying to fight the inevitable. I pressed my palm harder against his skin, willing him to hold on, to keep breathing, to not slip away.

His eyes, which had been searching mine just moments before, slowly glazed over, the light dimming until they were nothing more than glassy mirrors reflecting the cold room around us. The warmth drained from his face, his features slackening into a blank expression that tore through me with brutal finality.

My thumb lingered over the pulse point in his neck, counting the slowing beats until there were none. His breaths became shallow, irregular, each inhale a whispered struggle that seemed to steal more from him than it gave back. I counted them silently, desperate to will the next one, and another, and another.

But then they stopped.

His chest no longer rose and fell beneath my hand. The life I had felt moments ago slipped away like water through clenched fingers, impossible to grasp, leaving only a hollow silence.

A sob caught in my throat as I leaned closer, heart breaking in fragments too sharp to bear. I traced the lines of his face gently, memorizing every detail, as if by holding on tighter I could keep him here, could hold back the darkness closing in.

Around us, the room seemed to tilt, colors dulling and sounds fading to a distant hum, like I was submerged underwater, disconnected from everything but the crushing weight of loss pressing down on me.

He died in my hands. I felt the shiver of his last breath pass against my skin, and then… nothing. The warmth bled away, leaving a strange heaviness in his place. It was almost hypnotic, watching the life drain from him, how quickly the body becomes just a body. No one talks about that part; how quiet it is. I didn't flinch. I just kept holding him, as if I'd been waiting for this moment all along.

Cassie's quiet sobs broke the silence, and Indigo's trembling breath filled the space between us. I didn't want to look away, but the grief was so raw it burned behind my eyes.

Eli was gone. His blood pooled under his body, mixing with the blood still slowly spreading from Mason's lifeless form.

And none of us could pretend it wasn't real.

"What is wrong with you?" Maya whispered, voice trembling.

Finn's head snapped toward her like he'd been yanked on invisible strings. His eyes, dark and unreadable, locked on hers. No flicker of remorse. No hesitation. Only the kind of cold calculation that made the air feel heavier.

"What's wrong… me…" His words broke apart, uneven and sharp-edged. "You want to know what's wrong with me?" His voice pitched up, not in volume but in pressure, as if every syllable was squeezing through a clenched jaw.

Finn slowly sank to the floor, pressing his palms hard against his temple, fingers curling and uncurling in some restless pattern.

"My head… what I did… what *we* did… it was necessary…" His gaze sharpened, narrowing on Maya like he'd forgotten the rest of the room existed. "Nick… he deserved it."

Slowly, he pushed himself back onto his feet.

The revolver dangled from his right hand, the muzzle swaying lazily, never quite still. The faintest curl of a smile ghosted across his lips, an empty smile, something that didn't belong on the face of someone holding a gun in a room full of bleeding bodies.

The silence thickened, broken only by the faint metallic sound of his thumb brushing the hammer.

I could hear my heartbeat in my ears.

His foot scraped against the floor, a slow step forward.

No one breathed.

The gunshot split the air with a vicious snap. Light flared from the muzzle, and the smell of burnt powder hit before the ringing in my ears had even settled.

Maya jerked backward, a startled gasp tearing out of her before she crumpled, hitting the ground with a dull, final thud.

The acrid sting of gunpowder filled my throat, making each breath feel sharp and sour.

Cassie's scream ripped through the air, jagged and endless. She dropped hard to her knees beside Maya, hands hovering over the wound like she didn't know where to touch first. "No, no, no… come on, stay with me—" Her voice cracked, splintering into desperate sobs. "You can't leave me, Maya… no, no you can't…" She pressed her hands harder to the blood, shaking her head like that would change anything.

Maya didn't move.

"Breathe, Maya, please—" Cassie's words collapsed into raw, wordless sounds, her tears splashing onto Maya's shirt. Her shoulders shook with every sob.

Indigo pressed herself to the wall, her body rigid, fingers digging into the plaster as if she could claw her way through it. Her mouth moved, but no sound came out.

Ryan was frozen in the doorway, his knuckles white on the frame. "You're sick," he finally managed, the words trembling like they didn't want to leave his mouth.

Finn didn't even glance at him.

He stood over Maya's body like he was considering his work, breathing steady, revolver still hanging loose in his grip.

I looked at the gun. Six chambers. Two emptied into Mason. One into Eli. One into Maya.

Two left.

My mind ticked over the number like it was a fact in a math problem. Two more. Two more lives before the cylinder was empty.

Cassie's sobs blurred into the background hum in my ears. All I could hear, all I could focus on, was the sound of the revolver's weight shifting as Finn's hand adjusted, the faint creak of his knuckles, and the slow, steady rhythm of his breath.

Finn's gaze didn't linger on Maya for long. It flicked up, slow and deliberate, scanning the room like he was deciding which piece to move next in some game only he understood.

Cassie's sobs hitched, turned sharp. She looked up at him, eyes red and wet. "You—" Her voice cracked in the middle. "You monster."

His head tilted slightly, the faint smile returning like a muscle memory. "Monster," he echoed under his breath, as though testing the shape of the word. "No… no, not monster."

Cassie flinched when he shifted his weight, but she didn't move from Maya's side. Her fingers stayed pressed to the wound, even though her hands were slick and shaking.

Indigo's back scraped against the wall as she slid sideways, trying to get further from him, eyes darting between the revolver and the door.

Ryan took one slow step forward. "Finn—"

Finn's head turned to face him so fast I'm surprised his neck didn't break.

Ryan froze.

Finn's breathing deepened, but not with exertion, it was controlled, even. Too even. "Don't," he said. The single word hung in the air, heavy and final.

The revolver shifted, barrel lifting just enough to make everyone hold still.

I watched him, my pulse steady despite the chaos. He didn't see them, not really. His eyes slid over Ryan, Cassie, Indigo… until they caught mine for the briefest second. And in that second, I saw it; the flicker of something that wasn't rage or calculation. Something else.

Recognition.

Then it was gone.

He turned the gun slightly, idly, like someone absentmindedly twirling a pen. "Tick… tock…" he murmured, the words soft but audible.

Cassie's sobs turned into shaky, angry breaths. "You can't just—"

The barrel swung toward her, and she shut her mouth instantly.

Finn took a half-step closer. The floor creaked. His thumb brushed the hammer again, slow and deliberate.

The smell of gunpowder still clung to the air, mingling with the copper tang of blood until every breath felt like it was coating my tongue.

Indigo finally spoke, her voice trembling. "Why… why are you doing this?"

Finn's lips twitched, not into a smile, but something closer to a grimace. "Because it needed to be done."

No one moved.

The silence stretched so long I could hear the faint tick of the old wall clock.

Two left.

My mind repeated it again, slow and certain. Two more. And the thing was… I couldn't decide if that number scared me. Or comforted me.

Finn's fingers flexed around the grip, a slow, deliberate motion, as if he could feel the lives left in the cylinder. His eyes wandered over each of us again, weighing something invisible in his mind.

Cassie stayed hunched over Maya, her sobs thinning into shallow, broken breaths. Indigo's hands were pressed flat to the wall, palms pale, as if she could melt right into it. Ryan hadn't moved since Finn looked at him, his jaw tight, his chest barely rising.

I didn't move either.

The revolver stopped swinging. It was aimed low, almost lazily, but we all knew how fast that could change.

Finn took a deep breath, his nostrils flaring like he was drawing in the scent of the room, blood, sweat, and gunpowder. "It's quiet now," he murmured. "Quieter than I thought it would be."

No one spoke.

A faint sound came from somewhere beyond the doorway, a floorboard groaning under weight. Finn's head tilted, listening.

My mind looped back to the gun.

Two bullets left. Two more lives. Two more of us that weren't getting out of here alive.

He wasn't finished yet.

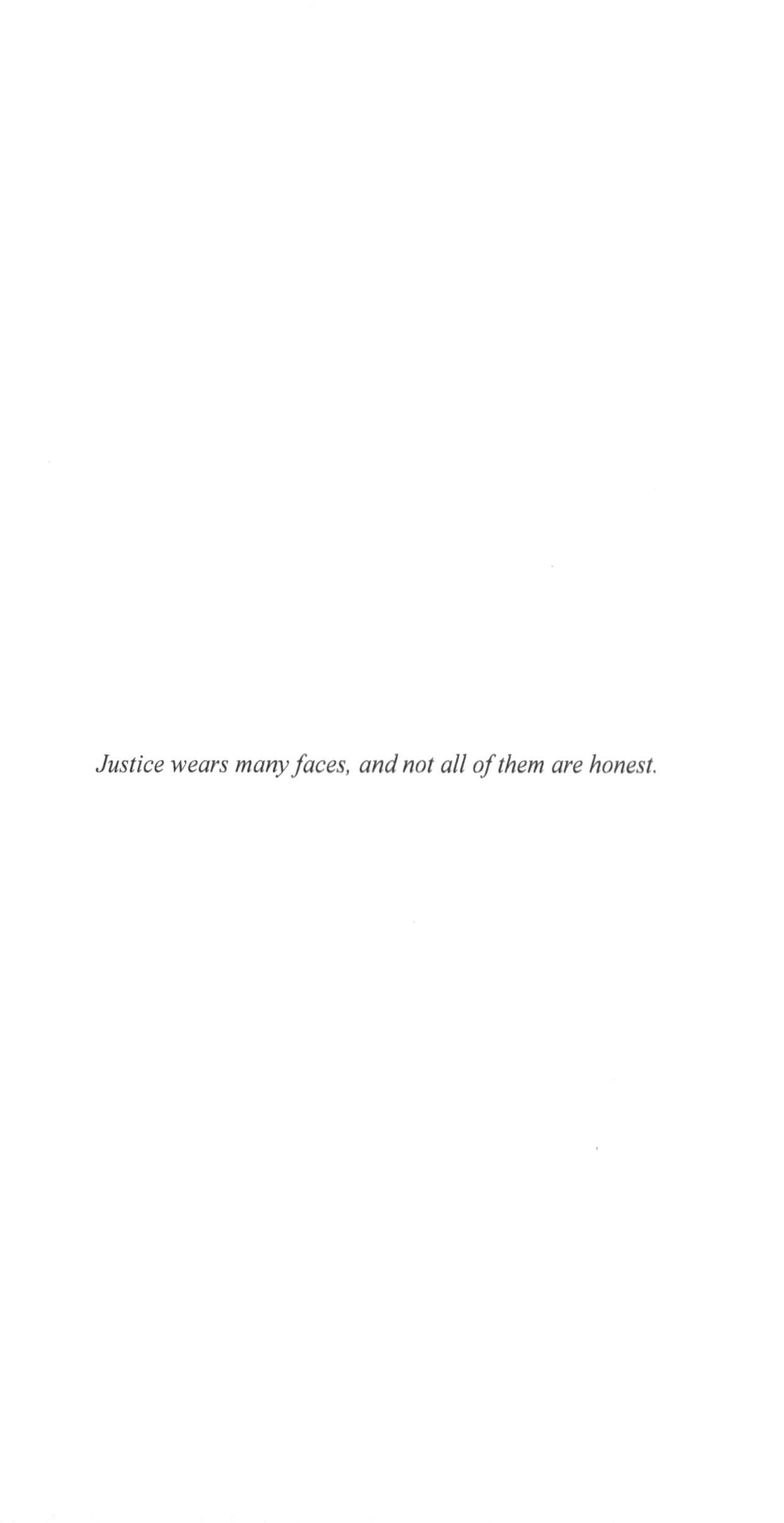

Justice wears many faces, and not all of them are honest.

Chapter Twenty-Six

Madness is never sudden, though it often looks that way from the outside.

By the time someone points and says *there*, there is where it began, the roots have already tunneled deep, tangled through thought and memory until even the sufferer can't tell where one ends and the other begins. Madness grows quietly. It waits. It studies the contours of its host's mind the way ivy spreads across a wall, patient and deliberate, knowing it will win in the end.

The poets say grief is the match that strikes the flame. The philosophers say it's the mind's attempt to make sense of the senseless. But Hamlet knew better. Or perhaps he only pretended to. *An antic disposition*, he called it, a performance wrapped so tightly around himself that no one could tell where the act stopped, and the man began. Was it strategy? Or surrender? Was the madness a mask… or the truest face he ever wore?

Those who watched him thought him reckless, erratic, dangerous. They saw only the splintering edges of his grief for a father stolen from him, for a crown stolen from his blood. They didn't see the careful pattern beneath the outbursts; the way each feigned wildness had a place in the design, each cryptic word bent toward revenge. That's the trouble with madness: it wears the same clothes whether it's genuine or deliberate. Sometimes even the wearer can't tell the difference.

It's tempting to believe madness must be loud. That it comes with shouting, or sobbing, or the smashing of plates against a wall. But there are softer kinds. There is a madness that moves like water seeping into wood grain, imperceptible at first, until the structure begins to warp. There is a madness that makes people smile in all the wrong places. A madness that lets them stand perfectly still while the world burns behind their eyes.

And there is the madness of revenge, a fever that eats the boundaries between justice and cruelty. That is the kind Hamlet understood best. He knew the taste of a grievance so raw it could rot a man from the inside. He knew that to strike back is to step willingly into a kind of performance where every gesture, every word, every silence serves the story you want others to see. He knew, too, that once you step into that role, you might never find your way out of it.

Here, now, in this small corner of the world, no crowns have been stolen. No ghost has stepped out of the dark to speak its vengeance. And yet, the air feels thick with the same fever Hamlet carried. People are beginning to move as if their strings are being pulled by something they can't see. Words come with barbs hidden beneath them. Glances linger too long. Even silence has started to feel like a loaded weapon.

Maybe it began weeks ago. Or months. Maybe years. Maybe madness has been here all along, crouched in the shadowed corners of every friendship, in the cracks between every truth told and every truth swallowed. The tragedy is not in the moment it appears. It's in the moment you realize it's too late to tell the difference.

The room held its breath. Cassie's sobs were ragged, spilling out in broken gasps as she clung to Maya's still form. The quiet around us felt heavier than the gun in Finn's hand.

I couldn't tear my eyes away from Finn. His fingers flexed slowly around the revolver's grip, the barrel swinging low like a pendulum marking time we didn't have. His eyes scanned us, cold, unreadable, but I could feel him weighing something, like a scale balanced on silence.

Cassie's cries became sharper, rawer. Her body shook as if she wanted to break apart, and suddenly, something fierce snapped inside her. Without warning, she pushed off Maya's lifeless chest and lunged at Finn.

"Cassie—!" I barely got the word out.

She was on him, grabbing at his jacket, her nails raking the fabric. Only Finn's hand moved, it jerked upward in a flash, while the rest of his body stayed frozen.

The shot tore through the air.

Cassie fell without a sound, her body folding in on itself like a broken thing.

Cassie didn't make a sound when she hit the floor. No cry, no gasp; just the dull thud of flesh meeting wood. I stared down at her, heart hammering so loud it felt like it might tear right out of my chest. Blood bloomed dark and quick against the floorboards, spreading like ink in water.

This *really* had gone too far.

Finn's face was unreadable. His eyes didn't flicker with regret or panic. He just stood there, the gun still in his hand, as if waiting for something else.

Maya's body was still at my feet, but now it was Cassie who was broken too. I couldn't breathe. My throat tightened. The weight of what just happened slowly settled over us.

Indigo was pressed flat against the wall, her hands splayed out on the peeling paint. She didn't move. Didn't blink. Her eyes were wide, but empty. I could almost hear the frantic beating of her heart behind the silence.

"Cassie..." The name fell out of my mouth again, but it felt hollow.

Finn finally spoke. His voice was low, barely above a whisper, but the words landed hard.

"Too many. It wasn't—I wasn't..." Finn hits his head. "It never ends."

He took a step forward, slow, deliberate, like the gun was an extension of himself and not a weapon meant to kill. His eyes flicked to mine for the briefest second. Cold, distant. Like I was part of some equation running through his mind.

"None of this matters," he said. "Not really."

I wanted to shout at him, to demand he stop, to make it all stop. But my voice was gone, swallowed whole by fear.

Cassie's body twitched, a weak, broken movement. Her eyes fluttered open just a little, glassy and unfocused.

Someone, maybe Ryan, took a shaky step forward, but I was frozen. Watching. Waiting. Afraid to believe.

Finn's gaze swept the room again. "You think I want this? You think this was supposed to be easy?"

His hands clenched the revolver tighter, knuckles white.

Indigo finally swallowed a breath and shifted, her back sliding down the wall until she sat, trembling but still silent.

I wanted to reach out to her, to say something, anything, but I felt trapped inside my own head. *This is your fault.*

The noise in the hallway had stopped. The silence inside the room was broken only by Cassie's shallow breaths and Maya's stillness.

Finn turned away from us, pacing slow, back and forth, rambling more to himself than anyone else. "Justice... it wears many faces. Sometimes mercy is weakness. Sometimes silence is betrayal."

I wanted to hate him. I wanted to scream at the cruelty, the cold calculation that put us here.

But all I could feel was the chill creeping through my bones.

My mind spun, trying to make sense of the madness, of the broken pieces scattering around us.

It wasn't supposed to go this far.

I noticed the small things: the way Finn's jaw twitched, the shaking in his fingers, the way his eyes seemed to lose focus for a heartbeat before sharpening again.

The mask was cracking.

And I was the only one who knew what was behind it.

The seconds stretched out, each one heavier than the last. Cassie's shallow breaths came in ragged, uneven spurts, like she was holding on to a thread too thin to bear her weight. I could see the faint rise and fall of her chest, but the life bleeding onto the floor screamed otherwise.

I wanted to crawl across the room, to do something, anything, but my legs felt useless. Frozen by the shock that stole my breath and scattered my thoughts like leaves in a storm.

Finn's voice broke through the silence again, low and relentless. "You all think this is about right and wrong, justice and innocence. You don't see the bigger picture."

His gaze flicked to each of us in turn; sharp, accusing. Like we were pieces to be moved, sacrificed if necessary.

I swallowed hard, the taste of copper thick in my mouth. Fear curling in my belly, tightening around my ribs like a boa constrictor.

Indigo remained pressed to the wall, unmoving. Her fingers trembled against the rough paint, but she said nothing. Eyes wide, unblinking. The kind of shock that kills from the inside out.

Ryan finally found his voice, a hoarse whisper that barely broke the spell. "Why, Finn?"

Finn's lips twitched in something like a smile, but it didn't reach his eyes. "Because someone has to."

"Someone has to what?" I asked, voice small, barely a whisper.

"To end it," he said. "To stop the cycle before it breaks us all."

The words sounded like a twisted prayer. Like a promise made to no one but himself.

I glanced down at Cassie again. Her fingers twitched, just a faint, useless movement, and then stilled.

"No more moves," Finn said, voice dropping to a whisper that felt like a threat.

I blinked, trying to hold onto something real, but the room was spinning, the walls closing in.

Every heartbeat echoed like a warning.

I realized, suddenly, that this wasn't just about a game anymore.

This was survival.

And some of us wouldn't make it.

The air felt impossibly heavy, like the walls were pressing in, trapping us in a nightmare we couldn't wake from. Cassie's body lay still, but her shallow breaths reminded me she was still hanging on, barely. Her sobs had stopped, replaced by a quiet that was worse.

Finn's eyes met mine again, dark and steady. It wasn't just a look; it was a warning. Something in his gaze said there was no turning back. No mercy left in this game. No winners, only survivors.

"Clear the board," he muttered again, shaking his head slowly, as if trying to rid himself of some invisible weight. "No more mistakes. Play the game."

I couldn't hold it in anymore. The anger welled up inside me, burning hot and sharp. "You're insane," I whispered, voice trembling but fierce.

"This isn't justice or revenge." Ryan mumbled. "This is murder."

Finn's face twitched, maybe a ghost of a smile, or maybe a grimace. "Call it what you want," he said. "I'm done waiting."

Indigo finally moved, her voice a breathless rasp. "Please... Finn…just stop."

But Finn ignored her. He took a step toward Ryan.

Ryan scrambled back, eyes wide, mouth open but no words coming.

Finn's breathing grew heavier, ragged. "You don't understand," he said, voice cracking like the last fragile thread holding him together. "This has to end before it's too late."

I stared at him, searching for anything human beneath the madness, but all I saw was a man drowning in his own darkness.

The room fell silent again, except for the soft, broken breaths of Cassie, and the distant thud of something heavy settling in my chest.

I felt tears sting in my eyes, but I blinked them away. There was no time for that.

Because somewhere deep inside, I knew weakness wouldn't help me escape this alive.

My breath caught in my throat. The room felt smaller, tighter, every heartbeat thundered so loud I thought it might burst through my chest.

Cassie's eyes fluttered closed again, her body still as a stone. I swallowed the lump rising in my throat.

Finn's voice cut through the haze, low and urgent. "This ends tonight. No more lies. No more games."

Indigo shuddered against the wall, her face pale, lips trembling. She looked like she wanted to scream but couldn't find the sound.

I wanted to reach for her, to steady her somehow, but my own hands were trembling too badly to move.

Finn's gaze flicked to Maya's lifeless form again, then back to us. "You don't know what it's like to watch everything you love burn and do nothing."

My heart twisted. I knew exactly what that felt like. But this, this was something darker, colder.

"I'm not like you," I said, voice barely steady.

He laughed, a short, bitter sound that echoed in the room. "You think you have a choice?"

The gun shifted in his hand, the barrel pointed just a little higher, aimed right at my head.

I felt the cold rise up my spine and settled there like ice.

Cassie's shallow breath caught again, a fragile thread holding her to the world.

Finn took a step forward, slow and sure, eyes locked on mine. "You know Sadee, you're a lot like me."

I shifted my weight. "No. I'm not."

Finn chuckled. "But you are."

I didn't answer. Not because I didn't have one, but because anything I said now could tip the balance the wrong way. My mind flicked through every possible response, every angle, every mask I'd worn since this started.

He stepped closer, the gun still loose in his hand, but not casual. Never casual. "You think I don't see it? You think I don't remember who sent the first letter?"

My stomach clenched. It was supposed to keep me from being a suspect. That was the plan. His voice wasn't just sharp, it was clean, aimed exactly where it would hurt.

Indigo's head moved, not much, just a slight tilt, but her eyes were on me now. Ryan, too. I could feel them both looking, like the air between us had thickened.

I kept my face steady. "You're not making sense."

That earned me a small, sharp smile. "Aren't I?"

Indigo's head turned just slightly, her eyes flicking between us. Ryan didn't move, but I felt the shift in the air, the kind of stillness that meant someone was listening too closely.

Finn's gaze swept over the room, pausing on Maya's body, on Cassie's slumped form, on the wall Indigo was pressed against. Then it landed back on me.

"You've been here since the beginning, don't you remember?" He said, almost conversationally. "You've seen every step."

I didn't flinch. "And I've seen enough to know you need to stop."

For a moment, his eyes softened, not with pity, but something stranger. Like he was remembering something only he and I knew.

He tilted his head. "You've changed."

My pulse jumped, but I forced my voice even. "So have you."

That smile again, slow and knowing. "The game changes everyone."

He started to pace, the revolver swinging loosely in his hand. Each turn of his steps brushed the air with threat, a reminder that a flick of his wrist could mean an ending for any of us.

Cassie's breath rattled in the corner. Indigo's fingers pressed harder against the wall, like she could sink straight through it if she tried hard enough. Ryan's gaze moved between Finn and me like he was trying to work out which way the storm was going to break.

Finn's voice cut through it again. "Funny thing about games… once you start playing, you can't just quit. You either win or you don't walk away."

"You can walk away," I said quickly. "Right now."

His eyes narrowed. "That's not how this works."

I held his gaze, willing my heartbeat to stay quiet enough that it wouldn't drown my thoughts. "It's how we make it work."

His laugh was short and humorless. "You think you can make your own rules? You think there aren't consequences?"

Indigo shifted just enough to catch his attention. "You're scaring us," she said, her voice low but firm.

Finn's eyes slid over her, weighing, then dismissed her like she wasn't even worth the bullet. "Fear makes people honest," he said. "It peels them open. Makes them show you who they really are."

His gaze snapped back to me. "You've been honest, haven't you, Sadee?"

The room seemed to shrink around me, the walls pressing closer. "I don't know what you're trying to say."

"You do." His tone was quiet now, too quiet. "You just don't want them to hear it."

I took a step forward, just one, slow enough not to startle him. "What I want is for this to end."

He smiled faintly, and it felt like watching the surface of water before it swallows something whole. "It will."

His pacing stopped. He was only a few feet away now, the revolver hanging at his side but always, always ready.

Outside, the wind groaned against the walls. Something loose banged in the distance, sharp enough to make Indigo flinch.

"Tell me something," he said suddenly. "When you look at them—" he gestured lazily toward Indigo and Ryan "—do you see the same people you started with? Or do you see the ones who survived?"

I didn't answer.

Because the truth was, I didn't see the same people. I hadn't for a while.

And the way he was looking at me told me he knew that.

Finn's gaze drifted to Cassie's body, sprawled on the floor where she'd fallen. His expression didn't change. No grief. No guilt.

Indigo's voice cracked, "Don't look at her like that."

He didn't answer. Just studied the stillness, the finality of it, like it was another piece in a puzzle only he could see.

I took a step forward, my voice sharp. "Leave her out of this."

His head tilted slightly, almost curious. "Out of what, exactly?" He gestures towards Cassie's body. "She's already out."

The silence that followed was worse than the talking. Every sound seemed too loud, Cassie's labored breathing, Indigo's unsteady exhale, the faint ticking of something metal cooling in the corner.

Finn took a step back, leaning slightly against the wall, and I realized he was waiting. For what, I didn't know.

Or maybe I did.

No one spoke.

Finn's knuckles flexed around the revolver's grip, the motion slow, deliberate. He wasn't in a hurry, and that was worse than if he'd been shouting. People who shouted were desperate. People who were quiet had already decided how this would end.

My legs ached from standing still, but I didn't dare move. My mind kept replaying Cassie's fall, the way her body had folded in on itself, the sound it made when she hit the floor. I kept my eyes off her now, because if I looked, it might break whatever thin thread was keeping me upright.

Finn spoke, almost idly. "You know what the problem is with endings? People think they're supposed to come with closure." He glanced toward Maya, then Cassie. "They don't. They just… stop."

Indigo's breath hitched, the smallest sound, but it made his gaze slide toward her. She stared back, pale and rigid, but her hands trembled where they pressed against the peeling wall.

"Finn," Ryan said carefully, "we can talk about this. You really don't have to—"

"Yes, I do," Finn cut in. "You think you know what's going on here, Ryan, but you've only been watching the surface. None of you see the rest of it."

I swallowed hard, my throat tight. "Then tell us."

He smiled faintly, not a kind smile. "Would you believe me?"

I didn't answer. Of course I would. Because deep down, I knew what this was about.

The revolver hung loose in his hand again, but my eyes stayed locked on it. One bullet left. The thought pulsed in my head like a heartbeat.

He took a slow step toward me. "You're different," he said softly. "You understand the cost. You've been paying it all along. Don't you know what you're giving up?"

And the truth is, I did.

I met his gaze, steady, unblinking.

And I knew exactly what it was worth.

The line between justice and vengeance blurs in the dark.

Chapter Twenty-Seven

The air hung thick and still, like the calm before a storm that refused to break. My heartbeat was irregular, each thump echoing loud enough to drown out everything else, the shallow breaths, the creak of the floorboards beneath our feet, even the faint hum of the world outside that somehow felt miles away. Finn's words, the weight behind them, pressed down on me like an invisible hand tightening around my ribs, squeezing the air out of my lungs.

I didn't blink. Couldn't. Not yet.

The room smelled like cold metal and something darker, something raw and sharp, like iron mixed with the scent of old wounds. Cassie's body lay motionless on the warped wooden floor, a fragile reminder that the line between life and death was thinner than I ever wanted to admit.

Finn leaned against the peeling wall, the shadows playing over his face like a mask. His eyes never left mine, dark and unreadable. Waiting. Calculating. Like this had been laid out on a chessboard only he understood, and I was the last piece left to move.

"Do you really want to know?" His voice dropped to a whisper.

I swallowed hard, words stuck somewhere in my throat, tangled with the dry panic clawing at my chest.

Around us, the others were frozen, breaths caught, eyes wide and raw, waiting for the moment to shatter the silence that pressed down on us like a weight. It was a silence so thick it almost had a sound, an oppressive quiet that screamed louder than any words.

But I already knew.

Indigo shifted against the wall, her pale face tight with something fierce and fragile all at once. Her breath was shaky but determined. "Don't let him win," she whispered, barely audible.

Ryan swallowed hard, his Adam's apple bobbing as his eyes flicked between Finn and us. His jaw was tight, muscles clenched, but there was fire in his eyes, a quiet resolve that tried to ignite the heavy air. After a long beat, he lifted a hand slowly, as if asking permission to speak in a room that barely breathed.

"If I may?" His voice cracked the silence, soft but steady.

Finn's head snapped toward him, eyes narrowing with an edge sharp enough to cut glass. "Am I going to be able to stop you?" His voice dripping with boredom.

Ryan's lips twitched in a grim smile, the kind that never reaches the eyes. "Probably not."

Finn let out a bitter laugh, one that sounded like it came from a place I didn't want to visit. "Then why even bother? This whole thing's already over."

Ryan's gaze hardened, holding Finn's with unflinching intensity. "No. It's not over. Not yet."

There was a flicker in Finn's expression, something sharp and dangerous, like a corner of a broken mirror catching the light. His eyes drifted to me, a sick smile twisting the edges of his mouth. "You think she's with you? That she's on your side?"

Indigo straightened, voice shaking but fierce, trembling like a leaf in a storm. "Don't drag her into this."

Finn's eyes glittered with something darker, something that made my skin crawl. "Why wouldn't she be my accomplice? Maybe she's the one who really helped me make all of this happen. Maybe she's the one who planned it all."

"No, she didn't!" Indigo yelled, her voice breaking free like a dam giving way, raw and desperate.

"Who are you to say what she can and can't do?" Finn snapped back, voice cold and sharp.

"She's my best friend!" Indigo shot back, the words trembling with all the years of loyalty behind them.

"I'm your boyfriend!" Finn hissed, the claim slashing through the tension like a knife. "You can never truly know someone as well as you think you do."

Indigo went silent.

My pulse hammered in my ears, drowning out the world, but I kept my gaze locked on Finn. There was something in his eyes, not just calculation, but something darker, a hint of madness lurking beneath the surface.

Ryan's eyes locked on Finn's, unwavering and steady, a beacon of defiance. "You didn't do this alone, Finn."

The room seemed to shrink around us. The faint buzz of a flickering fluorescent light overhead was the only sound that dared to interrupt the suffocating quiet. Sweat prickled at my temples, and the cold metal revolver in Finn's hand gleamed, one bullet left in the chamber, and four of us still standing.

I felt the weight of everyone's eyes on me, questioning, afraid, desperate, but mostly searching for any sign that I might break. That I might say something, do something, to stop this spiral before it consumed us all.

But I didn't move.

Because the truth was, I wasn't sure if I could stop it.

And part of me enjoyed that.

The sharp, icy edge of the adrenaline coursing through my veins was intoxicating. The danger, the power radiating from Finn like heat from a fire, it burned a strange trail down my spine. It was terrifying, yes, but it was also alive. Electric. Real.

For months, maybe years, I'd felt myself slipping into shadows I didn't want to name. I'd worn my careful masks, told my quiet lies, kept secrets folded tight in the back of my mind. But now, standing here with the weight of what was happening pressing down like a fist, those masks were cracking. Shards of who I was before were splintering off, sharp and raw.

The edges hurt, but I was still here.

Still standing.

Still fighting, even if the fight was tangled with something darker.

Finn's eyes locked onto mine, and I could see the faintest flicker of something behind his calm, hunger? Madness? Both? The way he held the revolver was casual, but there was a coldness behind it that made my stomach twist.

"What happens next, Sadee?" His voice was low, almost coaxing, as if daring me to answer.

I wanted to tell him to drop the gun. To put it down and stop this. To save us all.

But my voice was gone.

Instead, I swallowed the lump in my throat and met his gaze head-on.

Maybe, a sharp, strange thought flickered through me, *maybe I wish it were me holding the gun instead.* The cold weight of control, the terrifying power to decide, to stop feeling helpless. The thought unsettled me, more than I wanted to admit.

What did that say about me?

"What do you want me to say?" I asked, voice barely above a whisper.

Finn smiled, but it wasn't a happy smile. It was one full of shadows, a predator's grin.

"I want you to understand. To admit it."

"Admit what?" I challenged, though my heart pounded a rhythm I couldn't control.

"That you and I, we're not so different. You've been living on the edge, playing your own games, hiding behind your silence. You think you're innocent, but you're not. You and I both know that."

A cold wave washed over me, sharp and sudden. The truth cut deep, and so did the lie I'd been holding onto. I clenched my fists, nails digging into my palms.

"Maybe," I whispered, barely steady.

Finn chuckled, a low, bitter sound that seemed to hang in the air. "You believe the story you tell yourself. Over and over." His voice took on a dark humor as he shook his head. "I imagine you stand in front of a mirror at night, practicing those stories, trying to make them feel real. It's almost funny, lingering in the back of my mind."

He lifted the gun carefully, holding it close to his head but never threatening. His smile stayed fixed, eyes bright with a strange, unsettling energy.

Indigo shifted, stepping closer to me. Her voice was small but fierce. "Don't listen to him."

But I couldn't look away from Finn. His gaze was magnetic, pulling me deeper into a darkness I was scared to face but somehow drawn to anyway.

Ryan cleared his throat, breaking the spell. "You don't have to do this, Finn. We can find another way."

Finn's eyes flickered to Ryan, and for a moment, something like regret crossed his face, before the mask slid back on, colder than before.

"No. There is no other way."

The room held its breath.

My mind raced, searching for a way out, a plan, a solution, anything.

But there was only the gun. The silence. The weight of decisions I wasn't sure I was strong enough to make.

Finn's finger brushed the trigger lightly, a warning or a promise.

"Do you think you can save them all?" he asked, voice low, almost teasing.

I swallowed again, feeling tears prick the corners of my eyes. "I never said I was saving anyone."

His smile was a razor's edge.

No one moved.

No one dared.

And in that frozen moment, I realized something.

This wasn't just about survival.

It was about how far we were willing to fall.

Then Ryan's voice cut through the silence, steady but trembling with desperation. "Finn, this isn't justice. You're just hurting everyone now, including Indigo."

Finn's eyes snapped to Ryan, dark and wild, a dangerous gleam igniting in them. "You think you understand? You don't know what he did. What Nick did to her."

"But I do."

Finn's lip curled. "I sold him the drugs he used." He snarled.

Before anyone could react, the gun fired, sharp, echoing off the walls like a gunshot tearing through the fragile air. Ryan staggered back, clutching his stomach, his face pale but defiant.

Last bullet gone.

"Run if you want," Finn hissed, voice unraveling as his grip on reality slipped. "But this ends how it started. All of it... for her. For Indigo. For what he took from her."

His words spilled out in a torrent, jumbled and frantic. "Nick deserved it. Every bit. You don't get to walk away from what he did. No one does. You think it's clean? You think this fixes anything? No! It's just... it's just a pain that never goes away. Nagging at me. Always. It... it never... never... and now they all have to pay."

His eyes darted wildly around the room, landing on each of us like accusations, threats. The revolver shook in his hand, the last threads of control slipping away.

"I'm the reckoning," he muttered, voice cracking. "The balance. And I won't stop until it's done."

The air thickened with dread. The line between sanity and madness blurred, and I was stuck in the middle.

I couldn't stop staring at the revolver in Finn's hand. Six chambers. Six bullets. All gone.

He was empty. Weaponless.

Without thinking, I lunged.

Our bodies collided, crashing into the cracked floor with a thud. His grip was desperate, but I was fueled by a raw surge of adrenaline I didn't know I had.

A hand shot inside his coat pocket as we fell, a flash of steel appearing in his grasp.

He lunged at me; his face etched with fury and pain. I barely had time to react. The knife sliced into my side, a hot, burning sting that made me stumble back. Blood seeped through my shirt, pooling quickly. I gasped, staggering, fighting the shock that threatened to take over.

Blood welled up, hot and sticky, but I didn't slow.

I refused to go down that easy. My survival instincts kicked in. I clenched my fists, grit my teeth, and pushed through the pain. I fought back, swinging wildly, trying to get some distance between us. I managed to land a punch to his ribs; he grunted but didn't fall. Instead, he retaliated, coming at me again.

We grappled, our bodies twisting and shoving. My mind was only half there, focused enough to know I had to end this, to stop him before he hurt me more. Blood and sweat dripped down my face, my vision blurring at the edges, but I fought harder. A surge of adrenaline flooded through me, sharpening my senses, numbing the pain.

Every movement was a blur, fists, knees, desperate shoves, until I finally managed to wrench the blade free, gasping as it clattered to the floor. Finn's eyes widened in shock, and for a moment, I saw a flicker of something unhinged lurking behind the rage.

Without thinking, I grabbed the knife and pressed it against his throat, the cold steel a warning, a threat, a promise. His breath hitched, and his eyes darted between me and the weapon I held, a flicker of fear, or was it something darker?

Finn grabbed at my hands, trying to shove me away.

The knife pressed harder against his skin, and I felt a dark satisfaction, something I hadn't expected. A strange, twisted feeling appeared in my mind. Maybe it was relief.

A flicker of hesitation crossed his face, and then he suddenly twisted, catching me off guard. His hand shot out, grabbing my wrist, forcing the knife away. I stumbled back, pain flaring in my side, but I held onto the weapon as best I could. He was quicker than I thought, he always was.

He lunged again, and this time, I wasn't fast enough. His knife sliced across my side again, this time deeper. I cried out, stumbling backward, my vision swimming. The pain was sharp, blinding. I could taste blood in my mouth.

But I refused to give in. I saw my chance. With a desperate surge of strength, I drove the knife into his chest. He screamed, staggering back. Blood sprayed out in a dark arc, and he clutched at the wound, eyes wild.

He's down. He's finally down.

I stood over Finn, breath ragged, heart pounding like a war drum in my chest. My whole body was trembling, and my side burned fiercely.

The fight had drained from him, and for a moment, silence fell heavy around us, thick with the weight of what I'd just done. A strange, dark feeling swelled inside me, relief? Power? Or something else that lurked in the shadows I'd refused to acknowledge before.

The weight of the knife in my hand felt unreal, cold, heavy, a final punctuation to everything that had just happened. My breath was ragged, uneven, each inhale sharp and shallow, but the roar in my ears drowned it out.

I should feel horrified at what I've done. I should feel regret. Instead, there was a strange calm settling beneath my skin, a hollow, dark calm that made the world seem distant, like I was watching myself from somewhere far away.

Did I just kill a person?

The thought drifted through me, fragile and terrifying, but quickly swallowed by the flood of relief rushing in. I was alive. I was still here. Against all odds, I had survived.

And part of me liked it.

That cold flicker of satisfaction was a secret I wouldn't admit, not even to myself. But it was there, sharp and undeniable, coiling tight in my chest.

He had been so sure of himself. So, in control. And now, he was gone. Silent.

But the silence didn't bring peace. It brought something heavier. An emptiness that stretched out and wrapped around me, squeezing.

Only Indigo was left now. Just the two of us.

I swallowed hard, the taste of iron and smoke on my tongue. It coated my throat like ash, the ghost of violence still clinging to the back of my teeth.

Was I a killer?

No. I've never harmed anyone. Not directly. Not with my own hands.

But Finn just took my ideas and ran with them. That wasn't my fault. Not really.

Except—

He never would've thought of it if I hadn't said anything. If I hadn't *let* it happen. But that was a lie.

Because I didn't stop him.

And when it was me, when the blade was in *my* hand—

I didn't stop myself either.

I'd never wanted this. Never wanted to be that person.

But somewhere between the screaming and the silence, I became her.

The lines had blurred, melted away in the heat of survival and desperation. There was no good left in this. No clever twist or clean escape.

Only pools of blood. And bodies in every corner. And beneath it all, a whisper echoed…

You're not innocent.

You're part of this.

I didn't flinch when I heard it. I didn't deny it.

Because deep down… I knew it was true.

I closed my eyes, the darkness pressing in, and let it wash over me. Let the weight of what I'd done settle into my skin, into the hollow spaces where shame used to live.

But there was no room for shame now. No space left for guilt. Only the sick, steady pulse of reality thudding behind my ribs.

Because in the end, it wasn't just about surviving.

It was about what I was willing to become to stay alive.

And that should scare me.

But it didn't. Not in the way it should've.

What scared me was how easy it was to justify it.

How natural it had felt, his body heavier than I expected, the breath rattling from his chest as everything slowed down.

I didn't feel triumphant. I didn't feel relieved.

I just felt *changed.*

Like the person I used to be had cracked open, splintered in the pressure, and something else had stepped through the ruins.

Something colder.

Sharper.

Still wearing my face.

The air around me buzzed, thick with the electric weight of everything I couldn't take back. I felt my fingers twitch, not from fear, but from memory, muscle recalling the grip of the handle, the resistance of flesh, the heat of his blood on my hands.

I didn't cry. I didn't collapse. I just stood there, swaying in the quiet, like the wind might pick me up and carry me somewhere far away from all this.

But I knew better.

This wasn't something you could run from.

This was the kind of thing that followed you.

Clung to your shadow.

Waited for you in mirrors.

And when I finally opened my eyes again, all I saw was Indigo looking back at me.

And she didn't look away.

Her wide eyes locked on mine. Her jaw was trembling, but she wasn't crying. Not yet. There was something else in her stare, something sharp. Her mouth parted, but no words came out. Just breath. Just *shock*.

A thousand unspoken questions flickered across her face, the kind you could feel more than hear. I could see her mind turning, gears spinning too fast to hide the noise.

She was remembering things now.

Rewinding moments. Looking at them again, differently.

My hesitation. My questions.

Why Finn lied for me.

She blinked once. Slowly.

And then her expression cracked, just slightly. Like she didn't want to believe it but couldn't help the conclusion coming for her anyway.

"He was right, you know," I whispered into the heavy silence. "He had to have had a partner."

I hated Nicholas Donovan.

Not in the casual, eye-roll way people hate when someone cuts in line or forgets deodorant or breathes too loud in math class. I hated him like the body hates poison. Like a fever rising to burn something out. Every time I saw his smug, squinty little grin or heard that nasally voice, something in me recoiled. My skin would crawl. My jaw would clench.

I hated him because of what he did to Indigo.

Because he shattered her and laughed like nothing had broken. Because he walked around with that smug little half-smile, like he hadn't turned her world inside out and then dared us to say a word. Because every time she looked over her shoulder, flinched at shadows, or went quiet in the middle of a crowded room, I knew who the ghost was.

And he just kept showing up. Saying her name like it belonged to him. Looking at her like she was a secret prize to add to a collection. He made her small. He made her afraid. And he thought he could get away with it.

I hated how he looked at me. Like he knew I wouldn't do anything. Like I was too soft. Too slow. Too scared. He was wrong.

And maybe... maybe I hated him most because he made me wait. Because I had to pretend for so long. Because someone had to make sure he didn't get away with it.

And now?

Now he never will

Chapter Twenty-Eight

Indigo stared at me like a ghost.

Like something inside her had cracked straight down the middle and all she could do now was watch me through the fracture.

Her lips parted. No sound came out.

"Say it," I told her gently. "You've already figured it out."

I could hear the wind outside, thin, sharp, curling against the cracked windows like a blade searching for soft skin. The silence between us stretched, brittle and tight.

"You were in on it," Indigo whispered. Her voice was smaller than I'd ever heard it, like it had sunk into itself. "You and Finn."

I gave a little nod. Nothing dramatic. Just the truth, handed over like it wasn't the end of the world.

"You helped him."

"No," I said calmly. "He helped me."

That was when the panic sparked behind her eyes. She pressed herself harder into the wall, like she could force reality back, like distance might protect her.

"You're lying," she whispered.

I didn't answer. Not because she was right or wrong, because it didn't matter. The truth was already here, soaked into the walls, the floorboards. Into me.

"What he did wasn't the plan," I said. "He broke, Indi. I didn't want them all to die." My breath hitched as a sharp pulse throbbed from the two shallow cuts on my ribs, warm blood slowly seeping through my shirt. The ache was a dull, relentless burn, constant and grounding. I wiped a sticky smear across my side.

Her hands curled into fists. Her voice cracked with rage. "You knew he was going to kill people. You watched. You let it happen—"

"I was going to stop it." My voice didn't shake. "But then he killed Mason. And Eli. And Maya. Cassie. Ryan." I swallowed. "He wasn't supposed to go that far. It was supposed to be Nick. Just Nick. And then the third round, just to scare people, shake things up. Nothing was meant to happen after that. I swear."

Her expression shattered. The betrayal hit her like a slap, sudden, sharp, irreparable.

I looked at her, willing her to understand. "We did this for you, Indi. Because we love you. You shouldn't have to live in fear because of what he did. We were trying to make things right."

Her eyes narrowed, wet with fury. "And that's supposed to make it *better*?" she snapped. "You're standing here, trying to *justify* this?"

"It is justified."

Indigo moved like she might lunge, but she didn't. She couldn't. I think part of her was still trying to convince herself this was some sick joke.

"I loved you," she said, her voice shattering. "You were my *best friend*."

I nodded. "I loved you too. So did Finn."

She started crying. Or maybe it was something uglier than that, some combination of shock and grief and rage and helplessness all bleeding together in her throat.

"I'm sorry," I said. "But I can't let him take the fall alone."

Indigo's sobs hit the walls like broken glass, sharp and shattering. She sank down slowly, sliding until her back met the cold floor, knees drawn tight to her chest. Her breath came in ragged bursts, the fragile sound of a storm breaking inside her.

I stood over her, feeling the weight of everything that had come undone. The knife still heavy in my hand, though I barely noticed it anymore. The blood, the bodies, the secrets, the pieces of a nightmare that now belonged to both of us.

A faint dizziness tugged at the edges of my vision, the dull throb from my ribs pulsing in time with my heartbeat. I bit my lip, tasting iron again, my hands trembling ever so slightly.

"You don't have to do this alone," she whispered through trembling lips. "You could have stopped it."

"I tried," I said softly. "But once it started... Indi, do you know how nice power feels? Like to have true power over an entire freaking town? It feels nice."

Her eyes widened, disbelief flickering through the storm of emotions in her gaze. "Power? You think this, *all of this*, is about power?"

I nodded, swallowing hard. "It is. Power to make people pay attention. To make them stop pretending everything's fine."

Indigo shook her head, voice breaking. "You weren't controlling anything. You were losing yourself."

"That's just it," I whispered. "I stopped *losing* myself. I found something... something stronger inside."

She scoffed, bitter and raw. "Stronger? You call this strength? Look around you, Sadee. All of our friends are dead."

I swallowed the lump in my throat, the weight of my own words pressing down. "You don't understand. Not yet."

Her breath hitched, voice cracking like glass. "Then explain it to me. Because right now, all I see is my best friend turning into something I don't even recognize."

I looked away, hands trembling slightly, slick with blood. "I was scared, Indi. Scared of what I became... but even more scared of what I'd become if I'd stayed silent."

She wiped tears from her cheeks, voice softer now. "And me? Where do I fit in all this? Am I just collateral damage?"

I didn't answer.

Her jaw tightened. "You're insane."

I let a slow smile curl at the corner of my lips. "Maybe. Yeah, I guess I am. But you and I both knew that already."

Indigo stared at me, her expression unreadable. I felt the knife grow heavier in my hand, as if it had a pulse of its own.

"Who killed Nick, Sadee?"

"In reality? Finn did."

Indigo took a breath. "What about in your mind, Sadee?"

I look at her. "He hung himself."

Indigo looks at me. "That's the story you're going with?"

I didn't answer.

"So, who did? He hung himself? Was that it? Because no one's going to believe that. The cops already suspect foul play."

"You're right. No one will believe it."

"So, who killed him, Sadee?"

"You and Finn did, I guess."

Her eyes widened in shock. "What?"

I raised a hand, calm but unyielding. "Listen, Indi. I don't need to explain everything. You don't need to know every detail. Just this:

when the police come, you and Finn had snapped, and I had to defend myself."

She shook her head, tears spilling over again. "You can't do this."

"I have no choice." My voice dropped lower, steady. "Finn lost control. That was never part of the plan. I'm the one cleaning up his mess."

Her voice was barely a whisper now. "What if they don't believe you?"

I stepped closer, voice soft but ironclad. "They will. I'll make sure of it."

She looked away, breath shaking. "It's not going to work, Sadee. You won't get away with this."

I shook my head slowly, feeling the cold certainty settle in my chest. "No. You're probably right. But I'll be long gone by the time they figure it out."

The silence between us grew heavy, thick with everything left unsaid.

I looked her dead in the eyes.

The weight of the moment pressed down on us like the night settling outside the cracked windows. Neither of us spoke for a long time.

Finally, she whispered, "What are you going to say to the cops?"

I let a slow, cold smile spread across my face. "That I'm so, very lucky I managed to get away from you and Finn."

Indigo's eyes searched mine, desperate and wild, as if looking for a crack, a flicker of hesitation. But there was none. Just the cold, steady certainty that had settled in my bones like a shadow I couldn't shake.

"You don't have to do this," she whispered again, voice fragile, like a thread stretched too thin.

I shook my head slowly, feeling the knife pulse heavy and warm in my palm, slick with my blood and Finn's. "I do."

Her scream tore through the silence as she scrambled backward, hitting the wall with a sharp breath. "Sadee, please. You're not a killer."

I stepped forward, each movement calculated, slow. The pain in my side was sharp but distant, a reminder, a tether to what was real.

"I'm just trying to get out of this," I said softly, voice low enough for only her to hear. "And that means no loose ends."

She shook her head, tears streaming freely now, makeup smeared and eyes wild. "You don't have to do this alone. We can figure it out. We can fix this."

"No," I said. "This isn't about fixing. This is about finishing what I started. I never should've given Finn the idea. Never."

Her eyes darted to the door, then back to me. Panic rose, mixing with something fierce and broken. "You're insane." She repeated.

"Maybe," I admitted. "But in about forty-eight hours the cops will think you're the crazy one."

The moment stretched, taut as a wire, before I lunged forward. The knife moved before she could react, a swift, brutal slash.

Her scream was a sharp, broken sound, and she collapsed against the floor, clutching the wound spreading red across her side.

I knelt beside her, the blood warm against my fingers. Her eyes met mine, wide with shock and betrayal.

"Why?" she gasped, blood seeping from the corner of her lips.

I whispered, voice almost gentle, "Because I have to. Because no one can know."

Her hand fluttered weakly against my arm, and for a brief second, I saw the girl I once knew, the best friend I used to love. "The truth always finds it's way to the surface, Sadee." She whispered.

But then her eyes glazed over, and the light dimmed.

I stood, wiping the blood from my hands on my jeans, my breath ragged but steady.

Outside, the wind still scraped against the cracked windows.

And I was the only one left.

I pulled my phone from my pocket; fingers slick with blood. My breath hitched for a moment, the pain from my wounds pulsing sharp beneath my ribs, but I pushed it down. This was the part where I became the hero, the "final girl" who survived.

Dialing 911, my voice was calm, practiced. "There's been a shooting. I need help. My friend... she's hurt. And another..." I paused, letting the weight of my words settle. "He's dead."

The operator's voice crackled back, professional and calm, but urgent. "Stay on the line, ma'am. Officers and paramedics are on their way. Are you safe now?"

I glanced down at Indigo's still body, then back at the door. "Yes," I said smoothly. "I'm safe."

I looked down at my shirt. Covered in blood. My blood. My friend's blood.

The minutes stretched and bled together, a blur of distant sirens and footsteps that echoed like ghosts through the cracked hallways. When the cops arrived, I answered their questions without hesitation, every word carefully measured.

"Yes, I was there. Yes, I tried to stop him." I made sure my voice cracked just enough when I mentioned Finn's breakdown, the chaos he'd caused.

They asked about Indigo. I told them I couldn't save her in time. Tears welled in my eyes, real enough, rehearsed enough.

When paramedics arrived, I was suddenly the victim, clutching my side where the pain throbbed steadily.

The ride to the hospital was a haze of sterile smells and distant voices. I let them patch up the cuts, the warmth of the antiseptic sting contrasting sharply with the cold that had settled in my chest.

Through it all, I stayed silent about the parts they'd never understand, about the plan that had spiraled out of control, about the truth I was burying beneath layers of lies.

The days that followed blurred together like a half-remembered nightmare. Time lost meaning, hours melted into each other, each moment a fragile thread I clung to just to stay afloat.

The police interviews were a hollow formality, a performance I mastered quickly, the traumatized survivor who fought back against a madman. I wore the fear like a mask, voice trembling just enough to seem believable. The press swallowed it whole. Overnight, I became a symbol: *"Teen girl stops murderous rampage"*, *"Local hero saves community"*, *"Brave final girl facing unimaginable horror"*.

I sat through endless questioning, repeating the same carefully crafted lines, keeping my voice shaky but composed. "I was scared. I had to defend myself. Finn snapped, and I did what I had to do." Every word was a blade, cutting away the truth I couldn't share. The officers watched me with eyes that weighed me differently, some with sympathy, others with quiet suspicion. But no one could see past the surface, past the story I was telling.

At the hospital, nurses tended to the jagged cuts Finn had left along my ribs. The wounds seared with every breath, a slow-burning fire beneath my skin that refused to fade. The pain was constant, sharp, a cruel reminder that the line I crossed was real and unforgiving. I refused painkillers, insisting I wanted to feel everything. To remember. To own every scar, every sacrifice.

Outside those sterile walls, the world spun wildly, indifferent to the chaos that had consumed my life.

Social media exploded with reactions. Hashtags trended and tripped across timelines. Videos of my police statements leaked, dissected by armchair detectives and gossip-hungry strangers alike. Messages poured in, some filled with sympathy and praise, others dripping with doubt and venom. But I stayed silent. I let the story craft itself around me, a carefully spun narrative that didn't need my voice.

I spoke at wakes, in interviews, standing beneath harsh lights that made my skin crawl. The cameras adored the vulnerable strength I projected, the brave final girl who stared evil down and lived to tell the tale. My voice carried hope, survival, but never the weight of what I truly carried.

Inside, I unraveled, thread by fragile thread.

The quiet moments between cameras were the worst. Alone in my hospital room, the sterile hum wrapping around me like a suffocating shroud. My bloodied clothes tossed into a plastic bag at the corner, I lay back on the crisp white sheets, eyes fixed on the ceiling. The cracks in my own mind stretched wider, jagged fissures threatening to swallow me whole. The memory of the knife pressed heavy in my hand, the burning ache in my ribs, the faces of the dead flickered like a broken film reel, relentless, unforgiving.

Indigo's eyes haunted me most of all, that cruel mix of betrayal and heartbreak, the way she looked at me in those final moments. I shoved that image deep inside, locked it away behind a wall I prayed I'd never have to climb.

The police came and went like clockwork, praising my cooperation and "heroism." I fed them just enough truth to keep them satisfied, everything else carefully buried beneath layers of silence.

Finn was dead. There was no messy trial, no tangled web of questions. Just a body that had since been put six feet under. The story would never surface.

But the shadow of what I'd done stretched long and dark. The house where it all unfolded was cordoned off, a frozen crime scene haunted by whispers. The neighborhood murmured, some voices soft with sympathy, others sharp and cutting, filled with suspicion.

One afternoon, I sat quietly in a small, nearly empty café. The bandage wrapped snugly around my side hid beneath a loose sweater. A reporter from the local paper slid a notebook toward me, eyes curious and expectant.

"How do you feel now?" she asked, pen hovering.

I smiled softly, the practiced mask settling back in place. "Stronger," I said quietly. "I survived. I'm ready to move forward."

She nodded, satisfied with the soundbite, but no one ever asked the questions I couldn't answer, about the plan that spiraled into madness, about the secrets weighing me down, about the friends I had silenced forever.

Days wore on. I slipped slowly back into the fractured rhythm of my life, school calling from home, whispered teacher conversations, sidelong glances from classmates who barely recognized the shadow I'd become.

The wounds along my ribs burned with each breath, a constant, jagged reminder that the girl who walked into that house weeks ago was gone. Something colder, sharper, something darker had taken her place, and I wasn't sure if she'd ever let me go.

Weeks passed, and the world settled back into a brittle kind of normal. The chaos had faded from headlines, the flashing lights and sirens replaced by routine and whispered rumors. Classes resumed, hallways filled again with chatter and footsteps, but the air felt different, heavier, like something unseen had taken root beneath the surface.

I walked through the halls of school like a ghost drifting among the living. Everyone stared, some with sympathy, others with suspicion, but no one knew what truly lay beneath my calm exterior. No one knew what I had done. Only me.

The weight of that secret pressed against my ribs harder than the scars ever could. I didn't speak about it. I couldn't. The words were tangled in darkness, locked away behind a cold barrier that even I couldn't break without shuddering.

I caught myself wondering, sometimes in the quiet moments between classes, whether what I'd done was right. Justified. Necessary. The questions flickered like shadows, quick and fleeting, but I shoved them away with practiced ease. Because if I let them stay, even for a second, the whole fragile construct would crumble.

One afternoon, during a break between classes, I found myself scrolling through my phone in the empty school courtyard. The screen glowed bright in the fading sunlight, and there it was, a news article, sitting cold and accusing in the top headlines.

"Small Town Shaken: Finn Smith and Indigo Perez Terrorize Community"

The words stabbed through me like a jagged blade. The story was a warped version of the truth, Indigo and Finn painted as the villains, the instigators of a nightmare no one wanted to face. I knew the truth, of course. I knew what I'd done to keep that story from unraveling.

The article talked about fear, chaos, the "crazed couple" who terrorized the town. No mention of the real darkness lurking behind those headlines. No mention of me.

I felt a strange, cold calm wash over me. The world was convinced of the version I'd fed them. And I was safe, hidden behind the lie.

The bell rang, sharp and loud, dragging me from the spiral of thoughts. I shoved the phone into my pocket and headed inside.

Passing by Indigo's locker stopped me cold. The police had cleaned it out weeks ago. No books, no photos, no reminders left behind. Just an empty shell of cold metal, the silence of absence hanging heavy.

I ran my fingers along the cool surface, my breath catching in my throat. This locker was the last trace of the friend I'd lost, the friend I'd betrayed. The friend I'd killed.

A wave of guilt washed over me, sharp and bitter, but I swallowed it down. There was no use in drowning in what couldn't be changed.

I moved on, unlocking my own locker. The familiar click echoed in the quiet hallway, a small moment of normality in a world that no longer felt normal at all.

Then I saw it.

A single yellow Post-it note stuck to the inside of my locker door.

"Simon says it's your turn to play."

Acknowledgements

I'd like to thank my friends and family—you have been such huge supporters of everything I do, from sports to writing to music. You've pushed me to strive to be the best at what I do, and I wouldn't be who I am today if it weren't for you guys.

A special thanks to Ailynn and Josh for enduring countless hours of me rambling about plot points and half-formed ideas. Thank you for always picking up the phone or answering texts, even when you knew it might turn into a long, winding conversation that didn't quite land anywhere.

Ryan, thank you for reading every draft, for catching what didn't work and questioning what almost did. Your patience, honesty, and attention to detail shaped this book in ways I couldn't have managed on my own. Caleb, thank you for stepping in with fresh eyes and offering perspective that helped sharpen the story.

And to Jonathan, thank you for taking the vague, dramatic vibe I had in my head and somehow turning it into real, actual art. I don't know how you pulled it off, but the cover is everything.

I also want to thank my grammar school principal, Mrs. Cavender, who always told me I had to write a book before she would let me graduate high school. Look, Mrs. Cavender, I did it. I can graduate high school now.

And finally, my sophomore-year Western Civilization II class— Mrs. Washam, Edie, Kyler, Sebastian, and Ayden—thank you for our daily games of Hangman. You are, truly and completely, the inspiration behind this novel.

Kaitlyn Elyse is a student and writer from just outside Dallas, Texas. She spends most of her nights writing music, crafting stories, and wondering how much caffeine is too much.